A FITTING PLACE

By

Mary Gottschalk

Rising Sun Press First Edition 2014

Cover Design and Author Photo by Wendy Musgrave

Rising Sun Press
92 NE 64th Street
Des Moines, IA 50327
515-771-6675
www.risingsunpress.com

Manufactured in the United States of America
First Printing

Library of Congress Control Number: 201493413
ISBN: 978-0-9797997-7-8

To Kent, with all my love

— and with gratitude for all his

patience

Chapter 1

In her next life, Lindsey planned to be a perpetual student.

In this life, it wasn't an option. Between her job and her family, she'd barely managed to eke out enough time to audit a course at the New School for Social Research and that only by telling herself that "Mythology for Modern Times" was relevant to her social work. So many of the people who shuffled through the agency, battling everything from an abusive parent to schizophrenia, carried some culturally derived notion of who or what they ought to be ... an idealized image that often bore little relationship to the reality of their own family, their own education, their own talents. She hoped this course on modern myths would help her to better understand the demons her clients were trying to vanquish.

But coming out of her office into the crisp September evening, she knew she was doing it as much for herself as for her work. For months now, she'd endured recurring, energy-sapping stomachaches that her physician couldn't explain. She didn't expect to discover the cause in a class on mythology, but she hoped the academic setting would provide a bit of respite, a place where most questions had the possibility of answers.

Unfortunately, her husband's ebullient call that afternoon had triggered yet another stomachache.

"Lins, the defendants settled. The trial's off."

She wasn't surprised. Ted had lost only one litigation case in the ten years since they'd returned from Australia. "Congratulations. I'll make a reservation at Nobu." It was what they always did to celebrate his courtroom victories.

"Not tonight." He paused. "I have a huge pile of documents to sign, and the press is clamoring outside my door. I probably won't be done until after eight."

She'd refused to let him hear her disappointment, but she couldn't stop the knot forming in her gut. In the past, his associates always took care of the final paperwork. Why not this time? "We'll celebrate when you do get home."

"Absolutely. Why don't you pick up a good bottle of champagne and something to go with it? Maybe we can do a picnic—like old times."

It was a gorgeous evening, with a clear sky and a light breeze. The fall air was fragrant with the aroma of warm sugarcoated nuts hawked by street vendors. With Zoey already at a slumber party with her school chums, Lindsey had plenty of time to wander by the wine store and buy champagne—and an insulated bag to keep it cool—and hit a deli for paté and cheese.

As she waited for her deli purchases, she reminisced about the "at home" picnics she and Ted had in the early years of their marriage, before their evenings were consumed with bottles, baths and bedtime stories. Typically, she and Ted met after work at Zabar's or Dean & DeLuca, filling a basket with paté, cheese, cold salad, and wine. Sometimes they ate at the dining table, other times they made a picnic on the living room floor.

Those were the days, a decade ago, when they couldn't get enough of each other, when their need seemed insatiable. Her nipples hardened as she thought of those marathon lovemaking sessions, the time before work and a child became an integral part of their relationship.

She decided to stroll home through Central Park, and she ducked into the park near the Zoo, one of her favorite haunts. On her last visit, for Zoey's thirteenth birthday, the three of them had stood breathless as a huge polar bear tried to shove his mate off a sunny rock he obviously wanted for himself. The sow refused to move, growling each time he lunged at her. After several tries, he slunk into his cave.

Lindsey cheered for the sow. Ted and Zoey simply laughed.

Just as they were about to turn away, the bear reappeared. Sauntering over to the coveted rock, he lifted his hind leg and peed on the sow's head. She grunted and got up. That time, Lindsey laughed along with Ted and Zoey, but her smile faded as she thought about her female patients who were routinely pissed on by overbearing partners.

Once past the Zoo, she sauntered up the Mall, soaking up the gold-red sunlight as it filtered through the rustling leaves. After a dozen years in New York, she'd grown adept at observing people while appearing to be lost in her own thoughts—a way of conserving psychic energy. Ever the introvert, she found idle conversation with strangers exhausting. By accident as much as design, she'd chosen a profession that allowed her to watch and listen while others talked.

She stopped at the band shell to listen to a blues group. The knot in her stomach began to untangle as she swayed to the pulsing rhythm of the scruffy young musicians. They reminded her of the unkempt kids she'd seen crossing the sparkling white-and-glass atrium of the New School the night of her first mythology class.

She'd been one of the few who moved briskly and with a purpose. Most dawdled or huddled in small groups. Some, probably faculty, wore khakis and cotton shirts. Others, clearly students, wore frayed jeans and pierced everything. She could count on her fingers the number who, like herself, wore business attire.

The one standout in the crowd was a statuesque woman about her own age in an elegant cornflower blue pantsuit. Lindsey couldn't take her eyes off the woman. Her perfectly coiffed salt-and-pepper hair, the wiry kind that stays in place even in a high wind. Her oblong nails painted a crimson that seemed a natural color complement to her suit. Her leather purse with a blue cord running up through the gold chain-link strap. It seemed that nothing had been left to chance.

Now, recalling the woman's heavy, strikingly modern gold chain, with an opal pendant that matched her earrings, Lindsey reflexively fingered the simple gold rectangle resting in the "v" of her open-collared shirt. How wrong she'd been when she pegged the woman as more interested in flower arranging than scholarly pursuits.

The woman had appeared in her classroom a few minutes later and claimed the chair on Lindsey's left. "Hi, I'm Joan," she said, smiling brightly. "It's so nice to have a kindred soul in this class full of hippie young things."

Lindsey glanced down at her own tailored slacks and dark jacket. Kindred certainly wasn't based on style. Was age sufficient criterion? Not in her world. "I'm Lindsey. Nice to meet you."

The professor's loud cough, signaling the start of class, halted their exchange. As he reviewed the syllabus—America as melting pot, America as the land of opportunity, the nuclear family, and gender roles—Lindsey noticed his emphasis on the sexual dimension of each topic. His last example—vagina dentata—made her pelvic muscles contract.

"A lot of Vietnamese prostitutes inserted razor blades in their vaginas," he explained, "and many of our troops in Nam came home with serious hang-ups about sex. I bet not many saw themselves as a modern-day version of an age-old Christian and Jewish myth—the male fear of being castrated during intercourse."

As Lindsey stepped onto the down escalator after class, Joan appeared behind her. "How'd you like that story about the Vietcong hookers? Can you believe what they teach kids these days? I'm not used to talking about sex with boys half my age."

"Are you used to talking about sex with men your own age?"

Joan grinned. "Yeah. I was married for thirty years to a man who could bring sex into almost any conversation."

The social worker in Lindsey erupted before she could stop herself. "Is that why you're not still married?"

"Why do you ask?" Joan held up her left hand, displaying an angular gold band, set with diamonds.

"You said, '*was* married.' Past tense."

Joan's grin faded. "Actually, Brad and I separated two months ago."

"Sorry, I didn't mean to pry." Lindsey picked up her pace as she stepped off the escalator. She made her living listening to people's tales of woe and had no interest in doing it for free on her own time.

"It's okay. It was my choice." Joan swung into step alongside. "I just moved to New York from New Jersey. After a life as a stay-at-home mom, I decided to try out something new." She chattered on, about her luck at landing a job as assistant librarian at the Natural History Museum, her fabulous apartment, and her delight in finally having a granddaughter.

Lindsey listened with half an ear, just enough to nod politely. She was impressed by the woman's seemingly effortless ability to keep a conversation going all by herself.

As they came out onto 12th Street, Joan said, "Sorry if I've been babbling. Why are *you* taking this course?"

Lindsey said the first thing that popped into her mind. "I'm interested in comparative religion. Cultural anthropology more than theology. Myth plays a big role in religious traditions." As the words spilled out, she wondered what possessed her to give that answer. She hadn't done any serious study of religion since leaving Berkeley almost twenty years earlier.

Joan's face broke into a satisfied smile. "Well, we really are kindred souls. I've been studying Buddhism for more than a decade. I'd love to talk more. Which way are you going?"

Chiding herself for her snap judgment about flower arranging, Lindsey pointed. "Union Square. The uptown subway."

"I'm on 15th, half a block off the Square. Why don't we walk together?"

"All right." Even during her youthful fascination with religious diversity, Lindsey had never studied Buddhism. The walk might prove interesting.

~ ~ ~ ~

A jarring metallic noise interrupted Lindsey's musing. A hard rock band had replaced the blues group. It was nearly dusk and it didn't pay to be strolling alone in the park after dark. She headed briskly past Buckingham Fountain, thinking about the walk that never happened. As the two women had crossed 12th Street, a Domino's bicycle messenger barreled into Joan, knocking her off her feet. With a broken heel on her shoe and what looked like a sprained wrist, walking was out of the question. Lindsey bound Joan's wrist tightly with her silk neck scarf, hailed a cab and delivered Joan to her apartment before heading uptown.

A bit to her own surprise, she hoped she'd get that walk after a future class.

Chapter 2

When she got to her apartment, she was delighted to find Ted already stretched out on the couch in the den.

"Hi, sweetie." She gave him a radiant smile and dangled her bag in front of him. "Picnic delivery."

When he returned her smile, she was surprised to see tension lines still evident around his eyes and mouth. But he was obviously listening to a news report on the settlement, so she didn't comment. When he shifted his long legs to make room for her, she dropped onto the couch, set the bag on the coffee table, and slid her hand under the cuff of his pants to caress his leg.

Moments later, when the anchor announced that the chemical company had agreed to pay $65 million to the upstate New York community Ted represented, he raised his arm into a triumphant fist. Clicking off the TV, he turned to her. "Did I tell you we cut our fee in half? That's why I was late. There were documents that no one else could sign."

"What prompted that?"

"The folks in Millard need a new water filtration system more than the partners of Chandler Weeks need the money."

"I knew there was a reason I fell in love with you." She leaned over and pecked him on the cheek. "How about a little bubbly?"

"Absolutely. I'm parched."

Lindsey handed him the bottle. "Open this while I get some plates."

When she returned, he'd poured the champagne and was inspecting her food purchases. "This paté looks great," he said. "I'm starved. I never got lunch."

"It'll fill in the empty spaces." She served each of them, then sat with her knee brushing his. "How did you convince them to settle?"

"It wasn't me, actually. It was Lauren Glass. She has a background in chemistry and environmental law, and she's sharper than half the third-year associates." He handed her a glass of champagne. "Poring through the mountain of internal company documents, she saw that the production people knew the town's water filtration system wasn't adequate to protect from chemical contamination. If they'd told the town fathers when they set up the plant thirty years ago, they would have won this case. But they didn't say a thing. So we won."

She felt a burst of pride, not just because he'd won, but also because he was so willing to give credit to his partners and staff. She laid her free hand on his thigh, not a sexual gesture, but enough to suggest a next step.

Later, she would remember the pressure change in the palm of her hand as the muscles in his leg tensed. She would remember thinking the room was suddenly chilly.

"Lins, we need to talk."

"Sure." She gave him a come-hither glance over the rim of her champagne glass. "What about?"

She would remember later that he wasn't looking at her, that his eyes seemed fixed on her hand on his leg.

"I'm leaving."

"Leaving?" She frowned. "Leaving what?"

He got up and walked to the window overlooking the courtyard. With his back to her, he said, "I'm in love with ... someone else."

She fumbled for a response. "If that's a joke, it's not one of your best."

"I'm not joking."

Her mind flailed. It couldn't be true. When, over the past few months, would he have had time to fall in love? Long days poring over technical documents. Dinner on the run. Nights sleeping on the couch in his office.

It didn't make sense.

And then she remembered one of those long days in early August when she'd stopped in his midtown office on her way home from work, something she often did when he was preparing for a trial. His door stood ajar and his secretary waved her in. Ted sat on the edge of a massive conference table with papers strewn its full length. Lauren Glass, with her awe-inspiring crown of red hair, perched next to him.

He came and kissed Lindsey on the cheek. With his arm draped over her shoulder, the three chatted for several minutes about nothing in particular. When she left, he walked her to the elevator. Nothing seemed out of the ordinary. But on the subway home, she'd wondered why Lauren had been blushing—the bright red blush people make jokes about. It didn't fit the image of the smoothly confident young woman she'd met at the firm's winter shindig. Or with Ted's description of her as "talented, but wildly ambitious and manipulative."

"It's Lauren, isn't it?"

He braced his palms on the window frame, as if to prevent a fall. "What difference does it make?" He used the brusque, lawyerly tone he employed to unnerve an opponent's witness.

"And, Jesus ... why ask me to buy champagne if you had no intention of drinking it?"

"Lins, I didn't plan to do this tonight. I ... I ..." His voice came out throaty and thick. "I've tried to keep life normal for Zoey, but when you put your hand on my leg just now, I realized I couldn't lie to you anymore. It's killing me."

She had a bizarre urge to laugh. "Killing you? Is this the point in the play when I'm supposed to feel sorry for you?"

His head slumped down between his arms.

One question after another erupted in her brain, and she spewed them out as they appeared. "When did it start? Before the trial prep began? Or just recently? And why? I thought we were happy. Why didn't you tell me you weren't happy ... if I was doing something wrong?"

His shoulders sagged under her barrage.

"And Zoey. When were you planning to tell her?"

Zoey. Another flashback, this time to the previous weekend, when Zoey arrived home after Sunday breakfast with her dad. "It was great," she'd said, "until he got that phone call. When he saw the caller ID, he shut his phone off."

"So?"

"I dunno, Mom. But he went all weird after that. Like hard to talk to."

Lindsey stroked her daughter's toffee-colored hair, hanging loose and glinting in the sun. "I'm sure it was his office ... or a client. He didn't want to interrupt your time together."

She threw Lindsey a withering look. "He *always* answers his phone." Wrinkling her nose, she added, "Eew, do you suppose he has a lover?"

Lindsey laughed out loud. "Zoey Chandler, you watch too much television!"

But her feeble adolescent joke had been exactly right. Lindsey forced herself to focus on Ted's voice.

"You two go to the country tomorrow morning as planned. I'll come up Sunday morning for breakfast. I'll explain it to her then."

She barely resisted the urge to throw a wedge of cheese at his back. "You can't really think I'm going to maintain your charade until it's convenient for you? No way in hell. If you want to tell her, you damn well better be here tomorrow morning when she gets home."

He spun around. Without looking at her, he strode out.

She followed him as far as the doorway. Would he actually show up in the morning? What would she tell Zoey if he didn't?

Just before he left the apartment, Ted checked his image in the hall mirror, running both hands through his thick mass of greying curls. She'd seen that gesture a million times, his ritual way of readying himself to face the world. The walls started to swim and her knees buckled.

She had no idea what time it was when she finally crawled across the hallway to her bedroom. She pulled herself up onto the bed and fell asleep in her clothes.

~ ~ ~ ~

The next morning, she awoke in a cold sweat, exhausted after a rollercoaster night. One moment, she'd been angry at the deception that must have gone on for months. The next, she berated her failure to realize Ted's capacity for deceit.

Worst was the memory of the few times they'd made love over the summer, the humiliation of being sexually responsive to a man who wanted to be with someone else. At one awful moment, she imagined him in the spoon position with his hand cupped over Lauren's breast. She'd pulled the pillow over her head, but the image wouldn't go away.

By early morning, she'd tumbled into a chasm of despair, trying to fathom what she'd done to drive him into the arms of a woman half his age. Had she crowded him, not given him enough space? Was it...?

Shivering, she crawled under the blankets to get warm. She was still cold when she heard a door click shut. "Zoey, is that you?" she called as she scrambled out of bed.

No answer. Perhaps it had been a dream. But dream or not, Zoey would be home soon. She had to protect her daughter. How? Maybe Dee would know what to do. Lindsey called her number, but was dumped into voicemail. "It's Lindsey. Call me! Please! As soon as you can!"

After splashing cold water on her bloodshot eyes, she stripped off her clothes and pulled on her robe, then headed for the kitchen to, somehow, prepare Zoey for what was coming.

The sight of Ted at the table with the *New York Times* open in his lap left her befuddled. He'd changed into jeans, but wore yesterday's business shirt with the collar open and the sleeves rolled to his elbow. It was how he'd been dressed the first time they made love, fifteen years ago.

Her anger and confusion mounted.

He nodded toward the steaming coffee pot. "I made it strong."

Was he expecting a thank you? Tightlipped, she poured herself a cup and stood facing him, the small of her back braced against the granite counter.

"Lins," he said, meeting her eyes. "I didn't mean for this to happen."

The phrase "sucker punch" shot through her brain. "But it did happen." Her chest heaved as she struggled to breathe. "You let it happen."

She didn't expect a response. Even so, a slow burn crept up her neck when he raised the paper. Was he reading it, or just pretending, so he wouldn't have to look at her?

Staring at his grey curls above the paper, she wondered again what he'd say to Zoey. For years, she'd watched dysfunctional adults make their children miserable as they tried to escape their own misery. That's what Ted was doing—tearing his daughter's life apart for his own selfish reasons.

She couldn't stand back and let a train wreck happen. She snatched the newspaper. "Tell me what you plan to say to Zoey."

He reached out to grab the paper, then dropped his hands into his lap. "That we decided on a trial separation. That we thought it would be best for her to stay in familiar space."

She crumpled the paper and threw it at him. "We didn't decide any such thing."

It landed in his lap, and he brushed it to the floor. "She's too young to understand about Lauren. For her sake, we should say it's a problem with us."

"You hypocritical son of a bitch. You don't have the courage to say you want a good fuck more than you want your daughter." Lindsey wiped her eyes with the sleeve of her robe. "And she's not too young. She knows Lauren called you during breakfast last Sunday."

"No way," he spluttered. "I didn't take the call."

"She didn't know her name. But she made a damn good guess ... that the only time you wouldn't answer your phone was if you had a secret lover."

"I'm sure Zoey meant it as a joke."

"What did I mean as a joke?"

They both pivoted toward the voice. Zoey stood in the doorway. From her unusually pale cheeks, Lindsey wondered if she was coming down with a cold. But offering TLC for a cold would have to wait.

"Your dad wants to talk to you." Lindsey tightened the belt of her robe and walked toward the kitchen door.

"Lindsey, please stay." He'd used her full name. It was a command, not a request.

Sitting down opposite him, she motioned Zoey to the chair between them.

Zoey hung back, looking from one to the other. "Mom, are you okay? What's going on?" Her chin quivered as she edged into the seat.

Ted took both her hands in his. "I've rented a cool new apartment on Broadway, a few blocks from here. You'll really like it."

Lindsey gripped her chair seat to steady herself. His leaving was no spur-of-the-moment decision. He'd had enough of a plan to rent an apartment and stash clothes there.

"Why, Dad? You live here."

"No, honey, not anymore."

"I don't understand."

"Things with your mother and me—"

"Ted, don't you dare put this on me."

Zoey whirled around, the irises of her hazel eyes shrunk to pinpoints. "Mom, what's going on?" The confusion on her face wrenched Lindsey's heart.

Ted massaged Zoey's hands. "I need time on my own to think about what I want."

"Don't you want us?"

"Of course I want you. I love you. I want us to have lots of time together. You'll have your very own room at my place."

Zoey yanked her hands out of Ted's and tucked them into her armpits. "It's not true." She turned to Lindsey. "Is it?"

"I ... uh... yes, it is, pumpkin." Lindsey tried for calm.

Zoey leapt up, knocking over her chair. "You're cheating on Mom, aren't you? With that woman who called you Sunday."

Ted held out his hand toward her. "Zoey, let me expl—"

"I *hate* you!" Zoey tore out of the kitchen. Moments later, her bedroom door slammed.

Lindsey stood up. "I need to go to her." At the door, she turned to Ted. "Get out. Now!"

"I hate to leave her like that," Ted said.

"You should have thought of that before you started fucking Lauren."

Chapter 3

Lindsey sat curled in a corner of the porch swing. Her best friend had finally called back and was coming to offer a badly needed shoulder to cry on.

Lindsey wiped her dripping nose on the sleeve of her cotton jacket as she willed Dee to arrive. Through her sniffles, the peppery scent of the yellow mums by the porch wafted up—mums she and Ted had planted one summer, after laying the path of heavy flat bluestones. She rarely walked the path without remembering how often they'd ended up in the hot tub to relieve their aching muscles, how often they'd made love in the warm water.

She ricocheted between anger at Ted's deception and shame at her own gullibility. How could she not have noticed the changes in him during summer? Unable to come to the country on the weekends. Unresponsive with Zoey, the daughter he'd always adored. Unwilling to discuss his imminent trial. Uninterested in sex.

It was all there, if only she'd allowed herself to see it.

~ ~ ~ ~

When Dee finally arrived, she leapt from her car, leaving the door ajar as she gathered up her flowing voile skirt and raced toward the porch. She plopped down on the swing, wrapped an arm around Lindsey's shoulders and drew her close enough for their heads to touch. "You must be a wreck!"

Lindsey nestled into the shelter of Dee's arms, snuffling. When she went to wipe her nose on her sleeve again, Dee blocked her arm and fished in her own pocket for a tissue. She pressed it over Lindsey's nose. "Blow. You'll feel better."

Lindsey blew. The pressure shift cleared her mind. She drew back enough to meet Dee's eyes, choking out her words. "He's in love with someone else."

"When'd you find out?"

"Last night. His trial settled yesterday. I bought champagne to celebrate. And then he ... he announced he was leaving." She snapped her fingers in the air. "Just like that! I had no idea."

Dee handed her another tissue. "Blow again."

The humiliation that had swept over her during the night washed over her again. "Dee, why didn't I see it coming?" She twisted the tissue into a tight coil.

"Is he moving in with her?"

"Don't know. He's rented a place on Broadway, with a bedroom for Zoey."

"Where's Zoey now?"

"At the stable. She insisted on going, so I dropped her off on our way from the City. He told her this morning. She thinks it's her fault, even though she'd sort of cottoned to his affair. I'm hoping Wendy and the horses give her something familiar to hang on to."

"Well, at least the bastard had the courage to tell her himself."

Lindsey winced. Last night, she'd called him that herself—a bastard, a son-of-a-bitch, and a few other epithets besides—but it shocked her when Dee said it. What did it say about her that she'd spent fifteen years loving a bastard?

Her eye landed on her now very cold coffee. "I forgot to offer you coffee," she said, but made no move to get up.

"Well, now that you mention it, I'd love some," Dee got up and pulled her friend to her feet.

In the kitchen, Dee filled two mugs. "What are you going to do now?"

"Get through the day. Try to hold things together for Zoey."

"Is her stomach any better?"

"Her stomach?"

"Yeah, she complained of an upset stomach this morning. No big surprise," she said, rolling her eyes upward. "They snarfed down a huge bowl of kettle corn last night. I can't believe what teenagers are willing to put in their mouths."

16

"She didn't mention it. I'll ask her when she gets home."

"I'm sure it's nothing serious." Dee sat with her elbows on the table, cradling her cup with both hands. "Have you thought about a divorce lawyer? You need to find out what financial support Ted will provide."

Lindsey gaped, her cup poised in midair. Divorce. The last eighteen hours had been a nightmare, but in the recesses of her brain, she'd expected to wake up and find it over. If she could hold on long enough. Divorce. She hadn't even thought about it. "Gawd, I feel more stupid every minute."

"You're not stupid, you're in shock." Dee patted the chair next to her. "C'mon, sit."

Lindsey sat.

"Lindsey, how much do you know about your assets?"

"Every ..." She choked again. Did Ted have assets she didn't know about? "Everything, I thought. But now I'm not sure."

"All the more reason to get a lawyer ASAP. Do you know someone?"

Lindsey couldn't think of a single name. "No."

"I'd suggest Mike Switzer, a friend of Jim's. I'll call him and tell him you'll be in touch."

Jim. Lindsey's nightmare veered off in another direction. Dee's husband Jim and Ted had been buddies since they were boys. Thirty years later, they had a standing lunchtime squash game. Surely, Ted would have confided in Jim. And wouldn't Jim have told Dee?

"Lindsey, you look like you've seen a ghost."

"Did you know? About Ted's affair. Before I told you today."

Dee's mouth shriveled into a tight line as she lowered her cup to the table. She nodded.

Every muscle in Lindsey's body turned to jelly. "I don't believe this." She shoved back her chair and stumbled to the counter. With her hands burrowing against the bottom of her jacket pockets, she stared out into the yard, where leaves were already falling from the trees. Just as pieces of her life were falling away. Ted's betrayal. Dee's deception.

Why hadn't she seen it? Any of it?

She sensed Dee come to her side, but she would not allow herself to acknowledge her proximity.

Dee tugged Lindsey around and held Lindsey's face in her hands. "Jim was convinced it wouldn't last the summer. And you were always joking about Lauren, about how Ted spent more time with her than with you. Sometimes I wondered if you knew and simply didn't want to talk about it." Dee rested her forehead on Lindsey's. "I guess I did the wrong thing."

Lindsey drew back. "So, if I'd asked you if my husband was having an affair, you would have said 'yes.' Don't make me laugh."

"I wanted to believe it wouldn't last. I still think it won't. You two always seemed so ... well matched. I can't imagine why he's interested in that red-haired chippy."

"Red-haired chippy? How do you know she has red hair?" Lindsey braced herself against the counter, afraid her legs would fail her. "Don't tell me you've gone out with them."

"Of course not. We met her at the client party last winter, remember? Anyway, Jim told Ted he was a complete jerk to trade you in for an 'overeducated floozy.' In Jim's mind, you and she don't belong on the same planet."

"Fat lot of good that did."

"You must believe I never meant to hurt you."

"I ... I ... don't know what to believe. About anything."

Dee picked her coffee cup up and put it on the counter. "It's time to collect the girls from the stable. Why don't you come with me?"

Lindsey couldn't imagine being stuck in a car with Dee for the forty minutes it would take to get to the stable and back. "I'll get Zoey myself. She's pretty upset ... barely said a word on the drive up this morning."

"Don't be silly. It's my weekend to play chauffeur."

"I really think I should be with her."

"Lindsey, you're not making sense. If she's managed to get through the afternoon without you, she'll make it home without you. How about we get pizza on the way back, so you don't have to cook?"

"I ... I ... I really..."

"Lindsey, stop. You're in no shape to drive. I'll drop Zoey off."

Lindsey had no more energy to resist. She stood on the porch as Dee peeled out of the driveway and down the gravel road. When the hum of Dee's engine receded, she turned back to the house.

The house. The country house Ted had insisted on buying so he'd have a reason not to go into the office on the weekends. For a time, she'd resented the house, the way it kept her from going to museums, the theatre, and other city pleasures she had no time for during the week. But over the years, she'd come to love country life. Her garden, with shrubs and plants she'd nursed from seedlings and sprouts. The stream, a mere trickle now, but an abundant source of trout in the spring and early summer. The woods, with dozens of trails for both walking and cross-country skiing.

What if Ted wouldn't let her use it? What if he decided to sell it?

Her chest went tight as she pictured herself, age ten, standing on the sidewalk of a treeless street as the movers carried her beautiful white rattan bed into a dilapidated frame house. She'd been old enough to understand that, after her father left to marry his secretary, her mother's salary as a teacher wouldn't support the big Victorian house at the end of a tree-lined drive. But when they moved to the "wrong side" of town halfway through the school year, everything she knew got ripped away. Her best friend, Brenda, from the Hillside School. Her dog, Poppet, a caramel cocker spaniel. The white rattan dressing table that matched her bed.

Without Ted's income, she couldn't afford the apartment in the City, let alone the country house. Would she become like her mother, overworked, bitter and resentful of the demands of a teenager? And Zoey. She'd led a privileged life—private school, music lessons, and travel. Surely, Ted would continue to support his daughter's lifestyle. But what if he didn't?

And Dee. Her best friend for a decade. They'd shared so much. Hard things, like the death of Dee's twin sister in a skiing accident. Like Lindsey's stillborn baby when Zoey was four and the discovery soon after that she couldn't have more children. Good things, like Jim's awards for innovation in Internet technology. Like Ted's partnership in his father's law firm. Like Dee's promotion to head of a major New York hospital. They'd cried together and laughed together and often just passed the empty time together. How would she manage without Dee?

Lindsey stumbled into the kitchen. The blot of bright red lipstick on Dee's cup caught her eye. She carried the cup to the sink, determined to wash away the evidence of Dee's visit. But even as she scrubbed off the oily red mark, she wondered if she could ever wash away the memory of Dee's betrayal?

Chapter 4

Going to work Monday morning was a mistake.

Lindsey assumed that familiar routines would blunt the pain. She could not have been more wrong.

Things got off to a bad start when she had to stand in for a sick colleague and lead a morning-long seminar on case management for a group of social work students from NYU. Even though she'd been doing these seminars for years, she lost her train of thought every time someone interrupted with a question.

As if that wasn't enough, she then had to meet with a young case manager, a recent graduate who'd shown little patience with or empathy for mental health consumers trying to wend their way through the day-to-day bureaucracy of disability claims. She'd put him on probation two months earlier and now had to terminate him.

The young man smiled nervously as he shuffled into the small conference room where she and the HR director had arranged to meet him. She knew he was struggling with feelings of inadequacy, much as she had in her early days of social work. But the matter at hand was his inability to work with the clients.

She came directly to the point. "Daniel, your performance has not improved since our last review. Just this past week, three different clients complained that you seemed irritated by their questions. And you were late to four client meetings. We are terminating you as of today. We will pay you through the next week and, despite the performance problems, provide the necessary documentation for you to get unemployment."

"Geez, Mrs. Chandler, that's not fair. Some of these folks are impossible. They want me to fix things that can't be fixed … and they want it fixed right now, today. It drives me crazy."

"Daniel, many—probably most—of our clients have a none-too-solid grasp on reality. But your job is to make them feel you're concerned about their welfare. If you can't do that, you're in the wrong job."

Daniel sat taller, squaring his shoulders. "You can't do this! I'll get a lawyer ... file a complaint for wrongful termination. I graduated at the head of my class at Chapel Hill, and if I'd had anything like the proper training, this wouldn't be happening."

Lindsey was unfazed. "Daniel, you should do what you think is best."

Daniel snorted. "One of the worst things about this place is you. Your appalling lack of empathy for your clients or your staff. Everybody knows that."

That hit a nerve. Four days ago, she'd thought Ted loved her but he didn't. Two days ago, she'd assumed Dee was her friend, but now she wasn't sure. Minutes ago, she'd believed people at the agency respected her. Did they hate her as much as this young man alleged? She was desperate to escape his hostile stare.

"Daniel, as I said, you're entitled to your view. And now, Abby will go through the termination documents with you."

She walked out, hoping her legs would carry her back to her office. Once there, she collapsed into her chair and sat staring out at the traffic on Seventh Avenue, unable to form a coherent thought. When she felt strong enough to walk steadily, she put on her coat and left.

She arrived home only moments before Zoey, who headed for her room without a greeting. At dinnertime, Lindsey had to call three times before she finally appeared and slouched at the kitchen table, her arms crossed with her hands tucked into her armpits. The message was clear. "Don't even think of touching me."

Ignoring the hostile signal, Lindsey tried for a conversational tone. "Anything interesting happen in school?"

"No."

Another try. "Have rehearsals started?" Zoey had just been given the lead in *The Seven Ages of Anne*.

"Mom, don't you get it? I don't want to talk."

Lindsey rested her hand on Zoey's arm. "I know you're upset about your dad. But his leaving has nothing to do with you. He loves you so much, and he's so proud of you."

Zoey yanked her arm away. "Yeah. Right. He always said that actions speak louder than words. If he really loved me, he wouldn't leave me behind with you. He'd take me with him." She shoved her chair back and stomped out.

"Zoey ..." Lindsey called, but Zoey continued toward the bedroom hall. Lindsey flinched as Zoey's door banged shut.

Lindsey sat, forlorn. For years, she'd given thanks for her easy rapport with Zoey, so different from her fraught relationship with her own mother. But now she couldn't even manage to comfort her daughter. Had she driven Zoey away too?

She scrolled back over the past seventy-two hours. Zoey's tears of anguish Saturday morning after Ted left, exacerbated by her fear that she'd disappointed him without knowing how or why. By noon, she'd been composed again, determined to carry out her chores at the stable. She'd even made a salad to go with the pizza without being asked.

But then, around midnight, she'd crawled into Lindsey's bed, begging to be held. Barely able to hold back her own tears, Lindsey'd wrapped her arms around her sobbing daughter, crooning lullabies until Zoey's breathing grew even and soft.

Zoey had still been clingy on Sunday morning, but as the day wore on she grew increasingly distant. And now, Monday night, after a day at school, she'd morphed into a creature Lindsey'd never seen before, sullen and bad-tempered.

Lindsey wanted to hurl her dinner plate at the wall. Or at Ted. Or that stupid case manager. Or, as much as she hated to admit it, Zoey.

The phone startled her, and she dropped the plate she was ferrying to the dishwasher. It shattered, sending jagged pieces of stoneware skittering across the terra cotta tiles. Lindsey reached for the phone as her eyes followed the still-moving shards.

"Lindsey? Is everything okay over there?"

She recognized her mother-in-law's gravelly voice. Just what she needed to top off her day—an inquisition from Claire. "Sorry. I dropped a plate."

"Do you want to call me back?"

She stared at the fragments on the floor. "No, I'm fine. What's up?"

"I got our tickets for the Thursday symphony series. I have the six dates for you."

Lindsey almost dropped the phone as well. Was it possible Claire didn't know?

"Why don't you call Ted at his office?" Lindsey strained to keep her voice even.

"Lindsey, dear, you sound like you're about to cry. What's wrong?"

Lindsey swore under her breath. The bastard hadn't told his mother. All right, she'd do it, and damn the consequences. She rested her head against the wall and closed her eyes. "Ted's fucking a woman in his law firm," she said, aware that she'd never used a swear word in Claire's presence. "He moved out last Friday."

"Oh, my," Claire said. "I ... I never imagined ..." Seconds dragged by. Finally, she said, "Where's Zoey?"

"With me." Sooner or later, she'd have to face Claire's questions. But she didn't have to do it now. "Claire, I have to go." Lindsey hung up, damning Ted for leaving that job to her.

As she swept up the broken plate, Lindsey wondered how Claire would respond. Their relationship was cordial enough, but they weren't close. Certainly, Claire would stand by her son. But Claire adored her granddaughter, who worshipped "Gammy" in return. Zoey went to Claire's once or twice a month after school to play the piano. Sometimes it was duets on a single piano, other times dueling pianos, as Claire had two baby grands in her Park Avenue penthouse.

Lindsey was exhausted, and desperate for her mind to stop roiling. It was too early to go to bed, but she didn't know what else to do. She pulled on a nightshirt, then went to brush her teeth. As she switched on the bathroom light, she recoiled from the hollow-eyed face that looked back at her, a face from which all light and energy had been extinguished. She hurled herself into bed, expecting to fall asleep at once.

An hour later, her mind was still flailing, her limbs still twitching. She got up and fished Ted's bottle of sleeping pills out of the medicine cabinet. She didn't like taking pills, but it seemed that a medically induced calm was the only way she'd get any sleep. She twisted the lid, pulled out a single pill, and swallowed it without water.

When her alarm beeped the next morning, Lindsey couldn't face her office. She called Joel, the executive director, and arranged to take the rest of the week off. Although they'd been a collaborative team for nearly a decade, she offered no explanation and was relieved when he didn't ask. Then she called Elena, her Argentinean housekeeper and nanny since Zoey was three, and gave her the week off as well.

She spent Tuesday morning plowing through Zoey's closet, a long-overdue project that yielded four Goodwill bags of clothes Zoey had outgrown. After lunch, she moved to the walk-in closet she'd shared with Ted, and discarded anything she hadn't worn in the last two years. By midafternoon, she was working on her third Goodwill bag, filled mostly with elegant remnants from the era before pantsuits.

She was still sorting when Zoey came in from school and retreated, with nary a word, to her room. Within moments, however, she heard Zoey's door open and looked up to see her daughter's face contorted in rage. Zoey clutched a blue velvet dress with crocheted collar and cuffs of beige lace, her "Nutcracker" dress when she was seven. It was the first of what had become an annual tradition, a spectacular outfit from Claire to wear to the Christmas extravaganza at Lincoln Center.

"Why are you giving my dress away?"

"It hasn't fit you in years."

"I love this dress. I won't let you give it away."

Lindsey walked toward Zoey with outstretched arms. "Oh, pumpkin, of course you can keep it. I had no idea you still wanted it."

Zoey stepped back into her room as Lindsey approached. "I'm keeping them all. It's my stuff," she said as she shut her door. "You can't give it away. Any of it."

Lindsey stared dumbly at the door. How could she have not consulted Zoey? But having carefully packed up much of Zoey's childhood, an apology now would sound hollow, an attempt to excuse herself rather than comfort her daughter.

Not sure what else to do, she went back to her own closet. A few minutes later, Zoey's door opened again. Before Lindsey could turn around, the door banged shut. Four empty Goodwill bags lay strewn in the hall. Lindsey wanted to kick herself. In an effort to take her mind off her own distress, she'd ripped away a part of Zoey's world that her daughter would expect to be inviolable. She was no better than Ted.

Zoey refused to come out for dinner, so Lindsey left a tray with milk and a meatloaf sandwich outside her door. The tray was gone when Lindsey went to bed.

Wednesday morning, Zoey only grunted in response to her knock, but appeared in the kitchen a few minutes later, her cheeks pale, her eyes bloodshot as if she'd been crying.

Lindsey put down the morning paper. "Zoey, darling, I should have asked before I went through your things. I don't know what else to say, except I'm sorry."

Zoey fixed a huge bowl of cereal and left the kitchen without so much as a glance in Lindsey's direction. Ten minutes later, the front door clicked shut.

The day felt endless. Lindsey wandered from room to room, fleeing the unending stream of memories. The crystal cube Ted had given her on their third anniversary. A batik wall hanging they'd bought on a vacation in Bali. The prayer rug they'd purchased in Turkey.

For an hour or so, she sorted through stacks of art catalogues, mostly from contemporary and modern shows at MOMA, the Whitney, the Guggenheim, and BAM. They'd saved them with an eye to taking a course in contemporary art. With Ted's unpredictable trial schedule, the time had never been right. Now, of course, it never would be.

She intended to throw them all out, but with the bag poised over the trash chute, she had a change of heart. If she could make time for a course in mythology—something Ted had no interest in—she could certainly find time for an art course. She didn't need him to hold her hand.

But the realization that Ted would not be there to hold her hand threw her into a new bout of despair. She jogged over to the gym, hoping the dopamine hit from exercise would soothe her body as well as her mind. But pacing on the treadmill in front of the mirrored wall, all she could see were the lines starting to score her still-fit body. When a lithe young woman—with a halo of red hair, no less—climbed onto the treadmill next to her, she found herself obsessed by visions of Ted making love to Lauren. She fled.

Back in the shelter of her apartment, she took a long, hot shower and crawled into bed. She slipped into a dream in which she was waiting for Ted to call about the symphony. When the phone rang, she picked it up, only half awake. "Hi."

It was Dee.

The day after their conversation in the country, Dee had repeated her apology. Lindsey's reply was a chilly "There's nothing to apologize for. You did what you thought was best."

Since then, Dee had called daily, on the pretext of coordinating the girls' activities. While Lindsey tried to keep their conversations brief and superficial, Dee always managed to query her progress on finding a lawyer or changing the locks. Talking to Dee often left her feeling even more inept than she'd felt when the day started.

"How're you doing today?"

"Hummh. I was asleep."

"Sorry. I thought you'd be getting ready for class."

"Class? Geez, I forgot all about it."

"Want to come here for dinner?"

It was the last thing Lindsey wanted to do. How could she sit at their table, wondering what else Dee and Jim knew that she didn't?

She stalled. "Let me check with Zoey when she gets home. I'll see what she wants to do."

"You're in a fog, aren't you? Zoey came here from school. Since it's your class night."

Lindsey felt utterly deflated. Even a sullen angry child was better than being alone. The class would be something to do. "I think I'll go to class. I'll call you tomorrow."

Lindsey pulled on jeans, a dark turtleneck and a poncho. She grabbed a protein bar and left before she could change her mind.

For years after, Lindsey would marvel at how close she came to missing class that night.

Chapter 5

Lindsey made it through the lecture, but only by blowing her nose repeatedly to keep from crying. To avoid conversation after class, she kept her eyes glued to her notebook until the classroom was empty. Long after everyone else had left, she remained in her seat, an alternative to going home to an empty apartment.

When she finally came out into the corridor, she cringed at the sight of Joan standing by the escalator waving. She'd called Lindsey the morning after her accident to report that the swelling was down and she was in no pain. They'd chatted briefly after the second class, just long enough for Joan to return Lindsey's scarf. What reason could Joan have to wait all this time for someone she barely knew?

When Lindsey reached the escalator, Joan put out a hand. "Are you okay? You seem a little feverish."

"I'm fine." Lindsey stepped on the escalator, fumbling with her purse and notebook to avoid meeting Joan's eyes. "Just tired. A long day."

"How are you enjoying the class?" Joan stood on the step behind her.

"Fine." Lindsey wished this woman would leave her alone, but she wouldn't be rude.

"Wasn't that something? His discussion of hermaphroditism of the soul. I've never heard that term before."

Lindsey knew the word, one that came up in the context of gender identity. But she had no recollection of hearing it during class. "Umm ... I don't quite recall what he said."

"Are you sure you're all right? Why don't you let me get you a cab?"

Even as she replied, "That's not necessary," Lindsey knew her fogginess would make her vulnerable on the subway at nine o'clock at night. When they reached the street level atrium, she mumbled, "Perhaps you're right. A cab would be good."

She let Joan steer her to Sixth Avenue. Before she could stop herself, Lindsey said, "Would you have time for coffee?"

Joan gave Lindsey's elbow a gentle squeeze. "Sure. How about Café Loup, up on 13th Street? Do you know it?"

Lindsey nodded. She liked its bistro atmosphere. She pulled her poncho tight as they headed north.

To her relief, Joan did not attempt conversation during the walk, leaving plenty of time for Lindsey to wonder what had possessed her to suggest coffee with a near stranger. She hated small talk under the best of circumstances. Tonight she wasn't fit to carry on an intelligent discussion about anything, let alone Buddhism, the one interest they might have in common.

As soon as they were seated, Joan flipped open her menu. "I'm starved. Do you mind if I have something to eat?"

"Not at all," Lindsey said, wondering how they'd fill the time it would take Joan to eat.

"What would you like?" Joan said. "My treat."

Lindsey's stomach was rock hard. No way she could eat a thing. "Just a glass of wine. But you don't need to treat me."

"I'd like to," Joan said. "A token repayment for your kindness the night I fell. And you do seem like you could use a little something nice."

An unexpected surge of tears blurred Lindsey's vision as they ordered two glasses of wine and a bowl of onion soup for Joan. Lindsey swabbed her eyes with a tissue. She refused to cry in public.

"Is there anything I can do?" Joan asked when the waitress had gone.

"I'll be fine, really, I will." She set her hands, one atop the other, in front of her and flashed a smile she was sure looked fake.

Joan laid her hand over Lindsey's. "Okay. Let's just sit and enjoy the wine."

The warmth of Joan's hand on hers radiated through her whole body. It was the first human touch since Zoey had crawled into her bed Saturday night. Before she knew it, she'd blurted out, "My husband's having an affair. With a young woman in his firm."

Joan wove her fingers through Lindsey's. "You poor dear."

When the waitress brought their wine and a small bowl of steaming soup, Lindsey pulled her hands away. "I bought champagne to celebrate his victory ..." She blew her nose again. "I ... I ... just never expected..."

"It's okay." Joan's voice sounded velvety.

"The bastard wanted me to keep it a secret from our daughter for the weekend! To act as if nothing had happened, so he could tell her when it was convenient for him." Lindsey's throat burned from holding back tears and she tried to cool it with a sip of wine. "Ted wanted to say it was *our* decision. Like it was my fault, when *he* was the goddamned cheater."

"You must be kidding!"

"No. And worst of all, I didn't have a clue, even though there were warning signals all around me. I feel so stupid."

"Don't beat yourself up. You didn't do anything wrong—he did."

Lindsey sniffed.

"Your daughter. What's her name?"

"Zoey. She's always adored her dad, but now she refuses to speak to him. And it seems she's angry at me as well."

"Don't take it personally. She probably doesn't know what to think," Joan said as she attacked two thick, cheese-covered croutons in her soup. "She's a turtle, pulling into her shell because she's scared."

A turtle? An image Lindsey would never have picked for Zoey, who normally said whatever was on her mind to anyone who would listen. But Zoey's world had been shattered, and it made sense that she'd retreat into herself until she could sort it out.

Lindsey made a conscious effort to smile. "That's a nice image. I've seen so many teenagers caught up in an emotional maelstrom they have no way to understand. They *are* like turtles, closing themselves off from the world. But

Zoey's always been so resilient. It never occurred to me that she'd respond that way to anything."

"So many teenagers? Oh, I remember. You're a social worker. Where's Zoey now?"

"Spending the night with her best friend. She does that on my class nights."

"Can I interest anyone in dessert?" the waitress asked. "Our special is tiramisu."

Joan gave a beguiling smile. "That sounds awfully good. Lindsey, would you split one with me?"

"A taste, perhaps." She didn't care for sweets but whatever her earlier reservations, she wasn't ready for the conversation to be over.

"One tiramisu with two forks. And one coffee. Hi-test." Joan turned to Lindsey. "Does Zoey know why Ted left?"

Lindsey shook her head. "Not the details. But her antenna was up, long before mine. Ted muted a phone call one morning when they were together. She mimicked Zoey's sarcastic tone. 'He always answers his phone. So it must have been his lover.' I laughed at the time, thinking it was adolescent hyperbole. But she nailed it."

"So, this took you by surprise."

"I was stunned." She swirled the puddle of wine in the bottom of her glass. "The clues were all there. But I didn't want to see them."

"No one ever does. You make excuses for people you love. We all do it. All the time."

"I feel so stupid." How many times had she repeated that phrase in the last week?

"Don't," Joan said as the waitress laid a six-layered masterpiece in front of them. "There could have been a million reasonable explanations for Ted's behavior. If you trust someone, it's natural to give him the benefit of the doubt."

"Sounds like you've been there." Lindsey cut off a small corner of the pastry but knew she couldn't swallow it. She set her fork back on the plate.

"No. Brad was absolutely faithful, like a puppy that won't let you out of its sight. But I've watched lots of friends go through this."

Lindsey nodded in agreement. For years, she'd watched clients rationalizing the irrational behavior of a spouse. "Me, too. Not friends, but clients at the clinic. But most come from dysfunctional families. Or are mentally ill. It never dawned on me I'd make the same mistake."

"Did Ted ask for a divorce?"

Lindsey gave a long baleful sigh. Divorce seemed obvious to others, even if it wasn't to her. "No."

"Do you want a divorce?"

"I ... no. Well, I don't know. Do I even have a choice?"

"Maybe he doesn't want one. Maybe he's confused, trying to bludgeon his way through a midlife crisis."

Again, the image was jarring. Lindsey had never seen Ted when he wasn't in control of his environment. Could this be something he'd get over, as Dee and Jim had hoped?

Joan took another bite of the pastry and pushed it to the center of the table. "That's all for me. Would you take Ted back? If he said he'd made a mistake?"

"I don't know. I thought we had a good life." She laughed, sardonically. "But it seems I was wrong about that. I don't know, any more, what to want."

"Is he living with her?" Joan asked.

"I don't think so. He has an apartment on Broadway. Lauren lives in the West Village."

"Lauren?" Joan crinkled her eyebrows. "What firm is your husband at?"

"Chandler Weeks. Why?"

"Tell me it's not Lauren Glass."

Lindsey stared at her, incredulous.

"She's in my book club." Joan scowled as she tapped her fingers on the table. "She's very bright, but ridiculously self-absorbed. She's been singing Ted's praises for weeks. We all assumed she was having an affair with him."

Lindsey laughed in spite of herself. The small-world-ness was too bizarre not to laugh. "Guess you were right."

When the waitress dropped off their check, Joan took it. "I've got an early morning meeting, so I need to go. But I have an extra bedroom, if you don't want to be alone tonight."

Lindsey was tempted. Joan had thrown her a lifeline. She didn't want to let go but was loath to impose. "Thanks, but I'll head home. I'm feeling better. Really."

A few minutes later, as a taxi screeched to a halt in front of them, Joan said, "Call me when you get home."

"That's not necessary. I'll be fine."

In a nearly perfect reversal of the scene two weeks earlier, Joan handed her a business card. "My home number is on the back. Call me when you get home."

Falling back against the seat, Lindsey's muscles went slack, the way they did after strenuous exercise or a bad fright. It was nice to talk to someone who didn't think she was crazy or undisciplined or self-pitying. Dee, of course, never used those words, but her incessant nudges about things Lindsey needed to do only reminded her that her life was out of control. Joan had made her feel more able to cope.

More than that, Lindsey had a sense of possibility. If she wanted to save her marriage, there might be something she could do.

Chapter 6

Lindsey's heart beat double-time when she saw the clutch of empty hangers in the hall closet Sunday night. Pulling Zoey close, she scanned the apartment for other signs of a burglar.

Within moments, she realized it had been Ted. He'd come over the weekend to get his winter coats. She forced herself to think logically. Why, after all, did it matter when he got his things? Still, she felt violated, the way she had when their apartment in Sydney was broken into. How many other times had Ted been there that she didn't know about?

She almost laughed when she saw the drooping yellow mums on the coffee table. They looked like she felt, sad and bedraggled. As she drenched the plant with water, she noticed the library books were gone as well. Ted must have taken them when he got his clothes. But why had he taken hers? Without even leaving a note.

Blinking back tears, she shelved the groceries she'd bought over the weekend. As she emptied the last bag, she remembered Dee's admonition to change the locks. Ted didn't live here anymore? She'd call a locksmith in the morning.

One small step in getting some control over her life.

~ ~ ~ ~

When she returned to work the next day, she was far from in control. Almost every one of the case files stacked up from her weeklong absence had some detail—a cheating husband, a rebellious teenager—that brought her own ordeal back to the surface of her mind. By lunchtime, she'd managed to work her way through only four of a dozen files.

And while she'd never discuss her marital situation with her staff, the fact that no one asked about her week off reinforced her anxiety that she might be, as that horrid young man had claimed, a terrible manager that no one liked or respected.

It didn't help when Joel, who stopped by to update her, said casually, "I hope it wasn't anything serious."

She almost said, "No, nothing to worry about," but after a decade of sharing milestones in each other's lives, she couldn't blow him off. From his wide-eyed reaction, she knew he was as surprised as she'd been.

"I'm so sorry, Lindsey. You and Ted seemed so ... so compatible." At the door of her office, he turned in place. "If you need more time off, just take it. We'll manage just fine." And then he was gone.

Manage just fine. Had she been as wrong about her role at the agency as she'd been about everything else?

Joan called, shortly before noon, to suggest a picnic lunch in Central Park. Lindsey hesitated, concerned about the stack of untouched files, but decided fresh air would do her good. "I'd love to, but I have a meeting at one."

"So, a quickie. Columbus Circle in fifteen minutes?"

"You've got a deal."

Lindsey approached the Circle with a deli bag of tomato bisque and an oatmeal cookie. Joan, perched on the rim of the fountain, wore a gorgeous teal pantsuit. Lindsey's beige slacks and knitted jacket, stylish though they were, felt dowdy by comparison.

Joan wrapped Lindsey in a bear hug. "Isn't this Indian summer fabulous? I love it."

Lindsey wriggled out of Joan's embrace. New Yorkers didn't give bear hugs to near strangers. "It is a lovely day."

Joan held up a small rattan package. "I brought a beach mat in case we can't find a bench. I keep it in my desk. I often go out at lunch and sit on the grass in the Park."

"Now why didn't I ever think of that?" Lindsey pointed to a slope overlooking a ball field, where they could spread out the multicolored mat and watch what looked like a pickup soccer match. "But then, this isn't quite like the Jersey shore."

Joan laughed. "We won't get sand in our shoes, either."

As they started to eat, Joan asked about Lindsey's weekend.

"I was in the Berkshires. We have a weekend house in North Egremont, just over the line in Massachusetts. Zoey and her best friend spend most weekends at a nearby stable."

"Does she have a horse?" Joan asked.

"Doesn't she wish? Ted promised to get her a horse this past summer, but his trial kept him too busy. Now, who knows?"

"How's she coping?"

"She hardly said three words all weekend. Worst was Sunday morning."

"Geez, what happened?"

"Sunday's when Zoey and her dad used to go out to breakfast." Lindsey paused to sip her soup. "My darling daughter took her wrath out on me."

"Couldn't you take her out for breakfast?"

Lindsey's mouth went dry. "Sunday breakfast was not about food. It was about father-daughter bonding. No moms allowed."

Joan grimaced. "Oops. I guess I hit a sore spot."

Lindsey hadn't meant to sound cross. "I'm probably overreacting. Really, I've always been grateful Zoey had such a devoted father. Mine deserted when I was ten."

"It sounds like you felt a bit left out. Both times."

Beads of moisture pooled in Lindsey's armpits. She'd never admitted to anyone that she felt left out by the breakfast routine. But then, no one had ever asked her how she felt about it.

"When Zoey was little, I was the primary caretaker and it was Ted's way of giving me some time for myself. But somewhere along the line it turned into a father-daughter tradition. Zoey absolutely loved it. And no matter how busy he was, he always found time ..." Lindsey couldn't finish her sentence.

Joan drew her fingers slowly back and forth across Lindsey's back. "Did you ever talk to Ted about it?"

"And say what? That I resented the time he spent with Zoey? That I was jealous of my daughter? I was too ashamed. I was afraid ... " She couldn't make herself say the words and turned to watch the soccer game, avoiding the scorn she was sure she'd find in Joan's eyes. She wondered how the players, without uniforms, knew who was on which team.

"Afraid of what?"

She kept her eyes on the ball field, but wiggled her back, hoping Joan would continue her gentle stroking.

"Afraid of what?"

"That if I put too much pressure on him, he'd leave. I didn't want Zoey to be without a father too."

"Lindsey, listen to yourself. I don't believe for a minute it was just about Zoey losing her father. Wasn't it also about losing your husband? You must have felt lonely at times."

Lindsey winced. Lonely. That was exactly how she'd felt. And angry. But she'd refused to acknowledge her loneliness, telling herself that Ted was at the mercy of meetings that ran late, client dinners on short notice, out-of-town depositions. Had she been making excuses for him for years?

She wrapped her arms around her legs and rested her chin on her knees. "Sometimes I was very lonely. Trial periods, when he came home so late so often. And yes, Sundays, when he left me home alone."

Left me home alone. She was saying things to Joan she'd not allowed herself to even think, but she couldn't staunch the flood of bitterness. "Sometimes I wondered if he didn't love me any more, if he stayed only because of Zoey." The words triggered a searing image. Lindsey raised her hands and covered her eyes. "Omigod, I didn't even see it."

Joan arched an eyebrow. "See what?"

"That's what he said the night he left! That he'd stayed for Zoey." Lindsey hid her face against her knees, her hands over her head. "I've been such a fool!"

Joan rested an arm over Lindsey's shoulders. "That must hurt. Let it out."

The physical warmth of Joan's skin on her back broke down the last of Lindsey's defenses. Within the nest created by Joan's encircling arm, Lindsey sobbed while a woman she barely knew held her close.

When her tears ebbed, Lindsey said, "I'm sorry I got all maudlin and spoiled our lunch."

"You didn't spoil anything." Joan said as she pulled her arm back and wiped Lindsey's face with a napkin. "It's so easy, with the shock you've had, to lose your bearings."

Joan's reassurance didn't alleviate Lindsey's distress. Lindsey kept her eyes glued on the soccer field as she tried to sort out the broken pieces of her life, all the while wishing Joan had not taken her arm away. She grabbed at one of the loose threads dangling in her brain. "What I don't understand is why he hasn't let me know what to do about the bills and his mail. He came for clothes over the weekend, but didn't leave a note. It's like I don't even exist anymore."

"Does he talk to Zoey?"

"She still won't talk to him." Lindsey turned to query Joan. "Do you think I should make her talk to him?"

"She has every right to be angry. Trust your instincts on this one."

Lindsey sighed. "My instincts have been pretty rotten for a while now."

"Do you have anyone you can talk to?"

Lindsey shook her head with a wry smile. "That's one of my rotten instincts. It seems my closest friend, Dee—we've been friends since before the girls were born—knew about Ted's affair and didn't bother to tell me."

Joan let out a loud groan. "You can't be serious."

"I can. Our husbands have been buddies since grade school. Her husband told her, but she didn't tell me." Lindsey checked her watch. "You've been a real boost to my spirits, but I do need to go."

When they were packed up, Lindsey turned south toward the Circle.

Joan pointed north. "I'm heading toward 79th Street. If you need a shoulder, give me a call. Anytime." She gave Lindsey a one-armed hug, so brief that it was over before Lindsey could return it.

Halfway to the Circle, Lindsey passed a water fountain. She set her bag down, splashed cool water on her eyes, and dried them with a tissue. As she set off again, she saw Joan disappear into an underpass. Could this woman be one of those strangers—some called them guardian angels—who entered one's life at just the right moment?

Chapter 7

Lindsey arrived home late that evening. She hoped to get Zoey to take a break from homework while she ate. Given her daughter's crankiness, the odds didn't look good, but she'd ask anyway, if only so Zoey would know she was home and that she cared.

Zoey's room was empty. So was the den.

Where was she? Lindsey had not allowed herself to think that Zoey's acting out would go beyond sullenness. But what if it had? With her heart racing, she sprinted toward the kitchen. "Elena, do you know where Zoey is?"

"Here, Mrs. Chandler. In the kitchen with me."

The sight of the vase of bright yellow freesias on the dining room table, in front of a single place setting, caused her heart to clench again. Yellow was Lindsey's favorite color and for years, Ted had purchased a bouquet of freesias for the dining room on his way home from work. But Ted wouldn't have sent these. Where had they come from?

As she walked into the kitchen, she realized Elena had bought them, thinking Lindsey would miss having flowers on the table. For nearly a dozen years, that gentle woman, now a grandmother of eight, had been an utterly reliable support system for both Lindsey and Ted.

And a surrogate mother figure for Zoey. Elena was there when Zoey came home from school every afternoon. She took Zoey shopping for boots or a new backpack. In the early grades, she picked Zoey up after school, rehearsed spelling words and checked math problems. She stayed with Zoey on the rare occasions when Lindsey and Ted both had to be out in the evening. And now, after years of drying Zoey's childhood tears, she brought a measure of continuity and stability when Zoey's world had all but fallen apart. Lindsey wondered if she'd made things harder for Zoey by giving Elena the week off?

Elena stood at the sink scrubbing a skillet. Zoey slumped at the table with iPod buds in her ears, pushing a thick grey eraser back and forth across ruled yellow paper. She didn't look up when Lindsey came in.

Lindsey pulled out one earbud as she planted a kiss on Zoey's head. "Anything I can help with?"

"Mom, don't!" Zoey grabbed the earbud and replaced it. "It was a stupid math mistake. I've got it now." She picked up her pencil and started writing.

Lindsey couldn't help smiling. Zoey's response was not actively hostile. She was in the kitchen instead of hiding in her room. And she had a fuchsia ribbon woven into her French braid.

Lindsey scratched Elena's back lightly between her shoulder blades, then pulled her plate out of the microwave. "Your lamb chops smell divine. What *would* I do without you?"

When the phone rang, Zoey grabbed it from its wall mount above the table but halted her arm in midair when she saw the caller ID.

"Aren't you going to answer it?"

Eyes blazing, Zoey held out the phone, still ringing, at arm's length. "I won't talk to him."

Willing herself to sound calm, Lindsey took it. "Hello, Ted."

"Hello, Lindsey. How are you?" His voice was off-pitch, as if he had a bubble in his throat.

"Fine, thank you."

For an eon, they listened to each other breathing. Finally, Ted said, "Can I talk to Zoey, please?"

He hadn't called to talk to her. She wanted to hang up, but instead tapped Zoey's shoulder. "He wants to speak to you." She kept her voice level, all the while wondering if she was earning credits in purgatory.

"No," Zoey said.

"Zoey, please."

"*No.*" Zoey hunched up her shoulders, as if warding off a physical blow and drummed her pencil on the table.

"Ted, she doesn't want to speak to you." Lindsey couldn't take her eyes off Zoey's pencil, waiting for the sharp snap of the lead point breaking.

"Tell her it's about the symphony Thursday. I keep calling her cell but she won't answer." His voice was thin and reedy, nothing like the confident baritone Lindsey was used to.

She wanted to scream. It wasn't her job to play mediator. She held the phone out to Zoey again. "It's about the concert Thursday night."

Zoey looked up, her eyes bleary. "I'm not going."

Lindsey had made an honest effort. But enough was enough. "Ted, we're just sitting down to dinner. I have to go." She punched the off button, harder than was necessary, then turned to stroke Zoey's shoulder. "He loves you, pumpkin. You should talk to him."

"Yeah, you told me that already." Zoey shifted her shoulder out from under Lindsey's caress. "I don't want to see him. At all. Ever."

Stung by Zoey's gesture, Lindsey picked up her plate. She wanted to eat in the kitchen. But what if Zoey retreated to her room the moment she sat down? It was not a rejection she was brave enough to risk. Instead, she made her way to the place Elena had set in the dining room.

Her throat refused to let even small bites go down. For ten days, she'd been thrashing around in a sour soup of sadness, humiliation and rage. His call made it boil. Cheating on her. Leaving her to stew with worry about money. Breaking up their family. It was all she could do not to hurl those damned yellow flowers across the room.

"Mrs. Chandler, you haven't eaten a thing." Elena hovered over her. "What can I get you?"

"Nothing. I'm not hungry. I'm so worried about Zoey."

"She's a sad little girl," Elena said. "She misses her dad a lot." Elena took the plate and turned toward the kitchen, then swiveled in place. "Mrs. Chandler?"

"What, Elena."

"I don't know if it's anything, but Zoey finished off a whole pint of chocolate ice cream when she got home from school today. She's never done that before. And then, she ate a full dinner. I don't know where she put all that food."

"Teenagers do weird things. Do you know if she had lunch?"

"She said she did."

"It's probably just a quirk. I wouldn't worry."

"Okay."

Lindsey laughed bitterly as Elena returned to the kitchen. Talking to Joan, she'd allowed herself to believe something would work out, someday. But now, he wouldn't even talk to her. Why would she think he'd ever be back?

She'd call a lawyer in the morning. Not Dee's lawyer, but Angela Coleman, a woman she knew through work. And a locksmith. She'd been talking about it for days. Tomorrow, she'd do it.

~ ~ ~ ~

She tossed and turned all night, despite the sleeping pill. By midafternoon Tuesday, her head was throbbing. Her office phone rang as she was about to head home. It was Claire.

"I'm on my way out. Can I call you later?"

"I won't keep you. But Ted says Zoey won't come to the symphony. I'd like to see if she'll go with me, just the two of us. Would you mind?"

How typical of Claire to find a gracious way out of a thorny problem. But the gesture left Lindsey feeling utterly inept. Why hadn't she thought of it herself? "Of course not. I'll ask her when I get home."

"If it's okay, I'll call her myself. I'd like it to be between us."

Lindsey strove to match Claire's graciousness. "That would be wonderful. Thanks."

"Lindsey. One more thing."

"Yes?"

"I hope you won't let this come between you and me. I think Ted's behaving abominably. He may have lost his senses, but I haven't."

Lindsey wondered if she'd heard correctly. She'd assumed Claire would take Ted's side. The list of things she'd gotten wrong kept getting longer. "I appreciate that, Claire. You have no idea how much."

~ ~ ~ ~

At home, she found Zoey and Wendy in the kitchen with their science books, a large tree-like diagram with pictures of musical instruments, and the last few kernels of a bowl of popcorn.

Wendy gave her a toothy smile. "Hi, Mrs. C."

"Hi, ladies." Lindsey returned the smile and then planted a kiss atop each girl's head. "What are you working on?"

"My science project," Wendy said.

"What's it on?"

Wendy started to explain, but stopped when Zoey jerked her head up. "Mom, we've got to finish this so Wendy can get home for dinner."

The girls exchanged a look that Lindsey couldn't read and Wendy returned to her diagram without a word.

Swallowing hard, Lindsey reminded herself yet again not to take it personally. "Okay. Okay. I won't disturb you."

She watched the girls out of the corner of her eye as she rummaged through the cupboard for aspirin. The two had been inseparable since kindergarten despite their very considerable differences. Zoey, like her father, was tall and slim. Her features were too irregular to be classically beautiful, but with tawny skin and Ted's thick toffee-colored hair, Lindsey expected she would someday be stunning.

Wendy had Dee's ruddy complexion and wavy black hair. Unlike her mother, whose fine bones made her seem almost willowy, Wendy was stocky, already suffering from her father's risk of pudginess. Popcorn after school wasn't going to help.

Their personalities were as different as their looks. Zoey was totally at ease with strangers, while Wendy could be painfully shy around people she didn't know. Both were good students, but Zoey loved music and the theatre, while Wendy preferred science and wanted to be a doctor. What had cemented their friendship was a love of horses. For the last three years, they'd spent most of their weekends together at the stable.

Over the last year, a new dimension had emerged in their friendship. Wendy had sprouted hips and breasts, while Zoey still had the gangly limbs of a child. When Wendy got her first bra, Zoey had begged to get one as well. Lindsey knew that her slender daughter was unlikely to ever be buxom. Even so, she ached for Zoey each time she found one of the tiny training bras in the laundry.

Of perhaps more concern, their social roles were starting to shift. The once reticent Wendy now had a friend and regular texting partner in the person of an older brother of a Brearley classmate. To the best of Lindsey's knowledge, all of Zoey's friends—texting or otherwise—were other girls her own age. She'd wondered, more than once, if their developmental differences would erode their friendship. There was no sign of it so far, but she hoped Wendy would still be there, now that her daughter needed a loyal friend.

And then there was Dee, who'd always considered Zoey a second daughter. Despite Dee's insistence that she and Jim didn't socialize with Ted and Lauren, the men remained friends. Was Dee, intentionally or not, a conduit of information from Zoey to Ted about Lindsey?

She could hardly ask Zoey not to talk to Wendy or Dee. And she couldn't control what Dee said to her husband. Her headache, just beginning to abate, came roaring back.

At dinner, Zoey gave threadbare responses to Lindsey's questions about her day and the science project. Her questions about rehearsals were no more fruitful.

Finally, Lindsey said, "Hey, pumpkin, did you talk to Gammy?"

Zoey did not look up. "Yes."

"Are you going with her to the symphony?"

"Why do you care?"

"I wondered if you'll be here for dinner on Thursday."

Zoey glowered as she threw her fork on the table. "No. I won't be here."

"Zoey, I know you're angry, but that doesn't give you the right to be uncivil. If you're finished, pick up your fork and lay it on your plate where it belongs."

Zoey did not move.

"Zoey, I mean it. If you can't behave, I won't let you go to the concert with Gammy. Now, pick up your fork."

Zoey, her lips in a dramatic pout, moved the fork to her plate. "Now, may I be excused?"

"Absolutely."

As Zoey stomped out, Lindsey relished an unfamiliar sense of relief. For a change, something was going right. At least Zoey wouldn't lose her grandmother.

Chapter 8

Lindsey had been looking forward to Wednesday's class on "Gender as a Social Myth."

From a clinical perspective, gender identity issues were among the hardest to deal with, not because people with gender identity issues were mentally ill, but because people who didn't fit the heterosexual norm often struggled with the negative reactions of friends and family.

The professor introduced gender myths as social constructs. He pointed to the notion of feminine beauty, which had changed dramatically from the buxom women favored by Rubens to the almost anorexic creatures of modern advertising. He asserted that gender stereotypes— for example, men are stronger and more aggressive than women—reflect social and economic power structures as much as the physical or emotional characteristics of individual men or women.

His comment that gender is something you "do" also struck a chord. In his view, gender identity reflects the accumulation of day-to-day responses to social stereotypes. He argued, persuasively Lindsey thought, that gender discrimination is often self-imposed. For example, he argued that women often encourage male chauvinism by waiting to be asked for an opinion, instead of speaking up.

After class, Joan suggested going for a drink at a funky little jazz place on 10th Street, only a few blocks from the New School. "I don't know who's playing tonight, but it's always somebody good."

It was still early for the jazz club crowd and they got a table right away. As they waited for the first set to start, Joan asked, "Have you ever experienced gender discrimination?"

Lindsey shook her head. "Not much. I make sure I do my homework before I speak out. I've almost always had a respectful reception. How about you?"

Joan chuckled. "Not an issue as a stay-at-home mom and community volunteer. Women run that world."

What about the History Museum?"

"I've only been there three months, and it's a clerical job. Not much for me to have an opinion about." Joan propped her chin on her upraised fist and seemed to focus on the drummer.

Lindsey turned to look in that direction. "Do you know him?"

"No. I was just thinking."

"About?"

Joan brought her gaze back to Lindsey. "How come, if you're comfortable speaking out in your job, you never talked to Ted about Sunday breakfast? About feeling left out."

Lindsey's back stiffened. "That was different. If he'd wanted me to go along, he would have asked."

"Maybe he thought you still liked having time to yourself, like when Zoey was a baby? Maybe he would have asked you along, if he'd known you wanted to go."

"You think I've made it up?" Lindsey's voice sounded shrill to her own ears.

"I don't think that at all. But the way you describe yourself at work and with Ted ... they're so different."

"The two situations aren't at all the same." Lindsey reached for her purse. She wasn't going to be lectured to by a woman who didn't even know Ted. "Joan, I have to go. I have an early morning meeting."

Joan laid her hand on Lindsey's arm, holding her at the table. "I've upset you, haven't I?"

Lindsey shook Joan's arm off and put on her coat. "I'm fine. We can talk about this another time."

Lindsey fought to control her temper as her cab sped up Eighth Avenue. Ted had always known what he wanted and organized his life to accomplish it. If he hadn't asked—not even once—it was because he didn't want her to come along. She scrolled through other questions he'd never asked. How she coped with being so alone when he was preparing for a trial. Whether she wanted a weekend house. What she wanted to eat when they went out for dinner.

It hadn't always been that way. In the early years, he didn't have to ask how she felt or what she wanted. She loved the fact that, somehow, he just knew.

But after they returned from Australia, things changed. He continued to assume he knew what she wanted, but more and more often, his choices left her feeling foolish, as if she'd failed to want the right thing or to see things in proper perspective. Had the burden of taking over his father's law firm made him less sensitive? Had her needs changed once Zoey was in school and her career at the agency began to blossom? Or had she, in the blush of a new love, unconsciously bent her will to his, putting his pleasure above her own needs? She wouldn't have been the first—or last—woman to make that mistake.

As the cab jolted to a stop across from the Beresford, she realized that once again, Joan had zeroed in on an issue Lindsey hadn't wanted to think about. Looking back, she realized how often she'd let Ted take the lead, how seldom she'd challenged him or posed an alternative point of view. It occurred to her that she had imposed some of her loneliness on herself.

She owed Joan an apology.

When she called the next day, Joan brushed her apology off. "It's a tough time for you. Don't worry about it a bit."

After a brief chat about the readings for the next class, Joan mentioned that her older daughter and her husband were going to the Catskills with his family for the weekend. "I'll be at loose ends on Sunday. Any chance you're free for a movie? We could have brunch before the film."

Lindsey was about to refuse when she remembered that Wendy was hosting a slumber party Saturday night. If Dee would bring Zoey back to the city on Sunday evening, it might be possible. "Let me make a phone call and get back to you."

~ ~ ~ ~

Lindsey was delighted that Joan had commandeered a table in the café at the Angelika. Waiting in line for a table at noon on Sundays made her anxious. More than once, waiting for her bill, she'd missed the start of the movie or ended up sitting in the front row, her neck strained to look up at the screen.

As Lindsey approached, Joan raised her coffee cup in welcome. "When did you get back from the Berkshires?"

"About an hour ago." Lindsey noticed a brassy blonde waitress heading their way, and scanned her menu as she sat down. "I was going to come back last night, but I was too tired to make the drive. And, since I had to drop Zoey off, it gave me a chance to visit with Dee. Things between us have been a bit tense in the last few weeks."

"You said she knew before you did. Were you able to sort it out?"

Lindsey nodded. "She says she didn't know whether to butt in or not. I suppose I can understand that, but I'm still not sure how much to trust her."

Joan picked up the flyer with the movie schedule. "That's a hard call to make. I don't know what I'd do in your shoes. Anyway, I've heard good things about *Julie & Julia*. It's a can't-miss movie for a cooking nut like me." She patted her purse. "I got our tickets."

After the waitress took their orders, Joan resumed her classic pose, elbows on the table, chin on her fist. "Tell me about your country place."

"Ted was the one who wanted it. He may not want to keep it if Zoey won't go there with him."

Joan chuckled. "I suspect she'll get over her pissy mood one of these days and welcome him back with open arms."

"I hope so. He's always been her best buddy."

As the waitress delivered their meal, she searched for a way to turn the conversation to Joan. Over the past three weeks, every discussion had revolved around Lindsey. She needed a break from her own misery.

"That was quick." Lindsey said as she tucked her napkin in her lap. "Tell me about your girls." She watched in horror as Joan poured ketchup on a Swiss cheese and spinach omelet.

"Tammy's my firstborn. A dream child, a nurturing, caring human being. And she's a cuddler, like her mother."

Delight was written all over Joan's face. "She was adorable as a kid. I can still see her curled up on the couch with her dad, pretending to read the Sunday newspaper. And now, she's made me a grandmother at age 44. A gorgeous little girl."

"Do you see her often?"

Joan nodded. "She and Les live in Hoboken. He's an accountant, but he does pretty well, so she's a stay-at-home mother. I often go for dinner on Sundays."

"And your other daughter?"

"That would be Kelly. My Thursday child."

"Thursday child?"

"The old nursery rhyme. Monday's child is fair of face. Thursday's child has far to go."

"Sounds like she's been a handful," Lindsey said. "How old is she?"

"Twenty-one. She's had some tough moments, but she'll get her feet under her in good time." Joan halted a bite of omelet halfway to her mouth. "But I want to get back to you. From our conversation in the park, I gather your childhood was tough as well."

"Tough would be a good word. After my dad left and moved to the West Coast, it was like he forgot about me." As she talked, Lindsey played with her napkin, folding it in half and then into quarters. "My mother badmouthed him every chance she had. And things were hard financially. Her answer to anything I wanted was 'no.' We fought constantly."

"Is she still alive?"

"No, she died of a brain hemorrhage three years ago." Lindsey nibbled at her quiche as she thought back to the last years of her mother's life. "I didn't see her much in the five years before she died, since my stepfather was posted to Brazil. He works at Archer Daniels Midland, like my father. Zoey had just turned ten on their last annual stateside visit."

"Is there a juicy story there?" Joan asked. "That they both worked for ADM?"

"Not how you're thinking. Nick's wife died quite a while after my father left. I was a senior in high school when they married."

Lindsey signaled the waitress for more coffee. "After that, her mood improved considerably. But they were both too absorbed in his kids—three of them under ten—to pay much attention to me. I guess they thought I was 'old enough'—Lindsey made air quotes—to take care of myself. And within a year, I was away at college."

Lindsey waited while the waitress refilled their coffee. "I always thought it was a marriage of convenience. He needed a caretaker for his kids. And my mother ... she was desperate to recover her country club lifestyle. But they were still together when she died."

"She had a taste for the finer things, I take it."

"Yep. Before my father left, we lived in a big house and she was active in the country club and on the charity circuit. But they never saved much money. When Dad left, she had to go back to teaching. For a while, she took in boarders to make ends meet, but eventually, we moved to a shoebox house in a crummy neighborhood." Lindsey laid her napkin on her empty plate.

Joan cocked her head. "What did you call her?"

"Call her? Her name was Margaret."

"You always refer to her as 'my mother.' Never mom or mama."

"I called her Mother," Lindsey said. "She never felt like a mom. She wasn't exactly cuddly, even before my dad left."

"How was she with Zoey? Sometimes people are more relaxed with grandkids."

"She wasn't around enough to find out. The grandmother in Zoey's life is Ted's mother Claire."

"Do you and she get on?"

"She's lovely—generous, kind, caring, thoughtful—all things I aspire to be. But we come from such different worlds. She's New York society, the 'ladies who lunch' and work on charity boards. Stuff like the Central Park Conservancy and Sloan Kettering Hospital."

"Sounds a bit like your mother."

Now *that* was a connection Lindsey'd never made. Claire's role in New York society seemed like the air she breathed, not something for show. And Claire cared about the causes she worked on. Her mother—well, she'd only cared about causes that kept her hobnobbing with the right people.

"Nah. Claire comes from generations of those who make things happen in this town. My mother got to play the role only because she married successful men. Her father was just a dry cleaner in downstate Illinois."

Joan tilted her head, so she was looking down over her nose. "C'mon, Lindsey, Claire got to play the role because she inherited it. You don't think she'd struggle if she suddenly found herself without money and connections?"

Lindsey couldn't imagine Claire as anything other than gracious. But Joan had a point. Perhaps her mother hadn't been as shallow as Lindsey assumed. And her grandfather— she felt the heat of shame at her elitist comment. Was she in thrall to the same superficial values she'd criticized in her mother?

Lindsey glanced around the lobby, where people were lining up for the one o'clock film. "Maybe. Claire was certainly taken aback when Ted brought home a small-town girl from the Midwest. She had a different script for him— scion of a major law firm marries debutante from the Upper East Side. She had her money on a girl Ted dated through college."

As the waitress passed by, Lindsey handed her a credit card.

"You don't have to do that."

"You bought the tickets. Anyway, Claire didn't hide her disappointment when I turned down her invitations to luncheons and teas. But I was a newbie social worker. Who had time? And I wasn't interested, anyway. An endless round of mindless politicking. Who gets to chair which committee. Who gets to pick the colors for the gala invite."

Lindsey pushed back her chair and stood up, her eyes on the lengthening movie line. "Her desire for a socialite daughter-in-law put a lot of pressure on both of us. It's one of the reasons why Ted agreed to go to Sydney to oversee the opening of a new office. It gave us a chance to create our own life."

Lindsey tugged at the back of Joan's chair when the waitress returned with her credit card. "I think we should go ... the line's building up. Anyway, when we came back to New York, she had a granddaughter to dote on. But our relationship has never gone beyond the cordial. Until last week."

Joan arched an eyebrow as she stood up.

"She called about taking Zoey to the symphony. Just before she hung up, she said she thought Ted's behavior was 'abominable'—that was her exact word. I nearly fell off my chair!"

"Good for her. It *was* abominable." Joan tucked her arm into Lindsey's. "I think I'm going to like Claire."

~ ~ ~ ~

Zoey was ready to leave for the country when Lindsey got home the following Friday. She seemed in a fine humor, almost like old times. This, after stopping in Lindsey's room for a goodnight kiss when she got home from the concert with Gammy. Whatever Claire had done to brighten Zoey's mood, Lindsey decided she'd sign up for lots more of it.

"Hey, Mom, guess what!"

"No idea."

"Wendy's parents rented a four-bedroom condo in Cabo for Christmas. And they want us to go with them. It's okay, isn't it?"

"Us?"

"You and me."

Lindsey made a conscious effort not to let her astonishment show. Yes, the two families had vacationed together for years. But Lindsey and Zoey were no longer the same sort of 'family.' Yes, she and Dee relished the leisure to walk and cook and catch up on gossip. But things with Dee were, under the rosiest of interpretations, strained.

"It sounds terrific," she lied. "Let me talk to Dee."

"Mom, I really, really want to go. I don't want to spend Christmas here ..." Zoey's lower lip trembled ... "without Dad."

Lindsey gave Zoey a cuddle. "I know. It'd be nice to do something special—just for us."

To her delight, Zoey did not shrink from her embrace.

~ ~ ~ ~

After she dropped the girls at the stable the next morning, she called Dee. "Zoey said you've invited us to Cabo for Christmas? I wish you'd talked to me before you planted this cockamamie idea in Zoey's head."

"Wendy jumped the gun. Jim and I mentioned it the other night, but we haven't booked anything yet. But why's it a cockamamie idea? Wendy would love it ... and it would mean a lot to me if you'd come."

Lindsey ignored the personal plea. "I don't know if I can afford it. Ted hasn't yet said what kind of support he'll provide."

"Afford it? Lindsey, you've been saving most of your salary for years."

"But what if Ted won't cover the housing and school bills? I'll need that money."

"You're legally entitled to half of your joint property. You know that. And if you're concerned, use this as an excuse to discuss your finances. Ask him to buy Zoey's ticket."

Lindsey slumped in her chair, painfully aware that she still wasn't thinking clearly. Dee was correct. She was entitled to half and could certainly afford airfare. She tried not to sound as defensive as she felt. "There's nothing to be gained by pressing Ted until he's ready to talk."

"That's ridiculous. He may think you're not concerned about it. If you are, tell him."

Lindsey wanted to throw the phone at the wall. First Joan. Now Dee. But she had no intention of going to Cabo, and needed time to come up with a credible reason. "Dee, let me do a little figuring, and I'll get back to you."

"That's fine. But Lindsey..."

"Yes?"

"I know you're still angry at me. But I'd never intentionally do anything to hurt you. I hope we can get past this. I do want you to come."

Lindsey mumbled, "I'll call you later" and hung up.

Chapter 9

Lindsey's heart raced at the sound of someone turning the lock on the apartment door. Just as she grabbed a table knife and stood up, Ted strolled into the front hall, carrying a small suitcase. "Hi, ladies."

Fear gave way to white-hot anger. How could the bastard waltz in at dinnertime without knocking? As if he lived here. Scaring them half to death. Then anger morphed into annoyance at herself. Weeks ago, she'd decided to change the lock. Why hadn't she done it?

When Ted saw Lindsey clutching a knife, his grin gave way to a look of repentance. He waggled his hand in a silly, schoolboy wave. "I didn't mean to scare you."

Before Lindsey could react, Zoey shoved her chair back from the table and raced to the hall. "Dad," she shouted, hurling herself into his arms. "Wow! You're back!"

He swept her up in a bear hug and swung her around in a circle. "I'm so glad to see you."

Keeping one arm over her shoulder, he let her down and turned to Lindsey. "Sorry if I frightened you, Lins, but I thought if I came at dinnertime"—he tightened his grip on Zoey—"I could spend some time with my favorite daughter."

Zoey wrapped both arms around his waist and nestled her head against his chest. "Dad, I'm so glad you're here. I can't wait to tell you about the school play. I got the lead."

"Doesn't surprise me a bit. I'm sure you'll be terrific. When will it be?"

"Early November."

"I'll be there, tossing roses when you take your bow. Now, come with me and tell me all about it. What's the play? What part you have. What the tryouts were like."

"Where are you going?"

"To get some stuff from the bedroom."

Zoey drew back enough to quiz her father. "What stuff?"

Ted hesitated a fraction of a second. "My winter clothes. I'll need them."

Zoey's face deflated. She pushed his arm off her shoulder and stepped back, bumping into his empty suitcase. When it fell over with a hollow thud, she turned to follow the sound. "I hate you," she shouted as she flew down the bedroom hallway. The bang of her door echoed throughout the apartment.

Nodding toward Zoey's room, Ted managed to state the obvious. "I guess I upset her."

Lindsey dropped the knife on the table. "What the bloody hell did you expect? How was she supposed to know you only came to get clothes?"

"That's not true." He moved to the dining room doorway. "I came to talk to her."

"Are you completely clueless? You expect her to forgive you just because you came at dinnertime." Lindsey inhaled the familiar musky odor he often had at the end of a day, the aroma she associated with falling asleep in his arms. When the walls started to swim in front of her, she gripped the back of her chair. "Just get your things and go."

"Lins, why won't she talk to me?" Ted persisted.

The bastard. Using her pet name. Like they were in this together. Not a chance in hell. "Because the father she adored has walked out of her life and—in her words—'left me behind.'"

Ted shook his head. "I didn't leave her behind. She has her own room at my place."

"God save us from your legal reasoning." Her lips twisted in a sneer. "Zoey doesn't want another bedroom. She wants you down the hall from the one she already has."

She picked up the dinner plates and turned toward the kitchen. "Do you realize she slams doors at every opportunity? She hardly talks. She goes to school, but every time the phone rings, I wonder if it's the police or the hospital."

"What should I do?"

"Well, the obvious answer would be to come home."

He reached out and brushed her cheek with his fingertips as she went by. "Lins, you have no idea how sorry I am about all this."

Lindsey's skin burned where he touched her, and she backed out of his reach. "You're right. I have no idea. Now get the hell out."

He moved forward, again within reach of her. "Lins, I—"

"Get out."

She didn't know how long he stood there, staring at her, unblinking, unmoving. Only when she pushed past him to the kitchen did he turn toward the bedroom.

"I only need a minute."

After she'd cleared the table, she poured herself a scotch. That morning, she'd met with Angela, who reiterated Dee's advice to get an agreement on finances and parental responsibilities as soon as possible. Angela planned to draw up negotiating points and call Ted or his lawyer, but that would take weeks. Ted's unexpected invasion might be an opportunity to get some clarity a lot sooner. Sinking onto the living room couch, she rehearsed what she'd say.

"I'm leaving now." Ted's voice, only a few feet away, startled her. She'd been concentrating so hard on identifying every issue, she hadn't heard him in the front hall.

She bit her lower lip until it hurt. It was now or never. Without looking up, she said, "I'm changing the locks tomorrow."

"Why?"

Was it possible he didn't know? "You can't come in like this. Without warning." She turned to meet his gaze. "And something else. The September bills. Did you pay them?"

He cocked his head. "Did you think I wouldn't? I'll take care of whatever you and Zoey need."

She swallowed hard, to clear her head as much as her throat. "What in hell does that mean? All the expenses for this apartment? The country house? Zoey's school fees?"

"Of course. Why do you ask?"

Her laugh had the sharp edge of broken glass. "Everything I thought I knew about you went out the window a month ago. How would I know what you think about anything?"

Ted crossed his arms and shifted his glance toward the living room window. Finally, he looked back at her. "You're right. We should talk." He turned toward the front door. "I'll call you to set up a time."

"Ted," she called out again.

"What *is* it?" he said, his back to her, irritation evident in the rigid set of his shoulders.

"My lawyer is drawing up a separation agreement."

Ted made a half turn as if to say something, but changed his mind, picked up his suitcase and left.

As the door closed, Lindsey burrowed her way through a welter of emotions. Anger that she'd had to ask about their finances. Anxiety about Cabo. If he intended to cover all their expenses, she couldn't use money as a reason not to go. What would she tell Dee?

But the strongest emotion was an almost gleeful sense she'd evened the score a bit. He hadn't expected her to change the locks or call a lawyer. He'd expected—well, she didn't know what he expected, but she'd caught him off guard.

She wanted to share her triumph, however small, with Joan. But she had to attend to Zoey, whose trust had been abused for the second time. Lindsey didn't know how to comfort her, but she had to try.

She headed toward Zoey's room, girding herself for a repeat of the hysterical crying jag the day her father left. Halfway there, she changed her mind. Talking to Joan would ground her, and help her to maintain her own equilibrium as she tried to deal with Zoey's distress.

Joan's response was perfect. "Well done. Tomorrow, after class, we'll make a grand toast to taking control of your life. Now, go see about your daughter."

~ ~ ~ ~

Zoey didn't respond to her knock. She rapped a second time, and said "I'm coming in, pumpkin," but when she turned the handle, nothing happened. She heard only silence. No music. No crying. No bedsprings.

Icy fear gripped her. Zoey never locked her door. Lindsey jiggled the handle. "Zoey, let me in. Open the door."

Nothing.

Fighting panic, she pounded the door with her fists. "Zoey, say something. Please let me know you're all right."

"Go away and leave me alone."

"Zoey, darling, I know you're upset. I want to talk to you."

"Go away."

Lindsey stared at the door, not sure what she expected to happen. Zoey would have to come out at some point, but it might not be until morning. She couldn't stand there all night. But she couldn't go to bed without knowing Zoey was okay.

Finally, she pulled the armchair in her bedroom to a spot where she'd notice if Zoey's door opened. She tried to read the *New Yorker*, but kept losing her place. Glancing up at Zoey's door. Reliving her fright when Ted had opened the front door. Seething at the arrogance of his invasion. Eventually she turned on *Law and Order* to distract her from the endless loop of painful memories.

She woke with a start as the newscast began. Zoey's door was open. She crossed the hall. The room was empty. Wavering between relief and panic, she checked the den, and then headed to the kitchen.

Zoey stood looking out the kitchen window, a nearly empty bag of oatmeal cookies on the counter next to her. As Lindsey came into the kitchen, Zoey pulled the bag toward her, out of Lindsey's line of sight. Lindsey found the gesture curious, but assumed they were a sort of comfort food for an unhappy child.

Zoey didn't turn around. Lindsey reached out to stroke her back. "I know how sad you are, but—"

At Lindsey's touch, Zoey flinched and then spun around, her nose flaring, her eyes wide. She raised her arms to Lindsey's shoulders and shoved her mother backwards. "Get ... your ... hands ... off ... me."

Lindsey had the sensation of falling into the dark venomous pools in her daughter's eyes. As she struggled for balance, she flailed out. It was the sharp sound of flesh smacking flesh and the hard jolt of her palm against Zoey's jaw that brought her back to her spot in the kitchen.

What she saw was Zoey's wide-eyed look of shock above the bright pink cloud spreading across her pale skin. "Omigod, Zoey, I didn't mean to do that." She reached out again, but Zoey sidestepped away.

"I wish you were dead," Zoey hissed as she bolted out of the kitchen. "I wish both of you were dead."

Lindsey stared at the spot where Zoey had stood, trying to fathom the depths of an anger she hadn't known she possessed, trying to fathom how she could have turned that anger on an already wounded child. Her face burned from shame, her whole face, not just the spot that matched where she hit Zoey.

Chapter 10

Lindsey's stomach churned when she heard Dee's terse voicemail late the next day. Just when she thought things couldn't get worse, they had. It took her a full five minutes to work up the courage to return Dee's call. When she did, Dee's words surprised her.

"Lindsey, are you okay?"

"Me? I thought you'd be calling about Zoey."

"I am. But I can't imagine that you're in any better shape than she is."

"Did she tell you what happened?"

"Her side of the story. But I don't believe you slapped her for 'no reason at all.'"

"There's no reason that justifies what I did."

"You shouldn't have slapped her. But you had a reason. What was it?"

"She's been sullen, angry, and absolutely hateful for weeks now. I don't understand why she's taking it out on me. Like it's my fault—"

"What happened?"

"When I tried to rub her back, she flinched, as if I had leprosy. Coming on top of the scene with Ted, I ... I don't know, I was in such a fog, I couldn't ... she shouted at me ... to keep my hands off her. I ... I ... she was out of control ... she shoved me away. I just reacted without thinking." Lindsey let her head drop onto the back of her chair and closed her eyes. "She must hate me."

"She doesn't hate you. But it did shake her up."

"What did she say?"

"Her exact words ... 'She doesn't love me, either.'"

Lindsey's stomach contracted as if she'd been kicked. History *was* repeating itself. She was doing to her daughter what her mother had done to her.

Worse. Her mother had never slapped her.

"Dee, how do I make her understand that I love her?"

"I wish I had an easy answer. I know you love Zoey and she loves you. But this very minute, neither of you knows what cards to play—nor even what cards you have. Just keep telling her you love her, even if she doesn't seem to be paying attention."

~ ~ ~ ~

Her stomach knotted as she watched Joan leave the classroom, deep in conversation with a young, bearded student. Could Joan have forgotten they were meeting after class? What would she do if Joan had forgotten? Lindsey had betrayed every value she'd espoused for years. She wasn't sure she'd get through the night if she had to be alone.

She let out an audible sigh of relief when she saw Joan waiting at the escalator.

As they rode down, Joan chattered about the night's lecture. "I'm in over my head in this class. I don't get myth as part of everyday life. When I think about myths, I think about stuff I learned in grade school. You know, the rags-to-riches Horatio Alger sort of thing."

Joan's self-deprecating tone begged for a reassuring response, and Lindsey obliged. "Your experience with Buddhism has to provide a unique perspective on modern society."

"But Buddhism is a philosophical system, not a myth. It's a way of looking at life, not a tale about fictional events."

Lindsey offered a different perspective. "Myth doesn't have to be fiction. You can look at it as a narrative that captures the essential values of a community or culture. Stories about Buddha or the bodhisattvas are wonderful myths, even if they are true."

"Hummh. Have to think about that."

As they crossed the atrium, Lindsey wanted to talk about the scene with Zoey, but couldn't think where to start. She settled for a half-truth. "Things got a bit more exciting after we talked last night."

"With Ted?"

"No, Zoey."

"Oh, dear. Well, how about coffee at my place? We can talk there."

She nodded, comforted by the concern she saw in Joan's eyes.

Pushing through the revolving door into the night, they were greeted by a chilly drizzle. Huddling under their respective umbrellas, they trekked the four blocks to Joan's apartment without speaking.

The building, on 15th Street a few doors in from Fifth Avenue, was a large and elegant prewar stone structure with gargoyles carved into the corners on alternating floors. There was no doorman and only a tiny lobby. As she shook out her umbrella, Lindsey wondered whether Joan got frustrated waiting for the lone elevator.

Before she could ask, the elevator arrived. Joan slipped a key into the sixth floor slot.

"Do you always need the key, or just at night?"

"Always," Joan replied. "You can't get there unless I want you there."

"What about guests? Do you throw a key out the window?"

Joan snorted. "Thank goodness, no. I've got terrible aim. From my apartment, I can set the elevator to go to the lobby and come back to six."

Lindsey was pondering the mechanics of such a system when the door opened onto a small, parquet-floored lobby with a library table carved from tricolored lacquered woods. Above it hung a large mirror in an amoeba-shaped, bronze frame. Carved double doors, in a deep burgundy, led to the only apartment on the floor.

Lindsey tried not to gawk. How could Joan afford a floor-through in a prewar building on a librarian's salary? As they stepped into the inner hall, diffusely lit from panels near the ceiling, Lindsey heard loud rap music.

Joan shouted, "Kelly? You here?"

There was no answer. Lindsey set her purse on a small version of the elevator hall table. The mirror matched as well. Somebody with a designer's eye had done both spaces.

Joan said. "She lives in Newark, but camps out here when the spirit moves her. She wouldn't deign to turn off the lights or the stereo when she leaves."

From the hall, they entered a large, high-ceilinged room with a wall of windows at the far end. The discrete rooms typical of a prewar building had been converted into this airy loft straight out of *Architectural Digest.*

Joan switched the music to Norah Jones, at a noticeably lower volume. Meanwhile, Lindsey thought about her own place in the Beresford, spacious and comfortable with a stunning view of Central Park, but without the kind of intentional style this place had.

The longer Lindsey surveyed the space, however, the more impersonal it felt, a decorator's showplace. A sectional couch, three upholstered chairs and a grand piano sat at the far end, in front of the windows. In the middle, eight curved bronze chairs surrounded a massive glass dining table on a bronze base. Abstract art graced the walls. A dramatic black-and-white drawing caught Lindsey's eye. She was sure it was a Sol LeWitt.

A stark white corridor kitchen stretched out in front of them, a high counter separating it from the dining area. On either side of the loft, more or less opposite the dining table, were two hallways.

The décor said little about the apartment's inhabitants except that they had expensive taste. By contrast, Lindsey's apartment was a potpourri of things acquired when she and Ted saw something that struck their fancy. The oriental rugs, purchased in India, had been costly, but the art and furniture ranged from spur-of-the-moment purchases at a craft fair to well-considered choices from a gallery or showroom. Somehow, it all came together.

"Oh—and yes," Joan said with a wry laugh as she pointed to a pot of cold macaroni and cheese. "She never fails to leave dirty dishes. I'm the mother, so I get to clean up." She picked up the teakettle. "How about a hot toddy for this rotten night?"

"Sounds yummy." Lindsey perched on a stool to watch Joan. "This place is spectacular. Did you do the renovations?"

"No, I'm renting it from a couple that's overseas on assignment." Joan pulled two lemons out of a wire basket. She handed them to Lindsey with a sharp knife and an old-fashioned glass juicer. "Here, cut and squeeze."

"Sure." Lindsey attacked the lemons while Joan bustled around, gathering up ingredients.

"Why the hell did you turn off my music?"

Lindsey jumped at the shrewish voice, and turned to see a petulant young woman, all in black, in the hallway to the right of the kitchen, a backpack slung over one shoulder.

"My friend and I wanted to talk. You can't even hear yourself think with that noise."

"It's not noise. It's bitchin' good music."

"Be that as it may, this is my apartment. You're welcome anytime, but when I'm home, we'll listen to music I like."

"Well, you sure don't make me feel welcome." Kelly centered her backpack and headed toward the front door.

As she stomped across the apartment, Lindsey observed that the only relief from the girl's head-to-toe blackness came from a mop of short, spiky green hair and the silver rings threaded in the outer edge of one ear. Lindsey counted eight of them by the time Kelly reached the hallway leading to the front door.

"When will I see you again?" Joan asked.

Kelly hunched her shoulders. Her lower lip curled. "Dunno. Maybe never." She turned into the hallway and was gone.

Lindsey was astonished at Kelly's cruelty. She was even more astonished when Joan gave what sounded like a canned laugh. "Now you've seen my Thursday child. Isn't she a piece of work?"

"Piece of work" was not how Lindsey would describe her, but she sensed Joan was seeking a mother's shared perspective, not a clinical assessment. As a mother, Lindsey was awed by Joan's equanimity in the face of a seriously troubled child. Even with her social work training, Lindsey seemed unable to maintain her equilibrium with a child whose behavior was an altogether reasonable response to her situation. "It seems Kelly enjoys pushing your buttons."

"She's been trying for years, but I've grown immune to her wiles." Joan reached for the steaming teakettle. "Still feel good about your conversation with Ted?"

"Not exactly..." She pushed the juicer toward Joan.

Joan poured the pale yellow liquid into the mugs. "What happened?"

"When Zoey stormed into her room, she locked her door. She's never done that before. I knocked several times after Ted left, but she wouldn't open up."

"I wouldn't worry too much. She'll get over it."

Lindsey's throat burned. Her pleasure at catching Ted off guard had decayed into disgust at her own vindictiveness. And far from comforting her daughter, she'd made things worse. Having failed as a wife, now she'd failed as a mother. She had no idea what to say.

Joan handed Lindsey a mug. "Oh dear, you are upset, aren't you?" She put an arm over Lindsey's shoulder and nodded toward the living room. "Come, let's sit."

Encircled by Joan's arm, Lindsey let herself be drawn to the couch. The physical geography of their bodies evoked an image of late-night seduction, but she squelched the image at once. It was so not relevant to this comforting friendship.

Joan sat, patted the cushion next to her, then extended her arm along the back of the sofa, encouraging Lindsey to sit close.

As they sipped their hot toddies in a comfortable silence, Lindsey savored Joan's warmth through her thin silk shirt and pondered the contrast between Zoey and Kelly. What had driven Kelly to rebel in the face of a seemingly stable family life? And Zoey? Would she eventually settle down to a more adult version of the amiable child she'd once been, or would the divorce send her hurtling down a path of increasing hostility and anger?

She realized Joan had said something. "I'm sorry, my mind was wandering."

"Zoey. I presume she came out eventually."

Lindsey nodded. "A little after ten, for something to eat. When I tried to comfort her, she twisted away ... like I was a pariah. I can still hear her shouting 'Get your hands off me.'

You should have seen her face, Joan. Like she hated me. I was crazy with frustration. Angry at Ted. At her. At the whole damn thing."

Lindsey covered her face with her hands. She didn't want Joan to see her despair. "I can't believe I slapped her. My own daughter. I've never laid a hand on her before."

"Oh dear." Joan lowered her hand to Lindsey's shoulder and tugged her close.

Lindsey sat for a moment, then drew back to meet Joan's eyes. "Her face wilted. Like she'd been betrayed by her last friend. She locked herself in her room ... again! I kept knocking, but she wouldn't answer. She was gone when I got up this morning."

"Yikes. Do you know where she went?"

"School. I called. She's at Wendy's now. I called her on my way to class, but she wouldn't talk to me." Lindsey covered her face again. "Maybe she's right to hate me."

Joan drew Lindsey's head onto her shoulder and stroked her hair. "She doesn't hate you. But this is a tough time for her."

Lindsey slid down and settled into the curve of Joan's arm. She'd just revealed one of the worst things she'd ever done, and Joan had listened without judgment or criticism.

She didn't ever want to move.

~ ~ ~ ~

It was two in the morning when Lindsey's cab pulled away from Joan's apartment. Her heart hammered against the walls of her chest, the sound reverberating in her ears. She felt spacey, almost delirious, not quite believing what had just happened.

Was there a moment when she'd made a conscious decision to make love to a woman?

Was it when Joan drew her to the couch? When Joan pulled her close? When Joan rested her head against hers? When Joan stroked her hair? When Joan kissed Lindsey's wet eyes, the way you'd kiss a child's scraped knee? When Lindsey turned to thank Joan? Was it just then, when their lips met?

She couldn't point to the moment of decision. All Lindsey knew was that she'd been enveloped in a velvety cloak of well-being.

Chapter 11

Heading down 56th Street a little before noon the next day, Lindsey was as nervous as she'd ever been on a first date. Every few steps she stopped, wondering yet again if she should turn around and go back to her office.

Until yesterday, she and Joan were friends. But what were they now? Was last night a one-night stand, an unrepeatable confluence of too much hot toddy and her desperate need for comfort? Was it something they'd laugh about, and then go on as they had been?

Or ... Lindsey's pulse quickened ... was it the start of a new dimension in their friendship? She couldn't remember ever being physically attracted to a woman before. And yet, her body had instinctively responded to Joan's touch, instinctively reached out to pleasure her friend. Her newfound physical desire seemed of a piece with her connectedness to this nurturing woman.

And what did it mean about herself ... that she'd responded so powerfully to a woman? She slowed her pace as she tried to think it through.

If she were innately disposed to same-sex relationships, would she have gravitated only toward men for 40-odd years? It seemed improbable. But she'd read about sexual fluidity, the theory that sexual desire was often a response to a strong emotional attachment, regardless of gender. From that perspective, her attraction to Joan was a natural outgrowth of their deepening emotional intimacy.

Whatever, she'd slept with a woman, and was burning with desire to do it again.

Suddenly, the restaurant door was in front of her. Joan was waiting inside. Or was she?

Lindsey turned and walked back twenty paces in the direction she'd come. They'd made the lunch date as Lindsey left the night before. What if Joan had had second thoughts?

What if—Lindsey's heart missed a full beat—in the morning light, Joan viewed their liaison as 'odd' or 'sick?' Would it prove a barrier to the intimacy they'd shared until now?

She stared at her reflection in the window of a dress shop, trying to identify something in her face or her stance that would answer her questions. She saw nothing except a well-dressed social worker on her way to lunch.

Forcing herself to stand taller than she felt, Lindsey returned to the restaurant, opened the door and walked in.

Joan was already seated. A glass of champagne sparkled at each place. Joan lifted hers as Lindsey approached. "A toast to a wonderful—and loving—friend."

Lindsey hesitated—she didn't like drinking at lunch—but her relief at Joan's welcoming gesture overcame her caution. She clinked her glass against Joan's. "To our friendship."

Joan fingers played across the back of Lindsey's hand. "Are you feeling better today?"

Lindsey's skin tingled at the touch. It took every bit of concentration she had to give a sensible reply. "Absolutely. I needed a sympathetic ear a lot more than I realized."

"Sometimes it helps to talk, just to say it out loud. I loved being there for you." She gave Lindsey's fingers a concluding pat. "You're a lovely, generous woman, Lindsey, and you deserve to be fussed over."

Lindsey's eyes flooded. *Fussed over.* She wasn't used to being fussed over. She liked it.

After the waiter took their order, Joan reached for Lindsey's hand again. "Do you believe in synchronicity?"

Lindsey almost pulled her hand away, but seeing no one she knew at nearby tables, she let her hand rest under Joan's. "Umm. I've never given it much thought. Why?"

"Your breakup with Ted. My coming to New York. At the same time. Like it was meant to happen."

Lindsey nodded. "Maybe it was. I don't know how I would have made it through the last month without you."

"That's what friends are for." She kissed her fingertips and brushed them across Lindsey's cheek. "Now, tell me about Zoey? Have you talked to her?"

Lindsey touched her cheek where Joan's fingers had been, pleased by the intimate gesture but worried that others would notice. "I called her again this morning before school. When I tried to apologize, she muttered 'OK' and hung up." Lindsey shivered, reliving the chill that had run through her when Zoey's phone clicked off. "How do I get her to trust me? How do I convince her it won't happen again?"

"If it's never happened before, she'll come around. I'm sure."

Lindsey hoped, with every fiber of her being, that Joan was right.

"I'm looking forward to meeting her."

Lindsey nodded. "I think you two would enjoy each other." She turned to the question she'd been mulling over all morning. "Has this ever happened to you before?"

"Hitting one of my daughters? I certainly spanked them when they were little—"

"No, I meant being with a woman. I wondered—"

"I am *not* a lesbian."

"That wasn't my question. I just wondered if you've ever made love to a woman before?"

"Why would you ask such a thing? My god, I was with Brad for nearly thirty years and had two daughters!"

"Lots of married women have a same-sex relationship during or after a marriage. I never have, and I wondered if it was as extraordinary for you as it was to me."

"I have never slept with another woman." Joan's words were clipped, her face impassive.

Lindsey was taken aback at Joan's defensiveness. Like Clinton's line, "I did not have sexual relations with that woman." Why was Joan so loathe to share her reaction, to acknowledge whether or not it had been a significant experience? The anxiety Lindsey'd felt on her way to lunch simmered just below the surface.

"I'm sorry. I didn't mean to pry. I just want to know more about you." Searching for a neutral topic, she recalled Joan's study in a Buddhist school. "Tell me about the Buddhist center. What got you interested in it?"

"I remember it clearly—the moment I knew something in my life had to change." Joan rested her chin in the palm of her hand, her elbows on the table. "I was serving dessert after dinner, only half-listening to Brad and the girls. Maybe only a quarter. It was the same gossipy conversation we'd been having for years. About Brad's staff. About the girls' teachers or schoolmates. About our friends' children." Joan gave a small shrug, "Not a single new idea from one meal to the next."

Lindsey stifled a laugh. She'd never thought of Buddhism as the solution to a marriage gone flat. "Why Buddhism? Why not an art class?"

Joan smiled. "Synchronicity again! I signed up for a class on eastern religion at the local Adult Ed center. The teacher invited us to a Buddhist retreat center near Short Hills. The place spoke to a part of me that was starved for intellectual stimulation, if that makes sense. I loved the combination of classes, meditation and work-in-service. So I joined."

"What branch of Buddhism was it?"

"We studied different schools of thought—Mahayana, Theravada, Pure Land, Zen. It wasn't tied to any particular one."

"Which one appealed to you?"

"No one in particular. A lot of the difference is how different cultures handle day-to-day practices ... a monastic life or a family. What I loved were ideas that they mostly share."

"Like?"

"That suffering is a result of human desire to acquire things we don't have, or hang on to things we've already got. The idea of mindfulness, of living completely in the moment. And they go together. If you're living in the moment, you're not wasting energy and emotion longing for the past or yearning for something in the future."

Mindfulness. Lindsey had always liked the concept. Now, with her life falling apart all around her, it offered a way to focus on what she had to do today to protect herself and her child. Planning for the future was beyond her. And longing for the past would accomplish nothing.

"I'd love to read more about it ... about mindfulness. Can you suggest some things?"

"Better yet, I'll lend you a couple of quite good books. And some on meditation as well. I don't know how I ever survived without it."

"I tried for almost a year," Lindsey said, "but I never succeeded in stilling my mind. How often do you do it?"

"Every day, at least once. It centers me ... keeps me from feeling overwhelmed."

Lindsey wanted to probe the subject, but knew she wouldn't learn much about meditation techniques in the middle of crowded restaurant. Instead, she said, "Do you still go there?"

"No. It was one of the many things in Short Hills I needed to escape."

"Escape? Why?"

"Being taken for granted," Joan said. "Being expected to pinch-hit whenever anyone had a scheduling problem."

She held her knife to her ear like a phone and mimicked a deep bass. "Eleanor has a cold and can't come this weekend. So we'll need a salad for dinner Saturday. You don't mind making it, do you?" She shifted to a higher pitch. "Richard was supposed to shop for this weekend, but he's out of town on business. Is there any chance you could do it?"

"Couldn't you say no?"

"I was happy to help. I just got tired of always being the one they turned to."

Joan checked her watch as she replaced her knife on the table. "We need to get the check if I'm going to get back for my meeting."

Out on the sidewalk, Lindsey gave Joan a hug, the kind women give each other after lunch. Joan held on longer than Lindsey expected, but Lindsey didn't pull away.

Heading back to her office in the October sunshine, Lindsey luxuriated in a sense of possibility. Of a new chapter opening up in her life. Of a kind of intimacy she'd never known. She did a little three-step jig on the sidewalk.

Over the course of the afternoon, as she revisited their lunchtime conversation, she realized there was more to Joan than being Lindsey's guardian angel.

Like Joan's sense of being "used." People who felt they'd been taken advantage of almost always allowed it to happen, as a way of dealing with insecurity. Joan didn't strike her as insecure. Just the opposite. What had led her to see herself as a "victim?"

Like Joan's reaction to Lindsey's question about making love. She'd so wanted to share the wonder of last night's passion. Why wouldn't Joan discuss it?

~ ~ ~ ~

Euphoria gave way to guilt as Lindsey rode the elevator up to the 20th floor. She drummed her fingers on the back wall each time the car stopped to let another resident out. Once in the apartment, she headed to Zoey's room without taking off her coat and rapped on the door. "Are you there, pumpkin?"

She heard a low whoosh, the sound of Zoey landing on her bed.

"Zoey. I'm so sorry. It was an awful thing to do." Lindsey rapped again, fully aware that nothing she could say would make it all right. Her behavior had been as childish as Zoey's. Worse, because slamming doors didn't hurt anyone. Worse, because she was supposed to be the adult. "I was angry at your Dad and I took it out on you. It was an awful thing to do."

Nothing.

"Zoey, I love you."

Not a sound.

"Zoey, I know you're hurt and sad. I am too. I'm going to sit here by your door until you're ready to come out. All night, if I have to."

Lindsey folded her coat into a cushion and sat down, her back against the wall opposite Zoey's door, her legs out in front of her. She kicked off her shoes and began to sing "Country Road," one of her favorite James Taylor tunes, loud enough for Zoey to know she was there.

Not long after, Elena appeared in the foyer. Her eyes went wide. "Did you fall? Can I help you up?"

"I'm fine, Elena, thank you. I'm waiting for Zoey."

Elena glanced somberly at the door and then back at Lindsey, but said nothing.

"Did Zoey tell you what I did?"

Elena nodded, but visibly hesitated before she spoke. "She thinks it's because she's been so mean to you lately."

Lindsey suspected Zoey could hear their conversation. She raised her voice a notch. "Elena, I love her no matter how cranky she is. I was angry at Ted, not at her." She let out a long, deep breath, as if somehow she could exhale the pain.

"Can I get you something? A plate of food?"

Lindsey nodded. "And one for her."

When Elena returned with two plates of meatloaf and green beans, Lindsey set one on the floor next to her. "Zoey, Elena's brought dinner for you. Meatloaf. One of your favorites."

The only response was the sound of a toilet flushing.

Over the next half-hour, Lindsey switched back and forth among James Taylor, Norah Jones and lullabies she'd once sung to Zoey, stopping occasionally for a bite of food. Twice, she had to shake her legs to keep the circulation going. As she took her last mouthful of now-cold beans, the door handle twitched. With her eyes glued to the shiny brass lever, Lindsey took a deep breath and began to hum *Over the Rainbow.*

She got through two more tunes before the handle moved again, this time a full 90-degrees. She held her breath, waiting, hoping. And then Zoey was in front of her, tears streaming down her drawn cheeks, her tongue licking at the salty beads dribbling across her lips. Her eyes searched Lindsey's face.

Lindsey started to scramble to her feet, but instead reached up her arms and nodded toward the patch of carpet next to her. "Zoey, come sit with me. Have something to eat."

Zoey slipped to the floor, mimicking her mother's straight-legged position. She accepted the plate and popped a large piece of meatloaf into her mouth with her fingers.

Lindsey put an arm around Zoey's shoulder. She wanted to explain how stunned she'd been by Zoey's hostility, how angry she'd been at Ted. Words would not undo the damage, but she wanted to say them anyway. "My darling, I hope you can forgive me. I was so—"

Zoey dropped her head onto Lindsey's shoulder. "Mom, I thought you didn't love me either."

Either. As if she'd abandoned Zoey, along with Ted. Zoey was wrong on both counts, but Lindsey couldn't deny how her daughter felt.

Lindsey rested her head against Zoey's, reaching for a physical connection that words could never make. "Zoey, I do love you. So very much. But sometimes adults do hurtful things when they don't mean to." She shifted slightly and with the palm of her hand, turned Zoey's face to hers. "You are the most important thing in the world to me. I will never leave you."

Zoey eyes lingered on her mother's face for several moments. "Mom, can I sleep with you tonight?"

Lindsey thought she might faint with relief. "Of course. Tonight. Tomorrow night. As long as you want."

~ ~ ~ ~

As usual, they left for the country after work Friday evening. Zoey was still clingy, not like the weekend after Ted left, but in need of way more than the normal quota of hugs.

Once they merged into the steady hum of commuter traffic on the Henry Hudson Parkway, Zoey propped her back against the passenger door so she could watch Lindsey. "Mom?"

"Yeah?"

"I'm sorry I've been so mean to you since Dad left."

"I'm sorry, too. I wish I could make all this easier for you." She paused, her attention focused on passing a block of slower traffic, then said, "Why have you been so angry at me? Was it something I did? Something I said?"

"Why did you let Dad leave?"

Lindsey fought not to take her eyes off the road. Every part of her being wanted to look at Zoey, to read the emotion in her daughter's face. "I didn't *let* him leave. I thought we were happy, and then one day he was gone."

"Is he with her ... that woman who called him on the phone?"

"I dunno." Lindsey wasn't prepared to discuss Ted's affair with her daughter.

Zoey flinched, almost as if a bolt of electricity had seared her. "I hate him."

"He loves you."

"I don't care how many times he calls me, I won't talk to him."

"Does he call you often?"

Zoey nodded. "Every day. Sometimes two or three times."

Lindsey tried to think of a response. She didn't want Zoey to feel guilty about not talking to him, but the chasm between father and daughter saddened her. After several miles of silence, it struck her that the Cabo invitation might be just the thing. Whatever her ambivalence about Dee and Jim, the trip would be a tangible way to assure Zoey that mother and daughter were in this together. "Do you still want to go to Cabo?"

"Wow, yeah. Can we go? Please, please, puleeze."

"Okay. I'll call Dee."

"Wow, Cool. Can I call Wendy right now?"

Lindsey smiled to herself. Having Zoey announce the decision might avoid an awkward explanation. "Sure, pumpkin. Go ahead."

~ ~ ~ ~

Lindsey woke up to the sound of Zoey's soft, even breathing. It was a sound she could listen to forever. Only when her bladder forced her out of bed did she notice the clock. Nearly 8:40. It was her weekend to play chauffeur and they were supposed to pick up Wendy at nine.

She prodded Zoey. "Wake up, sleepyhead. C'mon, wake up. We overslept."

They managed to get out of the house in fifteen minutes and she delivered the girls to the stable a few minutes after 9:30.

Breathless from the frenetic pace, she stopped at the Old Egremont Country Store for a coffee to tide her over until she got home. As she savored the hot brew, her body grew warm with longing for Joan. Could she make it to the city and back in time to pick up the girls at 4:30? Two and a half hours to Joan's ... and two and a half back. That would give them two hours together.

Her hand shook as she pulled out her phone. What if Joan had other plans? What if there was an accident at the stable, and Lindsey wasn't here? Maybe Dee would cover for her. But what would she tell Dee?

She remembered that Dee and Jim were at an estate auction outside of Lenox and wouldn't be back until nearly dinnertime. With that, she gave a baleful sigh and dropped the phone back in her purse. She'd tough it out this weekend. But she could—would—invite Joan to the country.

Chapter 12

Ted called her late the following Monday, saying he'd be over that evening to discuss finances. Caught off guard, Lindsey agreed, but regretted it almost at once. When she called to get a faxed copy of her lawyer's preliminary recommendations, Angela had left for the day.

After dinner, Lindsey pored over her penciled notes from her conversation with her attorney. Halfway through, Dee called.

Annoyed by the interruption, Lindsey's greeting was curt. "What's up, Dee?"

"And a very good evening to you too. Is this a bad time?"

"Sorry. Didn't mean to be abrupt. But Ted's on his way over to talk about money."

"Is Angela there?"

"No. She'd left the office by the time Ted called."

"So, why are you meeting him? That's what you're paying her to do."

Lindsey was grateful Dee couldn't see her reddening face. "He's already on his way."

"Tough shit. He's had more than a month to work out a strategy. It's outrageous to expect you to be ready on a few hours' notice and without legal advice."

The buzzer rang. "He's here. I gotta go."

"Tell him to call your lawyer."

"I'll let you know what happens."

Pacing the hall as he came up from the lobby, she vacillated between being amiable and giving a barely polite "Please come in."

In fact, Ted set the tone the moment she opened the door. "Thanks for doing this on such short notice. I really appreciate it." As if he was the client and she was helping him out. He handed her a white bakery box. "I brought you almond biscotti. Your favorite, Lins."

Lindsey reached for the box, then pulled her hand back. Lins. Biscotti. He was wooing her. Like he wooed his clients. "I shouldn't have agreed to meet without my lawyer."

"You *are* kidding," he said with a look of disbelief. "You wanted to talk about finances. I'm here to do that."

"I can't agree to anything without my lawyer."

Ted set his briefcase and the box on the hall table. "I'm not here to negotiate. You two will have whatever you need. I'm here because you wanted to know *exactly* what that means."

Lindsey pursed her lips as he laid his coat on the hall chair, then picked up his briefcase and the box. She did want to know. "Okay. But I won't agree to anything without my lawyer."

"I'm not asking you to." He held up the box. "How about I make coffee to go with this?" Not waiting for her response, he strode toward the kitchen where he hung his jacket on a chair and loosened his tie. He seemed completely at ease grinding coffee and starting the percolator.

Just to be doing something, Lindsey set mugs, napkins, and small plates on the table.

When they sat down, Ted pulled out a yellow legal pad covered in handwritten scribbles, as if he'd thrown his list together on the way over. He dunked his pastry as he worked his way down the list of expenses he'd pay. The apartment. The country house. School fees and school trips. Other travel for Lindsey and Zoey. Insurance and clothing for Zoey.

Lindsey nodded dumbly as he checked off each item. His list sounded more generous than the one Angela was drawing up.

At the bottom of the page, he capped his pen and tapped it on the table. "Lindsey, there's a quid pro quo."

She knew it. There had to be something. She waited.

"I want a flexible custody arrangement ... so Zoey can spend as much time with each of us as she wants. No rules about number of weeks or months."

She had no reason to disagree. Assuming Zoey would reconcile with her father at some point, she was old enough to decide where to have dinner or spend the night. And yet, it couldn't be this easy. What was she missing?

In the guise of scraping the last bits of almond paste off her plate, she scanned her list. "What about my salary?"

"It's yours. You handle your personal expenses—as you always have. I assume medical insurance through your job is not a problem."

"That's okay. What about my retirement?"

"We'll need a finance guy to do the calculations, but you'll get what you put in, plus any income and capital gains on it."

"What about the car? If you want it, we'll need a way to get to the country."

Ted ran his eyes down his yellow pad. "I forgot about that. I'll let you know." He slid his pen and pad into his case and reached for his jacket. "Where's Zoey?"

"In her room doing homework."

"I'm going to speak to her."

"She doesn't want to see you."

He scowled as he put on his jacket. "That tune is getting old," he said as he strode out of the kitchen.

Lindsey, in mother-bear mode, was about to argue but thought better of it. Instead, she followed him to the corner of the front hall, where she could watch, but he wouldn't see her.

He hovered in front of Zoey's door, his knuckles poised in the air for several moments before he tapped with a two-three beat. "Zoey, I'd like to talk to you."

No response. He rapped again, sharply. "Zoey, please open the door. I miss you."

Again, nothing.

He raised his fist a third time, then dropped it. Lindsey ducked back into the kitchen. When she heard him in the front hall, she stepped out where he could see her. Knowing she was being wicked, she asked, "What did she say?"

"She wouldn't open the door."

Lindsey yearned to say something cruel, to wound him as he had wounded her. She bit her tongue as he put on his topcoat.

At the door, he made a half turn. "Lins, you keep the car. I'll get one if I need it."

When he was gone, she stood with her back against the door, unsure whether to laugh or to cry. To laugh at how easy it had all seemed compared to the horror stories of women who had to fight for their share of their marital property. To cry at how easily the fabric of her life had been shredded by a handwritten list on a sheet of yellow paper.

When she finally headed to bed, she rapped lightly on Zoey's door and said good night, but didn't wait for a response. She fell asleep almost instantly.

The next morning, on the bus down Central Park West, she began a new list of things Ted had missed—or chosen not to mention.

The mechanics of paying bills. What if all the bills went to him? She couldn't bear the thought that he'd question a bill, or worse, refuse to pay it. She circled that note, and decided to ask for a budgeted allowance. She'd use her salary to cover any extra expenses that came along.

And "I'll take care of everything" left a lot of questions. Would he want to use the country house? If not, would he pay for the minor maintenance he'd always taken care of?

And how long would "everything" last? Until Zoey finished school? Until she married? Ted hadn't drawn a distinction between child support and spousal support.

And wasn't she legally entitled to half of their retirement funds?

Her temples throbbed as she got off the bus. Ted was too good a lawyer to have missed so many important details. His proposal sounded generous, but was it?

Dee called midmorning. "I'm dying to hear. What did he say?"

Lindsey laughed. "You do love those administrative details, don't you? Anyway, he gave me everything I would have asked for, and then some."

"Well, guilt is good for something. Have you sent a copy to Angela?"

Lindsey wondered if she still had a brain. "Shit. He took his list with him."

"Do you have a record of what he said?"

"I made notes." Lindsey imagined Dee shaking her head in disbelief. "I'll call Ted and get him to send me his list. While I still remember the conversation."

"An excellent idea." Dee's tone was measured. "I hate to be tiresome, but you need a signed financial agreement. If not today, then tomorrow."

Chapter 13

When Lindsey got home from work Thursday, Zoey was tearing lettuce into bits for a green salad. She was back to being moody and distant.

Lindsey had considered finding a therapist for her, but moody and distant was not the same as emotionally disturbed. All too often, putting a child from a broken home into therapy sent the unintended message that it was the child who needed fixing. Lindsey didn't want to exacerbate Zoey's misguided concern that somehow she was at fault.

Still, she didn't know what else to do for her daughter. For the moment, her only option was to pretend that life was normal. "Hi, pumpkin, how'd the rehearsal go?"

"Okay."

"Would you like me to help you rehearse your lines?"

"Mom, I can memorize stuff by myself."

"I like rehearsing with you."

Ignoring her mother, Zoey set the salad on the kitchen table and sat down. "Can we eat now? I have a lot of homework."

Lindsey tried a different tack. "I thought we'd do something different this weekend. Maybe go to a movie in town tomorrow night. And we've been invited to my friend Joan's for dinner Saturday."

Zoey rolled her eyes. "No way. Janice has a wedding on Saturday. Wendy and I have to look after the horses while she's gone. It's a lot of responsibility."

"I wish you'd checked with me before you agreed."

"Why? I work at the stable every weekend."

"Well, I've already accepted her invitation."

Zoey's glare was evil. "Why didn't *you* check with *me* first?"

Lindsey was chagrined. She couldn't criticize Zoey for relying on a decade-long ritual. But she did not want to cancel dinner. Why couldn't they do both? "How long will you be at the stable?"

"All afternoon." Zoey looked up, suspicious. "Why?"

"What if we go up Friday night as usual and come back Saturday after you're finished?"

"No."

"Why not?"

"I don't want to. She's your friend, not mine." Zoey stood up and headed out of the room.

Ready to weep with frustration, Lindsey made a decision. In a stern voice, she said, "Zoey."

Zoey halted in the doorway but did not turn around. "What?"

"I'm sorry I didn't ask you before I made the date. But the Zoey I've always known would have mentioned the wedding as part of ordinary conversation. You've been sullen and moody for weeks. The fact is we're both at fault here."

She spoke slowly and with deliberateness. "We'll go to the country tomorrow night as usual. When you're done Saturday, we'll come back." She paused to lay her napkin on the table. "But we are coming back and we are going to Joan's."

"Unnh." Zoey stomped off.

While she cleared the table, Lindsey tried to parse Zoey's behavior. A reaction to her family falling apart. To being slapped by her mother. And perhaps, as had to happen, to being a teenager trying to carve out an identity of her own.

How would Zoey respond to Joan? Lindsey wanted them to like each other. She wanted it so badly it almost hurt.

~ ~ ~ ~

Zoey's chores took longer than expected—or so she said—and they didn't arrive at Joan's until after seven o'clock. During a drive endured in almost complete silence, Lindsey feared Zoey would spend the evening glowering at their hostess.

Joan took their coats and gave Zoey a one-armed hug. "I hear I bollixed up your weekend. I'll try to feed you something scrumptious to make up for my sins."

Zoey eked out a smile. "It's no problem, Mrs. Archer. I finished my chores at the stable. Thank you for inviting me."

"Oh, please call me Joan."

Zoey threw her mother a questioning glance. Lindsey nodded.

They followed Joan into the kitchen, where the counters were piled with vegetables. Lindsey whispered "thank you" into Zoey's ear.

Pulling out a stool at the counter, Joan motioned to Zoey. "Let's put you here. I'm making fondue. Can I get you and your mom to cut stuff up?"

"What's fondue?" Zoey clambered onto the stool.

"A Swiss dish. You dip bread, ham or fresh veggies into hot melted cheese." She winked at Lindsey.

"Yeah," Lindsey said, laughing, "It brings it from infinitely fattening to just outrageous." She ran her fingers lightly up and down Zoey's spine. "Fondue was one of my favorites when I was young enough to handle the calories. You'll love it."

Zoey's compressed lips suggested she wasn't convinced, but she turned politely to Joan. "What do you want me to do?"

"Lindsey, you do bread and ham. Zoey, cut the veggies into bite-sized pieces."

After organizing cutting boards, knives, and platters, Joan moved to the stove. As she dumped grated cheese and wine into a Corning Ware pot, she said, "Zoey, what were you doing at the stables today?"

Lindsey concentrated on cutting the bread into bite-sized cubes. She'd let Joan and Zoey bond on their own.

"Feeding and exercising eight horses. Janice—she's the owner—wasn't there today." Zoey's answer was polite but cool. She seemed determined not to like Joan.

Joan turned her attention to the melting cheese and they worked in a strained silence until she started to drizzle kirsch into the pot. "Zoey, your mom tells me you love horses."

Out of the corner of her eye, Lindsey saw Zoey's head bend ever so slightly toward Joan.

"Yeah. I learned to ride in second grade. My dad taught me. He promised to get me a horse last summer, but he was too busy with his trial."

Joan tasted the thick sauce without taking her eyes off Zoey. "Almost ready. So ...what does it take to 'get a horse'?"

While they ferried platters and the pot of hot cheese to the table, Zoey talked about the things a novice horsewoman had to decide.

How old a horse. For an inexperienced rider, probably one that was ten or twelve years old and trained as a jumper. *How many "hands" tall.* Should she get an animal that was comfortable for her now, but that she might outgrow, or a slightly larger one she could ride for many years. *How experienced.* A retired professional jumper would cost a lot more than a well-trained horse that a young horsewoman like herself had outgrown.

Lindsey had lived through many such conversations as Ted and Zoey scoured the Internet. Now, listening to Zoey and Joan, she added one more thing to the list of settlement items: the cost of boarding a horse.

Wielding a metal spear with a bright red ceramic handle, Joan demonstrated how to coat the bread with cheese and twirl it so it wouldn't drip.

Zoey laughed nervously when she lost her first piece of bread in the pot. On the second try, she got the bread out, but forgot to spin it and left a stringy trail of cheese on the dark green tablecloth. "Oh, Mrs. Archer, I'm so sorry."

"Joan. Don't give it a thought. It'll come off in the wash."

On her third try, Zoey mastered it. While the three worked their way through the mounds of food, Joan drew Zoey out.

About music (Zoey liked piano more than the violin).

About the Brearley School (her English teacher, Mrs. Sutton, was way cool).

About the school play (Zoey was thrilled about getting the lead). When Joan suggested coming to the play, Zoey absolutely glowed.

As she watched her daughter and her lover, Lindsey marveled at Joan's instinct about involving Zoey in dinner preparations. Zoey was chattier than Lindsey had seen her in weeks. Joan seemed to have much the same easy way with people that Ted did.

~ ~ ~ ~

After they cleared the table, Zoey headed for the bathroom. The moment she was out of sight, Joan wrapped her arms around Lindsey's waist and pulled her close. "I love having you here with Zoey." She flicked her tongue around the edge of Lindsey's ear.

Lindsey leaned into the warmth of Joan's breasts. She was ready to make love right there on the dining room floor, but pulled back. "Not with Zoey around, please."

"Don't be so anxious. Women hug all the time."

"I've never been a hugger. Zoey might think it was odd. We have to be careful."

"Whatever you say. Might as well get a start on the dishes."

The phone rang moments after Zoey returned to the kitchen.

Joan tossed her a towel. "Here, make yourself useful," then answered in a businesslike voice. "Joan here." A pause and then, "I have guests. Can I call you tomorrow?"

For a moment after she hung up, Joan's eyes remained fixed on a bulletin board of photos next to the phone. Then, in a resolutely cheery voice, she said, "Zoey, how about some piano duets?"

"Cool. Gammy and I play duets all the time."

"Okay. Sheet music is there." She pointed to the piano bench. "It's mostly Broadway stuff. Pick out what you like."

They played with gusto, starting with Broadway tunes, but soon drifted into music as diverse as Frank Sinatra, James Taylor, and the Beatles. Occasionally, Lindsey sang along, but mostly she observed, contentedly, from an overstuffed chair. From time to time, she ran her hands up and down her arms, a sort of self-hug, as she congratulated herself on arranging the first evening in a month where Zoey seemed her old self.

After almost an hour, Lindsey planted her hands on Zoey's shoulders. "We ought to go before we wear out our welcome."

"Do we have to? I don't have to be up early."

Snuggling her arm around Zoey's shoulder, Joan threw a sidelong glance at Lindsey. "Hey, don't spoil our fun."

"That's nice of you, but we should be on our way. Zoey, five minutes."

Zoey's lower lip stuck out in a mock pout. "I think you're mean."

Waiting for the elevator ten minutes later, Zoey volunteered that Joan was "really nice."

"Should we invite her to the country some weekend?" Lindsey asked.

Zoey replied without hesitation. "I think she'd be fun."

~ ~ ~ ~

The shrill sound of the phone pierced Lindsey's dream the next morning. Still drowsy and stifling a yawn, she picked it up. "I've been dreaming about you, about having you in my arms," she murmured.

"You what?"

Ted's voice jolted her wide awake. "Omigod." Her mind raced to cover her words. "I ... you woke me. I must have been dreaming."

"So you said." His voice was brusque. "I called to be sure you got the draft settlement. It should have been delivered yesterday."

It had been delivered, but she'd been too tired to study it when she got home from Joan's. "Yes. I need some time to read it. Can I call you later?"

"No need to call. If you have comments, call your lawyer." He hung up.

She slumped back on the bed, limp, dropping the phone to the floor. She always checked caller ID! How could she have been soooo dumb?

She'd almost recovered enough to think about coffee when it rang again, sending her adrenaline into overdrive. After the third ring, she checked the ID. It was Joan.

"Joan, you will never believe what just happened!"

"Try me."

"When the phone rang a few minutes ago, I answered by saying I was dreaming of having you in my arms."

"Who was it?"

Lindsey rolled onto her back. "Ted."

"Oyh. Did you say my name?"

"Un-uh. He must have thought I was dreaming about him."

"Why the hell is he calling so early on Sunday morning?"

"To find out if the separation papers arrived. We agreed his lawyer would do the draft."

"What's it say?"

"Some of it's easy. I get the car. He pays for Zoey's school and clothes. But the property ... our retirement fund—there are pages of legalese."

"So, you'll send it to your lawyer tomorrow."

"Ted sent a copy directly to her."

"Not leaving a stone unturned, is he?" Joan muttered.

"That wouldn't be Ted's style." She sat up and maneuvered her feet into her slippers. "How did you and Brad handle it? The paperwork for separating?"

There was a long silence. "We're not legally separated."

Lindsey remembered Joan waving her wedding ring that first night of class. She hadn't noticed whether Joan still wore it.

"So, is Brad supporting you?" Almost as an echo, she realized what she'd said. "Omigod, Joan, I'm sorry. I didn't mean to pry."

"It's okay. He covers the rent and insurance. I pay for day-to-day stuff myself."

"What if he stops paying?"

"He won't. He's hoping I'll come to my senses and go back."

"Was that him on the phone last night?"

"Yeah. He wants to have dinner next week when he's in town on business. He keeps asking if this New York life is what I want." There was a long pause. "I can't tell him I haven't a clue." Joan sounded desolate, so different from her normally upbeat self.

"Why not?"

"He doesn't understand why a loving husband, two adoring children—well, one anyway—and friends who dote on me isn't enough."

Another long pause. "If I say I'm happy, he'll accept it—not understand, but accept it. But if I say I'm not happy, he'll send flowers or suggest a trip to Europe. As if that will somehow make everything okay."

"It sounds like going back is an option you don't want to close out." Lindsey's stomach fluttered as she padded toward the kitchen. What would she do if Joan went back to Brad ... if she wasn't close by in New York?

"Not an option. I don't love him. But..." she added, her tone softer, her pacing slower, "I love you. I'll love you forever."

Forever. Lindsey wondered if she heard right. Before she could collect her thoughts, Joan raced on. "Gotta run. Tammy's bringing Becca in from Hoboken for brunch. Have a great day."

As Lindsey crossed the front hall, she came face to face with the mirrored image of a red-eyed, middle-aged woman in a bathrobe. The woman Ted had said he would love forever, but no longer did. Why? Had she misjudged his capacity to love ... or was she not worthy of being loved forever? What did it mean to love someone forever?

Her thoughts drifted back to the first tumultuous days with Ted. Almost from the moment they'd met at Berkeley, she'd slotted him into a story—a social construct, as her professor would say—of a family in a white clapboard house with a lawn. Ted in a Santa costume, entertaining a passel of children. Ted in a tux, playing host at a dinner party. Her head knew the reality would be different, but her heart bought into the 'I love you forever' model without reservation.

Tucking the phone into her pocket as she turned toward the kitchen, she realized she had no model for a "forever" relationship with a woman. Who ran the household? Who mowed the lawn? Who did the cooking? Who took out the garbage?

And did she even *love* Joan?

She loved so many things about her—her insights, her caring-ness, her enthusiasm, her passion. But if love was the forever-and-ever way she'd felt about Ted, maybe she didn't love Joan.

Turning away from the mirror, she wondered if that all-consuming feeling was even relevant? Was love at forty-three the same as at twenty-six? Maybe what she felt for Joan was "mature" love instead of barely-out-of-girlhood giddiness.

"Hi, Mom." Zoey lounged at the kitchen table, her script in front of her.

"Morning, pumpkin. Whatcha doing?"

"Rereading the script. We're rehearsing the whole play tomorrow. I'm double-checking my lines."

Lindsey's last offer to help had been spurned. Steeling herself for rejection, she asked, "Want me to run through them with you?"

"Sure. That would be great!"

As she sat down with Zoey, Lindsey realized that whatever her feelings for Joan, forever wasn't a part of the equation. She had a daughter to raise. Planning beyond the weekend was a challenge. There was no room for long-term dreams. For now, she had to live in the moment.

But, without a doubt, the moment included Joan.

~ ~ ~ ~

Three days later, she met with Angela, who'd sorted Ted's draft into two lists. The longer one detailed the proposals that provided adequate financial protection. The other—quite short—addressed things Lindsey needed to consider.

The moment she got home, she picked up the phone to call Joan. But given Joan's lack of attention to her own financial situation, Lindsey was reluctant to rely on her for advice. She needed good common sense, not moral support. She called Dee instead.

Dee answered on the first ring. "Hi. How was your day?"

"Do you have a minute?" Lindsey asked.

"Fine, thanks. I had a great day. We're going out shortly, but for you, I always have a minute."

"Sorry. I didn't mean to be abrupt, but my mind was on Angela. I saw her today. It seems Ted will take care of everything until Zoey finishes school or gets married. But she thinks he's stiffing me on the retirement."

"Stiffing you. That's not a very lawyer-ly term."

"That was her word. Under New York law, property gets split fifty-fifty. But Ted's only giving me what I put in, plus gains on that. Barely a fourth of what we've got."

"Does she recommend challenging it?"

"Not exactly. It seems the proposed living arrangements are more generous than the courts normally award."

"Bottom line, kiddo."

"Assuming Zoey finishes college, I'll have ten years to build up my retirement from my salary. But if I ask him to split the retirement fifty-fifty, he could demand that I pay for more day-to-day stuff. If, God forbid, I lost my job, I couldn't begin to support my half of this lifestyle. I don't want Zoey to have to live like I did after my father left."

"I'm not sure I followed all that. What do you want to do?"

"You once made a snide remark about Ted paying up to assuage his guilt. Maybe I can use that to my advantage."

"Lindsey, Jim's at the door glaring at me. Why don't you sleep on it and call me tomorrow."

Lindsey felt like she was lugging lead weights. If neither her lawyer nor Dee had an opinion, how in hell was she supposed to decide?

Chapter 14

Berkshire blue. Lindsey stood by the bedroom window, her gaze drifting out over the New England landscape. Of course, the November air didn't really have a color. But the phrase captured the unique quality of the light in the valley. In the summer, a blue haze washed over the trees and houses. During the winter, icy blue tinted the snow. In any season, the Berkshire peaks ranged from deep purple just across the valley to a blue-grey shadow on the far horizon. Lindsey had never understood why the blue aura made her feel warm and secure. But it did.

With the aroma of freshly ground coffee wafting up from the kitchen, she lingered at the window, savoring her deepening friendship with Joan. Her skin grew warm with desire. They'd agreed to avoid overt displays of physical affection when Zoey was around, so lovemaking opportunities were few and far between. With Zoey at the stables, they'd have the entire day to themselves. She ran her hands across her breasts, imagining how Joan's touch would feel.

Zoey interrupted her fantasy. "Hey, Mom, if you want breakfast, you'd better get down here quick."

Clomping down the worn pine board stairway, concave from a century of feet, she flashed back to the house tour she'd given Joan the night before. In her exuberant way, Joan had ooh-ed and aah-ed over this table and that etching, this quilt and that rocker. Knowing Joan's penchant for high design—in her home as well as her clothes—Lindsey was thrilled when Joan declared, "this house has such good bones."

The decision to preserve the farmhouse feel was one she and Ted had made together. They'd shored up the fieldstone foundation, put in a new furnace, and installed modern plumbing and electricity. But what was visible looked—and mostly was—from the original 19th century house. Odd-shaped cabinets tucked in a wall under an eave. Painted wide-board floors sloped from north to south where the foundation had settled. Most doors—except the bathroom doors they'd shaved to fit—wouldn't close all the way. The new master bath sported an antique marble sink and a claw-footed bathtub they'd rescued from a salvage yard.

In the kitchen, Zoey was cracking eggs into a bowl. Joan, standing next to her, was nursing a mug of something steaming.

Lindsey peered into the bowl. "And what mischief are you fine ladies up to?"

"French toast. Joan has a neat recipe with rum batter."

"Rum? For breakfast?" Lindsey mimicked shock.

"Just enough to give it some flavor," Joan said. "The alcohol cooks off anyway."

"I'm game." Lindsey flashed a smile at Joan as she reached for the coffee pot. "How was your first night in the Berkshires?"

Joan stretched her arms over her head. "Wonderful. I feel like a million dollars."

During breakfast, with enough French toast for a small army, Joan interrogated Zoey about her riding lessons. Zoey beamed.

Lindsey wondered if Joan was actually interested in horses or simply doing a masterful job, yet again, of drawing Zoey out. While Zoey was off brushing her teeth, Lindsey asked, "Do you ride?"

Joan snorted. "Not hardly. As a kid, I plodded around on the nags at local fairs, but that was about it. How about you?"

"I learned to ride in college, but never felt at ease on a horse. I haven't ridden in years."

"Hey, Joan, wanna come see the horses?" Zoey said when she returned to the table. "And watch my class?"

Joan gave Zoey a one-armed bear hug. "That would be very cool." She gave Lindsey a questioning glance. "Unless your mother has other plans."

Lindsey nearly choked on her toast. Why would Joan give up their few hours of assured privacy to tour a stable, when she didn't even like horses?

Determined not to show her disappointment, she picked up her coffee cup and headed to the kitchen. With a knot in her gut, she called back over her shoulder, "Nope, not a thing. As long as you're back in time to help with dinner."

~ ~ ~ ~

Over the course of the day, Lindsey worked herself into a tangled web of anger, frustration, self-pity, and guilt. Anger that Joan had accepted Lindsey's hospitality and then gone off to do whatever she wanted. Frustration that the urgency of her passion seemed not to be reciprocated. Self-pity that Joan didn't seem to care what Lindsey wanted or how she felt. And a vague sense that somehow Joan's going off with Zoey was her own fault.

She willed herself to be cheerful and pleasant through dinner, but she doubted she'd manage to mask her distress once she and Joan were alone.

After dinner, all three headed for the hot tub, which offered an uninterrupted view of a meteor shower. Orion seemed close enough to touch. The Pleiades were almost—not quite, but almost—visible to a direct gaze. For nearly an hour, they watched the celestial spectacle, with many of the meteors flaming till they reached the ground.

Lindsey missed out on much of the sky show, too absorbed in trying to decide what to say when they were alone. She was terrified that Joan would think her possessive and too demanding if she expressed her anger and resentment. Would Joan walk out like Ted had?

When the show ended and Zoey had gone to her room, Joan held her wine glass out toward Lindsey. "A toast to us. It's the first time we've had alone together all day. I'm absolutely aching for your touch."

"Well, that was your choice," Lindsey snapped.

"It was not," Joan snapped back. "Geez, why would I want to spend a day at the stables? I don't even like horses."

"So, why did you?"

"Lindsey, I gave you a chance to keep me here. I was flummoxed when you said we had no plans. I know you want Zoey and me to get along, so I felt I had to go with her."

Lindsey rested her head on the ledge. Once again, she'd read rejection where none was intended. Why hadn't she simply said she and Joan were having lunch in town?

"I'm sorry," Lindsey said. "Your enthusiasm was very convincing." She grazed her fingers along Joan's leg from knee to ankle. "I do want you and Zoey to get along. But today, I wanted to be with you."

Joan tucked her feet under Lindsey's leg and wiggled her toes, tickling the underside of Lindsey's thigh. "Have you ever made love in a hot tub?"

A wave of heat exploded in Lindsey's groin. She slid toward Joan, but the memory of being with Ted in the bubbling water stopped her. "We can't. Zoey could come out at any moment."

"How will I ever survive?" Joan said, her eyes rolling heavenward as she wiggled her toes again. "Can I ask you something?"

"Sure."

"Do you mind that I'm in a book club with Lauren?"

Lindsey had forgotten about the book club. "It's not my place to mind."

"If it bothers you, I'll drop out."

"That's your decision. But," Lindsey sought Joan's eyes, "promise you won't tell me what she says. Or talk to your book club about us. Please."

Joan dismissed Lindsey's request with a fluttery wave of her hand. "No problem. We only talk about books. And I never see her outside of book club."

"Really? I remember your telling me how she sang Ted's praises during book club ... talked about Ted all the time."

"She did mention him, but I was exaggerating. I was so surprised by the coincidence."

"Then it's an easy promise."

A lone meteor fell across the southern sky. Joan pointed to it with her glass. "Look. Another star. And yes, I promise."

As they waited, hoping for one last starburst, Joan asked, "Was Ted ever unfaithful to you before?"

"Not like this, with Lauren. But there might have been one-night stands."

"You didn't care?" Joan sat up, her eyes wide with skepticism.

"Times when he was out of town at a trial or a conference. Ending up in bed with someone he'd never see again. I don't know that it ever happened. But if it did, it didn't affect our relationship, so I didn't give it much thought."

The muscles around Joan's jaw stiffened. "I don't see it. Trust is so fundamental to marriage ... to any relationship."

Trust. She'd trusted Ted and he'd betrayed her. Suddenly, Lindsey itched to know if he'd ever cheated on her. "There was one time when I did wonder."

Joan cupped her ear. "Do tell."

"It was a month or so after Zoey was born. He was out of town at a conference, and sent a huge bunch of flowers with a very sweet card." Lindsey raised her palms in the air. "He'd never sent me flowers before."

"Did you ask him why he sent them?"

Lindsey shook her head.

"Why on earth not?"

Lindsey held up the diamond and ruby pendant lying just above her collarbone. "He gave me this when Zoey was born. What if he was just happy to be a new dad? Why turn a nice gesture into an ugly moment of suspicion?"

"If Brad ever cheated on me, even once, I would have thrown him out."

"But where do you draw the line?" Lindsey set her glass on the ledge. "To me, a one-night stand is much less threatening than close friendships over time, like Ted and Lauren. A day-to-day intimacy that competes with the relationship between husband and wife. Emotional betrayal may come long before sex begins."

"Well, maybe." Joan climbed out and slipped into her robe. "But if you're ready for a close emotional relationship with someone else, your marriage is already in trouble."

Joan's comment rekindled Lindsey's doubt. Had her marriage been in trouble long before Lauren showed up? And faithfulness. She and Ted had never discussed it. What if he'd read her lack of concern as indifference?

In the kitchen, Joan wrapped her arms around Lindsey for a goodnight hug. Lindsey returned her embrace, holding her tight.

The next morning she woke to the rat-a-tat of a woodpecker. As she swung her feet to the floor, she gasped.

Joan, in the doorway, held up a coffee mug. "You were sound asleep, lovey. I've been banging on this doorframe for a good twenty seconds."

"What time is it?"

"Nearly nine. Zoey thought you'd like breakfast before she leaves." Joan set the mug on the bedside table, turning the handle toward Lindsey. She was about to give Lindsey a kiss, and then seemed to change her mind.

"Don't want to break hotel rules." She winked. "But perhaps this lovely sunny spot will be available later in the morning."

Lindsey took a sip. "Absolutely. And thanks for the coffee!"

"I'm counting the minutes. Now I'll go help Zoey. See you downstairs."

Lindsey pulled on a sweat suit and ducked into the bathroom. As she went for her toothbrush, her hand bumped Ted's toothbrush, still in its accustomed slot. She was about to toss it into the wastebasket, but her fingers wouldn't do it.

She fled the bathroom without brushing her teeth.

~ ~ ~ ~

Once Zoey was out the door, Joan let her fingers play across Lindsey's shoulders and neck. "What shall we do with this wonderful day?"

As Lindsey swiveled in her chair, Joan bent down and kissed her, exploring the inner surfaces of Lindsey's mouth with her tongue. Every nerve ending in Lindsey's body was on fire. She loosened the belt of Joan's robe and slid her arms around Joan's hips, her fingers caressing Joan's warm skin through her thin white gown.

Joan pulled Lindsey up. "Let's move to someplace a bit more comfortable."

It was nearly eleven when she and Joan, limbs still entangled, began to think about how they might spend the rest of the day.

When they left Guido's—what Lindsey referred to as the "local Whole Foods"—they headed into Great Barrington for lunch. Afterwards, they visited Lindsey's favorite haunts. Their last stop was Gorham and Norton, an all-purpose grocery, wine merchant and delicatessen, where Lindsey bought several bottles of a Chilean red. As she signed the credit card slip, she heard a familiar voice.

"What a nice surprise."

She looked up. "Dee, what a happy coincidence!" She nodded toward Joan. "I've been wanting you and Joan to meet."

Dee took Joan's hand. "I've heard a lot about you. You've been a big help to my friend in the last month or so."

Joan actually blushed. "I haven't done anything, really," she said, tucking her arm around Lindsey's waist. "She's been good for me as well."

Joan's gesture struck Lindsey as proprietary, more intimate than women friends ordinarily do in a public place. She took a step back, trying to look casual, hoping Dee wouldn't notice. Joan let her arm drop. "Do you have time for coffee?"

"Love to, but Jim and I are meeting friends for a late lunch. I just dashed over to pick up fresh pasta. She glanced at Joan with an easy smile. "I'm sure there'll be another opportunity."

As Dee headed out, Joan whispered, "She sure knows how to make a fashion statement."

"Are you serious or kidding?"

"Serious. That felt jacket is gorgeous. And her skirt. It must be bias-cut … it just flows. It takes a real sense of style to put them together. Don't you like it?"

Lindsey chuckled. "Let's say I've come to appreciate it … a sort of high-end Woodstock. But people who like nice even hems—that would be me—can't fathom how to mix prints and colors and fabrics the way she does."

Joan laughed. "Well, I wouldn't mind taking lessons from her."

Halfway to the car, in front of a florist, Joan nudged her. "Look. Beautiful, isn't it?" Joan pointed to a tiger orchid, a dozen white blooms with purple spots and yellow centers. The plant had dozens more buds ready to burst open. "I want to get it."

Back out on the street, Joan held the plant out to Lindsey. "It's for you, m'dear. Each bloom reflects one of the ways I love you." She pointed to one of unopened buds. "Some of which I don't know yet."

Lindsey's eyes welled up and she kissed Joan's cheek. "You've been so good for me, Joan. I do love you and I've loved this last month together."

Chapter 15

From all appearances, Zoey's dress rehearsal went well. She skipped into the den where Lindsey was reviewing case management files and scrunched down next to the desk, her arms resting on the dark wood. "It was so cool. I didn't miss a single line."

"That's great, pumpkin," Lindsey said, stroking the soft golden fuzz on Zoey's arm. "I can't wait to see you on stage."

Zoey gave Lindsey a peck on the cheek and danced out. "Night, Mom."

Lindsey had no illusions that Zoey was back to normal, if she even knew what normal was for this thirteen-year-old straddling an abyss. But it was a relief to see her enthusiastic, instead of holed up in her room behind a locked door.

~ ~ ~ ~

Opening night, Lindsey left work early to offer a last blast of encouragement over dinner. She found Zoey dropping ice cubes into water glasses.

"Elena left pasta and salad."

"Great. You serve while I wash up."

When she got back, Zoey was tapping out a syncopated beat on the table with her fork.

"I know you're nervous. But you should eat something."

"Okay." Zoey snarfed a forkful of pasta, almost before Lindsey sat down. She filled a second fork but halted it halfway to her mouth. Her lips protruded and her cheeks got puffy.

"Zoey, are you okay? You look like you're about to throw up."

"Mom, my stomach has rocks in it." She pushed her chair back. "Can I go? Please?"

Zoey wouldn't starve for want of one meal. "Sure. I'll be over a little after seven ... want to make sure we get good seats."

Zoey stiffened. "We? Is Dad coming?"

"I'm meeting Joan. Remember, you invited her. But your dad is coming, with Gammy."

"I don't want him to come."

"Zoey, he's so proud of you."

"Tell him not to come."

Lindsey knew it wasn't up to her, but didn't press the point. "I'll see what I can do, pumpkin." She blew a kiss. "If I don't see you before the curtain goes up, break a leg!"

After Zoey left, Lindsey debated whether to call Ted. She did, finally, make the call and left a voicemail message.

~ ~ ~ ~

Milling around the lobby with other Brearley parents, Lindsey felt her knees go weak when Joan walked in with half a dozen pale peach roses. She wondered if her explosion of desire—her face felt flushed—was evident to anyone else.

"For the leading lady," Joan said as she came alongside Lindsey. "My favorite color. I hope she likes them."

"She'll be thrilled." Lindsey said, as she steered Joan toward the auditorium. They picked seats in the fourth row and chatted idly until the play began, ten minutes late. The moment the lights went down, Joan threaded her arm through Lindsey's. When Joan's hand came to rest on her thigh, Lindsey had to call on every bit of concentration she possessed to follow her daughter's opening lines.

At the intermission, she introduced Joan to several Brearley parents. It was almost time to return to their seats when she saw Ted walking toward her, trailed by Claire. He held a huge bouquet of red roses.

"Lindsey, are you okay? You're white as a sheet," Joan said.

"It's Ted. Zoey didn't want him to come tonight. I left him a message, but he's here."

As Ted threaded his way through the crowd, Lindsey floated in a time warp. Although she couldn't hear him over the babble, she knew what he was saying to the people he passed. As always, Ted would sling his arm around a shoulder and say something complimentary—tonight, perhaps, a comment on an offspring's thespian talent. She recognized the mock humble shrug of his shoulders as he accepted praise for Zoey's performance.

It was a role he played naturally. A lump formed in her throat as she remembered the two of them, years ago, stretched out on the living room floor, laughing about how Ted had charmed yet another client with his blend of bear hugs, flattery and self-deprecation.

Even as he chatted up the parents, his eyes were on Lindsey. When he reached her, his social smile evaporated. The muscles around his jaw went tight. "Why didn't she want me to come?"

Lindsey made no effort to hide her incredulity. "Opening night might not be the ideal time to have your first conversation in nearly two months. Where are you sitting?"

"In the balcony, where she can't see me."

"Thank you for that."

Discomforted by the unexpected intimacy, she squeezed her mother-in-law's arm lightly above the elbow. "Claire, Zoey will be so pleased you're here."

"I would not have missed my granddaughter's inaugural performance as leading lady. In fact, I'm coming to all three performances."

"That's wonderful! Want to go together tomorrow evening?"

"That would be lovely. Why don't you come by my place around six for soup?"

As she nodded in agreement, Lindsey realized Ted and Joan were standing, a bit awkwardly, outside the conversation.

"Ted, Claire ... meet Joan Archer. We met at the New School." Joan, of course, would know who Ted and Claire were.

Claire held out her hand. "I am delighted to meet you. Zoey tells me you are a piano maven."

Joan, clearly delighted at the recognition, gave Claire her signature one-armed hug. "We've had a bit of fun at the piano. But I gather she learned her duet skills from you."

"Zoey is a talented young lady. I don't know how much I taught her, but we have a good time." She turned to Lindsey. "Perhaps Joan can join us for a musical do sometime."

Joan beamed at Claire and then turned to Ted. "Lovely flowers."

Ted gave Joan his most winning smile. "They're for the leading lady."

"You're not planning on giving them to her yourself, are you?" Joan said.

Ted's smile evaporated. "Excuse me?"

"She doesn't want to see you."

Lindsey was flabbergasted. What had possessed Joan to say such a thing?

Ted's expression hardened as he glared at Joan. "I don't see that it's any of your concern."

"Joan, excuse us for a minute." Lindsey took Ted's arm and steered him toward the door. "Ted, I'm sorry. That was unforgivably rude."

"What gives that bitch the right to tell me what to do?"

"I said I'm sorry. But you *can't* give her those tonight."

"I'll make sure she doesn't see me 'til it's over."

Lindsey willed herself not to mock him. "Ted, it's possible your showing up with flowers is exactly what she needs. It's just as likely it will ruin her evening."

Without a word, he turned and headed back to his seat.

Lindsey's pulse beat wildly. Would Ted ruin his daughter's triumph just to prove he was the loving dad? And Joan? Damn her. She had no right to interfere.

She looked around. Joan was nowhere in sight. A good thing. If she'd been close by, Lindsey would have said something she might later regret.

She dawdled getting to her seat, arriving just as the curtain was going up. Joan was already seated. There was no time to say anything.

~ ~ ~ ~

Lindsey had calmed considerably by the time the play ended. After the applause died off, they made their way to the lobby. Joan was voluble in her praise of Zoey, joining the congratulatory chorus of parents and friends.

Suddenly, Joan tugged on her arm. "Lindsey, that SOB is waiting for you!"

She followed Joan's gaze. Ted stood just inside the door, twenty feet away. He glowered at Joan, distaste written in the lines of his mouth. Lindsey's heart rate spiked.

"Let me deal with him. I'll meet you in the reception room."

When she reached him, he thrust the bouquet at her. "I don't want to create a scene in front of her friends. You give them to her." He turned and marched out the door.

"At least the bastard was thinking about Zoey for a change." Joan's voice came from just behind her.

Lindsey spun around. "Joan, I asked you to let me talk to him alone." She pushed past Joan. "Just leave it be. Please."

She almost tossed the flowers into the trash. But Ted had done the right thing. Zoey didn't have to keep the flowers, but she'd know her father cared. Back in the reception room, Zoey caught her eye. With a broad grin, she pointed to the roses in her mother's arms.

Lindsey couldn't throw them out now. She poured herself a coffee and watched Joan weave her way into the bevy of girls around Zoey. She said something that made all the girls laugh. When Joan arrived back at the dessert table, Lindsey forced a smile.

"That girl is simply gorgeous," Joan said. "You should be so proud of her."

Lindsey strained to keep her voice even. "I've been very lucky."

"You're not an innocent bystander. She's a great kid because she has a fabulous mother." She put her arm around Lindsey's shoulder. "What are you going to do with those flowers?"

Lindsey extricated herself from Joan's embrace. "Give them to Zoey."

"You're not his messenger service, Lindsey. Throw them away and tell him to send 'em himself!"

Lindsey wanted to scream. Why couldn't Joan leave it alone? "Zoey's seen them."

"Then tell her they're from you. Don't say they're from Ted."

"I'm going backstage to help Zoey collect her things," Lindsey said through nearly clenched teeth. "I'll call you in the morning."

"I'll come with you."

Lindsey's self-control was on empty. "Joan, I need time—*alone*—with my daughter."

Joan's eyes reddened. "Did I do something wrong?"

"We'll discuss it tomorrow." Lindsey spun around and walked toward the stage door.

~ ~ ~ ~

The next morning, Joan's apology was heartfelt. "I butted in where I shouldn't have, didn't I? I get ahead of myself sometimes. It won't happen again. I promise."

Lindsey needed more than an apology. "What did you hope to accomplish?"

"I was trying to protect you ... and Zoey."

"From what?"

"That man walks all over you. You asked him not to come, but he came anyway. I wanted to stand up for you. And Zoey."

Lindsey felt the iceberg of anger inside her melting. How could she be angry with Joan for feeling protective? But Dee's advice—keep saying you love her, even if she doesn't seem to listen—applied to Ted as much as to Lindsey.

"I appreciate that. And the flowers did upset her. But that has to be better than thinking he doesn't care."

"Well, it's your life and I won't interfere again. But you need to stand up for yourself."

They chatted for a bit about the play and their plans for the day. Only after she'd hung up did Lindsey realize she had, in fact, stood up to Ted and he had listened. He hadn't given the flowers to Zoey.

The person she hadn't stood up to was Joan.

~ ~ ~ ~

Riding in the elegantly paneled elevator to Claire's penthouse, Lindsey wished she hadn't accepted the invitation. She and Claire had never, over the many years they'd known each other, shared as much as a cup of coffee without the company of Ted or Zoey or both. Whatever would they talk about for the time it took to eat ... even if it was only soup?

Zoey. Her music. Her triumph in the play. An easy quarter-hour. But then what?

Lindsey's job. Iffy. Claire's world was society boards and committees, while Lindsey's world was mentally ill people in poverty. Claire had never shown more than a polite interest in Lindsey's work.

The arts were a shared interest, but talking about something as abstract as music or the theatre seemed like avoiding the elephant in the room. She doubted Claire would breach any confidences Zoey had shared. And she felt sure Ted's mother did not want to hear Lindsey's side of the story. Even so, Lindsey had a nagging feeling Claire invited her to dinner for a reason.

When Lindsey stepped out of the elevator, Claire wore a welcoming smile.

"I'm so glad you were free." She gave Lindsey a quick hug. "We haven't had a chance to chat in ages."

"I'm delighted to be here," Lindsey lied as she followed Claire into the solarium. Claire had set out salad and white wine, but suggested Lindsey help with the soup.

While they ladled out the golden squash bisque, Claire drew Lindsey into a conversation about the play as well as Zoey's recent progress with the piano. The conversation, entirely predictable, got them through the start of dinner.

Halfway through the soup, Claire switched smoothly onto a discussion of the exhibitions at MOMA, the Met, and the Neue. Would Lindsey like to go with her to any of them? She was encouraging when Lindsey mentioned her interest in a Saturday film class at the Pittsfield Museum.

Throughout the meal, Claire was amiable and chatty. She didn't quite succeed in putting Lindsey at ease, but Lindsey appreciated her graciousness. It was a quality her son had inherited and had used to great effect in building his law practice.

When they finished, Lindsey reached for Claire's soup bowl. "I'll help you clear."

Claire put her hand lightly on Lindsey's. "Let them sit. There's something else before we go."

Yes, Claire did indeed have an agenda. Lindsey made an effort to sound casual. "Sure, what's up?"

Claire's fingers moved erratically around the stem of her empty wine glass. It was an uncharacteristically busy gesture for a woman who always seemed so self-confident and at ease. "I am concerned about Zoey. She thinks Ted left because of something she did ... or didn't do ... that she has disappointed him in some way. And that she has disappointed you as well."

Lindsey's mind was spinning. Did Claire know about slapping Zoey?

Claire stopped playing with her glass and put her hands together on the table in front of her. "Lindsey. You have been— are—a wonderful mother. But anger does strange things to people. I just hope you won't take your anger at my son out on her. I know how it happens ... because it happened to me."

Lindsey stared. Claire and Charles had been married for 40 years when Ted's father died. And Claire's parents— Ted's grandparents—were together at Lindsey's wedding. She waited.

"Charles and I had our differences in the early years. At one point, he walked out, leaving me with two small boys. It was a terrible time. I questioned everything I thought I knew about myself. I can't tell you how many times I yelled at those boys for things that weren't their fault."

Lindsey's jaw went slack. "I had no idea. Ted never mentioned it."

"He and Drew were only toddlers. Too young to put the experience into words. But Zoey is not too young. She will remember ... and I do not want it to be a crippling memory."

Lindsey closed her eyes and let her head fall back. She knew exactly what Claire was talking about: that sinking sense of despair when someone you love leaves and you don't know why. When your mother blames you—slaps you—for something that isn't your fault.

Claire was observing her when Lindsey opened her eyes.

"Claire, I'm afraid of that too. When my father walked out—I was a few years younger than Zoey—it left a gaping hole in my life. I never got over the feeling that it was my fault ... that there was something wrong with me. I didn't know what it was, but I assumed my mother did and that's why she was so awful to me."

Claire's eyes widened. "You don't really believe that, do you?"

"Intellectually, no. But emotionally, it's always there. I'm only now beginning to understand how it affected my relationship with—" She stopped mid-sentence. "I'm sorry, Claire, I don't want to put you in the middle."

Claire smiled, the lines around her mouth softening. "Lindsey, I don't ever want to find myself in the middle between you and my son. But I often wonder if I have some responsibility for his taking up with a woman half his age. I will do whatever I can to make your life as a single mother easier. I hope you will call on me if you need anything. Anything at all."

She pushed back her chair from the table. "And now, we should be on our way."

A lump welled up in Lindsey's throat. How could she have failed to notice, over the past decade, this caring side of Claire ... her ability to offer comfort without embarrassing Lindsey. What else had she missed along the way?

Chapter 16

Lindsey hesitated when Dee extended an invitation to Thanksgiving dinner in town. While the two women had resurrected their familiar pattern of daily give-and-take, Jim's friendship with Ted invariably gave rise to awkward gaps in their conversation. And Lindsey always found a reason not to linger when she dropped Wendy off on her chauffeur runs.

But she couldn't avoid Jim indefinitely if she and Zoey were to spend a week in Cabo. And she couldn't plead a long weekend in the country: Dee would know, from Zoey, that she had to work on Friday and would be in the City. Lindsey squared her shoulders, accepted the invitation, and offered to bring salad.

The evening proved surprisingly pleasant. The adult dinner table included the parents of twin girls in Zoey's class at Brearley. They were a delightful couple Lindsey had met at school functions, but did not know well. The table was rounded out with a Brearley father whose wife was in Europe on business.

The group spent much of dinner comparing notes on the arts, including the Met's opera season and the reviews of several recently opened plays that none of them had yet seen. Over dessert, they chatted about the City Council election and the age-old problem of the City's finances. Lindsey was grateful that the conversation remained on neutral topics and gave no hint of her discomfort with Jim.

The inevitable came a little before 9:30. As she went to the powder room, Jim was coming out and she found herself alone with him in the hall. She wondered if he could see the blood draining out of her face.

Jim was all smiles. "I'm glad you came tonight. I thought you were avoiding me."

She shifted from one foot to the other, unable to think of a clever response to shut down his obviously disingenuous comment. This was a conversation she didn't want to have.

Jim was undeterred. "I gather you think I've gone over to the enemy."

"At the very least, one could say you have divided loyalties."

"I think Ted's behaving like a complete jerk. I'll play squash with him, but no way in hell will I go out with him and that b ... woman."

"I appreciate that. But you must see how awkward it is. Knowing that he told you things about our marriage that he never told me."

"He didn't, Lindsey. When he told me about the affair, I told him he was making an ass of himself." Jim punched one fist into the other palm. "And that he shouldn't expect any sympathy from me. When he never mentioned it again, I assumed he'd ended it."

Lindsey stared in disbelief. She'd never thought of Jim as naïve. "You didn't think he'd tell you if it was over."

"Lindsey, I didn't think about it ... I didn't *want* to think about it. I was stupefied when I heard he'd left you."

At that moment, four giggling girls spilled out of the den, giving Lindsey an opportunity to end the conversation. Perhaps she'd been wrong to think Dee and Jim had betrayed her.

"Zoey, get your stuff. It's time." She turned back to Jim with a hesitant smile. "Thanks, Jim. I am glad I came."

~ ~ ~ ~

Lindsey invited Joan to the country again that weekend. As the two watched Zoey climb into Dee's car the next morning, Joan's fingers played across Lindsey's back. Exploding with desire, Lindsey sank to her knees and drew her lover down to the carpet. They made love where they were, unwilling to delay their passion for even the short time it would take to move to the bedroom.

It was nearly two hours before they got up and headed out for lunch. Snow was falling gently when they arrived back home. The large flat flakes melted almost as soon as they hit the ground. Lindsey suggested a walk in the woods.

"Sounds perfect," Joan said. "I want to see this countryside through your eyes."

For the next few hours, they trekked up and down and across the pine-forested hills, sometimes on the trails, sometimes bushwhacking through the undergrowth to find a particularly scenic spot. After a decade, Lindsey knew her way around these hills without a map or compass, much as Native American Indians had once done. She judged her whereabouts from the moss on tree trunks, from the species of bushes and trees, from the size and location of the streams. As they went along, she pointed out hunting blinds up in the now-leafless trees, patches of packed-down vegetation where deer slept under pine branches, and one nearly frozen waterfall glistening as it tumbled over a beaver dam. Twice, deer bounded across the trail in front of them.

By the time they got back to the house, dusk was falling, and Joan, visibly drooping from the strenuous exercise, opted for a nap before dinner. She was still asleep when Lindsey left to pick up the girls from the stable.

Dee called on her cell phone a few moments before Lindsey pulled into the Colberts' driveway. "Bring Joan in for a drink when you get here."

"She's not with me. She was dead to world when I left to get the girls."

"Any chance of coming back when she wakes up?"

The more Lindsey thought about her conversation with Jim in the hallway, the more she realized she'd overreacted to the discovery that Dee knew ... and made the situation worse by refusing to deal with it. She needed to make amends, of that she was sure. But she wasn't ready to do it tonight with Joan in tow. "I wore her out on our hike this afternoon. Can we have a rain check?"

Joan was up when Lindsey and Zoey got home. The two women lounged in front of the fieldstone fireplace with a glass of wine and sampled the Italian cheeses they'd bought that morning. When Zoey joined them, the conversation turned to her day at the stable. Only when they got up to start dinner did Lindsey mention Dee's invitation.

"I wish you'd told me sooner." Joan said. "Is it too late to invite them for dinner? We have enough spare ribs to feed an army."

"I hope you don't mind, but I was looking forward to spending the evening with just you and Zoey."

"Whatever you want," Joan said, not sounding entirely sincere.

~ ~ ~ ~

By the time they'd finished dinner, the snow had stopped and the sky was crisp and clear in the way that only a winter sky can be. Joan and Lindsey headed for the hot tub.

The warm water sapped what little energy Lindsey had left. She slid down so her head rested on the edge of the tub, her eyes closed. Her mind felt blessedly empty.

"Can I ask you something?"

Joan's voice intruded into Lindsey's subconscious. Just that fast, she'd almost fallen asleep. Reluctantly, she pulled up out of her reverie and opened her eyes. "Sure."

"Why didn't you want to go to Dee's—or invite them for dinner?"

"I'm still not quite comfortable around Jim. I didn't want to impose a potentially uncomfortable situation on you. And you seemed so tired after the walk ... I didn't know how long you'd sleep. There'll be lots of other opportunities."

She sat up, afraid she'd fall asleep if she closed her eyes again. "In fact, why don't you join us for our annual fruitcake bake-off. In two weeks. Dee and I've been doing it since we met, and the girls have been part of it for nearly a decade. It's a lot of work, but we have great fun."

"I'd like that." Joan moved in front of a corner jet and stretched her legs out, her feet up against Lindsey's hips. "I'd like to get to know Dee."

"I'd like that too. My two best friends." Lindsey ran her fingers across the top of Joan's toes. "But I've never had a friend like you. Someone I could share everything with. I feel so lucky."

Joan wiggled her toes. "I love being your best friend."

Chapter 17

Zoey was at the kitchen table, poring over a science textbook. She gave a half-hearted wave when Lindsey walked in after work, but did not look up.

"Looking forward to fruitcake this weekend?" Lindsey tousled her daughter's glistening, free-flowing hair. She hoped that two days of baking would lift Zoey out of her latest funk. "Do you realize you and Wendy were just babies when we began this tradition?"

She detected a barely visible nod.

"We'll drive up tomorrow night, so we can start early Saturday morning. Joan's meeting us here after work."

Zoey's head shot up and her eyelids narrowed. "Joan. Why's she coming?"

"I thought you liked her."

"She's okay. But doesn't she have anything else to do on the weekends?"

Lindsey's pulse quickened. Joan had become a more-or-less constant presence. They talked every day, sometimes more than once. She'd come to dinner with Lindsey and Zoey at the Beresford half a dozen times, since she worked just across the street. This would be her third weekend in the country.

It hadn't occurred to Lindsey that Zoey would mind. From all appearances, the two got along well and shared an interest in both music and cooking. "I thought she'd enjoy baking with us, since she's such a good cook."

"I wish she'd leave us alone." Zoey returned to her book.

Lindsey's hackles rose at this moody, adolescent outburst. It wasn't as if Zoey was clamoring to spend more time with her mother. But Lindsey knew she'd spent every spare minute of the last seven weeks talking to or thinking about Joan. Had she missed some signal Zoey had given?

"Zoey. Look at me."

Zoey's head inched up. "What?"

"Did something happen between you two?"

Zoey's look could have burned a hole in paper. "Mom, she acts like she's part of our family. When she's around"— Zoey's face crinkled in disgust—"you get so ... so gooey."

"Gooey. What does that mean?"

"You get this stupid smile on your face. Like she's said something amazing. Even if she's only talking about boiling eggs. I want my real mom back."

Every muscle in Lindsey's body went limp. Her daughter had described a simpering, lovestruck girl. Did she actually simper when Joan was around? Or was Zoey punishing her solely for the crime of being the parent of an adolescent?

Whatever her motive, Zoey had thrown down a challenge. Would she have to choose between her lover and her daughter?

~ ~ ~ ~

When Joan arrived Friday night, she was in high spirits. She held out a large insulated bag. "Since we're baking all weekend, I brought a chicken casserole for dinner tomorrow night." She winked at Lindsey. "I even tucked in some wine."

During the drive up, she directed most of her questions to Zoey. When did the fruitcake tradition start? How many kinds of fruitcake? Where did the recipe come from? Zoey was amiable and chatty, with no sign of the previous night's peevishness.

By the time Dee and Wendy arrived the next morning, shaking off a frosting of white from the heavy snowfall, they'd set out mounds of oranges and lemons, citrons, dates and nuts, as well as bowls of flour, sugar, and spices.

While the others grated, diced, and chopped, Lindsey retrieved metal tins from the storeroom and washed them. Years ago, she and Dee discovered a recipe to bake the fruitcake in the tins, slowly and at a low enough temperature the tins were not damaged.

As she came and went, Lindsey eavesdropped on conversations that flowed easily, with occasional outbursts of laughter. The one exception was in the late morning, when Lindsey arrived to complete silence. On her next pass, however, they were chatting easily.

By noon, the counters were piled high with chopped fruits and nuts. After lunch, the girls mixed the batter, while Lindsey lined the tins with foil and Dee filled them. Joan stationed herself at the sink, keeping a ready supply of clean bowls and utensils. By midafternoon, they'd filled the oven for one round, and prepared a second set of tins to bake the next morning. Before they left, all the fruitcakes would be laced with rum.

When the kitchen was cleaned up, the girls left to go cross-country skiing before dark.

Lindsey stretched to release the ache in her lower back. "Who's up for the hot tub?"

Joan rolled her eyes as she hung up her kitchen towel. "You ladies are made of sterner stuff than me. I need a nap."

~ ~ ~ ~

"Oh, my aching legs," Dee moaned as they stepped into the steaming Jacuzzi, each with a short glass of scotch. "Every year, I manage to forget how much work this is."

"This'll fix you up." Lindsey scootched down so the water bubbled up to her ears. "Move three inches to the left. That gets the strongest jets on your calves."

"Feels better already." Dee held up her glass. "To many more years of fruitcake." Reaching out from under the overhang, she let several snowflakes accumulate on her palm. "And to a couple more inches of fresh snow tonight."

"I'll second that." Lindsey raised her glass to Dee's.

They sat in an easy silence, watching the snowflakes drift through the blue-grey light of the Berkshire dusk.

"You haven't mentioned the separation agreement lately," Dee said as she laid her head back against the lip of the tub, her eyes closed. "What did you decide to do?"

"It's still sitting on my desk."

"It's been more than a month."

"If Zoey goes to grad school—it's 12–15 more years of school—Ted's proposal is a sweet deal. But God forbid she marries at eighteen, I'd have barely five years to save for my retirement. I'd be screwed."

Dee opened her eyes and swiveled her head to look at Lindsey. "Has Angela tried to negotiate it?"

"Yeah. Ted won't budge."

"You gotta put this to bed. He could change his mind any time."

Lindsey shifted to focus the jets on her back. "Did Zoey tell you we're going to the symphony with Claire this Thursday?"

Dee closed her eyes again. "You're changing the subject."

"Yeah. I know I need to do it. But I can't."

"Can't or won't?"

"Dee, can we change the subject?"

"Okay. Mother-in-law and discarded wife aren't the run-of-the-mill symphony companions. Do you realize how fortunate you are? A lot of women make life miserable for their ex-daughters-in-law."

"I do know that. I think we're better friends than when Ted and I were together. For years, every conversation was about Ted or Zoey. Now, we talk about more personal stuff. Our childhoods. My social work. Her charity work. The arts."

Lindsey finished off her drink and set her glass on the ledge. "Sometimes I'm my own worst enemy. I let myself be intimidated by her. Her society position ... her high profile charity boards. But she considers it just a job, what she has to do because of her family position. Do you know she hates the political jockeying almost as much as I do? She's a very wise woman."

"Too bad her son didn't inherit some of her wisdom."

Lindsey felt a burst of gratitude for Dee, a friend with whom she'd shared so much for so many years. "Dee."

"Umh?"

"You have no idea how sorry I am that I doubted you. You and Jim."

"Not to worry. You had a big shock to your system. It's natural to question everything ... everyone."

Dee opened her eyes and sat up. "And with that, let's change the subject once again." She gave a soft chuckle. "I guess Joan didn't know quite what she was in for."

"Guess not. But she chopped and diced, and then chopped and diced some more. She also brought dinner for tonight, which counts for a lot." Lindsey resisted the urge to rest her head on the ledge, knowing she'd fall asleep if she did.

"Jim's doing the honors for us tonight. Probably pizza or corned beef hash. Anyway, I can see why you like her," said Dee. "She's fun ... and good with the girls. Wendy isn't usually so outgoing with strangers. But Joan does have her bossy moments."

Lindsey remembered the odd silence as she came in from the storeroom. "Did something happen?"

Dee shrugged and shook her head. "It was silly."

"Tell me."

"I needed to grate lemon rind and Zoey was using the new slab affair for the oranges. When I went to dig out the old metal gizmo from the cupboard by the stove, Joan asked me what I was doing. I thought she was just being social and said I wanted the old grater."

Dee leaned forward, toward Lindsey. "She said ... and I quote ... 'If you need something, just ask me for it.'" Dee snickered. "I couldn't believe it."

Lindsey couldn't believe it either. How would Joan know where the metal grater was? It hadn't been used since they made fruitcake a year ago.

"It was amazing," Dee continued. "She searched five different places before she found it! I don't think she had any idea where it was. It was odd, you know—acting like she knew your kitchen better than someone who's been working in it for a decade."

Lindsey remembered the to-do with Ted at Zoey's play. "She can be a bit overbearing at times, but she means well."

"I'm sure she does. I'll trust your judgment on that."

~ ~ ~ ~

Lindsey arrived at work on Monday loaded down with fruitcakes, most of which she gave out at her weekly staff meeting. As people thanked her vociferously, she wondered how many liked fruitcake—and how many were mouthing the requisite platitudes that went with a seasonal gesture from one's boss.

Joel's response felt genuine. "Thanks. My wife waits by the door when she finds out your fruitcake's coming. And your staff was worried you might abandon the tradition," he hesitated, "under the circumstances."

Lindsey's separation was, by now, common knowledge around the office. "They like my fruitcakes that much?"

Joel gave a companionable laugh. "Some do. Some don't. But we're all concerned about you. You might say the fruitcakes tell us you're okay."

Lindsey's face flushed. She'd felt a bit alienated from her staff ever since the outburst from the case manager she'd fired. "Joel, do you remember the young man we let go in September?"

"A hard one to forget! Nice guy, but not cut out for this line of work."

"During the exit interview, he said my staff hated me— that I had no empathy. I assumed he was projecting, but it's worried me ever since."

"Lindsey, you have the most amazing blind spots at times. You're a great teacher, a patient and encouraging mentor, a role model for all of us. But you don't share much of yourself personally. What you did over the weekend. Where you're going for vacation. They all respect you, but most don't know you well enough to know whether they like you or not."

Lindsey blinked back tears. "I wish I were better at the social chitchat. But it always seems so artificial when I try it."

"It's not a big deal. I suspect you have more important things to adjust to at the moment. But we're all rooting for you."

"Thanks." She stood up. "I think I need to get out of here before I start to cry."

~ ~ ~ ~

Dee's urging about the separation agreement echoed in her ears.

The next day, she phoned Angela. "Most of it seems fine. But your retirement calculations don't work if Zoey marries at 18. I wouldn't be able to save enough for my retirement. Could we get him to make up the difference if Zoey marries before she's 25?"

Angela called back the next afternoon. "He offered to up the retirement split to 35/65—and you still keep all of your salary. I think you should take it."

Lindsey knew she should be pleased at Ted's concession, but she wasn't. She felt as hollow and depleted as she had in the days after Ted left.

For much of the last two months, Joan's nurturing spirit had been a soothing balm, giving her confidence that life would go on. But as she stared at the phone, she had an image of putting calamine on poison ivy ... it relieved the itch, but didn't fix the underlying ailment. Joan had done so much to fill the hole in her day-to-day life, but that didn't change the fact that Lindsey had failed to make her marriage work. And she still didn't know why.

She called Dee the moment she got home.

"It's over."

"What's over?"

"My marriage. I agreed to the new terms Angela negotiated. Ted will draw up the final papers in the next few weeks." Lindsey had been trying to be sensible, but suddenly the tears poured out. "It could be all over by early January."

"Are you going to be okay, sweetie?"

"I don't know. I really don't."

~ ~ ~ ~

The last mythology class of the term was the next night. Lindsey had not registered for the spring term, but had arranged for the Wednesday night sleepovers to continue. That would give her at least one evening a week to be alone with Joan.

After class, she and Joan went to Café Loup for champagne and found a table in a quiet corner. Joan rested her hand on Lindsey's knee. "Are you feeling better today? When we talked last night, my heart was breaking for you."

A surge of desire made Lindsey wish they'd gone to Joan's instead of stopping for a celebratory drink. She slid her hand on top of Joan's. "Yes, much better. You've taught me that nothing is as bad as refusing to think about it. Whatever mistakes I made with Ted, I have no chance of doing it better if I don't face up to them."

Joan looked at Lindsey over the bridge of her nose. "Doing it better? Last night, you said the settlement was final. Are you already thinking about reconciling?"

She squeezed Joan's hand. "Maybe this sounds like Psych 101, but you've given me the courage to be myself ... or at least try to figure out what myself is."

"Lindsey, you are a generous, caring, wonderful woman. I love you, just the way you are." Under the table, she turned her palm up and wove her fingers into Lindsey's.

An aura of warmth flooded Lindsey's chest. Meeting Joan's gaze, she whispered, "I love you too, more than you know." She tightened her grip on Joan's hand.

As she did, she felt the angular edge of Joan's wedding ring. "You still wear your ring."

Joan held her hand up and inspected the ring. "It's my favorite piece of jewelry. Brad had it made for me for our 20th wedding anniversary."

"But if you don't love him, why wear it? Why not buy yourself a new ring?"

"He likes me to wear it."

"How does he even know?"

"He sees it whenever we have dinner ... every few weeks."

Lindsey wondered if her amazement showed on her face. She'd had no idea that Joan and Brad met regularly. Why had Joan never mentioned any of those dinners?

She couldn't take her eyes off Joan's ring. What did loving each other mean if Joan still wanted to be married to Brad? Had she completely misread Joan's situation? She nursed a glass of ice water while she tried to make sense of this news.

"Lindsey, what's the matter? You've gone so pale."

"Are you planning to go back to him ... at some point?"

Joan snorted. "Not a chance in hell. I had enough of being his housekeeper and bed warmer. I won't go back. Ever. But it makes him feel better to know he can call on me if he needs something. I don't love him, but I don't hate him."

Joan's words were not altogether reassuring. Joan had become her lifeline and the thought of losing that lifeline was terrifying.

Chapter 18

"Lindsey, I can't believe how much I miss you after only one day."

Lindsey's longing for Joan was almost a physical pain. From the moment she left New York, she'd missed Joan. But with a houseful of people milling around, her reply was limited to "I'm so glad you called."

"Is this a good time to talk? Are you alone?"

She settled into a thickly cushioned chair. "I'm on the patio, waiting for the girls to come out for lunch."

"Guess not. So, how's Zoey doing?"

"Great! She's actually been quite chatty since we arrived ... not about anything of consequence, but a big improvement over the silent treatment I've had of late."

"So, she'll survive Christmas without her dad."

"We'll see," Lindsey replied. "Dee's put the girls in charge of lunch and dinner to keep them busy. And a Hobie Cat comes with the condo. The girls took it out for the junior sailboat races this morning while Dee and I explored the town. I'm hoping Zoey is too busy to think much about Ted."

"And you, lovey. Are you okay?"

"Yeah." Lindsey nodded as though Joan could see her. "I think it was serendipity coming here so soon after the negotiations with Ted. At least I'm not reminded of him at every turn."

"I get that," Joan said. "It's why I moved to New York instead of staying in Short Hills. No way I wanted to run into my old life every time I went to buy eggs. So, what's Cabo like?"

"Gorgeous. I bet there's a dozen surfers out there on the beach in front of us."

"Sounds delicious. How's the condo?"

"Large and ultramodern—all beige and white and chrome. The girls have the lower level to themselves, which works for everybody."

Just then, Zoey and Wendy appeared at the sliding screen door, juggling plates and milk glasses. As Lindsey got up to open the door, she waved the phone briefly in front of Zoey. "Hey, Joan, the girls just showed up. Can I—"

Zoey called out, "Hi, Joan, hope you're enjoying the holidays."

"Did you hear that? Anyway, can I call you back in about an hour?"

"Sure. Give my love to Zoey."

Lindsey tucked the phone into her pocket and returned to her seat. "How was the race?"

"Awesome!" Wendy's enthusiasm was contagious. "We finished third."

Zoey chimed in. "Pretty cool for two landlubbers" She plopped down on the chair next to Lindsey.

"Well, it depends on how many boats were in the race," Lindsey said, kissing her fingertips and brushing them against her daughter's cheek. "So what do you two partners-in-crime have planned for the afternoon?"

"Twelve boats," Zoey said. "I think we did pretty good."

"We're going to the mall after lunch." Wendy jumped in. "There's something I need to get for Dad." She pointed offshore. "Look. Dolphins."

They sat in an easy silence and watched half a dozen of the sleek grey animals cavorting just beyond the breaking waves. When they disappeared, Zoey murmured, without shifting her gaze, "I wish Dad were here."

Lindsey gave Zoey a light hug. It was one of the few times Zoey had mentioned her father without overt anger. "I know, pumpkin. Want to call him and wish him Merry Christmas?"

Zoey looked up, her eyelashes moist. "Do you think he'd mind?"

With the tip of her finger, Lindsey brushed the tears from her daughter's eyes. "I think he'd be thrilled." She noticed Wendy squeeze Zoey's arm and was grateful that the girls were still such good friends.

Zoey's tearful smile resurrected Lindsey's latent anxiety about Christmas Day. She was hoping the ritual of opening gifts, along with a flurry of Christmas Day activities—making brunch, modeling new clothes, swimming or sailing—would distract Zoey from the absence of her father and the long-promised saddle.

For a time, Lindsey had considered buying a saddle herself and shipping it to Cabo. She'd actually made the trek, in early December, to Manhattan Saddlery—"the" place for the horsey set in New York City—hoping to learn enough in an hour or two to make a selection. But it was clear, within minutes, how much she didn't know about riding: how Zoey "sat" in the saddle, whether she wanted English or Western. Ted, of course, would know all those details.

And the prices appalled her. The cheapest saddle was nearly $600 and had the feel of cardboard. To get one that was "fine-grain leather" with hand tooling would be at least $1,000, far too much to spend on a gift she wasn't sure was right. And probably too much to spend on a saddle for a first horse for a thirteen-year-old.

And then, of course, there was the possibility that Ted would buy a saddle, despite Zoey's persistent refusal to see or talk to him. The morning after her visit to the Saddlery, Lindsey had called him at his office. "I said I'd get it and I will," he'd snapped.

She heard no more about it, but nagging had never been her style. She wasn't about to start now that they were living separate lives.

Knowing there would be no saddle under the tree, she'd gone all out on gifts for Zoey. A tooled red leather jacket Zoey had admired. A gift certificate from Zoey's favorite cosmetic store. Biographies of Katharine Hepburn and Meryl Streep, inspiration for an aspiring actress. She hoped they would help to fill the hole.

~ ~ ~ ~

Christmas morning festivities began when Jim, dressed in an obviously snug Santa suit and tatty white beard, started banging on a metal pot.

The comic moments continued. Jim's gift to Dee was a pair of sapphire earrings, a gift on which Wendy had clearly played an advisory role. But Jim had made the giving of the gift as much a treat as the gift itself. The colorful box under the tree was right for a coffee maker or a small TV, but once opened, it contained a smaller box ... and another ... and another—a series of six mismatched boxes nested like Russian dolls. The earrings, when Dee finally got to them, were wrapped in emerald tissue and stuffed into an orange plastic pill container.

Zoey seemed to have been inspired by Jim's packaging ruse. Her gift to Lindsey—two tickets to a matinee performance of *The Book of Mormon*—was tucked into a blue velvet bag that might once have held an expensive piece of jewelry. Perhaps even a pair of sapphire earrings.

Lindsey was dumbfounded by Jim's gift to her, a $200 iTunes certificate. "Jim, I don't have an iPad or an iPhone," she said. "What on earth do I do with this?"

Jim gave her a mischievous wink. "Maybe Zoey will let you download a song or two onto her iPod."

Zoey's grimace did not suggest any enthusiasm for sharing her iPod with her mother. Perhaps this time Jim had been a bit too clever.

~ ~ ~ ~

When there was nothing left but empty boxes and streams of knotted ribbon, Jim retired to the den to check football scores, while mothers and daughters began breakfast.

They were ready to ferry food platters to the patio when the doorbell rang. "Jim, honey, are you expecting anyone?" Dee called out.

Jim came to the doorway, shaking his head. "No. Zoey, why don't you answer it?"

Something in his voice made Lindsey's skin prickle.

"Sure." Zoey set her muffin platter on the counter and disappeared into the front hall.

Lindsey held her breath. She didn't know what to expect, but she knew it would not be good.

"Dad! Wow!"

Lindsey braced herself on a stool, trying to comprehend why Ted was at the door. She turned to Dee, whose slack-jawed expression said she was every bit as shocked as Lindsey. And then she saw Jim's smirk. The bastard had known all along. Too shocked to move, she sat mute as Dee followed Jim and Wendy to the front hall.

Isolated phrases reached her. "… gorgeous … your flight … the Palace Hotel." The rich, sweet aroma of new leather made her nose itch. And someone was tugging on her arm.

It was Zoey. "Come see what Dad brought!"

She didn't need to see. She already knew.

With Zoey pushing her, she stumbled into the front hall. A lustrous sienna leather saddle, with a red ribbon around the horn, sat in the center of the terrazzo floor.

"Merry Christmas, Lindsey," Ted said. Ted smiled as if he'd just returned from getting the newspaper.

She recognized that smile—the one he'd perfected over years of working a crowd.

"I promised Zoey a saddle for Christmas," he said, laying his arm over his daughter's shoulder. "I came to deliver on that promise."

Lindsey froze as Zoey bathed her father in a smile that said "all is forgiven." The bastard had bought his way back into his daughter's good graces.

"Well, this is all great entertainment, folks, but my breakfast is getting cold," Jim announced. "Ted, you're welcome to join us."

Putting his arms around Dee and Wendy, Jim ushered them toward the kitchen. "Come, ladies, let me escort you to the patio."

With one arm still around Zoey, Ted pulled out a small box wrapped in an elegant red and gold foil out of his briefcase and handed it to Lindsey. "Merry Christmas."

She stared at the box, dumbfounded yet again. Why was this man, who had summarily tossed her out of his life, giving her a gift?

"Thanks," she whispered hoarsely. As she whirled around toward the kitchen, she tossed it on the hall table.

Dee linked her arm through Lindsey's as she came into the kitchen. "Honey, I had no idea," she whispered. "I'm going to kill that husband of mine first chance I get."

"If I don't kill him first," Lindsey said. "Dee, I can't sit across the breakfast table from him. I'm going for a walk on the beach."

"How about I come with you? The guys can manage without us."

Lindsey was shaking all over. She wanted Joan, not Dee. "Thanks, but I need breathing space. The sea air will calm me down."

"Okay, but if you're not back in an hour, I'm coming after you."

Lindsey hid in the powder room until they were all seated on the patio. To avoid any conversation, she decided to go out the front and use the public access to the beach. Crossing the foyer, she saw the gift box on the table. Without conscious thought, she stuffed it in the pocket of her shorts and made her escape.

Chapter 19

Lindsey stomped across the beach toward the waterline. She was desperate to talk to Joan. She needed a friend who would let her scream out her rage.

When the condo was out of sight, she collapsed on a flat, sunbaked rock and reached in her pocket. No phone. Only the goddamned foil-wrapped box.

She was on her own.

She sat hugging her legs, her chin resting on her knees. When she felt calmer, she pulled the box out of her pocket and peeled off the foil paper. A white box. An embossed silver apple. An iPod! Jim's iTunes gift certificate suddenly made sense. He'd not only known Ted was coming, he'd known about the gift. How long had they been orchestrating this?

She hurled the box toward the water. It fell short, landing a few inches below the high tide line. A breaking wave would eventually claim the box.

She had to figure out what to do. Demanding that Ted leave today would most certainly ruin her daughter's Christmas, bursting the bubble of delight his arrival had brought. And what if Zoey decided to go back with him? She couldn't bear the thought.

But what if he stayed? It wasn't within her power to carry off the charade of a family for the three days until she and Zoey flew home, to pretend the way Ted had pretended in the hall. And why should she even try? The bastard had breached the most basic rules of courtesy by showing up without letting her know. She deserved better than that.

A large wave broke on the beach, a few feet short. The box lay untouched.

The box. Was Ted trying to buy his way back into her good graces? Like he'd done with his daughter's saddle? And if so, why?

Her mouth puckered at a sudden metallic taste, one she recognized all too well. It was the taste of resentment—jealousy. How easily he had recaptured his daughter's heart.

She hated her own selfishness. What ought to matter was that he'd made Zoey smile once again. But, dammit all, he'd insinuated himself back into Zoey's life, just when her own relationship with Zoey seemed to be sending out new roots.

Her head throbbed. She wanted to close her mind as well as her eyes, to shut out all the questions she couldn't answer. She lay back on the rock and turned on her side to shade her eyes from the sun. She saw the iPod box, still on dry sand.

An iPod that almost any client or staffer at the agency would be thrilled to have.

She sat up. She couldn't throw it in the ocean in a fit of pique. She'd donate it to the agency. She plodded down to the tide line. No sooner had she picked it up than the cool water washed over her feet. Jamming the box into her pocket, she made her way back to the rock.

She stretched out on her side again, her head resting on her arm, her legs curled up in a fetal position and tried to concentrate on the rhythmic sloshing of the waves rolling up onto the beach.

~ ~ ~ ~

"Lindsey, sweetie, wake up."

She felt warm, gentle hands, moving up and down her back and mumbled, "Oh, Joan, I'm so glad you're here. I don't know what to do."

"Lindsey, it's Dee. Are you okay?"

Lindsey froze. Had Dee heard her say Joan's name? What else had she said that she didn't remember? She rolled onto her back. "I fell asleep. I must have been dreaming."

"C'mon, sweetie, put this shirt and hat on. We've got to get you home. You're gonna fry if you stay out here any longer." Dee tried to pull Lindsey up.

Lindsey locked her muscles. "I can't go back. I can't face him."

"No worries. He's already gone, winging his way back to New York as we speak."

Lindsey stared at Dee. "Did Zoey go with him?"

Dee shook her head. "He only came to deliver the saddle. Said he had to be back in New York for a meeting early tomorrow." She redoubled her effort to pull Lindsey up.

This time Lindsey let Dee guide her arms into the shirt. "Zoey was disappointed, of course. But they've got a plan to meet for dinner when you get back to New York."

Lindsey remembered tossing the box onto the table. "I hope I didn't make her feel guilty about spending time with him."

Dee gave an impish grin. "I told a bit of a white lie—that you left so Zoey could have time with him."

"You are good. Thanks."

They headed toward the condo, strolling barefoot at the waterline with the waves cooling their feet. After a few moments, Lindsey asked, "Why did he do it?"

"Who? Jim or Ted?"

"Jim. I can't believe he let Ted spring that on me."

Dee groaned. "He wants you two back together. You were his storybook marriage."

Lindsey kicked up clods of sand ahead of her. "And he thought Ted's visit would help?"

Dee squeezed Lindsey's upper arm. "I don't know what he thought, Lindsey. It seems Ted called him a couple weeks ago to ask about coming just for the morning, to deliver the saddle. He didn't want Zoey to know, for fear she'd rebuff him once again. And he thought you and I would put the kibosh on the idea if we knew."

"He got that one right."

They walked, arm in arm, listening to the lapping waves and shrieking gulls. After a minute or so, Dee said, "He talked about you during breakfast ... how Zoey had such a good mother ... how nice it was that you and Claire have stayed friends. He seemed genuinely disappointed that you'd skipped out on breakfast."

Lindsey gave a sardonic laugh. "The charismatic Ted we all know and love ... lots of feel-good compliments. But half the time, he doesn't mean a bit of it."

"You're really angry, aren't you?"

"The bastard didn't give a moment's thought to how Zoey might react to his walking out—he was going to let me tell her." She kicked a particularly large spray of sand. "And I'll bet he didn't give much thought to how his visit today will affect her—other than that he wants her to be devoted to him."

"Lindsey, give him a break. Zoey needs her father."

"I know that. But if he's back in her life, he's back in mine. I was just getting used to life without him. I don't like him dropping in without notice."

Dee snugged Lindsey's arm against her ribcage, and then let it go.

Lindsey found the gesture comforting. "I'm beginning to realize how far apart Ted and I had grown. Maybe his leaving was for the best."

"You don't really believe that."

Lindsey reached down for a shiny black stone at the water's edge. "I do. There are so many things Ted and I never talked about ... so many things he doesn't know about me."

"Like?"

Lindsey rolled the stone around in her upturned palm. Her comment about Ted was also true of Dee. While their lives had been intertwined for more than a decade, there were so many things she and Dee had never talked about. Her persistent stomachache. Her recurrent anxiety about losing Ted's love. Her irrational jealousy of his relationship with Zoey. Her recent fears that history would repeat itself.

But keeping secrets had not saved her marriage. She took a deep breath. "Like being jealous of Ted's relationship with Zoey."

Dee's eyes widened. "Jealous of Ted? Why?"

Lindsey ignored Dee's question, afraid she'd lose her courage if she broke her train of thought. "I was ashamed to admit it, even to myself."

Dee stopped and tugged Lindsey around so they faced each other. "What on earth are you talking about? Zoey has always adored you."

Lindsey looked wary. "Not the way she adored him. He has so much patience. He soaks up all her chatter about teachers and classmates. Even—god forbid—boys. She rarely talks to me about that stuff."

"Amazing." Dee shook her head. "For a smart lady, you sure are dumb."

Lindsey waited. The laughter in Dee's voice leeched out the sting of her words.

"Sure, he listens to her chatty gossip about school activities and her classmates," Dee said. "But then he pats her on the head, saying, 'You'll be fine. I know you can do it.' He's so dismissive. He doesn't want to deal with her doubts or anxieties. He wants her to be perfect."

Lindsey stared at Dee. Had Zoey felt as dominated by Ted as she herself had?

"She's always been in awe of him, scared she'll let him down. That's why his leaving was so upsetting to her. I can't believe you didn't realize that."

Lindsey wanted to kick herself. Yet again, she'd been so caught up in her own anxieties she'd failed to see what was right in front of her.

"Maybe you don't joke with her or tease her the way he does. But, sweetie, she's not scared of you. She loves that you're interested in the characters in her plays and the books she reads. That you like to rehearse her parts with her, not just show up for the performance."

Again, history was repeating itself. Not Lindsey and her father, but Zoey and Ted. Was Zoey a younger version of herself ... always treading lightly, avoiding conflict, afraid to reveal her flaws?

She pulled back enough to meet Dee's eyes. "I've never thought about it that way. He's so good with people, I figured he was that good with his daughter."

Dee gave a mirthless laugh. "Being good with clients is a trifle different than being good with your children." Almost as an afterthought, Dee said, "Or your wife."

"You know," Lindsey said as they started walking again, "there were several times in the weeks before Ted left that Zoey worried out loud about letting him down. She kept asking me if he was disappointed in her ... or mad at her. It puzzled me at the time."

"Do you hear what you're saying? That your daughter felt safe sharing her fear with you." Dee took a step back. "That's why she adores you."

"God, Dee, maybe I've spent years being miserable about something that never existed."

Dee butted her shoulder lightly against Lindsey's. "And I wish I'd understood how you felt. I'm sorry I wasn't the kind of friend you needed. After all these years, you must know I love you."

Hot tears rolled down Lindsey's cheeks and along her neck. She'd heard Dee say "I love you" a million times over the years, but almost always in the cheery, superficial way that meant "that was so nice of you" or "gee, that was fun." Out on the beach under the burning sun, Dee's affection washed over her like a wave.

"I love you, too, Dee. And I'm sorry I didn't know how to trust you."

"Maybe Ted's visit is a good thing, if only because it made us talk in a new way." Dee linked her arm with Lindsey's as the condo came into view. "By the way, Joan called. I guess she tried your cell three or four times and then called me when she couldn't reach you."

Lindsey checked her watch. 12:30 California time. 3:30 New York time. Joan would be sitting down to Christmas dinner at Tammy's. "Thanks. I'll call her back later this afternoon."

"How'd she get my cell phone number?"

Lindsey tried to sound offhanded. "I gave it to her. You know ... just in case."

"I gather you see a lot of her."

Moisture flooded Lindsey's armpits. Did Dee suspect? "Maybe twice a week, including class. Why?"

"Zoey's been feeling a bit ... umm ... she's mentioned a couple times that Joan gets more of your time than she does."

Lindsey unlinked her arm from Dee's and spun around. "Gawd, is there anything you don't know about my daughter?"

Dee gaped at Lindsey. "I'm confused. I thought the last ten minutes were about being more open ... trusting each other."

"Yes, but now you're telling me my daughter doesn't talk to me." Before her words were out, she remembered Zoey's protest at including Joan in the fruitcake day.

"That's not what I'm saying. What I'm saying is that your daughter—who lost her father three months ago—feels like she's losing her mother. I know Joan's been a big help to you, but Zoey doesn't understand that. All she knows is that she wants her mother, not a package deal of her mother-and-her-mother's-friend."

Lindsey brought her hands up to her shoulders, massaging them as if to ward off the chill of Dee's words. She forced a smile. "I'm sorry Dee. It's been a tough day and I'm feeling overwhelmed. I didn't mean to be short."

"Hey, Mommmmm."

Lindsey looked up to see Wendy and Zoey racing down the beach toward them. As Lindsey waved, she recalled how happy Zoey had been on the patio as they shared lunch the day before. Could Zoey's bad temper in the past two months have been anger at sharing her mother with Joan? Could her good humor now be because she had her mother to herself?

Dee put her arm around Lindsey's shoulders in a quick hug. "C'mon, my friend, let's go find out about Zoey's visit with her dad."

Chapter 20

When Zoey went off to do homework after dinner, Lindsey started her shopping list for New Year's Eve. She'd planned one of her favorite menus—marinated lamb chops, curried wild rice, and caramelized vegetables.

Halfway through the list, the phone rang. Ted's ID. He'd been calling Zoey at least once a day since Christmas. She let it ring until Zoey picked up.

Lindsey had chosen not to get involved in their interaction unless Zoey decided to share a conversation. But she couldn't ignore their plan to meet for dinner the day after New Year's.

She'd overheard Zoey and Wendy speculating about Lauren. Given the media, as well as the long list of divorces and unfaithful spouses among the families of her schoolmates, the girls were hardly ignorant of the concept of infidelity. But pubescent schoolgirls giggling in horror at the idea of illicit sex was a different matter than coming face to face with your father's mistress at the breakfast table.

She was pretty sure Ted's recent calls focused on Zoey's activities rather than his own. But what would happen when Zoey was part of his daily life. Would he expect her to slide smoothly into a routine that included Lauren? And, god forbid, what if he brought Lauren to their first dinner? He couldn't be that insensitive!

She gave momentary thought to talking with Zoey about Lauren. But what would she say, exactly? She knew nothing about their relationship: how serious it was, how much time they spent together, what plans they had for a future, if any. Then too, she doubted she could carry off such a discussion without sounding critical of Ted. She didn't want to go there. She wouldn't tear him down in his daughter's eyes.

As she finished her grocery list, the phone rang again. This time it was Claire, undoubtedly calling to make final arrangements for the New Year's Eve Pops Concert. She let it ring three times, but when Zoey didn't pick up, she grabbed it before voicemail kicked in.

"Hi, Claire. Happy New Year. Are you calling about tomorrow?"

Claire laughed. "To you as well. I'll come by about 5:30. I've got reservations at Gabriel's at six."

"I'm amazed you got a table on New Year's Eve. Who knows what celebrities you'll get to gawk at!"

"I think Zoey will enjoy it. And what are you doing for New Year's?"

"Joan's coming for dinner. After Zoey gets home from the concert, we'll head over to Central Park for the fireworks."

"Sounds like a late night. Should I keep Zoey overnight? Bring her back after breakfast."

"I think she wants to see the fireworks. She's never been in the City for New Year's, so it's a whole new experience. But I'll ask her."

"Lindsey?" Claire sounded hesitant.

"Umm?"

"If she does come, would you mind if Ted came for breakfast? He's dying to see her."

"Of course not," Lindsey responded automatically, if not truthfully. She *was* glad Zoey and Ted were reconciled. But Claire's request scraped at the scar left from all the other breakfasts she'd been left out of.

"I wanted to be sure. See you tomorrow."

As Lindsey was about to hang up, it struck her that Claire might have a suggestion about Lauren. "Do you have a minute?"

"Sure. What do you need?"

"Zoey knows there's a woman in Ted's life. She and Wendy make silly jokes about it all the time. But I worry she'll react badly if she suddenly discovers Lauren at the dinner table."

"She's never mentioned Lauren to me, but then she mostly tells me that she hopes you'll somehow get back together."

Lindsey wondered, for the umpteenth time, what Zoey had told her grandmother, but she wouldn't ask Claire to violate a confidence. She focused on the issue at hand. "I don't mean to pry, but is Lauren living with Ted?"

"He knows I disapprove, so she's never been there when I was visiting. I've never asked—and he's never said." Claire gave an uncharacteristic cackle. "I will tell you, Lindsey, it has taken some character not to check the medicine cabinet when I was using the ladies."

Lindsey smiled at the image of the ever-so-proper Claire sneaking a peek. "I don't want her to be shocked if Lauren suddenly appears."

"So, talk to Ted."

Lindsey bounced her head lightly against the wall. "That wasn't the answer I wanted."

"My dear, Zoey has two parents. You need to work together. I know you'll find a way."

"Don't I wish? See you tomorrow evening."

~ ~ ~ ~

For hours, she pondered what to say to Ted. Finally, at four, she couldn't put it off any longer. Hoping for some liquid courage, she poured herself a scotch and punched his number.

Ted picked up on the third ring. "Hi, Lindsey. What's up?"

She heard a football announcer in the background. She hoped Ted couldn't hear the banging of her heart. "It's about Zoey."

"Is she okay?"

"Yes, she's fine."

"Whew. So what's up?"

"I wanted you to know I'm very glad you two have reconnected." Lindsey's words, sincere enough, let her put off for a few seconds longer the question she dreaded asking.

"Me too. I've missed her."

Lindsey sank back in the desk chair, playing out the speech she'd rehearsed. "Have you said anything to Zoey about Lauren?"

Ted grunted. "Umm ... no. Why?"

"I don't think she's ready to deal with your mistress." Lindsey was talking too fast. She willed herself to slow her pace. "I don't want you to bring her into Zoey's life until you and I are officially divorced."

"That's a long ways off. And, in any case ..." he paused, long enough that Lindsey wondered if he'd hung up, "it's not your decision to make."

Lindsey tensed, bracing for a fight. "Ted, Zoey is only beginning to recover from your leaving. Please don't send her back into a tailspin."

"Hold on a minute."

As she waited, the football game grew fainter. With the click of a door, the sound of the game disappeared. She assumed he was watching it with Lauren.

"Lindsey, I know I didn't handle things well when I left. I—"

"You certainly didn't," she said, and immediately regretted it.

She heard a long and audible breath, the sound of someone trying not to lose his temper. "I took the apartment to be near Zoey. There's nothing of Lauren's here. But sooner or later, her name will come up. I won't lie to her."

"Promise me you'll let me know when that happens. So I'm prepared if she reacts badly."

"Yes. I promise." His too-patient tone was that of a weary parent humoring a cranky child. And Lindsey was the child.

She'd heard that tone too many times over the years.

Limp with relief that the call was over, she reflected on Ted's comment that there was nothing of Lauren's in his apartment. She counted out the months on her fingers. Assuming the affair started in early summer, they'd been together for six months. How curious that his home had no evidence of the woman for whom he'd left his family. What were the odds this relationship would last?

As she downed the last of her drink, she woke up to the irony of her situation. She'd been worrying all day that dealing with her father's new lover would unsettle Zoey. But she herself was asking Zoey to deal with Lindsey's new lover, a woman her daughter already resented. She wasn't lying to Zoey, but she wasn't being honest either.

~ ~ ~ ~

Halfway through dinner dishes, she mentioned Claire's invitation, but said nothing about Ted.

"I want to go with you." Zoey said with a sly look. "I'm hoping to get some champagne."

"I don't know. Thirteen's pretty young." Lindsey put on a stern face, then winked. "Well, maybe a sip."

"Cool."

"Can you stay awake that late? Do you want to take a nap after the concert, or have dessert with us?"

Zoey, about to load a plate into the dishwasher, spun around. "Us?"

"Joan. She's coming for dinner."

"Is she going to the fireworks?"

Lindsey nodded. "She's never seen them either."

Zoey's face clouded. "If she's coming, I'm going to Gammy's."

"Zoey, pumpkin—"

"Don't call me that." She dropped the plate into the dishwasher, then called Claire from the kitchen phone.

When Claire answered, Zoey managed to please her grandmother and lacerate her mother's heart with one stroke. "Gammy, it'd be cool to stay with you after the concert. Mom's going to the fireworks with Joan, so she won't miss me anyway."

Chapter 21

"I don't think I've ever been in Central Park after dark." Joan's eyes flickered from side to side, surveying the crowd. "I can't believe how many people are here!"

"It's not like Times Square, but between the costume party, the midnight race and the fireworks, we'll have lots of company. And"—Lindsey lifted up the canvas bag with the champagne—"it's the one time the police don't pay much attention to alcohol in the Park."

Juggling fold-up chairs and a canvas bag packed with drinks and blankets, they huddled together for warmth as they crossed the snow-covered lawn of Strawberry Fields. The frozen fog of their breath marked out a path in front of them. Lindsey hoped to find a spot where they could see both the race and the fireworks. The cold kept spectators from arriving too much in advance, but at 11:30 p.m., the best spots would soon be taken.

"Oh, my god, look at that." Joan pointed to a young couple in full-body black leotards, with furry, leopard-printed fabric draped, Tarzan-like, across their bodies. He carried a bamboo spear in his gloved hand. She cuddled a tiger cub, one Lindsey hoped was a toy. On New Year's Eve in New York City, that was not a foregone conclusion.

"Who knew all this went on in Central Park?"

Lindsey laughed. "The race and fireworks have been around since the late '70s. Somewhere along the line, some nut manufacturer became the sponsor and decided it should be called the Emerald Nuts Midnight Run."

"Cause the guys' nuts turn green from this cold?"

Lindsey groaned. "Jokes aside, it's still the best New Year's party in town."

Weaving their way through the throng of masqueraders, racers, and spectators, they found a spot with an unobstructed view of the fireworks. Once they were

146

settled, with fleeces draped across their shoulders and tucked around their legs, Lindsey pulled out a thermos of hot coffee and poured a mugful for each of them, mostly to warm their hands.

Lindsey watched the racers lining up on the transverse as well as the ever-thickening swarm of holiday revelers. Joan was agog at the array of costumes, delighted by the diversity of imaginative creations but curious about how the barely clad protected themselves from the frigid night air.

Shortly before midnight, popping corks punctuated the buzz of voices. As the crowd began the countdown—20 ... 19 ... 18 ... 17—Lindsey poured her coffee into the snow and pulled out the champagne. "We'll toast the New Year when the gun goes off."

While Lindsey popped the cork, Joan returned the mugs to the bag and drew out two tall plastic flutes. They stood up, arm in arm, glasses at the ready.

Joan pressed Lindsey's arm against her ribcage—4 ... 3 ... 2 ... 1. The race gun going off triggered the start of the fireworks. Lindsey stood rapt as a continuous stream of flaming orange daggers shot up into the sky, exploding into overlapping clouds of white crystals. When she remembered the champagne, she turned to clink her glass with Joan's. Tears, glistening white in the reflected light, were running down her friend's face.

"Joan, my darling, what is it?"

"It's just ... I'm so happy. Being here with you. I love you."

Her eyes locked on Joan's. "I love you, too." Lindsey's heart seemed to fill her entire chest.

As they watched the fireworks, their gloved hands intertwined, the words "I love you" echoed in Lindsey's brain. It was the second time in a week she'd said those words to a woman—and meant them. A week ago, it was with Dee. Now Joan.

She did love Dee, for her years of loyalty and support, for being all-around good company. But loving Dee had none of the intensity or sexual awareness of her love for Joan. During the week in Cabo, Lindsey felt an aching emptiness—

a hunger for Joan's voice, for the touch of her fingers —that wasn't allayed by daily phone conversations.

She turned to watch Joan, sitting forward in her chair, utterly absorbed by the spectacle overhead. Lindsey reached over and stroked her friend's back. Joan arched her spine, acknowledging Lindsey's caress, then turned, her face alight, and held up her still nearly full glass. "To our love," she whispered.

A wave of well-being swept over Lindsey. It was more than Joan. Since Christmas, her relationship with Dee had strengthened, as they talked more about the private spaces of the lives they had shared for so many years. And Claire. After a dozen years of being merely cordial, Claire had become a friend, an older woman to whom she could turn for counsel.

But that wash of contentment was laced with anxiety. She wasn't any more honest with Dee than she'd ever been. In the past, she'd hidden her feelings about Ted. Now she was keeping Joan a secret. And Zoey. The comfortable rapport they'd had in Cabo seemed far more fragile than Lindsey had allowed herself to think. If Zoey resented Joan's claim on Lindsey's time, how would she feel about her claim on Lindsey's affections?

~ ~ ~ ~

Joan was asleep when Lindsey woke the next morning and she slid quietly out of bed so as not to wake her. It was only when she got to the kitchen and saw the clock—9:10— that she remembered Joan was supposed to be at Tammy's house in Hoboken in less than an hour. Lindsey sped back and woke her with a kiss.

"Wake up, my love. It's after nine."

"You're kidding!" Joan flung off the covers and leapt up. She was dressed in less than ten minutes. As she dashed out the door, she pressed her palm against Lindsey's cheek. "Thanks for a wonderful evening. I love you so much."

Lindsey watched Joan, resisting the urge to run after her, to give her one last hug. When Joan looked back as she stepped into the elevator, Lindsey blew her a kiss.

It all seemed so natural, the evolution of her love for this remarkable woman who'd opened the door to a kind of friendship and intimacy she'd never known.

Chapter 22

Claire had invited Zoey to a Sunday afternoon piano recital in town, with dinner afterward on the weekend after New Year's. When Joan found out, she invited Lindsey to Sunday dinner at Tammy's, assuring Lindsey that she'd be home well before Zoey.

Lindsey recognized Tammy the moment they came out of the Hoboken ferry terminal. The tall brunette, with a chubby baby propped on her left hip, was a slimmer copy of her mother—the same square, athletic build and wide smile.

Joan held a black-and-white panda out to the baby and cooed. "How's my Becca?"

When the baby grabbed the plush animal, Tammy gave Joan a cuddle, a friendly arm-around-the-shoulder, peck-on-the-cheek. "How you doing, Mom?"

"I'd be a whole lot better if you let me hold that sweet thing."

Tammy handed Becca over, then turned to Lindsey. "Glad you could join us for dinner. It's surprisingly warm for January. Are you okay with walking?"

"A splendid idea," Lindsey said. It would give her a chance to scope out Hoboken. She'd read that it was a trendy place for young couples who wanted space for a family and an easy commute—ten minutes by ferry—to the City, but she'd never been there. And she suspected Joan would enjoy a chance to chat with Tammy without her son-in-law.

During the ferry ride, Joan had disparaged Les. "He's responsible and hardworking, and he loves Tammy. But that man has the personality of a toad," Joan had sniggered. "His only two topics of conversation are his job and sports. Any other subject and the man begins to fidget."

Lindsey had clucked in a gesture of sympathy, but said nothing.

Tammy reclaimed Becca and tucked her into the stroller and they headed up 14th Street. "So, what's new with you?" Joan asked, looking at her daughter.

"I'm fine, but Kelly's driving me around the bend, now that she's out of work again."

"Oh, no." Joan sounded weary. "What happened this time?"

"Last Thursday was her night to close. But Justin showed up early and she left with him."

"The Kelly we all know and love," Joan muttered.

"She had one of the girls cover for her. But Friday morning, there was $400 missing."

Joan's face went ashen. "Did Kelly take it?"

The social worker in Lindsey came alert. Did Joan believe her daughter could be a thief? She held her breath, waiting for Tammy's response.

"It seems not. But it's the third time she's left early, so he fired her, and won't sign her claim for unemployment. On top of that, she and Justin aren't getting along. She's afraid he's going to throw her out."

Lindsey breathed again. The girl might be a mess, but at least she wasn't a thief.

"Holy mother of god. I want to shake her sometimes." Joan grabbed the air in front of her and shook her fists.

Tammy gave a sarcastic laugh. "She's decided it would be a privilege for her to live with us. I don't quite see it that way. And Les would have a conniption."

"Why doesn't she go home to her dad?"

"Short Hills is too far from all her goth-y friends." Tammy eased her left arm through her mother's without stopping the stroller. "Sorry. I know this is tough on you."

As they turned a corner, Tammy said, "On a cheerier note, Les got a promotion last week—and a nice fat raise. We can fix up the back deck now. He actually wants to do it himself! A shocker, since he's never had a hammer in his hand that I know of."

"You'd be better off hiring someone who knew what they were doing," Joan said. "Get quality workmanship. And more likely to get it done in reasonable time."

Tammy brought the stroller to an abrupt halt. "Mom!"

Joan grimaced. "Sorry, sweetie. Didn't mean to interfere."

Tammy resumed her chatty tone as they walked. "I'm hoping it will keep him from going into work on the weekends."

"I'm in awe of your patience," Joan said. "I couldn't have survived those early years if Brad had worked as many long hours as Les."

"That's how his firm does things." Tammy gave her mother a curt glance. "And it does seem he's doing something right."

Lindsey remained silent throughout this exchange. Joan's inclination to intrude seemed to apply to her children as well as her peers. But Tammy handled it with good grace. She stood her ground, without the sharp edge of hostility so often seen in firstborn children of strong-willed, opinionated mothers.

~ ~ ~ ~

Les stuck his head out of his study as they came into the house. A nice-looking man, in a bland sort of way: regular features that, once she turned away, Lindsey couldn't quite remember.

"Nice to see you, Joan" he said. "This Sunday routine means a lot to Tammy and Becca."

Lindsey nearly laughed out loud. He clearly meant to be gracious, but it came out almost insulting. Perhaps he didn't like Joan any more than she liked him. Tammy, busy with the baby's coat, didn't seem to have registered the comment.

"It means a lot to me too." Joan replied. She took his arm to halt his retreat into his study. "I want you to meet my friend Lindsey."

Les managed a stiff smile. "Glad you could join us. I look forward to talking during dinner." With that, he was gone.

They followed Tammy to a large living area with a corridor kitchen. The late afternoon sun streamed in through a sliding door that opened onto a wooden deck in obvious need of new planks and railings.

As Tammy set Rebecca in her playpen, Joan asked, "What's for dinner?"

"Spareribs. On the grill."

"The molasses recipe I brought you last week?"

"No, one from my mothers' group."

"I really thought you'd use the one I sent you."

Tammy ignored Joan's whiney tone. "I tried it this week and it's delish ... I wanted to do something different tonight." She pointed to a brown bag on the kitchen table. "Can I get you fine ladies to clean the corn?"

"I'll clean it out on the deck. So we don't end up with corn silk all over everything. If you don't *mind*..." She swooped up the bag, yanked open the door and clomped out onto the deck, leaving a baffled Lindsey staring at her back.

Joan turned to say something, apparently assuming Lindsey had followed her. When she realized she was alone, she clamped her mouth shut, marched to the picnic table, and sat with her back to the glass door.

Lindsey watched with fascination as Joan ripped open the bag, abruptly enough that several ears of corn flew off the table onto the deck.

Tammy chuckled. "Oops. I guess I should have used her recipe."

Confused by this unfamiliar side of her friend, Lindsey said, "Should I do something?"

Tammy shook her head. "She has hissy fits from time to time, but she gets over them pretty quick. She'll be fine by the time she's done the corn. Can I get you to do salad stuff?"

"Be happy to."

Tammy pulled vegetables from the fridge and set them on the table with a paring knife and cutting board, then began to cut the rack of ribs into individual portions.

Lindsey started with the parsley. "Tammy, it's nice to finally meet you."

"I'm glad too. Mom says you've been a lifesaver for her. I'm not sure she could have managed alone in New York without you."

"I find that hard to believe. Your mom seems pretty self-sufficient."

Tammy snickered. "Don't be fooled by the fact that she's bossy and has lots of opinions. She likes to be needed and can get quite pissy"—Tammy pointed to the deck with a sparerib—"if she doesn't feel properly appreciated."

"Well, I certainly do appreciate her."

They chatted, mostly about Hoboken, until Joan came back in.

"Here's your corn, dolly. Clean as a whistle." Joan took a seat next to Lindsey and started chopping celery. The petulance that had driven her out to the deck had vanished.

"Thanks, Mom. Have you talked to Dad this week?"

"No, why?"

"He's called nearly every day, wanting advice. One time from a flower shop, ready to send you flowers. Another time, he wanted to show up at your place with champagne."

"And you said?"

"That I don't know what he should do."

"Well, keep telling him that."

"He does miss you."

"He misses his housekeeper."

Lindsey went on alert again. When Joan had first used that term, Lindsey imagined a marriage without much depth, but one to which Joan had been resigned. Now, in Tammy's kitchen, it struck Lindsey as a demeaning portrayal of Tammy's father. Whatever Ted's failings as a husband, she would never be so critical in a discussion with Zoey.

Tammy turned to face the two women. "You don't give him enough credit. There's nothing he wants more than to please you. To have you be happy."

"Perhaps, but by his definition. He never cared enough to ask what I wanted." Joan picked up the vase of pink carnations. "Tam, your father always gave me carnations. He never asked if I liked them. In fact, I hate them."

Lindsey coughed to mask her gasp of surprise. Joan, it seemed, had made the same mistake she herself had ... of waiting to be asked.

"Did you ever tell him you didn't like them?"

"I didn't want to hurt his feelings."

Tammy made no effort to hide her disbelief. "That's the goofiest thing I ever heard! How would he know if you didn't tell him? And the school. Having you gone one night a week and one weekend a month for ten years wasn't his idea of happiness."

"Well, that's a whole other issue." Joan brought the vase down on the table, hard enough that Lindsey expected it to crack. "I got woefully tired of everyone at that school taking it for granted that I'd fill in for any change of plans."

Lindsey was puzzled. What did school planning have to do with Brad's desire for his wife to be happy?

"Mom, face it. You love helping people. You never said no. Not to Dad, not to the folks at the school, not to your friends."

"I'm saying 'no' now, Tam. I want a life where nobody expects anything of me. Now tell me what you want me to do with this corn."

Lindsey stifled a laugh at the contradiction. A request to be helpful, even as she insisted she didn't want anyone to expect anything of her.

When Les emerged to grill the ribs, he was personable enough as long as the conversation focused on his job and his daughter. Once the discussion turned to other topics, he squirmed visibly, exactly as Joan had predicted.

When dessert was over, Joan put an end to Les's misery. "Well, my darlings, Lindsey and I have to work tomorrow. Can we help with dishes before we go?"

Tammy refused her offer but insisted on driving them to the ferry. After garnering seats for a 15-minute wait, they exchanged hugs and Tammy left.

Lindsey didn't mind the wait. The evening had raised so many questions. "Your conversation with Tammy was intriguing," Lindsey said, trying to sound casual.

"Which part?"

"Well, for starters, the bit about everybody taking advantage of your good nature. You've mentioned it two or three times."

With her hands clasped in her lap, Joan stared across the waiting room. Lindsey wondered if she'd overstepped some undefined boundary. She was about to apologize when Joan let out a heavy sigh.

"I've had a good life. Good friends. Good times. Lots of laughs. And Brad. A good provider, endlessly patient and a fine father."

Lindsey waited for the "but."

Joan still faced forward. "Brad's like Les. More personality, of course, but with few interests outside of work, sports, and his kids. And sex—lots of it on a regular basis. As long as I had his meals on the table and kept his bed warm, he had no complaints. But I don't think it ever occurred to him to ask whether I was satisfied ... socially, personally, sexually. He assumed that if he was happy, I would be too."

Lindsey waited.

"I always wanted to travel. We could afford it, and Brad always said he'd take me anywhere I wanted. But if I suggested something besides a Florida resort, he found a reason not to go. It was too far. He was too busy. It didn't sound very interesting. He couldn't speak the language." As she talked, she flexed her fingers repeatedly.

"It was the same with food. He said he'd be happy with whatever I served. But if I suggested something out of the ordinary—venison, for example—he countered with meatloaf or steak. For birthdays or anniversaries, I got to choose the restaurant—unless I chose Indian or Argentinean. Then he'd have an alternative with a conventional menu.

When Joan finally turned toward Lindsey, the set of her jaw was tight, not angry so much as determined. "Tammy's wrong, you know. He doesn't miss me. He misses the laundrywoman who kept his clothes clean and the mistress who kept his bed warm. But he doesn't have a clue about the person who lives in this skin of mine."

The longer Joan talked, the more Lindsey recognized a kindred soul, but not in the way Joan had first imagined. Both women had felt trapped by marriages in which they were reluctant to speak up, and often felt guilty when they did.

What made them different was that Joan had recognized the trap she was in and done something about it. Despite her social work and therapy training, Lindsey hadn't acknowledged there was a problem until Ted walked out. "Why *did* you leave?"

Joan shoved her hands into the pockets of her trench coat. "I don't know anymore. I've lived my whole life within thirty miles of Short Hills. Most of my friends—including Brad—have known me since high school. I hoped the anonymity of the City would help me find out who I am when I'm not playing the role I got cast in forty years ago."

"What role was that?"

"The kid who put a positive spin on anything, who made you laugh no matter how grim it got. The fun-loving girl who wanted everyone to have a good time. I filled that role in school, on the hockey team, in my marriage, with my daughters, with my friends." She turned to Lindsey. "And then one day, I didn't want to play it anymore."

"And now?"

"It's fun meeting new people and trying on different personas. But"—a tear trickled down Joan's cheek—"I miss being part of people's lives. I don't like being on my own as much as I thought I would."

"You are certainly a part of my life. And Tammy's, surely."

"Yours, yes. Tammy, not so much. We—"

The announcement of the 7:20 boarding interrupted her.

As they headed for the gate, Joan said, "About Tammy. We get along, but it's clear she doesn't want my advice or help. And Kelly, you know how much she wants from me."

In the taxi up Eighth Avenue, Lindsey pondered the seeming contradictions in Joan's life. Frustrated when people took her for granted, but unhappy when no one needed her.

And Brad. Joan had repeatedly claimed he took her for granted. But her weekend school would have left him parenting two teenage girls—one a problem child—on his own. And now, he was paying for Joan to live in a fancy apartment while he lived alone and dined on takeout. That didn't sound like a man who was taking advantage. Or at least not intentionally. Had he responded based on the signals—or lack of signals—he got from Joan?

Here was yet another parallel to her own marriage. Had Ted ignored Lindsey's loneliness for the simple reason that she'd never told him about it? Stepping out of the taxi in front of her apartment building, it struck her again that not telling him how she felt might well have been a factor in the failure of her marriage.

Chapter 23

A few days later, it all went to hell.

Since Zoey's Wednesday night sleepovers with Wendy had continued, Lindsey was unconcerned when she arrived home a bit after 10:30.

Until she walked in the front door.

"Mom, is that you?" Zoey stepped out of the kitchen into the hall. "Where were you?"

"What are you doing home? You're supposed to be at Wendy's."

"Where have you been? I've been calling you for hours."

"Has something happened?" Her confusion notched up when she reached the kitchen and saw Ted at the table with a bottle of Sam Adams.

He did not look pleased. "How nice of you to come home to see your daughter."

"What are you doing here?"

He set his bottle down hard enough to rattle the table. "Somebody needed to be here. When you weren't home by nine-thirty, Zoey called and I came over."

Lindsey looked from Zoey to Ted and back again, trying to fathom why Ted was sitting in her kitchen. Making a conscious effort not to appear anxious, she planted a kiss on her daughter's head and walked to the cupboard for a mug. "I had dinner with Joan."

Zoey sat down at the table. "Don't you ever get tired of her?"

Lindsey spun around, "No, Zoey, I don't. Just like you never get tired of Wendy." Tempering her tone, she said, "But why aren't you there?"

"I decided to have dinner with Dad. I didn't know how late we'd be, so I told Mrs. Colbert I'd have him bring me home."

Lindsey tried to mask her surprise by concentrating on making tea—filling the mug with water and fiddling with the timer on the microwave. When she thought she could manage a coherent sentence, she said, "I thought you were skiing in Maine?"

"The snow was crappy, so I came home."

She turned to Zoey. "You should have let me know you changed your plans."

"Well, excuse me, but I did! I left a text message at six o'clock. I called a bit later, then texted you three times after that."

Lindsey fought to catch her breath. She'd set her phone on vibrate during an afternoon meeting and neglected to switch it back when she left the office. After dinner, she couldn't resist the opportunity to spend the night with Joan. But she'd had trouble falling asleep, and after tossing for an hour, got dressed and took a taxi home. She'd never even looked at her phone.

Weak with shock at how close she'd come to leaving Zoey alone overnight, Lindsey tried to deflect the hostility aimed at her. "Why didn't you stay at your dad's?"

"No p.j.s ... no toothbrush."

Ted grinned at his daughter. "We can fix that easily enough, can't we?"

Zoey didn't reply, but stood up and carried her bowl to the dishwasher. "I'm going to bed." She gave Ted a loud smooch and turned toward the door. "Night, Dad."

Lindsey tapped her lightly on the shoulder. "Don't I get a kiss goodnight?"

Zoey's lips barely touched Lindsey's skin. Her cheek burned, as if she'd been slapped.

When Zoey was out of earshot, Ted banged his bottle on the table once more. "I will not tolerate your leaving my child alone like that."

"I *didn't* leave her home alone! When I talked to her after school, she was at Wendy's. I had no idea she was having dinner with you."

"You'd have known if you'd checked your voicemail."

"That's true. But you're as much to blame as I am. You should never have left her off without checking to see that someone was home."

"She said you didn't have class, so I assumed you'd be here."

She almost laughed, his statement was so preposterous. Instead, she crossed her arms, taking an aggressive stance. "You're no longer entitled to make assumptions about what I'm doing. We need to set a schedule, so this doesn't happen again."

"I can't think about schedules now." He stood up and rammed the chair into place against the table.

"Fine. We'll do it tomorrow. But as long as she's living here, you've got to let me know if you make plans that include her."

~ ~ ~ ~

After Ted left, Lindsey went back to her tea. While she waited for it to steep, she gazed out at the snow, drifting down in huge flakes that left the crystalline structure of each flake etched on the windowpane for a brief moment after it landed. They were so beautiful. She wanted to catch one and give it to Joan.

"Cool snowflakes." A bolt of electricity shot through Lindsey at the unexpected voice. Zoey, in her pajamas, stood behind her left shoulder, watching the fleeting images on the window.

"Nice, aren't they?" Lindsey voice came out crackle-y.

"Yeah." To Lindsey's surprise, Zoey put her arms around her mother's waist and laid her head on Lindsey's shoulder. "Mom, I was so scared something happened to you."

Lindsey swiveled around and tucked one hand under Zoey's chin. "I'm so sorry. My phone was on vibrate and I left my purse where I couldn't hear it. Will you forgive me?"

Zoey's eyelashes glistened. "I'm just glad you're okay."

They lingered in a sort-of embrace until Lindsey tickled her daughter's chin. "So, why didn't you stay at your dad's? It wouldn't be the first time you slept in his shirt or shared a toothbrush."

"I can't, Mom. I just can't."

"Why?"

"It would make it real ... that he's not ever coming home again."

"Zoey, listen to me." Lindsey held her daughter at arm's length where she could meet Zoey's eyes. "He's not coming home. Your dad and I *are* getting a divorce."

Zoey wriggled out of Lindsey's grasp. "I won't stay in that apartment. Ever."

"It's your choice. But I don't want you to get your hopes up."

"I'm going to bed." She turned and trudged out.

Lindsey carried her tea to her room. She smiled as she passed Zoey's room, where her daughter was in bed playing a game on her iPad. Her lights were out, but her door was open, for the first time since late September.

~ ~ ~ ~

When Ted called the next afternoon, they settled on Tuesdays and Thursdays for him on a regular basis and Fridays twice a month, as well as a protocol for communicating the inevitable times when the schedule just wouldn't work with their job responsibilities. Toward the end of their conversation, she wondered why he hadn't yet sent the separation agreement to Angela, but she'd won this skirmish and didn't want to annoy him any further.

Lindsey was pleased with the schedule. If Zoey stayed at Wendy's on Wednesdays, she'd have three evenings a week and an occasional Friday to see Joan without provoking Zoey's ire. It would be even better if Zoey would stay with Ted, but for the moment, that wasn't an option.

~ ~ ~ ~

Tension escalated further a few days later. Having extended a weekend invitation to Joan for mid-January, Lindsey was reluctant to retract it. The forecast was perfect for cross-country skiing. Zoey would be at the stables all weekend. It had been a month since Joan's last visit. What harm could there be?

Lindsey knew she'd goofed when Zoey sneered at the mention of Joan's name. "I don't want her to come. She's creepy."

Lindsey read "creepy" as typical teenage exaggeration, but the underlying message was clear. She had to be more conscious about balancing Zoey's needs with her own desire to be with Joan.

"Sorry, pumpkin. I should have checked with you before I invited her. But it would be rude to un-invite her. I promise—just you and me next weekend. Okay?"

"Whatever." Zoey stomped off. A few paces on, she spun around. "And stop calling me pumpkin. I hate that name."

Chapter 24

"Caveat emptor." Joan shook her head. "I've never been on cross-country skis."

Lindsey laughed. "With your athletic ability, I suspect you'll get the hang of it pretty quick."

They rooted around in the garage until they found boots that fit Joan and then did some practice glides in the flat driveway. On the third driveway run, Lindsey applauded. "By Jove, I think you've got it. We won't go far. It gets dark early these days."

They set out on the trail along the Flint River, under the thick cover of evergreens, where the slope was minimal. The powdery snow, unblemished except for the occasional deer track, made for easy gliding; the only sound was the rhythmic squeak of the metal fittings where their boots joined their skis.

When they reached the sandy open area in the bend of the river, they spied a buck with an eight-point rack, foraging along the water's edge. As they stood in silence, shoulders touching, Lindsey's throat tightened. The last time she'd seen such a regal animal was a year earlier, she was with Ted, watching the buck from almost the same spot where she and Joan now stood, Ted had slipped his arm around her waist, pulled her close and nuzzled her ear. Without thinking, she put her hand over the spot where his lips had touched. Realizing what she'd done, she reached out and linked her arm with Joan's.

When the buck wandered back into the trees, they brushed a layer of white off a log and sat down to watch the shallow stream slithering under its icy crust. Lindsey knew they had to talk about Zoey. She'd been pleasant enough on the drive Friday evening. But who knew how she'd be at dinner?

Lindsey had to assure Joan that Zoey's crankiness was jealousy, not dislike. But it would be a painful discussion, no matter how she couched it. She decided to start with a topic that would bring them together before broaching a difficult subject. "Will you teach me to meditate?"

"Sure. You said you've tried it before."

Lindsey nodded. "Yeah, while we were living in Australia. But not since we've been back in New York. Seems I can't go more than a couple of seconds without some idle thought popping in."

"That's not unusual for beginners. What techniques did you try?"

Lindsey tried to retrieve images from her meditation group a decade ago. "Concentrating on my breathing didn't work at all. I also tried relaxing my muscles, starting in my feet and moving up my body to my head. I liked what it did physically, but it sure didn't stop my mind."

Joan chuckled. "Lindsey, if it had a positive effect on your body, you were doing something right. The point is to maintain calm, to stay centered on what's important. You don't have to empty your mind to do it. You can meditate on a flower or a sunset. Anything that helps you let go of trivial irritations."

"Does it work for you?"

"Absolutely. If I don't meditate at least once a day, I find myself getting angry at really stupid stuff. It's what keeps me sane when I have to deal with Kelly."

Lindsey flashed back to Kelly's hostility the night they'd met. Joan seemed so unflappable. Her one-liner about a "Thursday child" seemed like a moniker for an idiosyncratic kid, not a delinquent. "You don't talk about her much."

"Who wants to hear that my daughter can't hold a job? That her boyfriend is an ex-con. That she's into crack. Every time the phone rings, I wonder if she's died of an overdose."

Lindsey had heard dozens of similar stories over the years. None had ever moved her as this did now. Some of the difference, of course, was an intimacy she didn't have with patients. But what unsettled her most was the realization that Joan had kept her own pain bottled up while she put so much effort into supporting Lindsey.

She pulled Joan into a hug. "Oh, Joan, I had no idea."

Lindsey held Joan close, much as Joan had held her the night after she'd slapped Zoey. Lindsey ached for her friend.

Joan tried, not successfully, to blink back tears. When they abated, Joan wiped her eyes with the back of her gloved hand. "Don't want icicles hanging off my cheeks."

"Would you like to go back?"

Joan shook her head. "The exercise will do me good."

They continued along the stream to a small waterfall where an ice dam, frozen into dramatic whorls and jagged spikes, blocked the visible flow of water. Lindsey thought of Kelly as they glided by. A child whose emotions were blocked off chose instead to act in visually dramatic and potentially dangerous ways. What would happen when the ice dam in Kelly's heart or mind finally melted?

She turned to Joan. "Tell me more about her?"

As they skied, Joan drew a more nuanced portrait. "Kelly was so cute as a kid. She had this wonderful way of sidling up to me, crawling into my lap and tucking her curly head into the crook of my neck."

Kelly had been a model student through seventh grade. Popular. Good at sports. But in eighth grade—Zoey's age— everything changed. Disruptive classroom behavior. Truancy. Falling grades. The next few years saw an unending round of parent-teacher meetings.

"I don't know how many times she got suspended for smoking. And we suspected she was using drugs, but never caught her at it." Joan's face was a picture of despair. "Without the school, I don't know if I would have survived."

From time to time, Lindsey reached over to massage Joan's back. She'd seen so many kids, particularly in the foster care system, for whom every day was a battle of wills against a hostile environment. Poverty and parental abuse was often a factor, but many came from middle class families that seemed to provide loving homes.

"I didn't think it could get worse," Joan went on, "Then she got pregnant in her sophomore year. She threatened to get an abortion through her friends if we didn't help her." Joan searched Lindsey's eyes. "You don't really want to hear all this, do you?"

"Some advice I once got from a good friend ... sometimes it helps to talk."

"Advice that's easier to give than follow." Joan eked out a thin smile as they reached the clearing near the top of the hill.

It was snowing harder and the temperature was dropping, so Lindsey suggested turning back. They followed the trail down, single file and in silence. When the ground leveled out, Joan took up her story again. "I hoped it'd be a wakeup call for her. I should have known better."

Lindsey heard mountains of regret in Joan's voice. She wondered what Joan thought she might have done differently, but it didn't seem like the right time to ask.

"Days later, she disappeared. We called the police, but they couldn't find any trace of her. For all we knew, she was dead. When she finally called Tammy four months later, she was living with the creep who got her pregnant."

"Are the girls close?"

"As kids, but not now. After Tammy got married, it was hard to stay in touch. Between her job and a new husband, Tammy didn't get out to Short Hills very often. For a couple months, Kelly and her boyfriend showed up at Tammy's at dinnertime. And then Tammy asked for a financial contribution. Guess what. They stopped coming."

"Is she still with the same guy?"

"No. She's been through four others in the last five years, one worse than the next."

"This must be exhausting for you. How about a stiff drink when we get back?"

"Actually, I'll need a nap." Joan caressed Lindsey's face with her glove. "I'm sorry I ruined our walk with my tale of woe. I usually avoid the dark side."

"You didn't ruin our walk. In fact, I'm touched you were willing to share that burden with me." Knowing that she still had to talk about Zoey, she added, "You're not alone in having a child you don't understand."

~ ~ ~ ~

They skied in silence until the house was in sight, the point at which Lindsey could not put off the conversation about Zoey any longer. What had already been an emotionally draining day would be so much worse if Zoey erupted in fireworks for which Joan wasn't prepared.

"Joan, we need to talk about Zoey."

"Is something wrong?"

"It seems she resents our friendship. She made a comment a month or so ago. I didn't pay much attention at the time, but she's made a couple more since."

Joan's brow wrinkled. "Like what?"

Lindsey heard Joan's anxiety. "It's not about you. It's about how much time I spend with you. She feels like she's losing her mother ... on top of having lost her father."

"But she has her father back."

"Not how she wants. Not as a family."

"What's that got to do with me?"

"When they reconciled, I assumed she'd stay overnight with him from time to time ... that we'd have more time together."

"My thought exactly!"

At the edge of the driveway, Lindsey stopped and planted her poles in the snow. "Except she won't stay with him overnight."

Joan stopped in mid-stride. "Why on earth not?"

"In her mind, staying in Ted's apartment makes his leaving too final."

"Well, geez, Lindsey, it is final." Her brows drew together. "Isn't it?"

"Yes, of course. But she's still in denial. And I won't force her to do it."

"So, Wednesday is our only night together in town. I can handle that. We'll still have days here in the country."

"Well, no. Zoey doesn't want me to invite you to the country anymore."

Joan's face wrinkled with irritation. "Lindsey, she's just a kid. She doesn't get to pick your friends."

Lindsey's heart ached. For Joan. For her daughter. For herself. Whatever choice she made, somebody she loved would be unhappy.

"Joan, my darling, it's not about picking my friends. It's about having her mother be a stable factor in her life when so many things have blown up in her face." She sidestepped in her skis and put her arms around Joan's waist. "I love you so much, and I want to be with you as much as I can. But I can't let her think she's been abandoned."

Joan shook off Lindsey's arms. "You have to do what you think is best. But you're coddling that kid," she said as she lurched the last few yards to the garage. "I coddled Kelly for years, and you can see where it got me."

~ ~ ~ ~

The phone was ringing as they came into the house, but it stopped before she got to it. Ted had refused to get voicemail, viewing the country house as an escape: if they weren't there when the phone rang, they weren't meant to get the call. Just in case it was Zoey, however, she checked her cell but there was nothing. She tucked it back into her purse on the shelf in the mudroom.

While Joan napped, Lindsey showered, then settled in the window seat to read while she waited for Zoey.

The next thing she knew, someone was nuzzling her neck. She opened her eyes to see Joan squatting down next to her.

"Hey, lovey, Zoey's making a marinade for the pork chops. Want to come help or nap a while longer?"

Lindsey smiled as she rubbed the sleep out of her eyes, pleased Joan had recovered from the strenuous afternoon. Making an exception to her own rule, she checked that Zoey wasn't in sight and kissed Joan on the mouth. "I didn't realize how tired I was. What time is it?"

"6:30. You were out cold when Zoey got home."

"I've got to get up if I want to sleep tonight."

As she swung her feet to the floor, the phone rang again. She heard Zoey's cheery "Hi. This is Zoey," and then a shrill "Is she okay?"

Lindsey's pulse quickened and she dashed to the kitchen. Zoey's wan face confirmed that something was wrong. "What is it, pumpkin?"

Zoey handed her the phone, a look of terror in her eyes. "It's Dad."

She took the phone. "Ted, what happened?"

"Where have you been? I've been calling for hours."

"Cross-country skiing."

"I've been calling your cell phone. You have a bad habit of not answering it."

Lindsey remembered her purse in the mudroom. Where she couldn't hear it. No help for it now. "So, why are you calling?"

"Claire has pneumonia. She woke up with a cough and a fever this morning, and was having trouble breathing. Her doctor said to get her to the hospital and they admitted her as soon as we arrived."

"How is she?"

"They've given her antibiotics. If it's bacterial, she'll be fine, but they don't know yet. Pneumonia is always dangerous in the elderly."

"Should we come now? We could be there by ten."

"That's not necessary." He sounded tired. "But tomorrow morning would be good."

"Okay, we'll be there."

"Thanks. Give me a call when you hit the FDR and I'll meet you at Lenox Hill if I'm not already there."

Chapter 25

At dinner, Joan asked Zoey about her grandmother. "What's your earliest memory?"

Joan, by accident or design, tripped the "ON" switch. Zoey talked about visits to the Central Park Zoo and the museums.

Lindsey watched, part cynical, part fascinated. It seemed that Zoey liked Joan well enough as long as her focus—and Lindsey's—was on Zoey herself. Even so, she was glad she'd spoken to Joan that afternoon.

"When did you and your grandmother start playing the piano together?" Joan asked when Zoey paused for a bite of her pork chop.

Zoey nodded. "She started teaching me piano when I was four." She held up her hand to show how Gammy would take Zoey's index finger and press it to the key to make the sound. As she moved her hand up an imaginary keyboard, Zoey intoned the letter of each key. "C ... D ... D sharp ... E ... F ... F sharp..."

Lindsey grew weepy, not for Zoey but for the grandmother she herself never had. Her mother's parents had died in an automobile accident when Lindsey was a baby. Her only memory of her father's parents was a vague image of two elderly people sitting on a rocky beach near a big house. After her father left, they disappeared from her life.

Another poignant moment came when Zoey described going to the *Nutcracker* every Christmas. What she remembered, more than the magic of the ballet, was the annual pilgrimage to Madison Avenue for a holiday dress, invariably a dress that Lindsey saw as obscenely priced for something Zoey would outgrow in a year.

"Gammy let me choose. She wasn't sensible like Mom. If I wanted bows and ribbons and velvet and lace all on the same dress, she let me have it. I loved those dresses." Zoey glanced over at her mother. "Mom wanted to throw them out, but I wouldn't let her, even though they're all too small."

Lindsey bit her lip to keep from tearing up. She was so glad she hadn't succeeded in giving those dresses to Goodwill, but what hurt more was the memory of her own adolescent longing for someone to take her shopping, for someone who cared what she liked or wanted.

~ ~ ~ ~

After Zoey went off to finish a history assignment, Joan attacked the dishes. Lindsey sorted out leftovers and packed for an early morning departure.

"You were pretty mum during dinner," Joan observed as she stacked the dishwasher.

"You two were on a roll. It'll be hard on her when Claire dies. You started her on the road to dealing with it. Thank you, darling."

"I don't know why you think she resents me. She certainly didn't tonight."

"Darling, she doesn't resent you personally. She'd probably resent anyone who took my attention away from her."

"Lindsey, adolescent girls are beyond self-centered. You're imagining the whole thing."

Lindsey had seen self-absorbed teenagers by the dozens in her practice. But it took only a fraction of a moment to register Joan's implied criticism. From a woman whose own child was a delinquent.

She regretted her sniping thought almost instantly. Stifling her irritation, she suggested a cup of tea by the fire.

When she'd drained her second cup, Joan surveyed the living room, her eye lingering on the window seat, the fireplace, and the windows. "I have a decorator friend in Short Hills who'd love to take a crack at this place," she said. "Make it really spectacular. Would you like me to give her a call?"

Lindsey stifled another burst of irritation. "No thanks. I love this house just as it is."

By the time she was in bed, Lindsey had powered through her pique. After all, Joan hadn't criticized the house, only commented on its potential. And perhaps her comment about Zoey hadn't been meant as critical.

This wouldn't be the first time Lindsey'd taken offense when none was meant.

~ ~ ~ ~

When they reached the hospital the next morning, Claire was asleep. Ted looked exhausted. "Her fever's down but she had a restless night, so I stayed. Let's go to the cafeteria and let her sleep."

At the food line, Zoey said, "Can I go sit with Gammy?"

"Okay, but don't disturb her," Ted said.

Ted had always been fond of his mother, and Lindsey was tempted to take his hand, the way she would with any friend who was in pain. But he wasn't just any friend. How was one supposed to comfort a man who had deserted you? The silence, as they waited in the coffee line, felt awkward. "How are you doing?" she finally said, as they made their way to a corner table.

"I'm a wreck. It's ridiculous, I suppose. Since Dad died so young, you'd think I'd be prepared. But she's always seemed invincible. And in some odd way I can't explain, I've always felt she was protecting my back. I wasn't ready for this." The muscles around his jaw twitched.

Recognizing a vulnerability she'd not often seen during her marriage, Lindsey rested her hand on his. "Your mother's an amazing woman ... in ways I'm only now beginning to appreciate."

"Only now?"

"She's been wonderful to me in the last few months." Lindsey was opening a door she wasn't sure she wanted to walk through. "I expected her to take your side when you left. I don't know what she really thinks about you and me, but she's been supportive in a way she never was while you and I were together."

Ted pulled his hand away. "You think I kept you from being friends?"

Lindsey shook her head. "Not at all. I always felt like I fell short of what she expected in a daughter-in-law. So I kept her at a distance. But she reached out to me after you left. Sometimes it seemed like she understood me better than I understood myself." A lump of sadness lodged in her throat. "I love her now ... as a friend, not just a mother-in-law."

Ted sat mute, his eyes shifting from Lindsey to his coffee cup and back. He seemed at an uncharacteristic loss for words.

The longer he sat, the more awkward Lindsey felt. She searched for a topic that would ease their discomfort.

Before she could say anything, he placed his hand on Lindsey's and murmured, "I'm glad Zoey went to sit with Mother. It gives me a chance to apologize. And to say thank you."

A compliment was the last thing she'd expected. "Apologize for what?"

"I should never have shown up in Cabo. But I was afraid if I asked, you'd say no."

"Indeed I would have," Lindsey said, remembering her distress. "But if you hadn't, you two still might not be talking." She met Ted's gaze. "And that would be tragic for both of you."

"Which is why I wanted to thank you. Zoey says you've encouraged her to talk to me from the beginning."

Lindsey shrugged. "Ted, you were a good father. I didn't want her to lose that."

"She's very lucky to have you as a mother."

"You didn't seem to think so last Wednesday night."

"Zoey was hysterical. I overreacted. And it *was* partly my fault."

She agreed, but to say so would sound like a put-down. To her immense relief, Zoey appeared at their table.

"Gammy's awake."

En route to Claire's room, Zoey claimed the space in the middle, holding hands with Ted and Lindsey as they walked three abreast.

Almost as if we're a family, Lindsey thought.

~ ~ ~ ~

By Tuesday, Claire had responded to the antibiotics and was sitting up in bed when Lindsey dropped by. They chatted briefly about the biographies Lindsey had brought and then turned to the subject of Zoey.

"She seems a lot happier these days," Claire observed. "But how are you doing?"

"Me?"

"You have to learn a new style of parenting. I expect you'll have some rocky moments."

Lindsey's chest tightened. Did Claire know about the night Lindsey had come home so late? Keeping her voice even, she met Claire's gaze. "We've worked out a schedule. He lives close enough for her to go back and forth by herself, so we don't have to have much contact."

"Zoey tells me that you've gotten to be very good friends with Joan."

Lindsey's diaphragm wrenched tighter. This wasn't idle chitchat. She decided to meet the issue head on. "Absolutely. She's been a lifesaver for me since September. But Zoey obviously resents her, although they seem to get along fine when they're together."

"If I might offer a suggestion ..."

"Of course."

"Do you remember our discussion about Lauren? I think it's the same issue. She doesn't want to have to share you. She wants to know you'll be there whenever she needs you."

"And I will be there." Lindsey nodded as much to herself as to Claire. "But sometimes I think she expects me to sit alone waiting for her to spare me five minutes of her precious time."

Claire gave a sympathetic laugh. "I'm sure she does. Young girls are amazingly self-absorbed."

"Are you saying I shouldn't have Joan around when Zoey is there?" Lindsey had had exactly that thought, more than once.

Claire raised her hand, palm out and shook her head. "Of course not. Zoey'd find something to complain about if she didn't have Joan to pick on. But I'm concerned that my granddaughter, much as I love her, will start playing you and Ted off against each other if you don't work together."

Lindsey matched Claire's palm, then squeezed it lightly. "Any advice?"

"Sorry, but no. I trust you two will figure it out. But you do need to figure it out."

At that moment, a gaggle of interns arrived with Claire's physician for end-of-day rounds. Claire returned the squeeze and dropped Lindsey's hand.

Lindsey was trembling by the time she got to the hallway. She'd long since recognized the irony of asking Ted to keep Lauren away from Zoey when Joan was a constant presence. She'd rationalized it by telling herself that no one knew they were lovers. But what if Zoey complained to Ted? Referred to Lindsey as "gooey?" Would he understand the significance of her taunt? If he did, what would he do?

Chapter 26

Ted met Zoey at school Thursday afternoon, and together they escorted Claire home from the hospital. Along the way, they decided to celebrate by cooking a welcome-home dinner at Claire's on Saturday evening.

That left Lindsey free for dinner with Joan.

Ted said he'd bring Zoey home at 9:30. Accordingly, Lindsey was on the subway—a twenty-minute trip at most—by 8:45. But the gods were against her. A broken signal delayed her train, which didn't pull into the 81th Street station until 9:45.

She checked her phone the moment she reached the stairs to Central Park West. Zoey had called at exactly 9:30. Her phone had not picked up the signal.

She dialed Zoey's number, walking as fast as her high-heeled boots and the slushy street would allow.

Ted answered. "Are you planning on coming home this evening? So there will be someone there when I deliver my daughter."

"I'm outside the building. My train got stuck in a tunnel."

"So you say." There was a weighty pause. "But you weren't home when you said you would be."

"Ted, be reasonable. Subway delays happen all—"

"Then you should have taken a cab." He hung up.

"Goddamn him to hell," she swore. The man was turning mean, a word she would never have used to describe him before September. In fact, the first time she'd ever heard him use that tone was when she called him about Lauren on New Year's Day. But that call would have put him on the defensive. This time, she'd done nothing wrong.

On Sunday, he'd told her that she was a good mother. Now he sounded vindictive. Had something changed in the last four days?

~ ~ ~ ~

The apartment was empty.

Lindsey called Ted, but hung up when voicemail clicked in. She tried Zoey, and again got voicemail. "Zoey, I'm home. Call me!" She called Ted again and left a message. "Where are you? Where's Zoey?"

Waiting for one of them to call back, she paced the apartment. From the bedroom to the front hall. From the front hall to the kitchen. She called Zoey again. No answer.

She retraced her steps from the kitchen to the front hall. From the front hall to the bedroom. From the bedroom to the front hall.

Just as she was about to call again, the apartment door swung open.

Zoey glared at her mother. When Lindsey reached out to embrace her, she blocked the gesture with her arm and stomped down the hall toward her bedroom.

"Zoey, why didn't you call back? I was so worried."

At her bedroom door, Zoey turned her head just enough to catch her mother's eye. Her look was searing. "Now you know how it feels." She disappeared.

Lindsey heard the door click shut, followed by the metallic snap of the lock.

Staring at the empty hallway, Lindsey slid to the floor. She couldn't seem to get it right.

~ ~ ~ ~

Tuesday afternoon, she got a call from Kate Sutton, who taught 8th grade English and had directed Zoey's school play. In Zoey's argot, she was an "awesome" teacher.

Ms. Sutton delivered the news that Zoey had failed to turn in several assignments the previous week and then another on Monday. She noted that Zoey seemed distracted, and wondered "if there is something wrong at home?"

Lindsey wanted to believe that Sutton had called the wrong parent. Zoey had always been a good student, and the disarray in her life was not evident in the December grades she'd brought home only a week ago. Why now?

But she did know why. Zoey's favorite grandmother almost died. Zoey had lost trust in Lindsey to "be there" no matter what.

"Mrs. Chandler? Are you still there?"

"I'm sorry. You caught me off guard." Lindsey responded to Sutton's question. "Her father and I separated last fall. It upset her—a lot—but her grades last term were fine. Did she give any explanation?"

"Last week, she said she'd been throwing up all night. Yesterday she said she forgot to bring her homework home. Either seemed legit, but the two together ... it's not like her."

Lindsey slumped back in her chair. Zoey hadn't been sick to her stomach even once, let alone all night. The fact that she had lied was, in its way, even worse than not doing those assignments. Something was very wrong. How had she not noticed Zoey's mounting distress?

"Ms. Sutton, I'll check with Zoey and her father, and get back to you."

She tried to call Dee, but her hands trembled so badly she got the number wrong twice. When they finally connected, Lindsey didn't even bother with "hello."

"Dee, have you noticed anything unusual about Zoey? Since we got back from Cabo?"

"Unusual how?"

"I got a call from Brearley. It seems she's missed a couple of deadlines and then,"—Lindsey almost couldn't get the words out—"lied about it."

"You're kidding!"

"Have you noticed anything? Anything at all?"

"When she was here last Wednesday, she talked a lot about her grandmother, but otherwise seemed fine. But I wasn't paying much attention."

"Has Wendy ..."—Lindsey cringed—"noticed anything?" She was asking Dee to violate her daughter's confidence.

"Let me see what I can ferret out when Zoey's here tomorrow."

"Thanks. I don't know what I'd do without you."

She called Ted next. "Has Zoey said anything about problems at school?"

"No. Why?"

"She isn't paying attention in class ... and she's blown off a couple of assignments. Some she blamed on being sick to her stomach all night. For one, she said she forgot to bring the assignment home."

"If she was sick, I can understand, but it's not like her to forget."

"She hasn't been sick, let alone throwing up all night."

"Do you want me to talk to her tonight?"

"Well, one of us certainly has to. And you're the one having dinner with her."

"What's the hell's the matter with you, Lindsey? I'm trying to help and you sound like I'm the enemy."

Lindsey fought to rein in her anger. At Ted for creating this situation. At Zoey for her petulance. At herself, for being blind to what was happening to Zoey.

"Ted, I'm sorry. Kate's call took me by surprise. If you're willing to do it, that'd be great."

"Okay. I'll talk to her and call you after I drop her off."

~ ~ ~ ~

Zoey arrived home about eight, but pleaded homework when Lindsey tried to draw her out. Lindsey let it drop, opting to wait until she talked to Ted.

His call was unhelpful. "I didn't get much out of her except that her classes are harder this term." Ted cleared his throat. "If that was true, the old Zoey would have been talking about it at every turn, but she hasn't ... at least not to me."

"What about the missed assignments?"

"She said she was throwing up most of the night. Apparently she'd eaten too much at a birthday party at school."

"That's ridiculous. I would have heard her from the den or my bedroom."

"It's not like her to lie. Did you and Kate discuss next steps?"

"Not yet. But Zoey will be at Wendy's tomorrow. Dee's gonna see what she can find out."

"Let me know."

~ ~ ~ ~

Dee called her Thursday morning at the office. "Are you sitting down?"

"Tell me what she said."

"A couple things. She's worried that you care more about Joan than about her."

"That's ridiculous."

"I know that, but right now, she doesn't have much resilience. It scares her if you're not where she expects you to be. And she's not happy about the arrangement with Ted."

"I thought she was glad to see him."

"She is. But,"—Lindsey heard Dee hesitate—"she feels you're sharing her like a toy, when it's convenient for you and Ted. Nobody asked her what schedule she wanted."

"Ouch," Lindsey said. "But that we can fix."

"There's more."

Lindsey let her head drop onto the rim of her chair and closed her eyes. "What else?"

"She hates that Ted keeps pressuring her to stay overnight."

"I can't do anything about that."

"You could tell him to back off."

Claire had been right. Ted was back in Lindsey's life. And she didn't like it one bit.

Ironically, her next appointment was with a distraught teenager being used as a pawn in an acrimonious divorce. The child's mother needed counseling as much as or more than the child. As Lindsey wrote up her notes afterwards, the parallel to her own situation was too obvious to ignore. Zoey was crying for help and Lindsey didn't know what to do.

Her stomachache was back with a vengeance.

Before she left work, she made an appointment with Stacy Halstead, a family-practice therapist she'd met at half-a-dozen mental health seminars or conferences. Lindsey had instinctively trusted her, seeing her as someone who was direct and didn't pull her punches.

She knew pretty much how the initial session would go. Biographical information on herself, her parents, Ted and Zoey. A timeline on the separation and subsequent events, including Zoey's problems at school. Going through it took most of the hour, longer than she expected.

Stacy listened without comment until Lindsey mentioned her anxiety about alienating Zoey, much as her own mother had alienated her. "From what you've told me, your mother sounds like an unhappy woman who was very critical and blamed you for your father's leaving. That's not how you describe your relationship with Zoey. What makes you think you're like your mother, or that you'll repeat her mistakes?"

"My god, I slapped my daughter," Lindsey replied almost automatically. "That's worse than anything my mother ever did."

"Do you really believe that? Not that it's okay to slap your child, but that a one-time explosion when you were under a lot of stress is worse than..." Stacy looked down at her pad, "a mother who was emotionally detached ... who abandoned you for years on end."

"No, I suppose not. But I feel so out of control. I'm scared that one of these days, it will all be too much for me and I'll become like her without even realizing it."

"Lindsey, the very fact you're sitting here ... that it worries you as much as it does ... I think you've taken the most important step to make sure it won't happen. You'll make mistakes, of course. Maybe even lots of them. But making mistakes isn't the same as abandonment."

"A friend's mother told me Zoey already feels abandoned. And last week when I got home late because my train was stuck in a tunnel, she wouldn't talk to me for hours."

"She may think that now. And the thought can become a feeling. But if the thought is wrong, it will pass and the feeling will as well."

"Will it? This was the second time I've been late when I was with Joan. The first time I was so late Zoey got scared enough to call her dad."

"Joan?"

Lindsey's pulse skyrocketed. Not once, in her biographical rundown had she mentioned Joan. She hadn't consciously avoided bringing her up, but she was too good a social worker to think that leaving Joan out was accidental. She had to say something. But what? The best friend she ever had? Her first woman lover?

"Lindsey?"

The voice, along with a light pressure on her arm, made her look up. She read confusion in Stacy's eyes.

Stacy drew her hand back into her lap. "Are you okay?"

"Yes. But I can't believe I didn't mention Joan before now. She's a very nurturing woman who befriended me shortly after Ted left. She's been a great source of strength."

Lindsey gazed out the window, playing with the pendant around her neck and searching for a way to describe their relationship. When she looked back, Stacy had tucked her pen in the binding of her pad. "I'd like to hear more about her, but we're out of time for today."

Lindsey kept shaking her head as she made her way out to the 79th Street crosstown bus. How could she have not mentioned Joan? Her best friend. Perhaps the love of her life. And a big part of the dilemma with Zoey.

Chapter 27

A few days later, she called Dee at work. "Dee, I need your sage advice."

"Ah, flattery will get you everywhere. What's up?"

"I've been invited to speak at two back-to-back mental health conferences in Boston in April. I'm trying to decide what to do about Zoey for the ten days I'm gone. She still won't stay with Ted."

"She can stay with us."

"I had another idea ... maybe it's crazy."

"Sweetie, nothing you do is crazy. It's not in your genes."

"You might change your mind this time."

"Okay, you've got my interest piqued."

"Zoey wants Ted to stay here ... in this apartment."

"Well, not crazy, exactly, but drifting in that direction."

"Seriously, Dee."

"Do you really want him in your apartment? Where would he sleep?"

Lindsey ignored Dee's questions. "It's Zoey's home too. It's what she wants."

"You sure that's why?" Dee's voice had a noticeable edge.

"What?"

"Is this a ploy to get him back? Are you setting yourself up for a big disappointment?"

Lindsey chuckled softly, savoring the pleasure of waking up in Joan's arms. "No way."

"Pardon my skepticism, but you were a wreck when he showed up in Cabo. What ... barely six weeks ago."

Lindsey was not ready to share the truth of her relationship with Joan. "I was furious at his disrespect ... the arrogance of his intrusion. But we've had quite a bit of contact since then and I seem to be doing fine."

"Listen, kiddo, you know I love giving advice. But I'm not touching this one. Especially since you never seem to take my advice anyway."

Later that evening, Joan echoed Dee's concern that Lindsey was trying to lure Ted back. Unlike Dee, she didn't hesitate to offer an opinion. "You're nuts. Why would you want him making himself at home in your place? Checking your mail. Looking in your closets. Don't do it."

Lindsey gave a wry laugh. "He's Zoey's father. What she wants counts for a lot."

~ ~ ~ ~

Notwithstanding her assurances to Dee and Joan, it was late the following afternoon before she felt sure enough of her message to call Ted. His secretary put her through before she had a chance to change her mind.

"Hi, Lindsey. Are Zoey and I still on for tonight?"

"As far as I know. But there's something else. Do you have a minute?"

"Of course," Ted said, in the amiable way he'd responded to her calls during their marriage.

"I have a conference in Boston in April. Zoey wants you to stay with her while I'm gone."

"Sounds fine. How long will you be gone?"

He'd agreed too quickly. Had he caught the nuance? "Ten days. You're sure you don't mind staying in our"—she nearly stumbled over the ambiguous meaning of 'our'—apartment."

"No, no, no. She'll stay with me."

"She doesn't want to do that."

"Until now, I've agreed not to press her. But I can't rearrange my life because you're going on a business trip."

"But she can."

"Geez, she's thirteen."

Was Ted channeling Joan? "Yes, a thirteen-year-old who's miserable because you decided to do what you wanted, not what was right for her." She heard the antagonism in her voice and softened her tone. "You may lose her again, if you insist she stay with you."

"Are you threatening me, Lindsey?"

"As a matter of fact, I was trying to do you a favor. The last thing I want is you living in *my* apartment. But I can suck it up if it cements Zoey's relationship with you." She paused to let her point sink in. "What are you willing to do?"

"You're pandering to her, Lindsey. You do it all the time. I'll straighten it out with her tonight."

"Be my guest. But I suggest you tread carefully."

"Thanks for the advice. I'll call you tomorrow."

~ ~ ~ ~

It was only 6:45 when Lindsey heard the front door open. Zoey was home too early.

Wiping her hands on a towel, she came out of the kitchen to see Zoey in the front hall, her eyes swollen and her cheeks streaked with tears.

Lindsey knew exactly what had happened, but she played dumb. "Zoey, what's wrong?"

"I hate him!"

Lindsey wrapped an arm around Zoey's shoulder. "C'mon, I'll make you some hot chocolate."

Zoey let herself be led to the kitchen. Lindsey tugged off Zoey's parka, maneuvered her gently onto a chair, and started to fix cocoa. "What happened?"

Zoey folded her arms on the table and put her head down. Her snuffling managed to be both genuine and melodramatic.

Lindsey filled two mugs and sat where she could run her fingers through Zoey's hair. "C'mon,"—she caught herself before she said 'pumpkin'—"give the chocolate a try."

Zoey raised her head and blew on her mug to cool it. "Why can't I stay with Wendy while you're in Boston?"

"You can. But you said you wanted your dad to stay here."

Zoey snuffled again. "He said I have to stay with him ... that you agreed."

Lindsey almost slammed her fist on the table. Ted had lied, but she couldn't say that. "He must have misunderstood. We talked about his staying here, so you'd be in your own room."

Zoey looked up with baleful eyes. "He thinks I'm stupid. Can I have more chocolate?"

"Sure," she said, reaching for Zoey's cup. As she mixed the second cup of cocoa, she said, "He doesn't think you're stupid, at all. I know he doesn't."

"He said I need to ... to grow up." Zoey's face crumpled as she started to cry again.

Lindsey ached for her daughter. Ted was right, in a way, but it was the wrong thing to say. She regretted ever considering the idea of Ted's staying in the apartment. "Sometimes adults say things they don't really mean. I'm sure he didn't mean it. Now, drink this, and then I'll give you a back rub."

~ ~ ~ ~

Lindsey had an uncharacteristic case of jitters as she walked into Stacy's office for her next appointment. Her failure to mention Joan had bothered her all week. And her befuddlement at the end of the prior session would surely have set off alarm bells in any therapist's mind.

Stacey turned the subject to Joan as soon as they were settled. Lindsey did her best to give an account of their meeting, the early days of their friendship, and the blossoming of their love in the months that followed. "I think about her constantly. She's as much a part of my life as Zoey. I don't know why it took me so long to mention her." Playing for time, she stopped to blow her nose. "Or why I haven't told anyone else either."

"No one?"

Lindsey shook her head. "This is new territory. I've never been with a woman before. How do I explain it?"

"From what you've said, you have no religious or social scruples. And you've certainly read enough of the literature to know that dramatic breakups can lead to relationships like yours."

"You're right on both counts. But how do I explain it to Zoey?"

"Has Zoey met her?"

Lindsey nodded. "In the beginning, she thought Joan was cool. But now, she throws a tantrum if I invite Joan to the country. It's ridiculous, because Zoey spends most of the weekend at the stables with her horses, so the only time she'd see Joan is at meals."

"Sounds like she's jealous. And maybe angry that you've replaced her dad with Joan."

"How would she know? We're never physical when she's around." Even before she finished the sentence, Lindsey remembered Zoey's complaint about her being "gooey."

"Children often know things emotionally that they can't put words to. If she feels she's competing with Joan for your attention, it may not matter what your relationship is."

Lindsey nodded. "I know she does. So I stopped inviting Joan to the country. I rarely see her unless Zoey's with her father."

"Do you miss Joan … when you're with Zoey?"

"Yes. But Zoey has to be my first priority. I only wish Joan were more understanding. She keeps telling me I'm coddling Zoey, giving in to her too much."

"Are you?"

Lindsey shrugged. "I don't know what I should do anymore. For Zoey … for Joan … for me."

"Maybe this isn't really about Zoey. Maybe it's about you … about what *you* want."

"I don't know what I want."

Stacy tucked her pen into her pad. "I'm going to give you some homework. I want you to make two lists. One, things you're happy with or that you'd like to get back. Two, stuff you'd like to change or that you're glad to have gone from your life."

"By next week?" Lindsey could hear the note of panic in her voice.

"No. I suspect it will take you longer than that. But think about what you want at this point in your life. Not what

Zoey wants or what Joan wants, but what you want. It won't hurt Zoey to know you have a life too.

Stacy's challenge bedeviled her for the next few days, in part because her "like" list included more time with Zoey and more time with Joan. She couldn't do both. And then, one morning as she was drying her hair, she realized that Ted never took Zoey for the weekend because she wouldn't stay overnight. But surely she'd go to the Berkshires with him.

If Zoey and Ted spent an occasional weekend in North Egremont, she could stay in the City and spend more time with Joan.

~ ~ ~ ~

Ted finally called two days later. He "happened to be in the area" and "wondered" if Lindsey was free for coffee. She "wondered" how he'd spin his conversation with Zoey.

He was at a small table near the back of the coffee shop, his long legs stretched across the narrow aisle. When he saw her, he pulled out her chair. "I ordered you chai tea."

Lindsey suppressed a laugh. Classic Ted. Lindsey gave momentary thought to asking for something different, but it wasn't a point worth making. She wanted to focus on Zoey.

"So..." she said as the waitress delivered their drinks.

He leaned back, his arms crossed, his chair tilted on two legs. "You were right."

"About?"

"I've been calling her two or three times a day. She won't answer. Or call me back."

Lindsey sipped her tea and waited.

"It's like when I left in September."

Again, Lindsey said nothing.

He reached into his inner jacket pocket and brought his hand out, empty. "I don't have a saddle to pull out of the air this time."

Lindsey laughed in spite of herself. Whatever his faults, Ted had a fine sense of the comic in everyday life. "You'll need more than a saddle."

Ted brought his chair flat to the floor. "Lins, what should I do?"

"Ted, you made her feel stupid."

"Not stupid. But certainly childish."

Lindsey resisted the urge to roll her eyes. "Ted, she *is* a child. You made her feel stupid for acting like the child she is."

"What if I come over some night at dinnertime and talk to her."

This time, Lindsey did roll her eyes, to make sure he registered her disdain. "And say what, exactly? Perhaps a nice concise explanation of why she shouldn't feel like a child. I won't let you do that to her."

"She needs to know I love her."

"Your love isn't worth much if you don't respect how she feels. A telephone message with an apology might be closer to the mark."

"So ... what should I say?"

Lindsey dropped her napkin on the table and stood up. "Ted, I can't script your relationship with your daughter."

Ted's eyes were pleading. "Lindsey, please."

"You're the one who has such a way with words. Figure it out for yourself." She started toward the restaurant door, but halfway there, remembered how many times she'd felt as helpless as he seemed now. And maybe there was a positive side to this.

She retraced her steps. "Why don't you suggest going to the country some weekend. Go riding with her. Take her to Sunday brunch."

He grimaced and shook his head. "Going to the country with you and Zoey sends the message that we might actually get back together."

"Not with *me*. Just Zoey. I can find something to do in town for a weekend."

"Well ... there's Lauren to con..." He stopped, looking sheepish.

"Ted, do whatever you damn please." This time, she headed out without looking back.

Only when she was out on the sidewalk did she remember the separation agreement. It had been almost two months since they agreed on the terms, but he still hadn't sent the final version. She considered going back to ask about it, but that would put him back in control of the conversation. She needed to follow up, but she wasn't going to do it now.

Chapter 28

Meeting Zoey's needs took on a whole new complexion a few hours later, when Lindsey got a call from her dentist. According to the hygienist who'd seen Zoey that afternoon, the inner surfaces of her daughter's teeth were beginning to show the erosion associated with an eating disorder like bulimia.

Lindsey felt utterly inept as she toted up the many small incidents that she'd been too busy to notice or that had seemed insignificant at the time. How often Zoey took second helpings at meals. How often Zoey excused herself from the table during meals. How often she'd found empty packages for ice cream bars or cookies in the trash, never stopping to wonder why Zoey wasn't gaining any weight.

She wanted to sink into the ground as she recalled how easily she'd dismissed Zoey's insistence that she'd been throwing up that night in January because of too much birthday cake. "I was stupid and deserved to be sick," Zoey had said. "I tried really hard not to make any noise or wake you." It hadn't dawned on her that Zoey might be an expert at masking her vomiting.

Since the call from Brearley, she and Ted had worked out a more flexible schedule and he'd stopped pressing Zoey to stay overnight. Lindsey made a conscious effort to see or talk to Joan only when Zoey was studying or with her father. When she didn't miss any more school assignments, Lindsey had let the matter drop.

The problem had obviously not been solved. Before she left for the day, she made an appointment for Zoey with a therapist who specialized in adolescent eating disorders. She'd referred quite a few teenagers to her in the past, with good results. And then she left a message for Ted: "It seems Zoey has an eating disorder—bulimia, probably. I've found a therapist for her, but we need to talk."

Lindsey was appalled to realize how much she—a social worker trained to recognize troubled adolescents—had missed. And even more appalled at the thought that this was her fault … that it wouldn't have happened if she'd been a more supportive mother … if she'd done better at juggling Zoey and Joan … if she hadn't slapped her daughter.

Loathe to face Stacy's disapproval, she almost cancelled her Friday appointment, but knew it would only get worse if she didn't get some help for herself.

"What's the matter?" Stacy said as Lindsey followed her into her office. "You look like you don't want to be here."

"I almost didn't come."

"Why?"

"It seems I actually have neglected my child. Like my mother did, only worse. I … I … I knew you'd be so disappointed in me."

"What makes you think that?"

"I just found out that Zoey has bulimia … and I've missed it for … Omigod … five months. I wish I knew what to do."

"Zoey has two parents. Why are you taking on all the responsibility?"

"Ted didn't hit her. I did."

"Lindsey, I suspect this began well before you slapped her. You don't have a contented child one day and a bulimic one the next. You know that as well as I do. When you look back, what are the clues you think you should have noticed?"

Lindsey pulled out a list she'd started at the request of Zoey's therapist. "Elena was the first to notice … in early October." Lindsey would never forget that day, the first time Ted called after he'd left. She'd never forget the blinding flash of pain when she realized he didn't want to talk to her.

"That was quite a while before you slapped her. What else was going on?"

"Until Ted left, everything seemed fine. She was excited about having the lead in the school play and,"—Lindsey smiled at the memory of their visit to Macy's lingerie department—"she was quite chuffed because she'd just gotten her first bra."

"She's thirteen, right? I take it she was late to reach puberty."

Lindsey nodded. "I never worried much about it. With her build, she's not likely to have big breasts or hips like Wendy." The image of Wendy reminded Lindsey of the developmental gap between the two girls. "Omigod. I just connected a couple of dots."

"What?"

Lindsey edged forward in her chair. "Wendy got her first bra and period about a year ago. A month or so later, Zoey asked about getting a bra. She didn't need it, but that's what training bras are for. We didn't call it a training bra, of course, but it's only been in the few months that she's had anything to put in it."

"It sounds like you handled it just fine."

"There's another dot. Zoey's a people-person and has always had lots of friends. Since Wendy's pretty shy, Zoey almost always took the lead in their social activities. But Wendy's had a sort-of boyfriend since late last summer. If there are boys circling around Zoey, I haven't seen any signs of it. I don't think it's affected their friendship, but I have wondered."

Now, it was Stacy who leaned forward. "You know, of course, that the situation you've described is a classic trigger for bulimia. And if Zoey was already feeling unattractive and then the father she idolizes walks out ... those are some pretty important dots. And they don't have anything to do with your failings as a mother."

Lindsey shook her head. "But I should have noticed ... paid more attention to what Zoey was eating ... what she was doing in school."

"Let's suppose you had paid more attention. You might have discovered it sooner. But you couldn't have prevented it. It might have happened even if Ted hadn't left."

Lindsey slid back in her chair, unconvinced. "But I should have seen it coming."

"Lindsey, you can't control everything in everyone's life. You certainly can't control how Zoey feels. Perhaps she's upset about Ted's leaving or the fact that Wendy has a boyfriend and she doesn't ... or it could be something else entirely. You're setting yourself up for an endless round of guilt and anxiety by thinking that how Zoey feels is your responsibility."

"I hear what you're saying. It doesn't change my feeling that I've neglected her."

They talked for another few minutes before the session ended, but Stacy's assurances did little to alleviate Lindsey's feelings of failure. It was only on the crosstown bus that Stacy's words began to make sense. Zoey was playing from Lindsey's script ... keeping everything on the surface looking good, while denying that anything was wrong. Lindsey had never had bulimia, but she'd had unexplained stomachaches for years. Both mother and daughter were taking out their frustrations on their own bodies.

The best way to help her daughter, she realized, was to learn how to deal with her own conflict and discomfort, rather than ignore it.

~ ~ ~ ~

Over the next week, she read everything she could find on bulimia. She was discouraged to learn that there was little she or Ted could do directly to stop Zoey's cycle of binge eating and purging, other than therapy and a low dose of antidepressants. Monitoring Zoey's food consumption at meals was futile, as bulimics rarely indulged in binging behavior in front of others. Vital signs were empty candy wrappers or ice cream containers, but in a Manhattan high rise, Zoey would have no problem disposing of unwanted evidence in the trash chute on her way to school. And as much as they needed to be alert to Zoey's distress, an environment in which she felt she was being watched would almost certainly be counterproductive.

The literature consistently recommended that parents of a bulimic child avoid discussion of how the child "should" behave. But how was Lindsey to get Zoey to a therapist without acknowledging that Zoey's eating habits were inappropriate.

When she and Ted sat down with her, Zoey looked genuinely puzzled. She insisted that she was not bulimic, even when Lindsey explained about the dentist's call. "Mom, I'm fine. I only threw up a few times, when I ate too much sweet stuff. I'll be careful. Dad, I promise it won't happen again."

Despite Zoey's seemingly calm demeanor, Lindsey didn't believe her for a moment. She knew not to challenge her daughter's honesty. What she didn't know was how to be observant and supportive without making Zoey feel she was being constantly monitored.

Yet again, she felt powerless to help the child of her heart.

Chapter 29

News of the bulimia prompted Ted to call Zoey with an apology and an invitation to go to the Berkshires with him the last weekend in February. As soon as Lindsey heard, she and Joan made plans for something "special" over those two days.

That Friday, Dee called her at home before work. "I have a meeting in midtown this morning. Any chance you're free for lunch?"

By chance, she was. When Lindsey arrived at the restaurant, she found that Dee had reserved a spot by the window where the sport of people-watching was at its finest. From the earliest days of their friendship, they'd concocted stories about passers-by who, for whatever reason, attracted their attention. More often than not, their stories provoked gales of laughter.

As she waited, she tried to remember the last time she and Dee had lunched together during the week. They saw each other most weekends, and talked almost daily. There'd rarely been a need for lunchtime get-togethers.

After a moment's hesitation, Lindsey ordered a glass of white wine. She rarely drank at lunchtime, but something in Dee's tone told her she'd need more than iced tea.

Dee arrived exactly at noon. Heads turned as she strode through the restaurant, swathed in a green felt cape with a cowl neck and huge bling buttons.

As she approached the table and saw Lindsey's wine glass, she lifted the back of her hand to her forehead as her eyes rolled up into her head. "Lindsey, how could you start without me?"

Lindsey mugged, "Okay, enough histrionics. Let's order and then talk."

While they waited, they chatted about Dee's meeting with the same city bureaucrats Lindsey dealt with almost daily. As Dee relayed her news about cuts in city funds to hospital programs, Lindsey suspected there'd be cuts in social service agency funding as well.

At the very moment when Lindsey let her guard down, Dee tilted her head playfully. "I presume you know I had an ulterior motive for this lunch."

Lindsey halted her fork midair. "Actually, I thought you were in town for a meeting."

Dee laughed. "Actually, I was. But I wanted to see how you're doing ... being alone without Zoey this weekend?"

"I'm fine. Zoey needs time with her father. And he needs to see what it's like living with a bulimic child, worrying constantly about whether she's eating properly, looking for the signs of another binge. And if they go riding, it might prompt him to finally get her a horse."

Dee seemed to focus on her salad. "Will he sleep in your room or the guest room? What if he leaves his toothbrush on the bathroom sink? How will it feel, sharing the house with him?"

Lindsey sat back, her hand over her mouth, horrified to realize that Ted's toothbrush was still on the bathroom sink. The first few times she'd noticed it, it brought her to tears. And then, one day, she stopped seeing it. If Ted used the master bedroom, he'd for sure see it.

"Lindsey, are you okay?"

"His toothbrush—his old one—*is* on the bathroom sink. I could never bring myself to throw it away. It was too final. A bit like Zoey not wanting to sleep in Ted's apartment."

Dee patted Lindsey's hand. "Sweetie, I know how hard this is for you."

"No, I'm fine. I swear, Dee, I haven't noticed it for months."

"Don't you ever clean your bathroom?"

"Sounds ridiculous, doesn't it. But, really, I haven't noticed it."

"So, why the ghost-like response just now?"

Lindsey shrugged. "Embarrassment, I guess ... that he might think I kept it on purpose. That I still want us to get back together."

"You don't?"

Lindsey looked straight at Dee. "Not even a little bit."

"Sure?"

Lindsey pulled her hand out from under Dee's. "We've talked about this before. I'm tired of living with someone who thinks his charm is all I need."

Dee looked apologetic. "Okay. Change of subject. What are you doing for the weekend?"

"Joan and I are going up to a sweet little inn in western Connecticut. Hiking during the day. A quiet dinner with good food and good wine. I'm really looking forward to it."

"Sweet little inn. A quiet dinner. Sounds almost romantic."

Lindsey felt blood rushing to her face. It was indeed to be a romantic weekend. Her mind went completely blank.

Dee dropped her fork in her lap, obviously thunderstruck. "Good lord, I meant it as a joke! Lindsey, don't take it so—" She stopped in mid-sentence. "Lindsey? What's going on?"

Beads of moisture broke out on Lindsey's temples and in the crook of her elbows. She'd kept the secret for so long, she didn't know where to start.

Dee opened her mouth as if to say something, then shut it again. Her eyes were fixed on Lindsey's face. Finally, she said, "Are you two ... are you sleeping with her?"

"I'm not sure what to say."

"Go for something easy. Yes or no?"

Lindsey pressed her lips together in a tight line and nodded.

Dee flopped back in her chair. "Wow, I didn't see that coming. How long has this been going on? Were you sleeping together when we were in Cabo?"

Lindsey nodded again. "It seemed ... seems ... so natural."

"You *are* joking. Your face is beet red. If it's so natural, why are you having such a hard time talking about it?"

Lindsey wondered if Dee could see her squirming in her seat. "Because I didn't know how you'd react to my being in love with a woman."

Dee stared at Lindsey.

"I love her. She's woven into every part my life—in a way that Ted never was."

Dee shook her head, almost in slow motion. "I know Joan's been a good friend. And it seems a better friend than I've been. God knows I hate to admit that. But, good lord, if you thought a lesbian relationship was the right thing for you, you wouldn't be hiding it."

"I have Zoey to think of."

"I'm not talking about shouting it from the rooftops. But, look at you. You're tongue-tied trying to explain it to your oldest friend. You've kept it a secret for ... how many months now?"

It was Lindsey's turn to sit back in her chair, increasing her distance from Dee. "You obviously don't approve."

"What do you think I don't approve of?"

"My being in love with a woman."

"Lindsey, I don't care who you're in love with as long as you're happy. It's been good to watch you grow happier. If I have Joan to thank for that, I'll send her flowers. What I don't approve of is your having a secret life with someone who looks to me remarkably like a stand-in for Ted."

Lindsey's mouth fell open. "That's absurd."

"Think about it. She has many of the same characteristics as Ted. She's charming—sociable and outgoing, able to get people to talk about themselves. She likes to be in charge." Dee paused, while she drank nearly half her glass of water. "And she seems—I'm using your word—to be more than a little manipulative."

"You don't know her. She's encouraged me to open up about things I was never willing to face before. She's helped me to understand so much about myself."

"And you should be grateful to her for that." Dee drummed her fingers on the table. "Have you thought about why she's been so willing to fill all the empty spaces in your life—almost from the day you met? What's in it for her?"

Lindsey laid her napkin on the table. "Dee, I don't have to defend this." She put two twenties on the table. "This should cover my half of lunch."

Dee pushed them back toward Lindsey. "You haven't heard a word I've said, have you?"

As Lindsey got up, Dee reached for her hand.

"Sweetie, I love you … as a friend. If Joan is what you want, I'll welcome her into my home. But I can't ignore my doubts."

Lindsey stared at her hand until Dee let go, then she turned and walked out of the restaurant.

~ ~ ~ ~

The lunchtime conversation haunted Lindsey for the rest of the day. It came back with a vengeance while she brushed her teeth before bed … having to admit to Dee that she'd left Ted's toothbrush sitting in the bathroom of the country house. What she'd said to Dee was true—that she'd stopped noticing it—but she knew that at some level, she was still clinging to the idea of them as a family.

As she put her toothbrush down, the light caught the stones in her pendant and cast two small red discs on either side of a single white spot on the bathroom wall. She stared at them, fascinated by the myriad ways in which light could come alive, but they disappeared the moment she raised her hand to touch them. She rubbed the pendant between her fingers as she stared at the now blank spot on the wall. Although this tiny piece of jewelry was the repository of some of her most treasured memories, it had been years since she thought consciously about why she always wore it.

But now, she couldn't avoid thinking about the day Ted gave it to her, the day Zoey was born. He'd had it made by their neighborhood jeweler in Sydney. A ruby for each of the July-born women he loved, and a diamond for himself, an April Fools' baby.

She'd worn that pendant for thirteen years, rarely taking it off. For many of those years, as they lay in bed at night, he'd run his fingers along the chain around her neck, and tell her that she was more valuable than any jewel he could ever hope to buy.

When had he stopped doing that?

Turning to observe herself in the mirror, she reached up and opened the clasp at the back of her neck. She held her hands there for several moments, then slowly lowered them, and dropped the chain and pendant into the top drawer of the bathroom vanity.

The diamond in her world was gone, and she could no longer pretend it would return.

~ ~ ~ ~

"Hey, Mom, where's your necklace?" Zoey asked at breakfast the next morning.

Lindsey touched her neck where the pendant had been. She should have known Zoey would notice. "I took it off."

"Why? It's our birthstones. Yours and mine."

"I know, but it's about more than you and me." She placed her palm on Zoey's cheek. "We're not a family any more, not how we were when your dad gave it to me."

Zoey's lips trembled. "Maybe he'll come back."

Lindsey realized with a start how little of her own feelings about the separation she'd shared with her daughter. Even as she'd lectured Ted about respecting Zoey's feelings, she'd imagined Zoey still in a child's cocoon, oblivious of adult concerns.

"I'd love for us to be a family again. But even if your father moved back in tomorrow, it wouldn't be like it used to be. You and your dad could go back to swapping stories over cereal before bedtime. But he and I can't re-create the past."

"Because of ... her?" Zoey had never mentioned Lauren's name.

"I can't pretend Lauren doesn't exist."

"Have you met her?"

Lindsey nodded.

"She's never around when I'm with Dad. He talks to her on the phone, but I've never met her. What's she like?"

Lindsey was approaching a minefield. Anything she said had the potential for disaster. "I've only talked to her for a few minutes. I don't know what she's like."

Zoey got up to put the plates in the dishwasher. Her back rigid, she wiped the kitchen table far more times than necessary to get it clean. Lindsey likened her action to the stiff-upper-lip posture she herself had adopted for so many years. The two rubies were very much alike.

She remembered the pendant in the bathroom drawer. Ted might be gone from her life, but he was still a diamond in Zoey's life. "Zoey."

"Yeah, what?"

"Would you like it? The pendant."

Zoey stopped and looked at Lindsey, her head thrust forward. "You mean to wear?" She raised her hand to her neck. "For me to wear?"

Lindsey nodded.

Zoey's face lit up and then fell as fast as it had brightened. "Do you think he'd mind?"

"What matters is whether you want it. If you do, I'm sure he'd be very pleased."

Zoey sat for a moment, chewing on her lower lip. Then, her eyes tearing up, she tried for a smile. "Yeah, Mom, I'd love it. And I'll never take it off. Ever."

Chapter 30

When they scheduled Wednesday dinner the next week, Joan suggested drinks at her place. "I'll have champagne on ice," she said with an air of mystery.

When Lindsey arrived, Joan was waiting at the elevator door. She greeted Lindsey with a full-tongued kiss that set Lindsey's nerve endings aflame with desire.

Joan drew her into the living room, where crackers, cheese and two champagne flutes sat on the coffee table. "Sit, my darling, while I open the champagne."

When Joan returned with the uncorked bottled, she poured two glasses and handed one to Lindsey. "To our love."

"To our love." Lindsey held Joan's gaze over the rim of her glass as she sipped.

Joan put her glass down and began to shave slices of cheese and match them up with crackers, all the while making idle conversation. When Lindsey couldn't contain her curiosity any longer, she clapped her hands. "Tell me. What are we celebrating?"

Joan waved her left hand. "I took my ring off." She caressed Lindsey's cheek. "I love you. I'm so happy we're together. I want to shout it out to the world."

Lindsey rested her face in the warmth of Joan's hand. It thrilled her to think she could make Joan so happy. But within moments, her brain registered a different script. Why now? For months, Joan had preserved so many outward symbols of marriage to a man she professed not to love. More than once, Lindsey had wondered if she was hanging on to him until she found something better.

Was Lindsey that "something better?"

And shouting it to the world. The very thought set every fiber of Lindsey's being on edge. It wasn't anyone else's business. And what would it do to Zoey?

She laid her head on the upper edge of the couch. A silvery cobweb was woven into the corner above her. A beautiful net that drew in and trapped the unwary. She shivered with the sudden sense that she too was trapped.

She rejected the thought almost at once. It wasn't Joan's fault that Lindsey's life was out of control. Still, how could she commit to anyone when she still didn't know why her marriage had failed? When she had a bulimic daughter who resented sharing her mother's attention. When her financial situation was unresolved.

She needed to find out what prompted Joan's action. "What did Brad say?"

"I haven't told him."

"Why on earth not?"

Joan shrugged but didn't answer.

"I don't get it." Lindsey reached for a piece of cheese and chewed on it while she tried to organize her thoughts. "You left him nine months ago, but never officially separated. You continued to wear his ring. You talk to him and see him regularly. Why now?"

Joan's smile was radiant. "Last weekend in Connecticut was so wonderful. I knew I wanted to be with you. Forever."

Lindsey's heart lurched. She was indeed a replacement for Brad. Except she had not been consulted about her role in this drama. She scrolled through their conversations over the weekend. Had she, in some unintended way, suggested she was planning on a future together?

Setting her glass down, she took Joan's hands and kissed her fingers, one by one. "Do you believe I love you?"

"Absolutely."

"Do you believe I can love you but not be able to make a commitment?"

The small muscles around Joan's mouth quivered. "It's Zoey, isn't it?"

"No. It's me. Six months ago, I thought I had a happy marriage. A month ago, I thought my daughter was coping just fine. I was wrong on both counts. How can I commit to anything when I don't trust my own judgment?"

"I just know we belong together."

Lindsey drew her fingers along Joan's face and neck. "My darling, right this minute, I can't imagine life without you. I can't promise forever, but I'm here now. I love you."

"And I love you." Joan stretched out her arms.

Lindsey melted into her embrace.

~ ~ ~ ~

The next morning, when they talked by phone, Joan apologized. "I was so excited when you told me about taking off the pendant. I assumed you were ready to make a commitment to us. Maybe I was moving too fast. I can wait … as long as it takes to sort things out with Zoey."

Lindsey's stomach knotted tighter. Taking off the pendant hadn't been about Joan. But saying that would be so hurtful. "Joan, my darling, if I don't know from one day to the next who I am or what I want, how can I know what I'll want in ten years?"

"I'll wait. As long as it takes for you to be comfortable."

"You can't make decisions about the rest of your life assuming I'll be a part of it. Maybe I will, but I can't promise."

There was a long silence, punctuated by Joan's audible breathing.

"Joan, talk to me."

"I'm trying to understand that you don't love me as much as I love you."

Lindsey rolled her head back and closed her eyes, as if the response she needed lay on the inside of her eyelids. But nothing came.

"Joan, it's not about how much I love you. It's that I—"

Joan sniffled and hung up.

~ ~ ~ ~

In her therapy session that afternoon, she brought up her discomfort with Joan's decision to take off her ring, along with a concern that she'd unwittingly misled her friend.

Stacy zeroed in on her feeling of being trapped. "Most people in love want to share the happiness. Why don't you want people to know?"

"It would upset Zoey terribly. To know that someone besides her shares my attention."

"She already knows that. That's why you came to see me in the first place—you were having trouble juggling the two of them."

"I can't make the kind of commitment she wants."

"Have you ever had a relationship where you cared about someone without being willing to make a commitment?"

Lindsey nodded. "Twice ... before I met Ted."

"Did your friends know about those relationships?"

"Sure. But they were men I was dating. And I didn't have a daughter to worry about."

"Aren't you 'dating' Joan?"

Her question startled Lindsey. Dating was what you did when you were trying to decide if the relationship had a future. Until Joan took off her ring, she'd never given serious consideration to what a future with Joan might look like. "Of course not. I didn't plan to fall in love with a woman. It just happened."

"Did you plan to fall in love with Ted?"

"Well, no ... but that's different. Ted was everything I thought I wanted. I don't know what I want right now."

"What about those lists you've been making. What do they tell you?"

Lindsey recalled her shock, a few days earlier, at how many items on her "don't like" list were about life with Ted. "I seem better at saying what I didn't want."

"For instance?"

"I can give you a few." Lindsey began the increasingly familiar litany of her discontents. Feeling so alone when Ted was preparing for a trial. Being left behind when he and Zoey went to breakfast. Having Ted order for her when they went out. Spending every weekend in the country. "I can't remember the last time I went to the theatre or an art opening on the weekend," she grumbled.

"How did Ted respond when you suggested doing something differently?"

Lindsey shifted uncomfortably, embarrassed to admit how seldom she'd raised any of these issues with Ted. "Until Joan came along, I never allowed myself to think about the things I didn't like in my marriage. I tried to be what Ted wanted. Or what I thought he wanted."

"How did Joan change that?"

"She asked a lot of questions and encouraged me to talk about how I felt. About Ted. About Zoey. About my family."

"So, doesn't that tell you something about what you want from Joan?"

"I love that she's curious and asks a lot of questions. But she can be bossy as hell, and she can get her nose out of joint if she doesn't feel she's properly appreciated. I don't know how to balance those two things."

"Isn't dating Joan a reasonable thing to do until you figure it out?"

"That makes it sound so superficial ... like I'm using her."

"I don't mean to trivialize your love. But the only difference I see between Joan and the two men before Ted is gender. Are you afraid people will think less of you for sleeping with a woman?"

"Well, Dee certainly seems to. She thinks I'm making a big mistake."

"In what way?"

Lindsey's memory of the conversation was little more than an agonizing sense of Dee's disapproval. She tried to recall Dee's words. "Pretty much what you said ... that it couldn't be a good relationship if I wasn't willing to talk about it."

"That's not what I said. I merely asked why you're so reluctant to talk about it."

Lindsey had a sudden sense of being caught out in a lie. She'd read Stacy's question as criticism when none was intended. And she'd lumped Stacy together with Dee. Her social work training kicked in. "I'm projecting my own anxieties onto you, aren't I?"

"I think so. But tell me what you think you're projecting."

"I wish I knew. I love Joan in a way I've never loved anyone. She's the best friend I've ever had. But in today's world, I don't want to be labeled as a lesbian. It's too politically charged."

"That's understandable, but it leaves you with a hell of a dilemma," Stacy said. "We're out of time today. But I have another assignment ... what you want from Joan. And be specific. Is it that she listens to you? Is it that you have interests in common? Is it sex? What?"

As Lindsey made her way down the concrete steps of Stacy's brownstone, she wondered whether she would "date" another woman if things with Joan didn't work out.

Instinctively, she knew the answer was "no." She remembered their last evening together. As their lovemaking came to an end, she'd fantasized about the intensely powerful physical release she'd so often felt with Ted. A sensation she'd never had with Joan.

She'd banished the thought as quickly as it had come. Everything with Joan was different from Ted. Why would sex be the same? But now, crossing 79th Street in the midday traffic, her uterus contracted from the memory of Ted making love to her. She knew, as sure as she knew the route home, that if she ever thought about dating again, she would date a man.

~ ~ ~ ~

Joan was her normal upbeat self when they talked the next day. She repeated her desire for commitment, but in a good-humored way. Lindsey reiterated her demurrals in an equally lighthearted way, pointing out the irony of their situation: despite Joan's emphasis on mindfulness and living in the moment, she seemed fixated on the future while Lindsey was mired in the present. Joan laughed, although Lindsey did think it sounded a bit forced.

A few days later, her cell phone rang in the middle of a PBS special on German Expressionists. It was Dee.

She hit the TV mute button. "Hi, Dee, how are you this fine night?"

"Very well. I thought I'd call and see what you're up to."

Lindsey snickered. "Deanna Colbert, you've never called at this hour just to be social. What's up?"

"Something Zoey said."

Lindsey broke out in goose bumps. Her normally get-to-the-point friend was certainly taking the long way around. "Out with it."

"About Joan."

"What about her?" While they'd both apologized for overreacting at lunch, neither had brought up the subject of Joan again.

"You need to be more careful around Zoey."

"What did she say?"

"Nothing to me. But as I walked by Wendy's room, I overheard them giggling, the way teenagers do when they're looking at dirty pictures or telling off-color jokes. Zoey was mimicking you on the phone with Joan. 'Cooing like lovebirds' was how she described it."

A lead weight slammed into Lindsey's chest. "Do you know how she found out?"

"I don't think she's found out anything. I think it's two teenage girls doing their spin on the goofy ways of adults. But make no mistake, Joan is in her sights. And if she makes that kind of joke to Ted or Claire, they might very well know what it implies."

"Dee, what do I do?"

"Sweetie, you need to decide what kind of life you want. If Joan's a fixture in your life, get it out in the open. Help Zoey deal with it. And if she's not..."

Dee's pause drove Lindsey nearly mad.

"You don't want Zoey running around saying her mother 'coos' to a woman friend."

She closed her eyes, as if that would avoid the avalanche of criticism coming at her from all sides. Zoey. Ted. Dee. Even Joan. Now Zoey again. She couldn't seem to get it right, no matter what she did.

The last session with Stacy had prompted her to think back to the men she'd loved, each suited to the time and place, but until Ted, she never considered the possibility of forever. She now understood that a commitment to Joan wasn't the issue. If their relationship were meant to last, time would tell.

But what did it say about the quality of her love that she wouldn't acknowledge it? The question had nagged her for days.

"Lindsey? You still there?"

"Yup. I've got to figure this out. I just don't know how. I'll call you tomorrow."

She walked to the window and looked out at the Fifth Avenue lights on the far side of Central Park. This was the second time—that she knew of—that her daughter had accused her of behaving like an idiotic schoolgirl.

She'd made a conscious effort to keep Joan out of Zoey's sight lines. She hadn't invited Joan to the country house since the weekend Claire got sick. She hadn't invited Joan to dinner since discovering the bulimia. Their nightly phone calls always came after Zoey went to study.

Zoey's giggle with Wendy had to be drawing on old memories.

Or maybe not. Ted's distractedness had shaken Zoey's confidence long before he acknowledged the affair with Lauren. Was Lindsey doing the same thing? Was she pouring so much energy into managing a secret life that she no longer noticed when Zoey needed her? Was Zoey reacting more to a sense that she was being left out than she was to the temporal demands of the relationship with Joan?

Lindsey rested her forehead on the cool glass. She couldn't see a way out. She loved a woman who wanted a commitment she couldn't make. Even worse, she loved a woman she wasn't prepared to acknowledge.

But she loved a woman she couldn't get through the day without.

"Well, shit," she said to her reflection as she downed the last of her scotch.

~ ~ ~ ~

Lindsey woke up the next day knowing what she had to do.

Joan had been there when her world splintered apart. Joan had given her the courage and confidence to start over. She owed Joan so much. But her primary responsibility was to Zoey. She couldn't ask Zoey to adjust—not only to the fact of her mother having a lover, but a woman lover. Not now. Not in a world where same-sex relationships among women carried such stigma. Not when Joan resented Zoey's demands and discounted Ted's affection for his daughter.

There was no way she'd go public. But she couldn't let things drift, couldn't let Joan continue to hope for an improbable outcome.

~ ~ ~ ~

In the elevator, Lindsey reviewed her discussion points again. She'd rehearsed them a dozen times over the weekend—once with Dee—and each time, found herself going off on tangents. But she couldn't put it off any longer. She'd called Joan that afternoon to see if she could stop by after work. Joan had agreed readily.

With her hand poised over the brass knocker on the burgundy door, a wave of sadness swept over her. No matter how she explained it, Joan would be hurt.

Before she could knock, Joan opened the door, her face alight with anticipation. "I'm dying to hear. Must be something special if it couldn't wait until Wednesday."

"I'm not sure "special" is the right word," Lindsey said, knowing her comment could be interpreted ambiguously. "Let's get comfortable and then we can talk."

"Sure. Do you want a drink ... or wine? I've got both."

Lindsey almost declined, but realized it would put a harsher frame on the discussion than she wanted. "How about a short scotch. On the rocks."

Lindsey carried her drink to the couch and patted the cushion next to her. "Come sit by me."

Joan plopped down and planted a melodramatic suction-y kiss on Lindsey's cheek. "So, lovey, what is it?"

Lindsey made sure to meet Joan's eyes. "Do you remember when you took off your ring ... I asked if you believed I loved you even if I couldn't make a commitment?"

"I do. I said I was happy to wait." Joan's eyes brightened. "Are you telling me you're ready?"

Lindsey reached for Joan's drink and set both their glasses on the table. She took Joan's hands, letting her thumbs graze softly over the smooth flesh. "Joan, my darling, I can't do what you want. Not now. Maybe not ever."

Joan's expression sobered. "We've talked about this already. I know your life is so unsettled, but as long as we're together, that's all I care about."

Lindsey continued to massage Joan's hands. "That's why this is so hard."

"This?" Joan's eyes darkened.

"That I don't want us to go public. I'm not prepared to deal with the social repercussions of a same-sex relationship—and ask Zoey to deal with them—when I'm not sure our relationship is permanent."

"Are you expecting it to end?"

Lindsey took a long swig of scotch. "No. I love you and want to be with you. But until I'm ready to make a commitment, I not prepared to tell the world we're a couple."

Joan eyes lit up again. "Well, then nothing has changed. We'll take it a day at a time."

~ ~ ~ ~

One day at a time lasted two days. That evening, after returning from her book club, Joan called, frantic with worry that Lindsey was going back to Ted.

"Where'd you get that cockamamie idea?"

"He cancelled his vacation with Lauren. He said that if he had to choose between her and his family, he'd choose his family. Why would he say that if you're not getting back together?"

Lindsey was dumbstruck. "I have no idea. Where did you hear that?"

"From Lauren. At book club."

Lindsey's stomach clenched. "You promised you wouldn't share what Lauren said in the book club."

"I'm so afraid of losing you," Joan wailed.

"Joan, I love you. I want to be with you now. Today. Tomorrow. And a lot of tomorrows to come. But I don't want to hear about Lauren."

Joan hung up without a goodbye.

Well, damn her, Lindsey thought. The woman had broken a promise ... and immersed Lindsey in the gossipy details of a world she was trying to put behind her.

But try as she might, Lindsey couldn't ignore Joan's news. Choosing his family over Lauren might be nothing more than a conflict between the demands of his daughter and his lover, a conflict she knew all about. But could he be thinking about coming back?

Did she want him to come back?

She'd managed, of late, to cordon Ted off in her mind as only Zoey's father. But as she tried to silence the echo Joan had lobbed into her brain, she knew the wounds Ted had inflicted were far from healed.

Chapter 31

Friday's drive to the country felt interminable. Lindsey imagined herself in a Bond-genre movie where the hero waited to be crushed between two walls grinding slowly together. The hero always escaped. She wasn't sure she would.

It began Wednesday, when Ted and Zoey made weekend plans to investigate a horse in Connecticut. Lindsey invited Joan to the country for the first time since January.

And then it all went to hell.

Late Friday afternoon, Zoey realized it was the last weekend before Lindsey's Boston trip. At the last minute, she decided to go to the Berkshires with her mother after all. The moment Lindsey found out, she called to ask Joan to put off her visit. Joan didn't answer, so Lindsey left a message.

By the time she got home, Joan was already there and Zoey was well into a temper tantrum. Lindsey suggested that Joan might find a different weekend more pleasant.

Joan waved away the suggestion. "I can handle her tantrums. No reason to screw up our plans just because she changed hers at the last minute."

Zoey resisted every attempt at conversation during the drive to the Berkshires, and they rode for two hours in nearly complete silence.

Hoping to appease her daughter when they arrived, Lindsey made cocoa. No sooner had she poured out three cups than Zoey grabbed one and stormed upstairs, somehow managing to make the off-square door to her room slam hard enough to shake the house.

"The little darling is having a snit-fit, isn't she? But it's good to see you stand up to her for a change," Joan tsked. "She'll get over it."

For a change. In no mood for a debate about parenting skills, she let Joan's rebuke go unchallenged. But she did wonder how such a normally nurturing woman could be so insensitive to the needs of a bulimic adolescent.

When they finished their cocoa, Lindsey went to comfort Zoey, who was curled up on her bed, sucking her thumb, something she hadn't done since she was four.

Lindsey lay down next to her and wiped Zoey's tears away with her knuckles. "What's wrong, pumpkin?" She hadn't meant to use the endearment and braced herself for Zoey's protest.

"Mom, I wanted this weekend to be just us."

"You've been planning all week to be in Connecticut with your dad."

"But you said you'd miss me."

"I surely was disappointed you wouldn't be here my last weekend. But I didn't ask you to give up your plans. I'd never do that."

"Well, I gave up looking for a horse—for *you.* Why couldn't you give up time with *her* for me?" Zoey's misery was palpable.

"I'll tell you what." Lindsey propped herself up on one elbow. "Let's you and me do something during the day tomorrow. We'll leave Joan home."

"I want her to leave."

Lindsey rolled onto her back and stared at the ceiling. "Zoey, I invited her before I knew you were coming. I can't just send her home."

"Why not?"

"You don't do things like that to your friends." She pulled herself back up on her elbow. "But I'd love to spend the day with you ... just the two of us. Check out Mass MoCA and go to the Red Lion for lunch. I'll tell her I really need time with you tomorrow. Just us. Okay?"

Zoey sniffed. "I guess."

Lindsey tucked her fingers under her daughter's chin and tickled it. "C'mon. Gimme a smile." She kissed her daughter's nose.

Zoey managed a thin, teary smile.

Lindsey sat up. Laying her hand on Zoey's shoulder, she said, "If I'm not up when you get up, come wake me. It'll be our day. I promise."

This time, Zoey's smile seemed genuine. "Okay."

When Lindsey got back to the kitchen, Joan had gone to bed. Lindsey tiptoed to the door of her room and called her name, but got no response.

No reason to ruin Joan's sleep. She'd tell her in the morning.

~ ~ ~ ~

Still drowsy, Lindsey's nose twitched. Warm bananas. Banana bread.

Her mouth watered as she scrunched under the down comforter, luxuriating in the bed warmth, reaching for that magical moment between sleep and wakefulness.

The next thing she knew, her world was tilting. She opened her eyes, expecting Zoey but instead saw Joan perched on the edge of the bed.

"Hi there," Joan set a coffee mug on the bedside table and gave Lindsey a loud smooch on her cheek. "Did you sleep well?"

"Yeah. How about you?" She drew out a full body stretch and rubbed her eyes with her fists. As she turned, she saw the clock. "Oh my god, it's 9:30." She tugged at the covers. "Hey there, kiddo, move your bod."

"I was hoping to get in there with you." She reached down and, as she had so often done, ran her finger around the edge of Lindsey's nipple. "Zoey's gone, so there's no problem."

"Gone? Where?"

"The stable. She left a few minutes ago."

Lindsey pushed Joan's hand away. "She was supposed to wake me."

"You were so tired after that awful show of hers last night, I thought you needed sleep."

Lindsey tugged harder on the blanket. "I need to get up." When Joan didn't move, she shoved her off the bed with the heel of her hand. "Let me up!"

"If I must." Joan threw up her hands, feigning dismay. "But I don't see why you're so upset. Zoey has her horses and you and I have each other."

"Joan, we need to talk." She also needed to calm down before they talked. "I'm going to take a shower. I'll be down in five minutes."

~ ~ ~ ~

Lindsey let stinging hot water pour over her, a form of self-flagellation. She'd failed to deliver on a promise and it was her own fault. She should have awakened Joan last night. What could she possibly say to absolve herself in Zoey's eyes?

She got to the kitchen and stood leaning on the doorway. She was afraid of what she might do if she got too close to Joan. "What happened with Zoey?"

Joan ambled over and patted Lindsey's cheek. "Lovey, you sound upset."

Lindsey shoved Joan to one side and walked past her into the kitchen. At the counter under the window, she turned around. "I *am* upset. Why did Zoey go to the stable?"

"What's the big deal?" Joan said. "She always goes to the stable."

Lindsey was having a hard time standing still. Was Joan being deliberately obtuse? "Not today. Tell me exactly what happened."

"She came down while I was making muffins with those old bananas." Joan shrugged as she reached for the coffee pot. "She was her normal cheery self. Not the little terror from last night. Can I pour you a cup?"

"Forget the damn coffee! I want to know why Zoey left."

"Okay, okay! While she poured juice, she asked what I was doing today. I said we had no specific plans but she was welcome to join us if she wasn't going to the stable." Joan gave Lindsey a conspiratorial smile. "I thought you'd like that."

Lindsey locked her arms across her chest, a gesture she hoped Joan would read as hostile. "What did she say?"

"That she wanted to talk to you. When she picked up two juice glasses, I stopped her. Said you didn't want to be wakened."

Lindsey's fingernails dug into the flesh of her upper arms. "I asked her to wake me when she got up."

"How was I supposed to know that?"

Lindsey stared at her. Yes, she should have awakened Joan last night. But she didn't need Joan's permission to make plans with Zoey. "It doesn't matter what you knew. It's not your place to decide whether my daughter should wake me. You're my lover, not my owner."

Joan curled her lower lip, a stereotypic penitent frown. "I'll tell her it was my fault."

"No. You won't tell her a thing. I'm putting you on the next train to New York City."

Joan clapped her hands over her mouth. "Lindsey, you can't be serious!"

"Go pack. I'll drop you at the train station in Wasaic on my way to the stable."

Chapter 32

While Zoey had been mollified by Joan's departure, Lindsey's continuing guilt prompted her to skip the Saturday morning conference session and spend the day in New York with Zoey. As she buckled herself into her seat on the plane home Friday evening, she couldn't wait to put her arms around that slim little body and hug it tight.

Sunday was a different matter. Thinking Lindsey would be in Boston, Zoey and Ted made plans to go to the opening of the Flower Show at the Brooklyn Botanical Center. After the fracas of the previous weekend, it would be unseemly for Lindsey to complain.

Then, too, their outing would leave her free to meet Joan for lunch. Since the drive to the station in near silence, they'd talked every day, but the conversations felt stilted, as if each was trying to avoid saying something that would set the other off.

Even now, a week later, the thought of Joan's interference still made her heart rate spike. Joan had inserted herself where she didn't belong once too often. Her rudeness to Ted the night of Zoey's play. Her subtle but persistent criticisms of Lindsey's mothering techniques. Her decision to "share" the news of Ted's cancelled vacation.

A male steward with the beverage service interrupted her train of thought. His shock of wavy grey hair reminded her of Mark Hildebrandt, whom she'd finally met two days earlier at the Boston conference. Mark was the director of a mental health agency in Providence. They'd exchanged half-a-dozen emails and phone calls about an innovative training program he'd developed for high school teachers dealing with gay and lesbian students. She taught occasional seminars for a similar program in New York and found his training tools to be quite effective.

She'd been surprised when she met him. Based on their phone conversations, she'd imagined him to be a bit didactic, sure of the rightness of his own point of view. Like Ted.

He could not have been more different. While he was not shy about offering his opinion, he had none of Ted's arrogance, typically prefacing his comments with a self-deprecating remark like "another way to think it about might be ..." or "our experience in Providence suggests ..."

The difference in style was even more dramatic. Where Ted was fit and always impeccably groomed, Mark was a bit rumpled, reminiscent of a stereotypical college professor. His prematurely grey hair was only slightly shorter than Lindsey's and seemed to have been last cut with a kitchen shears.

They'd chatted about conference topics several times that first day. She liked the way his mind worked—she'd always been drawn to men who were curious and wanted to understand how the pieces fit together. And, she admitted to herself as she returned to her seat after a break, his deep baritone laugh was seductive. She was delighted when he suggested drinks, where they continued in a professional vein.

That was all. Wednesday night, anyway.

Thursday night, drinks led to dinner where conversation ranged further afield. An easy entré into personal topics was their children.

Lindsey described Zoey in some detail, and noted her appreciation for the flexible custody arrangement with Ted. She did not mention the bulimia.

Mark looked rueful as she talked. When she asked about his family, he said he was divorced from a compulsive shopper who had wreaked havoc with their finances. "We have joint custody of Jason. He's eleven. My ex-wife is a good mother, so I don't worry about him when he's with her, but she seems unable to have him at home and ready when I go to pick him up. I don't know whether it's just disorganization or a conscious ruse, but I often have to come back hours later, or even the next day, to get him."

After moving onto a series of neutral topics, they ended the evening swapping travel stories. Unlike Lindsey, he'd never been overseas, but had seen much more of the U.S., mostly on camping vacations as a child and now with Jason. Like Lindsey, he loved the colors of the desert—the grey-green gum trees, the red soil, the intense, purple/blue sky.

From time to time, he touched her hand as he made a point. When they were leaving, he helped her up from the table, resting his hand on the small of her back as they walked out. She knew the signals. She felt her nipples harden and a rush of warmth in her groin, a response to the gravitational pull of an attractive and intelligent man.

It had started that way with each of the men she'd loved, including Ted. But it had never been that way with Joan. Until they made love, she'd never responded sexually to Joan's touch.

As she undressed that night, she fantasized about how his hands would feel on her legs and breasts. She wondered what his hair would look like as he climbed out of bed. The image made her giggle. It would probably look worse than hers.

Now, with her flight looping out over Long Island, in the u-shaped formation of planes threading the crowded airspace into LaGuardia, she came back to the purpose of Sunday's lunch. Their relationship was about love and mutual support but that didn't give Joan the right to make decisions about Lindsey's life. She had to set some boundaries.

~ ~ ~ ~

When Lindsey came out of the shower Sunday morning, Zoey was on the phone with her father.

A few minutes later, she appeared in the bathroom door, a twinkle in her eye. "Hey, Mom, want to come to brunch with us? You might get some cool ideas for your garden."

Lindsey made a concerted effort not to look surprised. "I don't think your dad would like that."

Zoey sidled in and, as she was wont to do, wrapped her arms around Lindsey's waist and rested her head on

Lindsey's shoulder. "I've already asked him. He thought it was a great idea."

Lindsey caught the reflection of her daughter's eyes in the mirror. "That's nice of you both. But I don't want to horn in."

"I don't want you to be alone this afternoon."

"I won't be alone, kiddo. I'm having lunch with Joan."

Zoey dropped her arms and stepped back. "Geez, can't she leave us alone for one single weekend?"

Seeing her daughter's glum face in the mirror, she couldn't refuse the invitation. And what harm could come of strolling through the gardens as a family. In recent weeks, her dealings with Ted had been amiable enough. If Ted was willing to make the effort, she could do the same.

"Zoey, it was something to do while you were out. I'd love to come to brunch. But I have to be back to catch my flight at five."

Zoey's eyes regained their twinkle. "Cool. He's coming at 10:30."

~ ~ ~ ~

Joan answered the phone almost before Lindsey heard it ring. "I can't wait to get my arms around you."

"Joan, I so want to see you, but I have to go to the Botanical Center with Zoey."

Joan's gasp was audible. "Why?"

Lindsey hesitated. Because Zoey asked. Because Ted agreed. Because she and Ted needed to work together as parents. Because Zoey resented Lindsey's attention to Joan. Because she dreaded the conversation she had to have with Joan. "After all my speeches to Ted about respecting Zoey's needs, I couldn't say no when she asked."

"But you can say no to me."

"Right now, she has to come first."

"You're right. Sorry to be snippy." Joan's tight voice contradicted her conciliatory words. The line clicked off.

Lindsey stared at the phone. Joan was understandably hurt. She toyed with sending flowers in the morning, but decided it would make it even harder to put their relationship on the right footing.

~ ~ ~ ~

Ted arrived with two long-stemmed red roses. "One for each of my girls."

Lindsey accepted the rose, but laid it on the hall table without comment. His gesture was nothing more than good manners if he planned to bring a rose to his daughter.

As they strolled toward the subway entrance, Zoey prattled on about her weekend. The patchwork vest Lindsey brought as a gift from Boston. The Saturday matinee at *Wicked* with Dee and Wendy, followed by dinner at the Hard Rock Café.

Lindsey said little, but smiled or nodded each time Zoey looked to her to affirm the details. She wondered what would be left to talk about while they ate.

He shepherded them to the cafeteria, so they didn't have to sit waiting for food to arrive. He persuaded Zoey to share his sandwich, on the pretext that he wasn't very hungry. Lindsey almost believed him. As they ate, he inquired about Lindsey's conference and her role in the panel discussion on Wednesday evening. He chatted about Claire's visit to his brother in California. And falling back on a trick he'd learned from Lindsey, he pointed to a family with three children, each a different race, and encouraged Zoey to make up stories about them.

Ted clearly wanted Zoey to enjoy the day, and the sparkle in her eyes spoke to his success. Lindsey did her part to keep conversation lighthearted and easy.

After lunch, Ted sent Zoey ahead to save a place in the line at the exhibition hall. He gave her two twenties, in case she got to the ticket window before he and Lindsey arrived.

That left Lindsey strolling alone with Ted. He stayed close to her, not close enough for their hands or arms to touch, but it was a possibility if one of them were to misstep. After a few moments of a not-uncomfortable silence, she said, "Thanks."

He laughed. "It wasn't an expensive lunch."

"I meant making such a nice day for Zoey. I loved your ruse about not being hungry."

"It wasn't entirely a ruse. And we both know that mealtimes aren't the problem. What's been hardest, these last few days,"—he paused, looking a bit sheepish—"has been resisting the urge to check her bedroom wastebasket or her schoolbag while she's taking her morning shower."

"I know that feeling. But I don't think she feels that you're spying on her. And it clearly means a lot to her that you were willing to come and stay with her."

"I have you to thank for that."

Lindsey looked at him out of the corner of her eye. Was he saying what he thought would put her at ease?

Ted stopped and turned to her. "Remember that day in the coffee shop? When you walked out on me."

Lindsey nodded. "Mmmh."

"You'd never done that before, stood your ground like that. I felt your ... not anger, but scorn ... disgust. I couldn't believe you and Zoey both turned your backs on me. And then when Zoey came in wearing your necklace ... I don't know ... the fact that I couldn't charm my way into getting what I wanted. It really shook me up."

Lindsey said nothing, curious where he was headed.

Ted resumed walking. "Don't laugh, but I actually saw a child psychologist. We talked a lot about how kids react to divorce. About trying to find the boundary between appropriate discipline and recognizing a kid who's really in distress. He said exactly what you'd said. If I wanted Zoey in my life, I had to recognize what she needed, not just what I wanted."

She saw Zoey heading their way, waving tickets. "Well, you've figured out how to do that. On behalf of me as well as Zoey ... thank you."

Even as she said the words, Lindsey knew it was a lesson she hadn't yet mastered.

Chapter 33

Lindsey sat in bed, reading through the binder of papers for Tuesday's meetings. She kept drifting off, a combination of fatigue and dry academic prose.

It was after ten when Joan called. "Hi. Sorry, but my book club ran late."

"Must have been one hell of an interesting book."

"What kept us late was Lauren. She and Ted—"

A blaze of white anger flashed behind Lindsey's eyes. "I do not want to hear this."

"—have split up! You need to—"

"Joan, why are you telling me this?"

"I thought you'd be pleased things didn't work out."

Lindsey hit the off button before she said something she'd regret. It had to be nearly six months since that night she'd asked Joan not to share information about Lauren. And Joan hadn't ... until the cancelled ski vacation three weeks ago.

The next day, Joan had apologized profusely. "I couldn't keep something so important from you. I don't want any secrets between us."

"Where's the secret?" Lindsey retorted. "You're in her book club. You chat about each other's lives. That's fine. I don't want to hear about it."

Joan scrunched her lips together, looking abashed. "I guess I didn't understand how it would affect you. It won't happen again. I promise."

But it had happened again.

She concentrated on breathing slowly, deeply. When her pulse slowed, she switched off the light and pulled the covers tight under her chin. As she drifted off, Joan's news— "Ted and Lauren have split up"—broke through to her cortex. When? And who initiated it?

Her last thought was, indeed, satisfaction that Ted's new life hadn't worked out.

~ ~ ~ ~

She called Dee at work the next day.

"Lindsey, you didn't call in the middle of the day from Boston to be social. What's up?"

"Did you know Ted and Lauren have broken up?"

She heard Dee suck in her breath. "No way! When? Where'd you hear that?"

"Lauren told Joan's book club. I don't know when. He certainly didn't look like his life had fallen apart at the Botanical Center on Sunday."

"How are you?"

"My first reaction was to be furious at Joan for being a carrier of tales."

"And your second?"

"Unspeakable glee. Hope that it made him as miserable as he made me."

"Sweetie, I get that."

Lindsey saw the next presenter come to the podium. "Dee, I have to run. I'll call you later." As annoyed as she was at Joan, a part of her wanted the full story. She was sure she'd get it from Dee sooner or later.

~ ~ ~ ~

Lindsey's number-one concern, as she let herself into her hotel room late Wednesday afternoon, was the painful knots in her back and shoulders after three full days of lectures, each one interesting but collectively numbing. The pace of socializing—breakfast, lunch, dinner, and after-dinner lectures—had worn her out. Her brain was tired. Her spirit was tired. Her feet were tired. Her bones were tired.

Mark had soaked up the last of her reserves. He liked her. She liked him. But on the plane back to Boston Sunday evening, she knew she wouldn't sleep with him. She'd always been monogamous, and she was not about to make an exception now, no matter how attractive he was.

When he invited her out for a drink the next evening, she said she was "in a relationship" but gave no details. Half an hour ago, he'd pressed her to "come have a drink," but she begged off, saying—truthfully—that she needed to review her notes before an evening session in which she was a panelist in a discussion on new case management protocols.

Dumping her briefcase on the table, she turned her fantasies to the hotel shower, with its projectile streams of high-pressure water. She anticipated a bout of acute physical pleasure.

Stepping into the shower, she knew some of the tension in her back was anxiety. Since Joan's call about Ted's breakup, she'd had a recurring image of a scab being scratched, the scab that had only recently formed over the wound Ted had inflicted.

With hot water raining down on her back, she wondered how much Joan had shared about their relationship with her book club. The thought that Joan had channeled news to Ted via Lauren flooded her with rage yet again, nearly defeating the soothing effects of the hot water.

~ ~ ~ ~

As she stepped out of the shower, she saw the blinking message light on the bathroom phone. Probably someone from the conference. Ted or Zoey would have called her cell. It could wait, she thought, as she wrapped herself in the hotel's thick white terrycloth robe.

The clock read five. She set the alarm for six, leaving time to review her notes before she got dressed. She slid under the duvet, savoring the cool sheets against her hot, tingling skin.

She woke to a rhythmic tapping on the door. When she put her eye to the peephole, she blinked twice and then blinked again. It was Joan, a cosmic smile on her face. Bewildered, Lindsey opened the door. "What are you doing here?"

"I'm so glad you're here," Joan said, wrapping her arms around Lindsey. Lindsey stiffened but Joan seemed not to notice as she drew her lips softly across Lindsey's cheek.

Lindsey twisted to break the embrace.

Joan loosened her grip, but kept her hands planted on Lindsey's shoulders. "When we talked last night, I knew you were upset." Joan raised one hand to caress Lindsey's cheek. "I shouldn't have told you about Ted when you were alone. Tell me you can forgive me."

The image of a scab being scratched rose up again. Lindsey stepped back, causing Joan's arms to drop. "I can't talk now. I have to get dressed for a meeting. But bring your suitcase in and you can make yourself at home."

She knew Joan would automatically follow her to the bedroom, expecting to chat while she got dressed. Lindsey didn't want to be hurtful, but she did need time to prepare for her meeting. She took a keycard from the desk. "There's wine in the fridge. Help yourself. If you want to go for a walk, this'll get you back in. We'll talk when I get back."

As she closed the bedroom door, she saw Joan's reflection in the mirror. At the sight of her lover's waif-like stance, she realized she'd spurned Joan for the second time in less than a week. But there was no way she could manage this conversation now, before her meeting. She pushed the door until it clicked shut.

Just before she left the bedroom, she hit the blinking message light. It was Joan. "I'm at Logan Airport. I'll be at the Marriott before you know it. I can't wait to see you."

When she came out, a suitcase lay open on the couch, but Joan was gone.

~ ~ ~ ~

Lindsey was ready to drop when the panel discussion ended at nine. She wanted to fall into bed and sleep forever. But Joan was waiting, wanting to talk.

Lindsey considered booking a separate room for Joan, but it seemed the coward's way out. Instead, she ordered a pot of tea from the lobby bar and searched out a high-backed chair in an alcove where she wouldn't be interrupted. She sat down to think.

She remembered the night at Café Loup, when Joan had picked up the pieces of her shattered ego. Lindsey was swept away by Joan's unwavering concern, her willingness to listen, her open and generous spirit. Their drift into a physical relationship offered a whole new dimension of intimacy and mutual support.

When her tea arrived, Lindsey curled into the soft velvet of the chair. When had things changed from loving and supportive to what felt more and more like a struggle for control? Certainly, the night Joan took off her wedding ring was a turning point. But the roots lay deeper.

She recalled Joan's stories about being taken for granted, about people who hadn't bothered to thank her for her efforts on their behalf. Lindsey was more convinced than ever that Joan's commitment to the Buddhist study group had been a way of compensating for an empty marriage, a way to fill the void once her daughters began to measure her maternal services in units of laundry and meals.

Joan insisted she'd thrived on the blend of learning and service, but as Lindsey interpreted the story, Joan's penchant for being a caretaker eventually bubbled to the surface. Once her comrades at the school began to take her for granted, the void loomed again.

By moving to New York, Joan had escaped being taken for granted, but at the price of having no one to take care of.

Lindsey blinked at a sudden insight: she'd been Joan's latest caretaking venture. She recalled Dee's question, over lunch, about a woman so willing to provide so much support for someone she hardly knew. Joan's friendship was an undeniable piece of serendipity. But would they have become friends if Lindsey hadn't been so needy? And hadn't she, Lindsey, been doing exactly the same thing as Brad and the school—taking Joan's devotion for granted.

As she finished off the pot of tea, she realized her anger had dissipated. No one was perfect, and she owed Joan so much. She was ready for the conversation she knew they had to have. Perhaps Joan's unexpected arrival in Boston was serendipity of a different kind. With a light conference schedule on Friday, she could manage it even if they stayed up all night on Thursday.

Halfway to the elevator, she backtracked to the front desk and booked a room down the hall from hers. She was no longer afraid to face Joan, but tonight was not the right time. She hoped Joan would understand.

~ ~ ~ ~

Fishing for her room key and desperate to pee, she heard the television. It went off the moment she stuck her keycard into the lock.

As she came in, Joan greeted her with outstretched arms. "How was your evening? I can't wait to hear."

Lindsey reached into the depths of her being for a smile to mask her fatigue. She let herself be folded into an embrace, rounding her shoulders to fit into Joan's arms.

After a moment, she pulled back enough to look into Joan's eyes. "Joan, my darling, I'm glad you came. I really am. And I'm sorry if I seemed abrupt before. I wasn't prepared for my meeting, so it panicked me a bit."

"I do understand. But you're here now." She released Lindsey and turned toward the refrigerator. "Let me pour you a glass of wine."

Lindsey put out a hand to hold her back. "Not now. Joan, as much as I want to, I can't talk tonight. My day tomorrow starts early and I'll be a wreck if I don't get some sleep. I hope you'll understand, but I got you a room down the hall."

Joan shook off Lindsey's hand and walked to the window. With each step, she seemed to shrink in her skin. "How foolish of me to assume I'd be welcome."

Lindsey knew her friend could feel slighted by the smallest thing, and this wasn't small. She wrapped her arms around Joan's waist and rested her chin lightly on Joan's shoulder, their eyes meeting in the window glass. "Of course you're welcome. I should be done by midafternoon. At the latest. And then we'll party."

She stepped back and drew Joan around. Cradling Joan's face in her hands, she said, "I really am glad you're here, but now I have to pee and go to bed."

She had a change of heart when she saw Joan's hand-embroidered white nightdress on the bed. Getting another room made sense while she sat in the bar, but now it struck her as unconscionably cruel. How could she be so hurtful to a woman who'd been so good to her?

In the bathroom, her guilt mounted. Joan's toiletries were strewn on the shelf over the sink. As she sat on the pot, she ran the tip of her finger along the shelf, drawing an invisible line between each one of Joan's things. She couldn't let Joan sleep alone in a strange hotel room. She'd get through tomorrow somehow.

When she came out, Joan and her nightgown were already gone. Lindsey got halfway to Joan's room when a wave of dizziness made her grab the chair rail on the hall wall. Fighting equal measures of guilt and fatigue, she stumbled back to her room.

The next morning, she scribbled a note to say she'd be back by three, signed it "Love, Lindsey" and slipped it under Joan's door.

She called Joan at noon and left a message. "I'm really looking forward to three o'clock."

The panel discussion, with one member who apparently loved to hear himself talk, ran half an hour over. The moment it ended, she left a message. "Ten minutes and I'll be there."

At her door, she gave a rhythmic knock and slipped her keycard in the slot. "I'm here!"

Her greeting echoed in an empty room. Lindsey looked for a note and checked her cell phone. Nothing. Her pulse sped up. Where could she be?

She checked the clock. 3:45. Still early. Joan might have lost track of time ... might be on a bus in a traffic jam ... might have lost her phone. She willed herself not to worry. She picked up a conference paper for Friday's meetings, but couldn't concentrate. Every few minutes, she went to the window, as if she might see Joan on the street fifteen floors below.

When she went to change into comfy clothes, her anxiety spiked in a new direction. Joan's toiletries were gone. She scoured the closets. Joan's suitcase was gone as well.

Joan had left.

Chapter 34

During the Friday morning break, Lindsey tried Joan again. She'd left messages every few hours the night before, with no response. Genuine concern alternated with bouts of guilt. She could not escape the fact that, if the situation had been reversed, she might very well have made the same decision Joan had.

At the third ring, Lindsey prepared to leave yet another message. She blinked in surprise when she heard "Hullo, this is Joan!" An impersonal voice. A verbal douse of cold water.

Lindsey shivered. Joan would have recognized the caller ID. Her chilly response was intentional.

"Are you okay? Where are you? I've been calling since yesterday afternoon."

"Umm ... fine ... I'm at work."

"I've been frantic with worry. And I'm so sorry—"

"I didn't mean for you to worry," Joan said. "You were so busy, I didn't think you'd notice."

Another splash of cold water. It was what you'd say if you left a large party without saying goodbye. "Joan, that—"

"Sorry, Lindsey, but I have a meeting. I'll call you later." The line went dead.

Lindsey leaned against the wall for support. Joan's words—"I didn't want you to worry" ... "I didn't think you'd notice"—were disingenuous. Joan had let Lindsey dangle in a state of anxiety for nearly twenty-four hours. But was that any crueler than what Lindsey had done?

Lindsey's mental rant was cut short as the next speaker tapped the microphone on the podium. She was glad to have something else to think about.

~ ~ ~ ~

The conference ended a little after noon, but her flight wasn't till five, leaving her with three hours to kill before she had to be at the airport. Leaving the lobby, she drew salt air deep into her lungs. She thought about taking the ferry to Quincy and then catching a ferry back to Logan Airport from there. Open water and the smell of the salt air might blow the cobwebs out.

The April air cooled as she neared the ferry terminal at the seaward end of Long Wharf and she dug a fleece hat and gloves out of her pocket. She settled on the upper deck, out of the wind, with a steaming cup of tea. The water rushing against the hull offered a soothing white noise as the ferry flew across the Inner Harbor.

Surrounded by skyscrapers, she was reminded of the long-ago days in New York when she and Ted were newly married. A favorite Saturday activity was a picnic, cruising back and forth across New York Harbor on the Staten Island ferry, gawking at the breathtaking skyline and spinning out their dreams.

She smiled as she recalled their final picnic, the weekend after they returned from Australia. With Zoey still an infant in arms, they'd had to schlep a stroller, diapers, bottles, and baby food on the subway. It all seemed too much like work. And tending to Zoey didn't leave much time for soulful conversation.

Sitting near the stern rail of the Quincy ferry, high above the frothing wake, Lindsey felt a pang of sadness at the loss of those leisurely Saturday afternoons. There'd been so many other demands on their time in the years since. Ted's law practice. Her social work obligations. The country house. And, of course, Zoey.

A gust of wind brought Lindsey's attention back to the ferry. Maybe she and Ted could take Zoey on the Staten Island ferry. If they could spend an afternoon at the Botanical Center, why couldn't they go for a ride on the ferry?

A hard jolt as the ferry lined up with the Quincy dock caused her now-cold tea to spill. She tossed her cup into a bin, grabbed her wheelie, and followed the crowd into the terminal.

On the trip back to Logan, she laughed at her own silliness. A family ferry trip was a terrible idea. To Zoey, it would only be a picnic on a boat, fun perhaps but of no significance. And what was the point of reliving those days with Ted? Perhaps he didn't remember them as she did. Perhaps he didn't remember them at all. And what would be accomplished even if he did?

It was a foolish notion. Even so, it was progress of a sort that she remembered those days without a lump blocking her throat.

~ ~ ~ ~

Though the conference and boat ride kept her concern about Joan at bay for a few hours, once she got home, she never let her cell phone out of her sight. When Joan hadn't called by Sunday night, Lindsey was a wreck. Over the last eight months, they'd talked at least daily, and sometimes more than once. Lindsey couldn't count the number of times she'd picked up the phone to call, but put it down again, unsure of what she wanted to say ... or what she wanted Joan to say. She was angry with Joan. But she was also angry with herself for letting the relationship get so out of control, for being so hurtful to someone she loved.

Her internal disarray must have been evident in her body language. Even before they were seated, Stacy said, "What's wrong? Angst is written all over your face."

Lindsey sat stiffly on the edge of her chair, recounting the events of the last week in what she herself recognized as obsessive detail. "I can understand why she left Boston. But she didn't leave a note and wouldn't answer my calls. Stacy, I was worried to death for nearly twenty-four hours."

When Lindsey ended her recitation and reached for a tissue, Stacy asked, "When did all this start? The intrusiveness."

"She's always had an overbearing streak, but it's been impossible in the last few weeks."

"Since when, exactly?"

Lindsey scrolled through a mental calendar, starting with Joan's call about Ted's vacation. "The end of March, maybe. Not long before I went to Boston."

"Before or after you said you couldn't make a commitment to your relationship?"

"After. Definitely after."

Stacy nodded. "What do you want Joan to do?"

She repeated the phrase that had run through her mind in the hotel bar. "I want the loving and supportive friend she used to be. Someone who seemed to understand what I needed without my having to tell her."

"So, are you upset because she did something wrong, or because she wants something different than you do?"

"She keeps assuming she knows what I want or what I need, without asking."

"But you just said you loved the fact she knew what you wanted without your having to tell her. Now she thinks she knows, but she gets it wrong. Has Joan changed? Or—," Stacy paused for a count of five, "—have you?"

Her question startled Lindsey, and she had to sit back and consider it before admitting, "It's probably me. When we met, I could barely decide what I wanted for breakfast. But over the last few months, I've had to make decisions for me and for Zoey. Now that I'm coping, sometimes just barely, but coping ... " Lindsey let the sentence hang, ashamed to say what she was thinking.

"What?"

"I know she's glad I'm doing better. But I don't need her the way I once did. I've actually wondered if she does things in order to upset me—like talking about Lauren and the book club—so I'll go back to needing her."

"Do you still love her?"

"Of course. But the last few weeks have been a constant struggle. Joan pushing me to do something. Me resisting. Ever since Joan took off her ring."

Took off her ring. Another puzzle piece dropped into place. What if taking off Brad's ring hadn't been a gesture of love? What if Joan was trying to corral a lover she sensed was drifting away? Lindsey shivered as she remembered the cobweb, the feeling of being trapped.

Whatever Joan's motives, Lindsey had responded with a degree of selfishness she'd never tolerate in Zoey. She'd assumed Joan would be content to fill in the empty spaces in Lindsey's life, even as she made light of Joan's pleas for a future. Lindsey was as guilty as Joan of presuming that she knew what her lover wanted, without ever stopping to ask.

"Lindsey. Talk to me."

Gazing up at the ceiling, she shook her head slowly. "I've been so self-absorbed I didn't see what was in front of me. But Dee saw it months ago. That this relationship was about two needy people propping each other up."

"What's wrong with that, if she met your needs and you met hers? But if you've changed, perhaps your relationship needs to change."

"I've handled this badly, haven't I? Never acknowledging what she wanted. Presuming she'd always know what I wanted. When I don't even really know what I want."

"I think you do know what you want, at least for now. But you owe it to her—and to yourself—to talk to her."

"I should have talked to her a long time ago."

Chapter 35

The moment she left Stacy's office, Lindsey called Joan to confirm their Wednesday night dinner.

When she arrived, Joan greeted her with a glass of champagne. "A toast to a wonderful—and loving—friend," she said.

Lindsey recognized the script, a reprise of their lunch the day after they'd become lovers. Remembering her own response, she raised her glass and repeated: "To our friendship."

But instead of tasting it, she said, truthfully, "I've got a splitting headache. I couldn't handle champagne."

Joan drew her in. "Let me get you some aspirin."

Lindsey set her champagne glass on the kitchen counter, then tucked herself into the corner of the sofa where her knees would create a barrier between them when Joan sat down.

Joan handed Lindsey the aspirin. "Lovey, can I get you something else?"

"No, thanks."

Lindsey waited while Joan bustled about, serving cheese and crackers onto individual plates, then perched stiffly on the sofa, her hands folded in her lap, much like a child expecting to be scolded. "You're still angry, aren't you?"

"Angry? No, not any more."

"I've thought about it. I shouldn't have mentioned the book club. But I was so afraid," Joan's lower lip quivered, "you'd go back to Ted. And Boston. That was so stupid of me. To surprise you, and then leave without letting you know. I'm so sorry that—"

Lindsey pressed her hand lightly over Joan's mouth. "Don't apologize. I'm not angry. But," she said as she lowered her hand, "I think you've fallen in love with someone who doesn't exist. Maybe we both have."

"I don't understand."

"It's always been a point of pride for me not to need anyone, to be able to manage on my own." She lifted Joan's hands and kissed them, the palms first and then the backs. "You've taught me how delicious it is to be cared for by someone you love. But I'm still the same piss-ily independent person I always was. It's not in my DNA to need anyone the way I needed you during the month or so after Ted left."

Tears began to slide down Joan's cheeks. "All I've ever wanted was to make you happy."

With her fingertip, Lindsey wiped away the tear streaks. "You have made me happy. Happier than I thought I could be ever again. But I need more space than I think you do. We need to talk about that. We need to learn how to negotiate what I want versus what you want."

Joan stretched across Lindsey's knees and kissed her full on the mouth. Her left hand found Lindsey's breast. "What I want now is to make love to you."

Lovemaking was the furthest thing from Lindsey's mind; it would be a temporary salve, a papering over of the conflicts they needed to address. She rested her hand against Joan's shoulder and pressed her back gently. "Joan, not now, not tonight. I love you. But making love won't make this go away."

Joan slid forward on the couch and picked up the cheese knife. She cut thin slices of cheese, matching each one with a cracker, meticulously laying each one on the platter, as if she was preparing hors d'oeuvres for a party. "I wish I knew what you wanted from me."

"Joan, you can't live your life based on what you think I want. We need to talk about what you want as well as what I want."

The absurdity of her statement stopped Lindsey dead. Joan had, in fact, told Lindsey what she wanted. Commitment. Public recognition. To be helpful. As often as not, Lindsey had rejected what Joan wanted without defining what it was she wanted instead. And she'd just done it again.

Knowing her friend was in pain, Lindsey shifted her legs and put her arm around Joan's shoulder. "In those early months, when I needed you so badly, I let small things slide. I didn't want to make you angry. I was afraid you'd walk away if I made demands or told you what I really wanted. I pretended to be what I thought you wanted ... just like I used to do with Ted. But I can't pretend any longer."

Joan looked up from the platter, her eyes bloodshot. "I don't know how to be what you want. I love you in the only way I know how."

Lindsey was at a loss for how to define the line between loving support and intrusiveness. A postmortem on past conflicts would make it seem as if it was all Joan's fault. Which it wasn't. "I'm not sure what else to say right now. I think we have to take it day to day, with each of us doing a better job of sharing what we each want as we go along."

Lindsey couldn't believe how trite her last words sounded, but they described what she believed. She kissed Joan's cheek and then got up. "I'm going now, but I'll call you tomorrow."

Halfway across the living room, Lindsey looked back. The sight of Joan still arranging cheese and crackers was heartwrenching. "I hope you know how much I love you," she said as she turned into the hall.

~ ~ ~ ~

The next day, Joan was cheery and upbeat, which Lindsey saw as a meaningful effort to go forward on a new basis. Joan seemed to take it in stride when Lindsey had to turn down her suggestion that they go to a Sunday afternoon movie in town. "I'd love to, really I would, but Zoey's got stable duties."

The following morning, Joan called her at work twice, each time asking if Lindsey still loved her. Lindsey tried to reassure her, but sensed she was pouring water into a bottomless cup.

They continued to meet two or three times a week. Joan was volatile—sometimes effusive in her love for Lindsey, other times desperate for reassurance. The more they talked about the "quality" of their relationship, the less they shared the day-to-day things on which their companionship had been built. Lindsey almost never discussed anything about Zoey. They made love less and less often, and on one occasion, Lindsey begged off. Making love had become a task rather than a pleasure.

Lindsey could see their love affair coming to an end. The turning point came in mid-May when an agency fundraising event kept her from Wednesday dinner. Joan suggested stopping by afterwards, but she pleaded the late hour and an early morning meeting. The truth was she couldn't face Joan's neediness after four hours of intense socializing.

The next evening, as Lindsey stepped out of the elevator in the lobby of her office building, Joan looped an arm through hers. She was breathing hard, as if she'd just been running and her eyes were puffy.

"Joan, what are you doing here?"

"You can't shut me out like this."

Lindsey moved quickly out of the building, pulling Joan with her. Once out on the street, Lindsey spun around. "How did you know I'd be here? It's after six."

"I got here before five and called up. They said you were in. I've been waiting."

"Over an hour? Why?"

"I can't bear it when you shut me out. We have to straighten this out." Joan's words poured out so fast they almost ran together.

Lindsey stood mute as Joan raved on. She had to stop this ... not only the scene on the street, but also the daily stream of apologies and pleas for reassurance. She grasped Joan's arm above the elbow and squeezed hard. "Stop it, Joan. Stop talking."

Joan stopped mid-sentence, her eyes locked on Lindsey's face.

"Joan, I have loved you so much. But all we do anymore is argue. Whether I love you. How you should take care of me. Whether we 'belong together.' We need to take a break. For a few weeks at least."

Joan grabbed Lindsey's arms. "No. Please no. I love you."

Lindsey stepped back to free her arms. "Joan, the fact is, I need a break. I don't know for how long, but I'll let you know when I figure it out." She turned and walked toward the bus stop. It took every bit of willpower she possessed not to turn around to check Joan's reaction.

Lindsey's sense of relief grew each day she didn't hear from Joan. After a week, her stomach stopped clenching every time the phone rang. Even so, she mourned the loss of the closest friend she'd ever had.

If Zoey noticed Joan's absence, she didn't mention it. Lindsey chose not to ask. She did notice, though, that Zoey's mood was more upbeat than it had been in months.

Chapter 36

She'd arranged to meet Claire and Ted outside Carnegie Hall for the final concert of the season, an all-Mozart program. When they arrived, Ted greeted Zoey with his normal enthusiasm, but he gave Lindsey only a cool nod. Not even her name. For the first time in the five weeks they'd been doing activities together with Zoey, he did not return her smile.

While they waited for Claire, Zoey chatted excitedly about their imminent trip to Connecticut for a second look at a 20-year-old gelding being sold by a girl just going off to college. They would make the final decision on Saturday. Lindsey had the odd sensation that Ted kept shifting his position so she couldn't catch his eye.

Once inside the concert hall, Claire piloted them into their seats, positioning Zoey between herself and Ted, with Lindsey on Ted's far side. Lindsey wondered if Claire's seating maneuver had a larger purpose. Claire had made no secret of her pleasure that Lauren was out of the picture and that Ted and Lindsey were willing to attend social functions with Zoey.

When they got to their seats, Lindsey opened the program. Knowing that Mozart piano sonatas were among Zoey's favorites, she leaned across Ted to point it out to her daughter. As she touched his arm, Ted flinched and jerked it out from under hers.

She gave him an apologetic smile. "What's wrong? Did I hurt you?"

He muttered, low so Zoey wouldn't hear, "You know perfectly well what's wrong."

Lindsey looked at him blankly. "I'm sorry, but I don't."

"Does the name Joan mean anything to you?"

"Yes, of course. She was in my mythology class. You know that."

"Apparently that isn't all she was in."

Lindsey's jaw literally dropped. If Ted knew, his comment was as vulgar as anything she'd ever heard him say. But how would he know?

"So, the rumor is true," he said.

"What rumor?"

The lights went down and applause drowned out Ted's response. The concert hall began to spin and Lindsey gripped the arms of her seat. In the few seconds between the end of the applause and the start of the music, she whispered, "We have to talk."

"Not any more we don't." He shifted in his seat so his back was to her.

Lindsey barely heard the music. By intermission, she was afraid she might throw up, and dashed to the ladies' room. Her nausea abated, but she delayed returning to her seat until a few moments before the second half began, blaming her absence on a typically long line.

Since it was a school night, there was no question of socializing after the concert. She gave Claire a hug and sent Ted her most gracious smile, but she made sure there was no opportunity for her arms or hands to touch his.

The message light was blinking when she and Zoey got home. It was Dee. "Call me the minute you get in. No matter what time it is."

Drained from the encounter with Ted, she wanted only to cry herself to sleep. But Dee's message was not to be ignored. She collapsed on the couch in the den and punched out Dee's number.

Dee picked up on the first ring. "Lindsey, Ted knows about Joan. She called him this morning."

Ted's bizarre behavior suddenly made sense. "How do you know? What did she say?"

"I have no idea. But the boys played squash today and Jim said Ted was absolutely enraged. I wanted to get to you before he does."

"Too late. The last of our Thursday concerts with Claire was tonight. Ted flinched when I accidentally touched his arm and he made a comment about Joan that was shockingly obscene." Lindsey stared up at the ceiling. "Tell me what Jim said."

"Not much, just that all thoughts of a ..." Dee stopped mid-sentence.

Lindsey heard Dee take a deep nasal breath. "Of a what?"

"I didn't know until tonight, but ... Ted's been thinking about a reconciliation."

"With Lauren? What's Joan got to do with reconciling with Lauren?"

"No—with you."

"Where did that come from?"

"All I know is what Jim told me today ... that he started thinking about it before he stayed with Zoey. It's why he broke up with Lauren."

"So, what am I supposed to do now?"

"About Joan or Ted?"

"Start with Ted. Do you care that he was thinking about getting back together?"

"Dee, I don't know what to think. But after tonight, I don't see how we can even continue with family activities for Zoey."

"Can you talk to him?"

"And say what, exactly? When I have no idea what she said to him."

"You need to find out."

"To do that I have to talk to her ... to let her back in my life.

"Lindsey, she's back in your life, whether you like it or not. You can't just ignore it, hoping she'll go away."

"I swear to God, Dee, I could kill her."

"You don't mean that literally."

"No, but it's a good thing she's not standing in front of me right now."

"Sweetie, you have every right to be upset, but I think you should get some sleep and we'll talk tomorrow."

As Lindsey hung up, she wondered how a relationship—*two relationships*—that had once seemed so magical could have gone so wrong. She pulled a sofa pillow over her face and sobbed.

~ ~ ~ ~

Ted's response to her request to meet after work had been a rude "What for?" After she stressed how important it was to Zoey to maintain the appearance of getting along, he agreed. Reluctantly.

Lindsey made of a point of getting to the restaurant before Ted. She hadn't wanted to meet in a public place, but her apartment was out of the question and Ted didn't suggest his place. A five-dollar bill got her a table where their conversation would not be overheard.

As soon as she was seated, she requested ice water, downed the whole glass and asked for a second. She debated whether to have a drink to calm her nerves or tea to keep her head clear. She settled for a scotch, but seconds later called the waiter back and switched to tea, with another glass of water. Every few moments she looked at the door, hoping Ted would actually show up.

When he did, he wore a scowl and his expression did not change as he sat down. "So, what do I need to know"—his voice was acerbic—"about my wife sleeping with a woman?"

He was baiting her. She'd seen him do that when he cross-examined a witness in court, or when he was angry with an associate who'd made a careless mistake. But he'd never done it to her. Lindsey steeled herself for his barbs.

"I was devastated when you walked out on ..." she chose her word, "... us."

"So, you replaced me with a woman?"

"It was a rebound thing—something mature adults shouldn't do. I was in a desperate place. It's over now."

"I'll bet you learned some new tricks. Maybe you never liked being in my bed."

"Ted, stop it." She tried to sound firm, but it felt like begging.

"Stop what? Being upset about having a fifteen-year hard-on for someone who prefers women? Being upset that you've exposed my daughter to a bunch of dykes? I'm supposed to be polite and understanding? Give me a break."

A bunch of dykes. Where had that come from? He'd never been homophobic. Was he trying to humiliate her? She made a conscious effort to not slump in her chair. "I do not prefer women. Joan was what I needed at a low point in my life. It's over. It won't happen again."

"And you know that how?" he asked, rubbing his chin between his thumb and forefinger.

He was out to get her. This was a side of him she'd never seen. What could she do or say to make him stop? She thought of Mark. "Because I still get turned on by an attractive man. Because I've never been attracted to a woman before Joan, and I'm not attracted to women now. Because I can't see raising Zoey in a world of only women."

"Ah, Zoey. My daughter. The one you didn't want to know about Lauren. But you certainly didn't mind if she knew about Joan."

She didn't know how much longer she could manage to think in a straight line. Her arms and legs were trembling. She folded her hands in her lap, where he was less likely to notice. "She didn't know about Joan. She still doesn't."

Ted's smile was contemptuous, as if it was beneath his dignity to even talk to her. "If she knew about Lauren"—he picked up his fork and poked it toward her as he talked—"why would you think she couldn't see what was right in front of her? She clued me in ages ago."

Lindsey felt as if she had just fallen into an abyss. Dee had warned her this could happen.

Dee. Dee's call the night before. Her mind cleared. He hadn't been 'clued in' months ago and he hadn't learned from Zoey. He'd found out from Joan only a few days earlier.

"Zoey does not know. And if she'd told you ages ago, you wouldn't have been thinking about a reconciliation."

Ted's jaw twitched. "What makes you think I have any interest in a reconciliation?"

Lindsey's mouth went dry. She'd made a mistake. Hoping her hand wouldn't visibly shake, she reached for her water and sipped it, searching for a way to undo her gaffe. "Dee warned me that you were angry. The bit about reconciliation just slipped out."

"Well, I'm not thinking about it now. What I'm thinking about is having you declared unfit and suing for full custody of Zoey."

Her water went down the wrong way, and she started to cough, her eyes tearing up from the exertion. Ted watched, unmoving, as she struggled for air. When she thought she could control her voice, she said, "You wouldn't!" It came out as a squeak.

"I would." He leaned across the table so his face was inches from hers, his standard technique for intimidating a witness. He was so close she had trouble focusing her eyes on his face. "You've neglected Zoey so you could get it on with a woman."

"I have not." She had her voice back, but only barely.

"She thought you did. She was always complaining about how much time you spent with Joan. How you two talked every day. How often you brought Joan to the country. How you didn't have time for her."

"For a while, she did resent the time I spent with Joan, but once I realized it, I stopped including Joan in our dinners. I stopped inviting her to the country. I did everything I could to show Zoey she was my number-one priority."

"It seems she didn't get the message."

Lindsey pushed back. "What are you talking about?"

"Well..." He sat back, thrumming his fingers on the table. "I don't think bulimia is the sign of a child who feels secure. And to make matters worse, it was going on under your nose for months. We still might not know if she hadn't gone to that damn dentist."

His shot hit the mark. The guilt she'd been carrying around for months before she learned about the bulimia burst to the surface. Slapping Zoey. Leaving her unattended. Breaking her promise about their day together. She hadn't neglected Zoey intentionally, as her mother seemed to have, but it was neglect nonetheless. She sat, mute and defeated, wringing her hands in her lap.

Ted sneered again as he put his napkin down and stood up. "Not so long ago you said that to be a good father, I needed to play by Zoey's rules. Perhaps you should have taken your own advice."

She watched as he strode off. When he was gone, she stumbled out of the restaurant into the pouring rain. She'd been determined not to cry, but in the rain, no one would notice.

Losing her daughter was beyond comprehension. Worst of all, it was her own fault. In her search for comfort, she'd let herself be distracted from her obligations to her child. And she could have, months ago, taken control of the way people learned about her relationship with Joan. She'd ducked the issue, denied its urgency. And now she was paying the price.

~ ~ ~ ~

As she walked the few blocks home, she rehearsed all the things she might say to Zoey, but none of them made any sense. When she reached the Beresford, she couldn't go in. Despite the rain, she trudged around the block twice, willing herself to believe that Ted wouldn't expose his daughter to public humiliation and a litany of prurient details just to avenge his bruised ego.

When she was finally calm enough to go inside, she found Zoey setting out silverware and glasses on a tray.

Zoey looked up as she came in. "Wow, what happened to you?"

"It's pouring out there, and I didn't have an umbrella. But I'm fine. What's with the tray?"

"Since we're not going to the country until tomorrow morning, I thought we could eat dinner while we watch a movie. *Gilbert Grape* came from Netflix today."

"Sounds like a fine idea. Let me get into some dry clothes." Lindsey headed off to her bedroom, relieved that she could put off dealing with the gathering storm for a few more hours.

Or so she thought.

When she came into the den with a tray of food, Zoey was fiddling with the movie and talking on the phone. "It's Dad," she mouthed.

Lindsey set the tray on the coffee table, keeping her back to Zoey, and started to distribute the food. She didn't want Zoey to see the anxiety she was sure had erupted on her face.

"Can't," Zoey mumbled into the phone. "I'm at the stable both days."

A pause. Lindsey held her breath.

"I dunno ... 11:30 or 12, I guess."

A long pause.

"Wow. That'd be cool. Let me check with Mom." She turned to Lindsey. "Dad wants to come to the country and take me to brunch on Sunday. It's okay, isn't it?"

No, it's not okay, Lindsey wanted to scream. Not once, since January, had he come up just to have Sunday breakfast. Why now? Was his plan to turn Zoey against her? Lindsey sank to the floor, her legs no longer willing to hold her up.

"Mom ... are you okay?"

"I'm a little woozy. A glass of water would be good."

Zoey barked into the phone, "Dad, I'll call you back."

By the time Zoey returned, Lindsey felt in control, but only barely, of her senses again. Whatever Ted's intent, she couldn't refuse to let Zoey go with him.

She downed the water in one long gulp. "Thanks. I'm okay now. I'm gonna get an aspirin." She kept a hand on the wall, steadying herself as she went toward the bathroom, wondering if she'd ever be calm again.

~ ~ ~ ~

She bolted awake the next morning, dripping wet, with a horrific memory of shouting "stop it, stop it" as she tried to escape from Joan's bear hug, from her insistence they were destined to be together.

She kicked off the covers and lay hugging her pillow, waiting for her body to cool off, for her dream-stoked frustration to abate. But even as she put distance between herself and the dream, she knew that some variation of it would come true.

Chapter 37

Lindsey had agreed to meet Dee at the café in South Egremont after she dropped Zoey at the stable the next morning. When she arrived, Dee was staring out the window, her fingers tapping out an erratic rhythm on the table. Lindsey slid into the booth and settled into the corner, against the side.

Dee gave her a commiserating look. "How *are* you?"

Lindsey dropped her head into the palms of her hands. "Ted's taking Zoey to breakfast tomorrow. I'm terrified he'll say something to her—about Joan or about filing for custody. *Say* something to turn her against me."

"I can't believe he'd do that."

"I don't know. I've never seen him like he was Friday. Vulgar. Crude. Mean."

"You know why he's reacting this way, don't you?"

"No, I don't. He's never been even vaguely homophobic."

Dee cupped her hands to mimic a foghorn. "Calling all social workers."

Lindsey gaped at Dee. This was hardly the time for jokes.

"This had to be an emotional earthquake for him, Lindsey. Shaken his view of himself as a man ... as an attractive male."

"Geez, why am I being punished when he rejected me?"

"Jim says he's been thinking about getting back together for a while. The fact that he still found you attractive when you were sleeping with a woman ... well, it must make him question everything he thought he knew. Not just about you, but about himself and his judgment. He's flailing, like you were after he left."

"But it's over!" Lindsey pounded the table with her fist.

"Is it? Are you sure? You were talking to her nearly every day until a few weeks ago."

"It's over now. I have to make him understand that."

Dee rested her hands on Lindsey's. "Why, if you're not interested in getting back together? What matters is Zoey. Focus on what it would do to her to have you fighting in court. The publicity. The jibes from kids at school."

Lindsey rolled her eyes. "I've been thinking about practically nothing else for the last twenty-four hours."

"And you have less than twenty-four hours to decide what to do."

~ ~ ~ ~

Lindsey headed back to the house to call Ted. What would she say?

If this were about Ted's ego, it would serve no purpose to argue about being a good mother, or how it would kill her to lose her daughter, or about Ted's misreading of the situation. If he didn't understand yesterday, he wouldn't understand today.

But she had to believe he would not willfully hurt his— their—daughter. She had to appeal to his parental instincts.

Her hand shook as she called his cell. After the fifth ring, she got his voicemail and left a message. "Ted, we need to talk before you see Zoey tomorrow. Call me."

By midafternoon, he hadn't called. Since he never went more than a couple hours without checking his phone, it seemed he wasn't going to call her. She'd have to leave a more detailed message. She wrote out what she'd say.

I hope you don't plan to say anything to Zoey about our last conversation. ~~You must realize that you cannot obtain full custody of our daughter without her learning~~ *She doesn't know about Joan and she doesn't need to. But if you try to separate her from me, you will have to tell her why. If you open that door, I will make sure you have to walk through it too.*

She read the note and reread it and read it again before she picked up the phone. His number rang five times before going to voicemail, a clear sign he'd picked up her earlier message. She read her lines, then tore the paper into miniscule pieces.

When her hands stopped shaking, she headed out to the porch to work a pile of case management files. Halfway through the top file, her cell phone rang. It was Claire.

"Hi. How are you today?"

"Not as well as I might be." Claire's usually cultured voice seemed reedy.

Lindsey's already sagging spirits drooped another notch. She didn't think she could handle yet another crisis. "What's wrong?"

"I just heard the most outrageous story from Ted."

Lindsey didn't know whether to laugh or cry. Ted was actually going forward with his threat. "What did he tell you?"

"That you are a lesbian. Is it true?"

"No."

"Why would he make up such a thing?"

For months, Lindsey had made a conscious effort not to involve Claire in her disputes with Ted. But now that her mother-in-law had brought the subject up, Lindsey would speak her mind. "Because his ego is wounded. I guess Ted thinks I should have sat at home pining for him. I was devastated when Ted left, but Joan swooped in, offering comfort and consolation." She let the sentence hang for a long beat. "We had an affair at a time when I wasn't thinking clearly. It's over now. "

"Does Zoey know?"

"No."

"Ted says she does."

A familiar blaze of white anger shot across the back of Lindsey's eyes. Was Claire trying to trap her? And if so, why? Whatever Claire's motive, there was nothing to be gained by being evasive. "Claire, did Zoey ever say anything that made you suspect?"

For several beats, she heard only Claire's steady breathing. Lindsey waited, holding her own breath, not sure she was prepared for Claire's answer.

"She certainly complained about having Joan around all the time. But I never paid it much mind. You needed a friend and Joan seemed very caring. And now that I think about it, she hasn't mentioned Joan for a while ... since April, I think, when you went to Boston."

Lindsey let the air flow back into her lungs. Claire's answer appeared to be no.

"Did he tell you he wants custody of Zoey? And plans to have me declared unfit."

"Yes," Claire replied. "I told him he was out of his mind."

"Do you think he'd really do it?"

Claire snorted. "Not if I have anything to say about it. After that ridiculous business with Lauren, he's in no position to lecture you on good parenting. If you want my opinion, he knew Lauren was a mistake from day one. It's why he's never had the final divorce papers drawn up. And I suppose I encouraged him not to be hasty."

Lindsey listened in amazement. As supportive as Claire had been over the months, she'd never betrayed her son. Lindsey had assumed that Claire, at some level, wanted them to get back together, but she'd never said a word.

"Well, he's not coming back now. And he wants to take Zoey away from me."

"Lindsey, he *will not* do that." Claire's tone brooked no opposition. "A custody fight would devastate Zoey and embarrass this family."

"But how will you stop him?"

"I don't know. But stop him I will."

Lindsey could only hope. As she returned to her case files, she wondered if Ted had shared details of Joan's call with his mother. Perhaps Claire would have some insight on how to deal with Joan. She reached for the phone, but then thought better of it. If Claire did know, she might not be willing to say. And if she didn't know, Lindsey's query could make an already fraught situation even worse.

~ ~ ~ ~

Ted knocked on the front door Sunday morning. Since he and Zoey had been spending weekends there, Lindsey expected he'd let himself in. Was this small courtesy a good sign?

When Zoey opened it, Ted scooped her up in his arms, lifting her off the ground. Over Zoey's head, he caught Lindsey's eye. "I'll be sure to get her to the stable on time."

When the door closed, Lindsey stood shaking her arms and kicking her feet, trying to fling away the nervous energy coursing through her body. She wasn't sure how she'd make it through the six hours until she could pick up Zoey and find out why Ted had come.

She went for a long walk, and then set herself to mindless tasks in the garden. Weeding and deadheading daffodils calmed her, but not much. If she'd been a nail-biter, Lindsey would have bitten every finger to the quick.

Zoey was waiting when Lindsey pulled up to the stable door.

"Am I late?"

"Nope. Dad wanted to walk around the stables for ideas on training my horse. Except I had work to do. So he helped. Made it go much faster."

"What did you guys talk about?"

Zoey shrugged. "Mostly about the horse. Dad's arranged for us to go pick Dude up in two weeks. I'm so excited."

Zoey's casualness did not relieve Lindsey's anxiety. Ted was an expert lawyer, and he'd get all his ducks in a row before he took any formal action.

When she climbed into bed Sunday night, Lindsey still hadn't decided what to do about Joan. What she wanted was to scream out her anger and frustration, throw books or dishes at her, berate her for her appallingly immature behavior ... anything to make Joan feel as miserable as Lindsey did now.

What she needed to do, however, was to persuade Joan to leave her family alone. But how? Should she call, state her case and then hang up? Or arrange to meet, on the assumption they could have an adult discussion? Should she send her a threatening letter?

Many times, over the years, she'd gone to bed noodling some work-related issue, and awakened the next morning with a solution clear in her mind. She hoped it would happen this time.

It did. She woke up with a plan.

~ ~ ~ ~

She called Joan at work Monday morning. Since Joan didn't have her own office, there was no chance of an unscripted telephone conversation. She suggested they meet that afternoon at a café on the Upper West Side. Joan agreed, with a degree of enthusiasm that exacerbated Lindsey's already considerable anxiety.

Lindsey arrived ten minutes early and picked a booth near the front. It was roomy enough to be private, but the steady flow of passing patrons would preclude any emotional scenes ... and give Lindsey an easy exit when the conversation was over. To make it even easier, she put two tens in her jacket pocket, enough to pay for whatever they might order, without having to wait for the bill.

Even so, Lindsey was jittery, unsure of her ability to stand firm in the face of Joan's professions of remorse, unsure where to draw the line between gratitude and resentment. The memory of their love counted for a lot, but a love that depended on destroying her family was not a love Lindsey could accept.

Her jitters eased when Joan came in, looking for all the world as if she was meeting her best friend. If Joan was as oblivious to the impact of her action as she appeared, Lindsey could say her lines, listen to Joan's response, and then leave, knowing—well, hoping—they'd never meet again.

Joan's words, as she slid into the booth, matched her exuberant aura. "I was so pleased when you called. I have missed you."

Lindsey was all business. "Let's order, and then we can talk." She signaled for a nearby waitress.

When they'd ordered, Lindsey sat up straight, the way she did when she had to deal with difficult staff. "Do you know why I called you today?"

"I ... umh... no." Joan adopted her standard pose, chin on upraised fist. "But there's so much to catch up on ... so much I want to tell you."

As Joan's shoulders eased forward, Lindsey edged back on her seat. "Let's start with why you called Ted. What the hell did you think you were doing?"

"I wanted him to know how lucky he was to have you back," Joan said, too quickly to have required conscious thought.

Lindsey didn't know what answer she'd expected, but that certainly wasn't it. If it was true, Joan was even more deluded than she'd imagined. "I'm not back with Ted. More to the point, Ted is suing for full custody of Zoey. Suing to take my daughter away from me. Do you have any idea why he's doing that?

Joan dropped her hand onto the table. "No. Of course not. You're a wonderful mother."

Lindsey leaned in, so her eyes were level with Joan's. "Because," she spoke slowly, enunciating each word, "you told him something that makes him think I've been neglecting Zoey. I don't know what you said, but whatever it was, it has destroyed my life."

Joan sat back, her smile gone. "I've done it again, haven't I? Made you angry when I was just trying to help."

"Angry. I'm beyond angry. I'm about to lose my daughter. Because you decided you needed to help. How did you imagine that calling Ted would help?"

"I thought if Ted knew I accepted your relationship with him, that we—you and I— could—"

"Ted and I don't have a relationship."

Joan reached for Lindsey's hand. "Then I just don't understand why you left me? We were so happy together."

Here it was ... the scene from Lindsey's nightmare, the conversation she'd dreaded. She had to bring this to an end. Except that Joan across the booth seemed even more clueless than the Joan of her dream. She drew her hand back and rested it in her lap. "Yes, we were, at a time when you helped me through a crisis in my life. Now, you're the one who has created the crisis."

Lindsey saw tears pooling in Joan's eyes, the small muscles around her mouth trembling. She pulled out a ten and laid it on the table as she slid out of the booth. "Joan, I do not want you to contact me or anyone in my family again. Is that clear?"

"Lindsey, please, let me ..."

Lindsey did not wait to hear the end of Joan's sentence. She did not turn around as she walked out. She did not want Joan to see the tears in her own eyes.

Chapter 38

Angela called early Tuesday morning. "Were you aware that Ted was going to change the terms of the settlement?"

"No," Lindsey said. It wasn't true, but how would she explain what had happened?

"The new draft has 50/50 custody with court-approved terms. And the financial terms are very different."

They agreed to meet at four that afternoon, by which time her concentration was shot for the day. A 50/50 split meant he'd wasn't going to declare her unfit. That had to be good. But Angela's vagueness about the financial details triggered bruising memories of her childhood. Would Ted put her on the verge of financial insecurity? Would she, like her mother, struggle to make ends meet?

More than once, Dee's advice echoed in her brain. "You need to get that settlement signed as soon as possible." Why hadn't she listened?

Angela had two copies of Ted's document, along with a detailed schedule comparing the new proposal with the earlier draft. For twenty minutes, Lindsey listened, mute, as her lawyer drew lines through parts of her life that she had taken for granted. She barely understood half of what Angela told her.

When Angela sat back, her recitation finished, Lindsey said, "I got lost in all that detail. What does it actually mean for me? For me and my daughter."

Angela laid her pen down, parallel to the top edge of the page of numbers. "He'll buy out your half of all the assets including your retirement based on September 21st of last year. So you'll have a very sizeable pile of cash to invest. Child support will cover Zoey's expenses plus half the expenses of the co-op. But he does not propose to pay spousal support. That means you have to cover the balance of the co-op expenses from your salary or the cash. And of course, your own clothing, entertainment, travel, and health insurance."

Lindsey's brain felt paralyzed, unable to make the pieces fit together. Had the custody threat been nothing more than a ploy? Were the diminished financial terms his way of punishing her without embarrassing his family? "Can I challenge it?"

Angela steepled her fingers. "Lindsey, you won't have the luxuries he provided in the earlier agreement—the country house, for example—unless you're willing to live off your assets. But based on your income, the settlement seems fair. Unless there's something in your favor that you haven't told me, this agreement would be hard to contest in a court."

"The country house?"

"The assets ... remember, he's buying out your interest. You won't have access to it."

Lindsey stared dumbly at the page of numbers. She no longer had the strength to reach for her water or even to cry. Along with splitting her daughter's life in half by fiat, Ted had sliced off much of Lindsey's life outside of work ... a life she had created to please him.

The moment Lindsey left Angela's, she phoned Dee, who agreed to meet her at the apartment.

Dee was waiting in the lobby when Lindsey arrived. "I rang, but no one answered."

"Zoey's out with Ted tonight."

"Good." Dee opened her bag to reveal a bottle of Courvoisier. "You need something stronger than scotch. Didn't know if Ted left any of this good stuff in your larder."

In the apartment, they headed for the den, where Lindsey poured the amber liquid into snifters.

"Tell me," Dee said even before they were seated.

Lindsey scanned her notes. "A 50/50 custody split. A 50/50 split of our assets, but I get cash." Her eyes burned with the effort of not crying. "Child support, but no spousal support. I have to pay half the apartment expenses and can't use the country house."

"Whoa. Slow down." Dee sipped the brandy. "Ooh. Try it. It's good. Does 50/50 custody mean Zoey has to stay in his apartment? Whether she wants to or not."

Lindsey took a cautious sip. "Yup."

"And the country house? What about weekends when you have Zoey?"

Lindsey took a larger slug, grateful for the way the golden liquid warmed her core as it went down. "I can't use it. We'd have to stay in the City."

Dee swirled her snifter under her nose. "You're not going to like what I have to say." She held the glass toward Lindsey like a pointer. "Sign the damn thing and consider yourself lucky."

Lindsey's brandy went down the wrong way. When her coughing fit subsided, she gaped at Dee. "You're kidding."

"No, sweetie, I'm not. Three days ago, he was making threats that would cause untold pain and embarrassment to you and Zoey. You stood up to him. You matched his threat and he backed down. No embarrassment ... no public spectacle." Dee made a check mark with her finger on an imaginary column in the air. "That's a point for you. But what he's offering is what most women in your position would be grateful to get."

Lindsey banged her glass on the tabletop. "But Joan didn't happen until *after* he left me! And it's *over*."

"That's a fact. But you no longer have the moral high ground." Dee put her hand over Lindsey's glass. "Make no mistake, duckie, if you challenge him, you'll be the one causing the embarrassment and public spectacle."

~ ~ ~ ~

Lindsey lay awake for hours. There didn't seem to be many options. If any. He'd offered what the law required. Challenging him in court would be devastating and likely unsuccessful. How could she take that step, after begging Ted not to?

She couldn't.

But even as she understood that the fabric of her life was about to be torn apart once again, she knew Ted's proposal was wrong. At two in the morning, she got up, made tea, and parked herself at the desk to draft an email. She commented on things she felt were wrong for Zoey, but said nothing about other terms of the agreement. When the draft was done, she went back to bed and promptly fell asleep.

She proofread her email the next morning. It was, she decided, too confrontational, a "my way or the highway" challenge. Clutching the unsent email in her hand, she called Ted.

He answered on the third ring. "Is Zoey all right?"

"Yes, she's fine. I want to talk about the new agreement."

"That's why we have lawyers. So we don't have to fight about it."

"I don't want to fight about it."

"Then sign it."

"Zoey will be very unhappy with some of this. She's not going to understand."

"Zoey's been unhappy since the day I left." Ted stressed each syllable of each word. "I've tried my best to deal with her upsets, but at thirteen, she doesn't run the world. This is as good a time as any for her to learn that the world can be a shitty place."

"Ted, please hear me out."

He gave a long-suffering sigh. "Okay. I'm listening."

Lindsey willed herself to focus on Zoey. "You're forcing her to stay in your place against her will. Once her horse is finally here, you'll deprive her of access to the stables twice a month. And I'm worried about her eating if no one is there when she gets home from school."

"Did you hear me? About Zoey and reality. She's staying with me, all night, every night, every other week. We'll have Elena come here during my weeks to keep an eye on her after school. And if you think the stable is that important, you can drive her there."

"That's ridiculous, Ted. Two hours up and two hours back, two days in a row."

"I've given you the car."

"But I can't use the house and I can't afford a motel twice a month."

"So, stay with Dee and Jim. Or better yet, let her go to the country with them."

"But then I'd never see her."

"Precisely," Ted said, his voice clipped. "Now, if you have any other questions, I suggest you direct them to your lawyer." He hung up.

~ ~ ~ ~

Lindsey debated all day whether to call Dee. She was embarrassed to admit she'd ignored Dee's advice yet again.

Through sheer force of will, she managed—or so she thought—to get through dinner, as if everything was normal. But on her way out of the kitchen afterward, Zoey asked if Lindsey was "getting the flu or something." Lindsey assured her it was nothing more than a long day at work.

But stress was taking its toll. How much longer could she keep up this charade for Zoey's sake? Perhaps she should sign the agreement and be done with it.

When she finally called Dee, her friend wasted no time in social niceties. "What did you decide?"

"I called Ted today."

"You did *what*?" Dee's voice rose nearly an octave. "Lindsey, why do you even bother asking for my advice when you have no intention of taking it?"

"I was worried about Zoey. About his forcing her to stay with him. About making it hard for her to get to the stables on my weekends."

"And?"

"He said he didn't care. That it was time for Zoey to grow up."

There was a long silence. "Lindsey, you can't go on fighting forever. Kids survive divorce. She will too."

"He said something else."

"Yeah?"

"That Zoey should go to the country with you if she wants to work at the stables. On the weekends I have custody." Her throat was burning. "So she won't be with me."

"That's ridiculous. Zoey would never agree to spend half her weekends without you."

"Once she has her horse, she might."

"Look, you can both stay here. You know you're welcome."

"I can't take up weekend residence with you until Zoey goes off to college. But I also can't face four years of weekends without her."

Lindsey waited for a response, but got none. "Are you still there?"

"Lindsey, I don't know what else to suggest."

~ ~ ~ ~

By midday Thursday, Lindsey was feverish and achy, and went home to bed. There was no need for her to pretend to carry on an ordinary conversation with Zoey.

She called in sick on Friday and slept most of the morning. When the phone rang shortly before noon, she let it ring. It rang again a few minutes later. It was Ted.

"Hullo." Her voice came out low and phlegm-y.

"Your office said you were home with the flu. Are you well enough to listen for a moment?"

Did she have a choice? "Yeah."

Ted cleared this throat, as if he was about to make a speech. "I've thought about our conversation. Zoey is going to be with me every other week, period. But if you sign the agreement, as it is, you can use the country house on the weekends that you have custody."

"Like guest privileges."

Ted let out an impatient sigh. "Call it what you like. You made a valid point, and—like you—I really am thinking about Zoey."

"Ted, I'm too sick to think clearly. Can I give you a call back?"

"Yes, of course. But, Lindsey, if you care about Zoey as much as you say you do, you'll sign the agreement before I change my mind again."

Chapter 39

The first month after she signed the agreement was the hardest.

The first Sunday, Zoey loaded up a backpack with her pajamas, underwear, a school uniform, and her books and stormed off to Ted's. That week, she spent hours each evening on the phone with Lindsey, much of the time tearful, despite Ted's promise to take the day off on Friday to pick up Dude.

When Zoey was with Ted, the apartment felt hollow and barren. And Lindsey was angry. Angry at Ted for making her pay for his wounded ego. Angry that he'd upset Zoey once again. Angry at herself for not taking Dee's advice to get divorce terms finalized months ago. Angry at herself for allowing the affair with Joan to threaten her relationship with Zoey. Many nights, she worked late to avoid going home to an empty space and the bitter taste of her own resentment.

In fact, Zoey settled quite quickly into a new routine, much as Ted and Dee had predicted. Lindsey's own anger gradually ebbed as well. The arrangement with the country house worked out surprisingly well. She fought tears as she moved her things into the guest room, but it was a beautiful room with a cathedral ceiling. The French doors opened out to a porch overlooking the river. Falling asleep to the burbling of the stream, she wondered why they hadn't converted it into the master bedroom long ago.

A month or so after Zoey's horse arrived, Ted came up to the apartment with Zoey when he brought her home Sunday evening. "I'm sorry to show up uninvited, but I wanted to talk to you about the weekend arrangements."

His words sent a flicker of anxiety running up Lindsey's spine. It must have shown on her face, because he held his hand up and continued without a pause. "Lindsey, you can still use the house. In fact, from now on—," he pulled a credit card from his shirt pocket and handed it to her—"I want you to put your gas and food expenses on this card. It will be billed to me."

Lindsey was dumbfounded. After trying to keep her away from the country house, now he was offering a financial incentive for her to go there. Moreover, the cost of gas was trivial in the context of her overall budget and they had to eat no matter where they were.

"Why this sudden change of heart? Six weeks ago, you didn't want me there at all."

"It's not so sudden. I've been thinking about it ever since Zoey signed up to compete in the showjumping event the end of September. It's a big stretch with a new horse, and she'll need all the training time she can get. I want to make sure that money concerns aren't an obstacle to getting her to the stable every possible weekend between now and then."

"Between now and then." She held the card out in front of her. "You want the card back when the show is over?"

"No. It's yours." He gave a rueful sigh as he shook his head. "Lindsey, trying to keep you and Zoey apart was one of the dumbest things I've ever done. She needs her mother, every bit as much as you've always said she needs her father. I want to make it easy for you to use the house as you always have."

She appreciated his apology, but found his earnestness discomfiting. She tried to lighten the mood. "So, I can start gardening again?"

He laughed out loud. "I'd be grateful if you would. The garden's been looking pretty sad this summer."

"So I noticed."

"You can do whatever you want with it. Consider it yours. And now, I'll go say good-bye to Zoey."

The next weekend, she used the credit card for the first time and spent much of Saturday afternoon in the garden, rooting at least a month's worth of weeds. It felt awkward, that first time, but three weeks later, she was hard-pressed to describe how life in the country had changed from the months before the settlement.

And the new custody schedule offered unexpected benefits: substantial blocks of time when she didn't have to worry about Zoey. She signed up for a contemporary art course at MOMA and joined the Lincoln Center Film Society, to catch up on years of films she'd missed. She decided to brighten up her image and asked Dee to help her shop for new summer clothes in something other than navy blue, black or maroon. She was particularly pleased with a poplin pants suit in pale peach.

She arranged a series of museum afternoons with Claire. One Saturday in mid-June, they met in the café at the Whitney Museum. As they sipped coffee after a very pleasant lunch, Claire asked in a casual tone, "Do you ever see Joan?"

Lindsey's pulse flickered. "No. Why?"

"I ran into her at Bloomingdale's last week. She asked about you, but I pleaded a doctor's appointment, so we didn't talk. But then she called me the next day, wanting my opinion on how to make up for the trouble she'd caused you with Ted."

Lindsey clenched and unclenched her fists beneath the table. There wasn't much more damage Joan could do, but she seemed undeterred by Lindsey's demand to leave her family alone. "What did you say?"

"At first I was too surprised to say anything. But once I got my wits back, I said it was between you and her, and I did not care to be involved."

Claire's response did nothing to relieve Lindsey's apprehension. "Did she tell you that we met just after her call to Ted?"

"No." Claire settled back in her seat as she shook her head. "I don't mean to pry, but I've often wondered what happened between you? She was a good friend to you for a while."

Lindsey made a show of folding her napkin. "She was indeed. Joan filled in so many empty spaces after Ted left. But the more I learned about her, the more I realized she gravitates toward people who are needy. I was certainly needy after Ted left. But that's not who I am. As I began to get my life in order, she became demanding ... suffocating, even."

Lindsey described her dilemma in the weeks after Joan took off her wedding ring. She readily admitted her own culpability for the situation by having ignored Joan's repeated comments about loving Lindsey forever and her repeated requests for commitment. "I did love her. But it had no future. And, honestly, I prefer men."

Claire smiled warmly as she took the check from the waitress. "My dear, I don't give a damn whether you love men or women. All I care about is that you are a good mother to my granddaughter." She folded her napkin neatly on the table. "Now, let's go look at art."

They had many leisurely conversations over the summer. Lindsey was amused to learn that Claire, the oh-so-proper society matron, had been a hellion in her youth. Her tales of misadventure during her college years often had them both laughing until their ribs hurt.

While they still avoided "who did what to whom" discussions, Lindsey talked openly about the insights she'd gained in the months since the separation. Claire, in turn, shared some of the lessons she learned as she'd tried to get her own marriage back on solid ground. Lindsey felt a burst of love for Claire when she discovered that this elegant society woman, who always seemed so self-possessed, had struggled for many years to learn to speak up for herself in her marriage. Just like Lindsey.

~ ~ ~ ~

The schedule also gave her time for Mark. Given how they'd left things in Boston, she was surprised—and delighted—when he invited her to dinner during a business trip to New York in late June. They spent most of the meal talking about the conference and the outcome of ideas their agencies had tried to implement. It was an interesting discussion, but she did wonder if he was intentionally steering clear of personal topics.

On the theory that he wouldn't have called if he weren't still interested in her, she turned the conversation to his son as they were finishing dessert. "How's Jason doing? Has the custody situation gotten any better?"

He groaned. "No. Not really. I've petitioned the court to enforce the agreement, but it's still pending. But at least I'll have real time with him this summer. We're going camping in Yosemite for three weeks in August." He paused to finish his coffee. "And Zoey. How is she doing?"

"Okay. I don't know if I told you when we were in Boston that she was bulimic. We've gotten her help, and we try to keep pretty tight control on what she eats, but we're not out of the woods yet." She debated whether to tell him about the new custody arrangement, but decided against it. It was far too personal if this was only a "professional" dinner.

When they left shortly afterwards, she noticed, with some disappointment, that he did not take her arm or guide her out of the restaurant. When he delivered her to the lobby of her building, however, he asked about her "other relationship."

"It's been over for a while now."

He kissed her cheek gently. When he stepped back, he grinned like a kid who'd found the prize in the cereal box. "I hoped that was the case. Can I give you a call in the next week or so?"

"I'd like that." She smiled. "Very much."

As she rode up in the elevator, she hugged herself, savoring her delight at having an attractive man interested in her. She knew that long distance relationships had challenges all their own, but on balance it seemed like a good thing. It would force her to take her time.

He called a week later with an invitation to meet him in Hartford, some weekend when Zoey was with Ted. She accepted. Since that lovely, languorous weekend in mid-July, they'd stayed in touch by phone or email every few days. He'd come to New York for a weekend in August, and would be back on business in early October.

During the Hartford trip, he'd expressed surprise at the harsh terms of Lindsey's divorce. Blaming it on Ted's change of heart wasn't untrue. But if Mark couldn't empathize with her unconventional rebound love affair, they wouldn't have much of a future.

Screwing up her courage, she told him about how Joan had swooped in when she was at her lowest, about the unexpected intensity of their love affair. "I loved her. I really did. But what drew us together—both emotionally and physically—was based more on neediness than on shared interests and values. For me, it wasn't about loving a woman, it was about loving anyone who would take care of me at that point in my life."

Mark's response went well beyond empathy. "I'm glad you told me. But you didn't need to. After last night, it would never have occurred to me that you preferred women."

She went limp with relief when he kissed her and then added, "Consider the subject closed."

~ ~ ~ ~

Except the subject wasn't closed. Two days after the Hartford weekend, Dee called. "Have you and Joan taken up again?"

"I haven't talked to her in almost two months. Why?" Lindsey knew she wasn't going to like the answer.

"She just called me to get my advice on a birthday gift for you. Something special ... I quote ... 'to make up for how badly I've behaved.'"

"Oyh. What did you say?"

"I made up some nonsense about your not liking birthday gifts. Said I couldn't help her."

Lindsey tried to quell a sense of panic. Why was Joan doing this? Was she still trying to rekindle the relationship?

"You there, sweetie?"

"Mmmh. I can't sit back and let her intrude on people I care about. But I don't know what else to do. If she didn't listen in May, why would she listen now?"

"I wish I had some words of wisdom."

"I am aware, my friend, that you warned me about her. I should have listened."

"Actually, I wasn't warning you about her. I just knew you weren't thinking as clearly as you normally do."

"Well, I should have listened."

~ ~ ~ ~

The following evening, Joan's caller ID appeared when the phone rang. Lindsey let it ring. When it went to voicemail, Joan hung up without leaving a message. When she then tried Lindsey's cell, Lindsey switched it off.

Joan called again an hour later. This time, Lindsey answered, certain Joan would keep calling until she did. "Hello?"

"Lindsey, I'm so glad to catch you. I called to see if I could treat you to dinner for your birthday. It's next week, isn't it? The 22nd of July."

Lindsey listened, aghast. Joan's chatty tone implied they were on the best of terms. She willed her voice to come out cool and flat. "Joan, I told you not to call me again."

"Lovey, I miss you so much. I know I acted badly, but I can make it up to you."

Lindsey wanted to reach through the phone to shake Joan. "Joan, nothing you could do would ever make up for almost losing my daughter." She hung up.

Still holding the phone, she headed for the den, where the landline came into the apartment, and pulled the plug. She felt an almost physical sense of relief when the tiny screen on the phone went dead.

The next morning she found three voicemails, one more pleading than the last. What would it take for Joan to get the message?

Chapter 40

On her birthday, Lindsey's staff threw a surprise party for her at lunchtime. She left the office around three and met Zoey for afternoon tea at the St. Regis. That night, since it was Zoey's week with Ted, Dee and Jim treated her to dinner at the Boathouse in Central Park. It was a lovely day, made even lovelier by a dozen yellow roses from Mark.

The next morning she found a small square package, wrapped in foil paper with an extravagant fuchsia-colored ribbon, on her desk. Still aglow, she untied the ribbon and pulled off the paper to find half a dozen CDs by musicians who frequented jazz and blues spots in the Village.

There was no card. She scrolled mentally through her client roster, but couldn't think of anyone who'd associate her with jazz. She tossed the box onto the stack of materials for the next staff meeting, and turned to check her voicemails.

She froze at the sound of Joan's voice. "Happy birthday. I left you a memento of those lovely jazz evenings in the Village. I look forward to doing it again one of these days."

Instinctively she reached for the CD case. Ruffling through it, she saw that each was by a musician they'd heard in person in one of the many jazz joints they visited. She shivered at the thought that Joan was stalking her, trying to hold on to a past that could not be retrieved.

But the reality was that Joan was still calling. Not just calling. Actually showing up—and at her office. She dropped the CDs into the wastebasket.

What would Joan do next?

She gasped as she realized that Joan's next call might be to Zoey.

Zoey, who knew nothing of the love affair, nothing of the acrimonious breakup, nothing about Joan's call to her father. Zoey, who had been at the core of so many of their disagreements, the child Joan so clearly resented. Would Joan try to get to Lindsey through Zoey?

She couldn't allow that to happen. Without conscious thought, she dialed Ted's number.

His greeting was curt. "I'm in a meeting. Has something happened to Zoey?"

"No. But I'm concerned that something might."

"Lindsey, I don't have time for intrigue."

Lindsey didn't know where to start, especially over the phone, where she couldn't read his reactions and he couldn't read hers. "Can we meet today?"

"Lindsey, this is ridiculous."

"It's serious, Ted. Please."

"Just a second." Ted put her on hold. A few moments later his secretary came on the line. "Mrs. Chandler, I've made a reservation at Aquavit at 11:30. Mr. Chandler will meet you there."

When she arrived, Ted had already ordered. At her place sat a small smorgasbord of herring, gravlax and shrimp that she was far too anxious to eat. She was barely seated when he said with obvious impatience, "I don't have much time. We can eat as we talk. What's this about?"

She took a deep breath, one she wanted him to notice. "I'm afraid Joan will do something to Zoey."

"That bitch. What's she done now?"

Choosing her words, Lindsey described Joan's behavior, starting with their confrontation in late May, Joan's calls to Claire and Dee, and now the CDs. Ted picked at his food as she talked. He made no comment, but tension lines etched deeper and deeper around his mouth as her story unfolded.

Her throat was parched and she paused for a drink of water. "I don't know why she'd contact Zoey, but after today, who knows. I don't know what else to do."

Ted cracked his knuckles as he stared into the middle distance. She waited, her eyes locked on the beautiful food she couldn't possibly eat.

Finally, he said, "I knew she called Claire, and she called me a second time a while back. I just hung up on her. But this does begin to sound like stalking. Do you think she'd harm Zoey?"

"Not physically. But I cringe to think what she'd say."

"Well, one possibility is a restraining order."

Lindsey had worked with enough abusive families to know that an order of protection against someone not a family member required evidence of an "intimate" relationship.

"Is that the only option?" she implored. "It could be as traumatic for Zoey as anything Joan might say or do."

"Another approach would be to get a lawyer—at a different firm, so she won't connect it to me—to tell her he's drawing up a restraining order on your behalf. He can say that if she has any further contact with anyone in your family, he'll file it." He wiped his mouth, folded his napkin, and laid it on the table. "That should give her a good scare."

"You'd do that for me?"

"No, not for you. For Zoey. But you'll have to warn Zoey that if Joan contacts her, to call you or me immediately." He slid out from the table and stood up. "I have to run. Don't worry about the bill. It's on my account." As he turned to leave, he added, "Think about it. I'll check with you later."

Lindsey tried to sort out her emotions as he strode out. She was relieved he was willing to help her get through this. Now, she had to figure out how to explain it to Zoey.

Zoey treated the "warning" about Joan with aplomb. "Mom, she was weird. I don't want to talk to her anyway."

While Zoey had tossed it off, Lindsey couldn't. Although the threat of a restraining order appeared to be effective, it was more than a month before her pulse stopped jumping every time the phone rang, and even longer before she stopped looking around in all directions when she left her office or apartment.

And then on the Sunday of Labor Day weekend, when she was out for a run in Central Park, she saw Tammy and her family at the Carousel. She didn't stop, but when she came back the other way ten minutes later, they were still there. This time, Tammy saw her and waved, proffering the bright smile she'd obviously inherited from her mother. Lindsey reluctantly stopped to say hello.

Almost immediately, Les and Becca wandered off as if they'd been instructed to make themselves scarce. Tammy's face turned sober. "I suppose you don't know about Kelly."

Lindsey knew the news was not good. "No, what?"

"Kelly OD'd a couple weeks ago. They found her in time, but she's pretty sick. Mom took her home to Short Hills and stayed to take care of her."

"I'm so sorry. Was it accidental or intentional?"

Tammy shrugged. "Who knows? Kelly's been living on the edge ever since high school." She glanced around as she talked, keeping her eyes on Les and Becca. "Something awful was bound to happen sooner or later. If there's a positive side, it's that Mom feels needed again."

Tammy slapped her fingers across her mouth "Oh, I shouldn't have said that. It makes it sound like she's glad it happened. That's not what I meant."

Lindsey rested a hand on Tammy's shoulder. "I know it's not what you meant. But your mother did seem like a bit of a lost soul while she was in New York. Perhaps being home will help her sort things out." Lindsey pulled out her phone, using a time check as a polite way to end the conversation. "I've got to run."

Tammy put her hand on Lindsey's arm. "Do you have another moment?"

Lindsey drew in a sharp breath, then nodded. She wanted Tammy to observe her impatience.

"Maybe I'm out of turn here, but your friendship meant a lot to Mom. I think she'd appreciate hearing from you." Tammy pulled a small notebook out of her pocket, scribbled on one page, and tore it out. "Here. It's her address and phone in Short Hills."

"Thanks." Lindsey stood frozen in place as Tammy headed toward her family. Only when the three disappeared did she realize she was clutching the paper so tightly her fingers had cramped. She looked at Tammy's scrawl. Would she actually use this information?

How could she not? As a mother, her heart broke for a friend who'd nearly lost a child. As a social worker, she knew Joan had to be tormented by both guilt and anger. How could she not reach out to Joan, who'd been there when Lindsey's world had all but fallen apart? But it would be cruel to call if all she did was mouth trite words of sympathy, if she was unwilling to offer the support and assistance Joan needed.

And she was unwilling. This tormented mother was also the possessive and manipulative woman who'd almost cost Lindsey her own child. The thought that Kelly's problems were of Joan's making flashed through her mind. Even as she chided herself for the more-than-unkind and wholly unwarranted thought, she knew nothing would persuade her to re-entwine her life with Joan's. She crumpled the paper and stuffed it into her pocket.

A few days later, doing laundry, she came across the wadded paper. She opened it, crumpled it again, and tossed it into the wastebasket, but a few minutes later retrieved it. Flattening it, she focused on the address. She wouldn't call, but she would write a short note, acknowledging a mother's pain in dealing with a suffering child and offering a referral to a therapist who might be able to help. She would not offer to play a role herself.

It took her several tries to draft a letter that would reflect her sympathy, without offering a link for the future. By the fourth attempt, she was satisfied enough to put it in an envelope and stamp it.

The stamped envelope sat on her desk for two weeks before she picked it up and dropped it in the wastebasket.

Chapter 41

It was a gorgeous September. Balmy days perfect for capris and a cotton shirt. Crisp cold nights that started the leaves turning.

The Saturday of Zoey's show jumping event with her new horse was no exception. The skies were cloudless as Lindsey dropped her off at the stables. She blew her daughter a kiss and said she'd be back in time for the event.

Driving to the country house, she reflected on the past three months. Being a single parent wasn't the life she would have chosen but—in a flash of insight—she realized she'd never actually lived "the life she would have chosen."

That was certainly true of her marriage. The image of herself and Ted and Zoey as a close-knit, happy family had masked, especially in the last few years, an increasing level of tension and anxiety. Over the summer, in sessions with Stacy, she'd begun to understand more about what happened to her marriage. Not why Ted left—she'd probably never know that—but where things had started to go wrong. A goodly share had been her fault.

As with Joan, the early days of their relationship offered a marvelous sense of well-being, a delight at being with someone who seemed to understand her so well. But as their lives got busier, she and Ted rarely talked about the emotional consequences of their changing lifestyle. Fear of rejection had led her to bury her own needs, to gradually shave off little bits of her personality. Somewhere across the years, she'd ceased to be the intelligent and assertive woman Ted had married and had become a hollow shell called "wife and mother."

Through Stacy, she'd seen that her affair with Joan, whatever its problems, had been a watershed moment, the point at which she began to take responsibility for her own actions and feelings. She couldn't undo the damage to her marriage, but she could do it better the next time. If there was a next time.

On balance, she was content. She hadn't had a stomachache in more than two months. Perhaps for the first time in her life, most of the pieces of her life seemed to fit together comfortably.

~ ~ ~ ~

When she returned to the stables, Ted's Lexus was already there. It was her week with Zoey, but there was no way he'd miss the public debut of his daughter's equestrian skill.

She made her way to Dude's stall. Ted and Wendy were brushing the gelding's dappled coat, while Zoey braided his mane.

"Hi, sweetie. Are you excited?"

All three looked up.

"Hi, Mom. Doesn't he look beautiful?"

Lindsey stroked the horse's muzzle. "Indeed he does."

"Morning, Lindsey." Ted pointed his brush toward Zoey. "Pretty nifty, isn't it? Our very own horsewoman."

Ted was going to make this a good day. She would do her part. "What can I do to help?"

~ ~ ~ ~

She intended to join Dee and Jim in the spectator seats, but she was with Ted and Wendy in the barn when the show began, and they watched from the railing nearby. Wendy provided a running commentary on the accomplishments and challenges of each of the jumpers.

When Zoey cantered into the arena, Lindsey climbed onto a hay bale to get a better view.

Zoey had practiced the course with Dude daily for weeks. Even so, Lindsey's heart was in her throat as Zoey approached each of the hurdles. She let out an audible breath each time Dude took a hurdle with ease. Zoey completed her routines with a time penalty of only three seconds, an outstanding performance with a horse she'd only had for two months.

Lindsey joined the enthusiastic applause when the routine ended. In her excitement, she lost her balance on the irregular surface and stumbled backwards into open space. Ted caught her under her arms, breaking her fall. "Careful, hon."

His voice echoed in her brain. The timbre, the gentleness, the endearment. She felt the warmth of his palms and the pressure of his long, tapered fingers against her ribcage. "Thanks, my love." The words were out before she knew she'd said them.

Ted pulled back as if his hands touched acid. Their eyes met for a moment, then he spun around and walked away.

Breathless, Lindsey sat down on the bale. When she fell, Ted had reached for her out of instinct. It was something anyone would do. Calling her "hon" was not. Was it an automatic response in a tight moment ... or a sign his anger had faded?

And she had given a reflexive response to the familiar, if unexpected, aura of affection. Was she still connected to him in a way she no longer thought about consciously?

Zoey trotted out of the arena. Ted appeared at her side and walked with her toward Dude's stall.

At least five minutes went by before Lindsey was calm enough to walk to the barn with any measure of poise. When she got to Dude's stall, Jim and Dee were perched on the tack box in the corridor. She heard giggling inside the stall where the girls were presumably bedding Dude down for the night. Ted was watching them from the far wall and didn't notice Lindsey's arrival.

Jim gave her a military salute as she strolled up. "We wondered where you disappeared to. We want to toast"—he reached for an insulated bag on the floor and pulled out a bottle of champagne—"the mother and father of our star equestrian."

Dee rolled her eyes and tsked. "Jim, we can't drink here in the stable."

"Okay, then let's take the girls out for pizza and we'll buy a bottle of plonk to celebrate."

Ted glanced at his watch. "I'll pass on pizza. I'm heading back to the city."

"Oh, c'mon," Jim protested. "Drive back in the morning."

The giggling stopped and Zoey's head appeared over the stall wall, a clown-like grin on her face. She was obviously following every word. "Dad, you gotta stay. We could go to brunch in the morning." She disappeared without waiting for a response.

Ted grimaced. "I suppose I could ... but only if it's okay with you, Lindsey."

For the second time in an hour, Lindsey was caught off guard. His tone was, what ... conciliatory ... respectful ... cooperative? After a pleasant day, she had no reason to stand in the way of father-daughter bonding. "By all means, stay. You two have been planning this day for years." Lindsey waited a nanosecond, "But if you go to brunch, I'm coming with you."

~ ~ ~ ~

During dinner, the girls prattled on about the riders— who'd done well ... who'd done poorly ... whose horse was gorgeous ... whose horse was a nag. The adults got in a few toasts, but one bottle of mediocre red had little impact on anyone's sobriety.

Out in the parking lot after dinner, Ted announced that he would, in fact, drive back to New York City. "I don't have a change of clothes or a toothbrush."

Zoey's comeback was immediate. "You do too! At the house."

Lindsey wondered if he had an obligation in the City or was trying to avoid the prospect of her company at brunch. Or, as she had wondered earlier, was he actually being respectful of the fact that it was Lindsey's weekend. Whatever his reasons, coming to the show had created a set of expectations in Zoey, who was not going to let him off easily.

Lindsey gave Ted a sincere smile. "Come get whatever you need. In fact, there's no reason to schlep your stuff over to Jim and Dee's. You might as well stay in your own house."

Zoey nodded furiously. "Yeah, Dad, that'd be cool. We could hang out in the hot tub." She pulled at her father's arm. "C'mon. You gotta stay."

Lindsey noted the furrows of indecision in Ted's brow. "Are you sure, Lindsey?"

"Ted, you're already here. What's the point of leaving now?"

Ted held Lindsey's eyes for a long moment before he turned to Zoey, who was nodding furiously. "All right, ladies. You've talked me into it."

Zoey high-fived Wendy. It seemed the girls had been plotting this outcome all along.

Dee tucked her hand around Lindsey's elbow. "Are you sure you know what you're doing?"

Lindsey squeezed Dee's hand. "It'll be fine."

~ ~ ~ ~

It had been fine. Back at the house, Zoey and Ted headed for the hot tub. In response to her daughter's plea, Lindsey joined them, but kept a watchful eye. When she saw Zoey's energy level starting to run down, she pleaded fatigue and excused herself, leaving before Zoey did.

Once in bed, it took Lindsey a while to fall asleep. She could still feel Ted's fingers against her ribcage, hear the warmth in his voice as he called her 'hon,' remember the physical sense of something missing when his hands were gone.

But his response to that moment of intimacy had been to slink away. She had a sense of *déjà vu*, from their last time together in the country, barely a week before he walked out.

That Saturday, as they'd put away groceries, he'd placed his hand on her back as he reached for a higher shelf. He caressed her fingers as they walked in the woods, warming her to her toes. He brushed crumbs from her mouth, letting his fingers linger on her face, then raised his glass of champagne for toast. And then, when she clinked her glass to his, pouring all her love into his eyes across the rim, he looked away.

As sleep began to overtake her, Lindsey saw these two scenes as bookends of what was best and worst about her marriage. Ted was a master of romantic gestures, but too often they were unrelated to what he was actually feeling.

And then, of course, she'd never known how to match her actions to what she was feeling.

She woke Sunday morning to the aroma of coffee and the sound of puttering in the kitchen. When she got there, Zoey was cracking eggs into a bowl and Ted was browning sausages in a skillet. The table was set for three.

"What happened to brunch?"

Ted looked over his shoulder. "Zoey has a recipe for French toast with rum. It sounded interesting. Hope you didn't have your heart set on going out."

Lindsey's pulse flickered. Had Zoey told Ted where the recipe came from? But he seemed relaxed. She poured coffee and sat down to watch the two of them at work.

Ted was at his most charming throughout breakfast. Zoey was still on a high and chattered on about her goals for the opening show in the spring. When the opportunity arose, Ted asked about life at Lindsey's agency. She got him talking about one of his newest legal cases. He asked her opinion of the Klimt exhibit she'd seen with Claire at the Neue Gallery. She knew he'd seen it, and enquired about his own reaction to it.

Conversation flowed easily, reminding her, once again, why she'd fallen in love with him. But it was a nostalgic moment, rather than a bitter one.

After Zoey left for the stables, Ted stayed to help with dishes. She watched him moving easily around the kitchen, knowing exactly where things belonged.

When he closed the cupboard door and turned to face her, he was less than a foot away. He was looking directly at her, smiling.

Notwithstanding her assurance to Dee, she hadn't expected his visit to be as comfortable as it had been. She matched his smile. "Thanks for making this such a nice weekend for Zoey."

"I was worried about horning in. You made it easy."

"I'll do anything to make sure Zoey doesn't grow up without her father." She hesitated. "And turnabout is fair play. You've been more generous financially than you had to be."

Ted poured himself coffee and stood next to her at the counter. "You know I didn't mean for this to happen."

He shifted from one foot to the other as he talked, and she felt his shoulder touch hers. Her pulse fluttered again. The exact words he'd used that Saturday morning he walked out. She played for time.

"This?"

"All of it. Lauren. Getting so angry about Joan. Making it hard for you financially. I wish I could take it all back."

Lindsey's pulse fluttered faster. "Well, there are lots of things I wish I'd done differently, too."

"We both made mistakes." Ted set his cup on counter and wrapped his long fingers around her upper arms.

His palms felt warm on her skin, his breath warm on her face. He was so close. Close enough to kiss her. She felt a surge of desire.

He raised one hand and cupped her cheek gently, his eyes searching hers. His voice came out as a whisper. "I never should have left."

Unprepared for how strong her attraction to him still was, she pulled her head back. Passion hadn't been enough before. Why would she expect it to be now? She'd changed and matured. Had he?

She met his gaze. "But you did leave. And now we're divorced."

"That can be fixed."

"Oh, Ted." She removed his hand from her cheek and pulled his other hand from her arm. She straightened her own arms, forcing him back a step. "I'm not the same person I was when you left. I don't want the same things I wanted a year ago."

"What *do* you want?"

"I'm still trying to figure that out. But I know what I don't want." She dropped his hands, then gently pushed him back another step. "Did you know I had a stomachache for much of our last three years ... and almost always when you had a trial coming up? I always thought something was wrong with me."

His drew lips into a tight, thin line, then said, "Why didn't you tell me?"

"I didn't know how. Somewhere along the line, we stopped talking about who we were and what we wanted. And once we stopped ..." Lindsey sipped her coffee to give her time to complete her thought. "That's what I don't want. A life where you're hardly ever there and when you are, I feel like you're controlling the conversation. I know it was as much my fault as yours, but I won't go back there."

"Can't we start talking again?"

"To what purpose?"

"To see if we can get back to what we had when it was good." He moved toward her, close enough to put his hand on her arm again. "There *was* a time when things were good."

Lindsey met his gaze. "You're right. A time when it was very good. But it hasn't been good for a long time. You realized it before I did, but right now ..." She shrugged as her mind flitted across the pleasures of the summer just past.

Ted watched her, waiting.

"I guess I have a sense of possibility in my life that I haven't had in years. I want to go forward, not backward."

He edged over to the counter by the window. Looking out, he said, "I'd like to think I've learned from this experience ... to think that we could go forward." He turned to face her. "Could we have dinner this week?"

"You and me and Zoey?"

"No ... you and me."

"I have to think about that."

Ted smiled. "Fine. As long as you say yes."

Lindsey couldn't help but laugh. "There you are, the same old Ted, controlling the conversation. I'll give you a call in a day or two."

"Point noted. Now, I'm going back to the work I should have been doing this morning."

They walked in silence out to his car. Lindsey stood at the edge of the driveway as he left. Twenty yards down the gravel road, he stopped and rolled down his window. "Just remember. I'm expecting your answer to be yes." He waved and was gone.

Lindsey watched until his car disappeared. She would probably say yes. But if she did, she'd insist that Zoey join them.

And she'd insist on ordering her own meal.

Acknowledgements

Boundless gratitude goes to Carol Bodensteiner, my writing buddy of nearly a decade, and my two editors, Catherine Knepper and Calla Rongerude. At every step along the way, Carol has been a source of ideas and inspiration. Catherine provided structural guidance early on, while Calla was invaluable in polishing off the rough edges. What particularly distinguished these three women was their determination to make me dig deeper, to reach for the small nuances that bring a fictional character to life.

Major thanks goes to my beta readers—all of them lovers of the written word—who made the time commitment not only to read a work-in-progress, but to provide the thoughtful and detailed feedback that made Lindsey's story so much richer. My heartfelt appreciation goes out to Pat Boddy, Eleanor Day, Phyllis Goodman, Donna Langer, Susan Loots, Eileen Lundberg, Julia Martinusen, P.J. McEvoy, David Lawlor, Laura Sands, Marcia Safirstein, and Ellen Taylor. Mark Lunde was a "sort-of" beta-reader, who read the final version for both word usage and grammar.

I am also grateful for the inspiration and insight offered by personal and professional friends who helped me wend my way through the practical and emotional dimensions of divorce, teenagers and same sex relationships. Friends who walked me through the vagaries of contemporary adolescents included Lori Chesser and Mary van Heukelom. Therapists who offered helpful perspectives on the psychodynamics of divorce included Mary Riche, Sheila Pottebaum, Judy Rinehart, and Suzanne Link. Friends who explored concepts of sexuality fluidity and same sex relationships include Penelope James and Carolyn Jenison.

Particular thanks also go to two therapists in the field of human sexuality. The first is Lisa Diamond, whose 2008 book, *Sexual Fluidity: Understanding Women's Love and Desire*, provided a sound conceptual framework for a story I have wanted to tell for several decades. The second is Paul Joannides, a psychoanalyst on the editorial board of the *Journal of Sexual Medicine*, who introduced me to Diamond's work and sensitized me to the generational differences in views of sexual identity and sexual attraction.

A special note of wonder goes to my cover designer, Wendy Musgrave. Within a matter of days, she came up with the perfect cover concept, based on little more than a one-paragraph summary of the novel. I have loved her cover since the first minute I saw it.

Discussion Questions

1. Lindsey has a long history of withholding important information about herself without realizing it. How do you think that pattern affected her marriage? How did it affect her relationships with the key women in her life (Joan ... Dee ... Claire)?

   What sorts of information do you withhold in your relationships? Why do you do it? What has been the result?

2. Same sex relationships remain controversial even as more states allow same sex marriages. How was Lindsey's view of her sexual identity affected by her love affair with a woman? How has Lindsey's story influenced your view of same sex relationships?

3. The concept of sexual fluidity (see Chapter 11) offers a new perspective on same sex relationships? How comfortable are you with this as an explanation for Lindsey's love affair? How common a phenomenon do you think sexual fluidity is in the everyday world?

4. Lindsey hides her new love from everyone. How do you think this secret affects her relationship with Zoey ... Dee ... Joan ... Claire ... Ted? How might things have turned out differently if Lindsey had not hidden her new love affair?

   How has keeping secrets affected your life? How has this book influenced your view of the consequences of keeping secrets?

5. Lindsey vacillates between imposing appropriate discipline on a sassy teenager and offering comfort to a

distraught child trying to cope with divorce. Do you think she handles Zoey well or badly? Do you think she is to blame for Zoey's behavioral and health problems. Why or why not?

How have you dealt with this sort of conflict? What things might you do/have you done differently? What advice would you have given Lindsey?

6. Lindsey struggles to balance the conflicting needs of her daughter and her lover. What do you think about the way she manages it? Is she a model for how you would handle conflict? What would you have done differently?

7. Psychologists and therapists tend to caution against rebound romances. Do you think Lindsey's love affair was a rebound relationship? Why or why not? Do you think the net impact of the relationship on Lindsey was a positive? On her lover? Why or why not?

8. What do you see as the biggest changes in Lindsey over the course of the novel? Do you find her changes credible? Why or why not? What are the two or three most important factors contributing to that change?

www.ingramcontent.com/pod-product-compliance
Lightning Source LLC
Chambersburg PA
CBHW021217250626
47155CB00008B/2837